ANADARKO

ANADARKO

A KIOWA COUNTRY MYSTERY

TOM HOLM

THE UNIVERSITY OF
ARIZONA PRESS

TUCSON

The University of Arizona Press
www.uapress.arizona.edu

Printed in the United States of America
20   19   18   17   16   15   6   5   4   3   2   1

ISBN-13: 978-0-8165-3181-3 (paper)

Cover designed by Leigh McDonald

Publication of this book is made possible in part by the proceeds of a permanent endowment
created with the assistance of a Challenge Grant from the National Endowment for the
Humanities, a federal agency.

Library of Congress Cataloging-in-Publication Data
Holm, Tom, 1946– author.
   Anadarko : a Kiowa country mystery / Tom Holm.
      pages cm
   ISBN 978-0-8165-3181-3 (pbk. : alk. paper)
   1. Prohibition—Oklahoma—Fiction. 2. Distilling, Illicit—Oklahoma—Fiction. 3. Kiowa
Indians—Oklahoma—Fiction. I. Title.
   PS3608.O494325A84 2015
   813'.6—dc23
                                      2014039736

♾ This paper meets the requirements of ANSI/NISO Z39.48 1992 (Permanence of Paper).

ANADARKO

PROLOGUE

Khōn Charging Horse awoke with a smile on his deeply creased face. Now in his early eighties, he had taken regularly to sleeping in his tipi rather than in the clapboard house his son George had built for the family. George's youngest two sons had married, moved a few miles away, and established their own households. But two of Charging Horse's many grandchildren were still in the same house with George and his wife, and as *khōn*, a revered grandfather, he loved to sit with his grandchildren and tell them of the old ways when the Kiowa people had many horses, fought the blue coats, ate buffalo, and took part in the ancient Sun Dance religion.

All those things were gone now, except for the tipi and the old buffalo robe covering Charging Horse's scarred but remarkably strong body. He loved sleeping in the tipi because it felt as if he were recapturing the days of his youth. This was the one that his wives—he had married sisters—had made long ago. He rarely saw his wives lately. They were always off visiting grandchildren and great-grandchildren. The new tipi, which his wives had lent their expertise in constructing, had been carefully taken down, folded and stored away for use in the new religion—the religion of Chief Peyote. It would be raised again for a meeting in a few days. His son George was a chief in the new way, and Charging Horse attended every meeting because he loved the songs, the prayers, the medicine, and the good feelings that were part of Grandfather Peyote's ceremonies.

Ironically, Charging Horse had been one of the last instructors of the Sun Dance religion and one of the first Kiowas to take the Peyote Road. He had guided the last four young men through the eight-day-long Sun Dance ceremony that renewed, rejuvenated, and ensured the prosperity of the Kiowa people. In those days Kiowa prosperity depended on horses and the buffalo. But the buffalo were gone now, and he had learned Grandfather Peyote's new songs. He had gone along with the painful decision to put the Sun Dance away in the face of the white peoples' objections to it and in the hope that the Peyote Way would bring back unity and happiness to his people once again. The Peyote Road was narrow, and many could not stay on its strict pathway. But the Kiowas needed a spiritual reawakening. They had suffered so on the reservation and had even had that last bit of land taken away under the government's policy of allotment.

Charging Horse rubbed the sleep out of his eyes and breathed in the cedar smoke smell of the small fireplace in the center of the tipi. He slept opposite the east-facing door and could see the light of a new sunrise around the edges of the door flap. It was the gray light that comes just before dawn. He quickly got up, walked in a clockwise direction to the door, put his hands in the bucket of cold water there, and splashed his face. He took up his pipe and his tobacco pouch and prepared to go out and greet the morning sun.

He stood waiting for the sun to rise over the small copse of trees by the creek bed east of the tipi. The light was getting stronger, and out of the corner of his eye he caught an unnatural movement coming from the base of a blackjack to his right. He turned and took in a sight that ran chills from the back of his head to the base of his spine. Under the scraggly branches of the tree lay the body of a white man. All Charging Horse could see was the top of the man's head. The wispy long blond hair moving in the slight breeze of the early morning was what caught his eye. He'd seen that blond hair before.

Charging Horse calmly returned his pipe to the tipi and went over to the small tree. He kneeled down to get a better look under the branches and saw the body; it was only then that he caught the metallic smell of blood and the rancid odor of the man's bowels.

He had seen the horrible consequences of battle as a young man. But the sight of the white man's body was enough to make him wince. The man was young, with plenty of blond hair. He wore glasses, which drew Charging Horse's eyes to the man's mutilated nose and mouth. Someone had cut the man's nose completely off and had bashed his teeth so that his mouth was cut wide open below the hole that had been his nose. The man's mouth was actually caved in.

Worse still was the fact that the man appeared to have been gutted. Charging Horse could smell the odor, but the man's intestines had been pulled out. His shirt was still buttoned at the neck but had been spread open from the throat down. The man's belly was slit from the sternum to the groin, and the skin drooped inside the stomach cavity. Only remnants of the man's intestines and other organs were left in the body; they had obviously been left elsewhere. No blood or organs were under the tree with the corpse. The white man had been killed, mutilated and eviscerated, and then brought to the Charging Horse allotment. Khōn decided that somebody was tying to pin the white man's death on his family.

Charging Horse sat back on the ground beside the tree, crossed his legs, and wondered how the man had come to rest under the blackjack. He saw no blood trail, no obvious footprints in the dirt, no disturbance in the grass around the area. Nor could he understand how the dead man had been brought there without waking him up or causing the numerous dogs that lived on the Charging Horse property to sound a warning of intruders. Strange, too, that the dogs had not worried the corpse. Surely they would have detected it. The old man thought about that; something truly evil must have taken place. The dogs must have known it and kept their distance. There weren't any traces of coyotes either.

Charging Horse reached over and carefully brushed the blond hair back from the man's forehead. His eyes showed deep sympathy. "You poor white man," he said in Kiowa, "you must have had hateful enemies."

The old man squinted and looked deeply into the dead man's clouded-over eyes. He was the man his son George had let camp just over the ridge. Charging Horse had seen the man before, but the cataracts over the old man's eyes made things seem as if they were seen through a mist. The blond hair was easily recognized though. Charging Horse had rarely come in contact with people with yellow hair. He shook his head, stood, and walked over to the clapboard house. He had to talk to George. No good could come from having a dead white man under a tree on your allotment. Especially if the poor man had been left there with the purpose of making trouble for the Charging Horse family.

»«

The heavyset man staggered and put his hand against the wall of the alley for support. He was wearing his faded blue work clothes and a black fedora with the brim pulled down. One strap of his bib overalls hung down his back. He turned to the wall, put his other hand against it, and looked down at the brick alleyway and vomited on his lower overall legs and work shoes. He shook his head in disgust and dizzily looked up at the wall.

"Too much to drink," he said out loud.

"You okay, mister?"

The voice came from directly behind him. He wiped his chin with his right hand and turned. He stood weaving back and forth like tall grass in the wind; the motion was making him sick again. His eyes were out of focus, and he could only see a tall figure in an old-time driving slicker and a wide-brimmed hat. The man's face was a white blur.

"Watch it," he growled, "gonna be sick again."

The man in the slicker stepped back to the other side of the alley while the drunk turned his head and threw up once again.

"You're in bad shape, old man. Why don't you let me help you out?" the man in the slicker said calmly.

"Yeah . . . yeah, need help. Automobile's a couple of streets down."

"Well, just walk on, and I'll take your arm. Tell me if you're gonna upchuck again."

"Sure . . . sure, I'll let you know."

They walked two short blocks and turned into an alley. The man in the slicker patted the drunk man on the back and said, "Ain't the usual payday, this bein' Monday. What you celebratin'?"

"Ain't celebratin'. Got canned."

"Sorry to hear that. Where was you workin'?"

"Diggin' ditch for a pipeline 'cross the river. They hired a Portugee on the cheap. Lousy bastards, firin' a white man for a foreigner. Probably a Bolshevik to boot."

4

"Damn sorry to hear that. What you gonna do now?"

"I'll find somethin'."

They came to a T where another alley met the first, turned right, and walked over to an automobile parked close to a brick wall. The drunk shook his head and pulled open the driver's side door. The black Ford Model T had seen its better days. The rag top was down, and in the space behind the front seat, a shovel and pick were leaning almost straight up against the rear seat. The drunk pulled himself behind the wheel and shut the door.

The man in the slicker looked directly into the drunk's eyes and asked with a slight smile on his still blurry face, "Your name Cunningham?"

Surprised at the question, Bryant Cunningham groggily answered, "Yeah, so . . ." Then he looked curiously at the man in the slicker. "You . . . I . . ."

In one fluid motion, the man in the slicker took up the pick, raised it high, and buried the point in Cunningham's skull. In that single instant, all the breath left Cunningham's lungs and he died without knowing what hit him.

Chapter I

COOPER'S PLACE

The two men standing close together on the platform of the Anadarko train depot were about as unlike as two men could possibly have been. The first was undoubtedly an Indian. He wore a "Montana Peak" or "lemon squeezer" army campaign hat and a dark brown wool suit coat. If somebody looked close enough, they could see a small bullet hole in his hat brim. His white shirt with its gleaming stiff celluloid collar almost shined through the smoke and steam of the still-puffing engine. His black trousers met the highly polished round toes of his ankle-high brown military shoes. He stood beside a thick bedroll stuffed with articles of clothing and with a well-oiled old .44-40 Winchester rifle slipped in the leather belt that held everything together and served as a carrying strap.

The man standing next to him was a beefy, scarred older white man with a heavy multicolored moustache. He wore a dark bowler hat and a black suit coat with a blue shirt, white collar, and striped tie. The one incongruity with his outfit was that he had stuffed his gray trousers into knee-high lace-up brown field boots. He looked like a cross between a rough-cut field rig-fitter on the bottom and a no-nonsense city businessman on top. He held a cardboard suitcase in his right hand and was checking his gold pocket watch with his left.

"By God, Hoolie," said the man with the multicolored moustache, "that rancher was supposed to meet us fourteen minutes ago. By the looks of things here, he's probably the only person with an automobile for fifty, sixty miles. And the heat . . . well, goddam."

"He'll show up, J.D.," Hoolie said, "you just gotta have some patience." Then he tried to change the subject. "Anadarko's a small town, ain't it?"

6

"Sure is. I'm still not quite sure why I took on this job. At least I got an electric fan in Tulsa."

"Tell me again what it's all about," Hoolie asked, more or less to kill time.

"Well, my lawyer, Sam Berg . . . you met Sam?"

"Yep."

"All right. Well, one of Sam's boys readin' for the law has a brother that came out here and was nosin' around, lookin' to put some cash into the cattle business. The main thing is that a good deal of the land around here is allotted to Indians—Wichitas, Caddos, Delawares, and Kiowas. Anadarko's the main government agency for most of them, and you have to work leases through the Indian Office."

"Same o'd thing where I'm from."

"Well, yeah. But they figure if you can lease a big enough spread then raisin' cattle can be profitable. Especially since Anadarko's got a railroad link. You could operate a slaughter and packing house right here."

"I don't like it," Hoolie muttered.

"I didn't think you would. But it's a way for the people around here to make some money."

"That depends."

"I know, now." J.D. said, slightly frustrated. "Your people have been done pretty bad by the Indian Office. And your wife's people have more than paid the price for livin' over an oil field . . . and things look like they're gettin' worse."

"J.D., if they know what they've been doin', why don't they let us alone?"

J.D. brushed his moustache with his right thumb, sighed, and put on his best fatherly smile. "You just gotta understand how business works."

"All right, then how does business bring a man who don't know anything about cows out here to look into the cattle business?"

"Okay, you have to know that the first rule of business is to diversify. Invest your money in money-making businesses so your business will grow along with your other businesses. See?"

Hoolie smiled. "I thought you said the first rule of business was 'supply and demand.'"

J.D. scowled, shook his head, and then smiled. "There's just no getting around you, is there?"

"I guess not."

J.D. looked at his watch again.

Hoolie remained silent. He was deep in thought. Knowing that Hoolie didn't use the telephone, J.D. had traveled to Osage County to recruit him for this expedition to western Oklahoma, and Myrtle, his pregnant wife, was none too happy about the operation.

J.D. had worked with Hoolie long enough to know what he was thinking. "How's your wife and the rest of the family?"

"They're fine."

"I don't know how you do it," J.D. began, "livin' with an old grandma, your mother-in-law, your wife's sister, and a half dozen relatives visiting you all the time."

"Used to it, I guess. I keep my mouth shut. Sometimes it's good not bein' able to talk Osage. They leave you be when you don't. But then, all of 'em like me and I like them. Now that we got a baby on the way, the relatives are comin' around more and more. You came when there's a lot of 'em visitin'."

Hoolie looked across the fields and turned his gaze toward town. J.D.'s eyes followed suit. A black Packard touring car was coming down the street toward the depot.

"I bet this is him," said J.D.

The touring car stopped and a young blond man wearing bib overalls and a blue work shirt hopped out. "You Mr. Daugherty?" he asked J.D., giving Hoolie a squint-eyed once-over.

"That's right," answered J.D., "and this is my associate, Mr. Smith."

The blond man's clear dismissal of Hoolie registered on J.D. "And who are you, boy?" growled J.D. in an even clearer effort to put blondie in his place.

The young man looked down and spoke out the side of his mouth, around the wooden match in his teeth. "I'm Eric Cooper, sir. My pa sent me to get you all. I'll take you out to the ranch and then bring you back to town afterwards. Got a room in town, yet? You could go to the Bryant."

"Not yet, but that'd be just fine, Mr. Cooper. We need to talk to your pa. We'll get a room when we get back to town."

Hoolie sat in the front seat of the big automobile. As a mechanic, Hoolie admired the finely tuned Packard engine, the suspension, and the comfortable seat. The car's heavy springs, sturdy wheels, and big tires smoothed the ride over the bumpy red dirt road. Blackjack trees dotted the swells of the prairie lands. A good deal of barbed-wire fencing was being erected alongside the road. The thought that the days of the open range were over popped into Hoolie's mind. Except for the red dirt, the prairie was about the same as his wife's people's country. His own people, the Cherokees, lived in the rocky, heavily wooded hills of northeastern Oklahoma.

As they drove along, Hoolie's mind wandered for a while but finally focused on J.D.'s plans for this case. Being from the big city of Chicago, J.D. was always negatively comparing rural to city life. Although J.D. thought of his Tulsa home as a hick town, he nevertheless looked upon the growing "magic" city as his kind of place. Tulsa was maturing with its paved streets, clanging trolley cars, tall buildings, rich churches, and big houses. Museums, parks, and even a college had found homes in Tulsa. The terrible race riot of two years before had been swept under the carpet. Tulsa high society was doing its best to cover up and forget the massacre and destruction that had occurred in the city's black part of town.

The whites were doing a pretty good job of forgetting; the blacks, whose neighborhoods, churches, and businesses had been burned out and who had suffered the loss of friends and relatives, were not going to forget so quickly. Besides, the KKK was still in operation and a large number of black people were being beaten up or flogged on a regular basis. The coppers were doing little or nothing to stop these new acts of racial violence.

J.D. was in with the city's most prominent oil families. Still, he could not fail to remember the fact that a group of white men had shot him and beat him senseless during that riot. Most importantly the same rioters had killed a beautiful young woman he had been interviewing and who, he continually reminded Hoolie, had been in his care at the time. Her murder, Hoolie noticed, continually gnawed at J.D.'s own conscience.

Hoolie knew J.D.'s thoughts almost as well as his own. J.D. had already declared Anadarko to be a "one-horse town" several times during their journey from Tulsa to Oklahoma City to western Oklahoma. J.D. would interview Mr. Cooper, a wealthy cattleman, and then return to town and try to make friends with local law enforcement. J.D. told Hoolie that Anadarko had a town police chief and a county sheriff's office. It was the seat of Caddo County, with a fine courthouse and sturdy jail. Hoolie guessed that the town's lawmen were neither more nor less corrupt than in any other small jurisdiction. Since there was a large Indian population around, both Hoolie and J.D. figured that the bootleggers were everywhere and that they paid heavily to keep the constables and deputies off their backs. This kind of graft was normal in areas of Oklahoma with large Indian populations—and large Indian populations were everywhere in Oklahoma. J.D., Hoolie thought, was going through a precise list of things to do in the hope that his thorough approach to the detective business would pay off in a quick return home to Tulsa.

Hoolie had been brought along to look into what J.D. called the "Indian angle" of the operation. The missing person, one Frank Shotz, was primarily interested in securing new leases on Indian allotments. In order to get the grazing land, he would have to buy out the current leaseholders, negotiate new deals through the Indian Office, and hire the men to look after the cattle. If no leases on Indian allotments were held by white men, Shotz would have to obtain them, once again, through the Indian Office. Shotz hadn't been in contact with Sam Berg's acquaintance in two weeks. So Sam decided to ask J.D. to look for him.

Hoolie still didn't understand Shotz's interest in the cattle business. From what J.D. had found out, Frank Shotz was a geologist who had detected two relatively large oil and natural gas fields in eastern Oklahoma and northern Texas. With his earnings from the discovery of the underground wealth, he invested in Shelby Oil for one and a Texas tool company that patented hard rock drill bits for another.

J.D. had made inquiries in Tulsa, especially of his contacts in high society, in particular Big Bill and Rose Shelby. The Shelbys had apparently worked out their problems. Big Bill had acknowledged that Rose Chichester was his blood daughter and had begged E.L. Chichester's, his wife's, Miss Chichester's, and his children's forgiveness. And he had seemingly been forgiven, although J.D. told

Hoolie that he suspected that no one really had done so. "I think they're just putting up a front . . . Big Bill's still pretty powerful, you know. And I don't think Rose Shelby's the forgiving type and neither are the Chichesters, father or daughter. Big Bill better keep his eyes peeled and watch his back."

Big Bill had convinced everyone except J.D. and Hoolie that Rose Chichester's abduction and imprisonment had been engineered by the Hominy, Oklahoma, town police chief who called himself "sheriff" as if he were back in the Wild West and an Osage County judge who had been intent on blackmailing the Shelby family. The story was plausible because the judge had committed suicide and the sheriff and his murderous nephew had suddenly disappeared from the face of the earth, leaving the Shelby family with no other alternative than to believe Big Bill. Hoolie's opinion of white families and their domestic relations was none too good. He'd seen brother turn on brother, and Big Bill's treatment of his blood daughter Rose Chichester was hardly commendable. But Hoolie also knew that Rose Shelby had taken in her grandson by Little Bill and a black girl named Minnie; his feeling about Little Bill could be dead wrong.

When J.D. had questioned Big Bill, the oilman had told him that Frank Shotz was more of an entrepreneur than a geologist, even though the man knew a good deal about finding oil deposits. It followed that Shotz was indeed attempting to diversify his investments. But J.D. thought that Shotz would have been more inclined to buy into more oil companies or into the booming coal mines or into construction. Tulsa was, after all, rebuilding. Or at least covering up the destruction left by the '21 riot.

Hoolie really thought that Frank Shotz was looking for oil once again in the red dirt around Anadarko. He thought the notion that Shotz was going into the cattle business was a cover story for snooping around Indian lands. If people knew that Shotz was prospecting for oil around Anadarko, others would flock to the area and start drilling without sound knowledge of what did indeed lie beneath that red clay. When Hoolie told J.D. about his suspicions, J.D. wrinkled his nose and nervously thumbed his moustache. "You know, Hoolie, you're probably right," said J.D., "and I'd bet a hundred dollars to a pig's ear, that Big Bill's in on the deal. Shotz not only has a brother working for Sam but he's also well-known around the oilmen."

That, of course, simply confirmed in Hoolie's mind that Shotz was just another snooping, land-grabbing oil magnate. Hoolie often spun out his friend John Tall Soldier's ideas about how businesses were interlocked to the detriment of all Indians. Without the railroads, there wouldn't be the mining, oil, cattle, coal, steel, timber, textile, and agriculture businesses. All of them required more and more land, and the only land available nowadays was Indian land. Maybe Shotz *was* looking to get into the cattle business—once again, to the detriment of Indian people.

Sitting on the front porch of Hoolie's home near Hominy in Osage County, Hoolie and John would talk about how white people did things. John thought—and Hoolie had to agree—that white people were just the opposite of true warriors. Cherokees and Osages, although ancient enemies, shared the idea that generosity, honesty, humility, and courage were the foremost virtues in life. According to John, white people were greedy liars who hid behind masks, their women, the Indian Office, lawyers, and the courts.

Hoolie always told John that not all white people are like that. J.D., although somewhat miserly, was honest and brave. Rose Shelby and Rose Chichester were generous and truthful. John had witnessed Rose Chichester's courage. John would counter with the argument that those three were extraordinary white people and would then point to the continued murders of Osages for their headrights and the Tulsa race riot as examples of white cowardice, dishonesty, and avarice. "Look at that Ku Klux Klan," John would say. "They're probably the worstest, but whites do the same things here in our country without even tryin' to hide under their bedsheets."

At that, Hoolie would remind John that the new governor, Jack Walton, was carrying on what looked like a one-man war against the Klan. The Klan had carried out hundreds of floggings of black people in the last few years. To top everything off, the Klan had kidnapped a Negro deputy sheriff in Tulsa and cut off his ear. After listening to this catalogue of Klan violence, John just looked at Hoolie with narrowed eyes and said, "Just what you said, a one-man war."

Hoolie shook off his thoughts and decided to engage Eric Cooper in conversation. Before he got in the car, Hoolie noticed that the Cooper boy had a trench knife from the war on his belt. "Mr. Cooper," he said, "you weren't in the war, were you?" Hoolie was certain Eric Cooper didn't look old enough to have served.

"No, sir."

"You're carryin' a '17 trench knife, a knuckle duster, right?"

"Yeah, it was my brother's."

"He in the war?"

"Yep. He got kilt couple of years back. Train hit his automobile."

"Ahh, sorry to hear about that. What's his name?"

"Ben," Eric said without emotion.

"I'm sorry too," J.D. said from the backseat. "I'll say the same to your pa."

Eric Cooper guided the big Packard onto an even rockier dirt road that led to a large, prosperous-looking ranch house. A hay barn, several outbuildings, a big horse corral and stable, and a bunkhouse for the cattle wranglers were all spread out on what Hoolie guessed was about two acres. The Cooper ranch was of course much larger, and the cattle herd or herds were probably grazing at least a mile away from the house.

A small man in high boots and a soft felt ten-gallon hat stood on the porch as Eric Cooper parked the touring car on the side of the road fifty or so feet from the house. Hoolie immediately noticed that there were no chickens, guinea fowl, geese, or even dogs around. That struck him as unusual—even cattle ranchers kept chickens for a welcome change from eating beef all the time, and they always had one or two dogs around to protect the chickens from badgers, raccoons, coyotes, and foxes. Guinea hens went after snakes, and geese were among the best watchdogs a person could have around. Cooper must be a pure cattleman who had no time and no wife to deal with anything else.

Cooper stepped down from the porch and extended his hand to J.D. He gave Hoolie a quick once-over and did not offer his hand. Cooper turned to J.D. and said with a smile, "Name's Paul. I got the letter from the lawyer and your telegram. I'm glad to cooperate with you. Please come inside."

He glanced at Hoolie again and said to J.D. in an offhand manner, "Your boy can go 'round to the kitchen and get him a biscuit."

J.D. glowered at Cooper. "Mr. Cooper, Mr. Smith here is my associate. I would ask you to treat him as such. He is no servant."

Cooper dropped his eyes to the ground and frowned. Clearly he was not used to being told that his behavior was unacceptable or that Indians were "associates" of white men. "All right, come in," he whispered through his teeth. Cooper led them into the front parlor and had them take seats. Eric disappeared.

"You boys want some water? Don't got coffee and I don't have liquor 'round the house. Christian and temperance. Don't smoke neither. Got a colored gal workin' here. She'll be in shortly to run and fetch you somethin'."

J.D. pulled off his hat, rested an ankle on one knee, and placed his bowler in the figure four of his legs. Cooper had offended him. He chose to forget offering condolences to the man.

"Don't worry about that," J.D. said brusquely, causing Hoolie to look at him incredulously. "Now, Mr. Cooper, I want to know everything you know about Mr. Shotz. Sam Berg said you might have some information about what he was doin' while he was here."

Hoolie kept his mouth shut and watched Cooper intently, tying to measure the lift of an eyebrow or the casual twitch of the man's lips.

"Berg?" Cooper paused for a moment and remembered. "Oh yeah, that Jew lawyer in Tulsa called me on the telephone. As a good Christian, I usually don't have no truck with Jews. But this was about Shotz, so I went along." Cooper paused again. "Well, Shotz wasn't here that long, seems to me. He asked me about how much acreage I got and if I lease from the local redskins." He raised an eyebrow, but both Hoolie and J.D. let the derogatory word pass. "Anyways, he was askin' lots of questions about leasin' and who owns what hereabouts."

He took a deep breath and darted his beady gray eyes back and forth between J.D. and Hoolie. Finally he added, "I tried to put him in touch with Alonzo Hughes down to the Indian agency office. Told him Al would help him out with lookin' into leases and such." He looked at Hoolie, raised his right hand to scratch his chin, and put in, "Said that there's nothin' 'round here says that oil is down there. But he was talkin' about runnin' cattle. I told him that he'd have to make a deal with the Indian Office and the local Indians. Chargin' Horse family has the most land. That's a big outfit—that's what I told him. The old man is still alive, but his son George . . . well, he's a real old fogey. He's around fifty and one of them cactus eaters. He was just a papoose durin' the Indian Wars. Two of his older brothers got killed in the '70s. George is the oldest of the boys the old man's got left. He don't like white men. Goes around sayin' we stole their lands. Takin' that peyote put him to preachin' against us in his meetings. They gotta learn that we won and that this is a Christian country."

Paul Cooper paused for a moment and took another deep breath. Unlike Hoolie and J.D., he had not removed his hat when he entered the house. He leaned back against his chair and pushed the brim of his hat up. "You know," he began, looking straight at Hoolie, "I think the gut eaters somehow got rid of Shotz."

"The who?" J.D. asked, taken aback.

"You know—the Indians. They eat beef gut, so we call 'em that."

"Well, why do you think the Indians did something to him?"

"I think he went out to the Chargin' Horse place, and they worked some kinda evil spell. Probably run him off or made him forget who he really is. You know them peyote eaters can do things like that. That's more than just singin' songs in a tipi. They get drugged up on that stuff and cast evil spells on people. The drum and the rattles call up devils. They're still savages. Cut your throat soon as look at ya." He looked at Hoolie and back to J.D. "You know that," Cooper said flatly.

J.D. shook his head. "No, I didn't know that, Mr. Cooper." Unsettled, J.D. rose from his chair. Hoolie followed suit and put on his hat, ready to leave.

"I'm sorry to have bothered you, Mr. Cooper. I think we should get back to town. We've got a lot to look into around there, and it doesn't look as if you know much about Frank Shotz's disappearance. So I'll bid you farewell."

"You're right. I don't know where he went. But I'll always cooperate with the right people. I know the people who hired Berg and sent you here. They're good folks."

"Well, them good folks are rich," mumbled Hoolie.

A quiet settled between the men at Hoolie's words. Mr. Cooper smiled; J.D. wrinkled his brow and let his face fall into a deep frown. One side of Hoolie's mouth went up into a half smile. "Good-bye, Mr. Cooper," he said. Hoolie walked out of the parlor and out the door. J.D. followed uncertainly. The Cooper boy was waiting by the Packard, chewing his matchstick and looking up at a cloudless sky.

Chapter II

THE SHOTZ OPERATION

Hoolie and J.D. checked into the K.C. Gregor Hotel. The Bryant was booked solid. They shared a room because of J.D.'s penchant for keeping expenses—even though he was always reimbursed—at a dead-level minimum. There was only one bed, and Hoolie said he'd sleep in his bedroll on the floor.

"O'd man like you," Hoolie kidded J.D., "needs a bed for his rheumatiz."

"Yeah, you just keep on thinking that, and I'll run circles around you at the next footrace. But thanks, sometimes I do need a soft place to lay my poor old Irish head."

Hoolie just grinned, stacked his rifle and belongings in a corner, and walked downstairs and out on the front sidewalk. Like other towns in Oklahoma, Anadarko was gradually replacing its boardwalks with concrete. Businesses like the hotel, bank, and haberdasher's came first. He looked up and down the wide street and grinned. Everything was redbrick, and all the buildings were connected with arched window frames. Hoolie knew that Anadarko was the home of the Riverside Indian School and the big agency for all the western tribes. He had heard that there were more Indian Baptist churches here than anywhere else. Funny, he thought, everything seemed red—from the street to the brick buildings to the dust in the air.

Hoolie knew that J.D. liked to unpack his cardboard case and put things meticulously away. Neither man had brought much clothing, but luckily Anadarko had a Chinese laundry one street over from the hotel. They could get their shirts and underwear washed. Hoolie smiled and mumbled to himself, "Either that or go down to the creek bed."

Hoolie walked over to a lamppost, leaned against it, rolled a cigarette, and struck a match on the seat of his trousers. Slowly smoking, he surveyed the main thoroughfare of what looked to him like a thriving little city that served the surrounding farms and ranches as well as the government officials who ran the Indian schools, the local Indian health field nurses, and the Indian Office services. There was probably a feed store on the edge of town, and likely as not, Anadarko supported a few honky-tonks further out. Funny thing, Hoolie thought to himself, these one-room shacks that sold liquor and played some music on the Victrola for people to dance to appeared all over the countryside after Volstead. The poor white sharecroppers and cattle wranglers frequented them, and the bootlegger operators got wealthy. Sometimes a fiddle player showed up and the croppers would drink and dance until daylight. The poor black sharecroppers had them too, but they called them juke joints. Most of them had live music—usually a couple of old men with guitars and maybe a harmonica. Hoolie had been into both and preferred the black peoples' music. He wondered if there were any juke joints around Anadarko.

J.D. came out of the hotel, spotted Hoolie at the lamppost, and strolled over. "You takin' in the sights?" he asked sarcastically. Hoolie just lowered his eyes and grinned in a lopsided way, shaking his head at J.D.'s own particular brand of sarcastic humor.

The older man pulled out a gold case and took out a pre-rolled, factory-made cigarette. "This place ain't any better than the rest of the hick towns in this state. No trolleys, only a few cars, and a bunch of Bible-pounding hayseeds with no brains."

"Damn, you're harsh on these people," said Hoolie. "They're pretty much just quiet farmers and cattlemen."

J.D. smirked. "Didn't our visit with Cooper tell you something about these people? Let me tell you about these 'quiet farmers.' Ten years ago they caught a colored man named Simmons, took him to a trestle, hanged him, poured coal oil over him, and burned him up.

"Tell you something else—three, four years ago, this town just about emptied out so that the same bunch who did the lynchin' could go to one of that ex-baseball-bum-turned-preacher Billy Sunday's tent shows. He played ball in Chicago when I was a kid— the White Stockings then—and he didn't play that much. Did you know that now he's taking money from J.D. Rockefeller, the Standard Oil fella, to preach to these saps that liquor is bad but puttin' their hard-earned money in the hands of big business is good? And they usually throw what money they got left at Sunday's shiny brogans. So he's got the cash to pal around with the Rockefellers. I'd need a stiff drink of hooch just to listen to Billy Sunday for half a minute. They call it the sawdust trail to Jesus. These hicks, they're dumber than the dumbest jackasses."

It was Hoolie's turn to smirk. "I'm glad I'm not on your bad side. Why are you so mad at everybody?"

J.D. drew deeply on his cigarette and fastidiously brushed a piece of lint from his coat lapel. "It's that Cooper fella. I know damn good and well that he knows more about Shotz than he lets on."

"I kinda thought so too."

J.D. just nodded thoughtfully. "Well, I'm off to see the coppers in this burg. Why don't you snoop around town? Maybe some of the locals will let somethin' slip." J.D. looked down at his knee-high boots and grimaced. "Shoulda put some shoes on. Well, too late for that. Let's meet up around six. They say there's a good café down the street. Called Violet's. We'll meet up there for supper. That leaves us a couple of hours."

"All right. See you later." Hoolie stepped down from the sidewalk and crossed the street. He had seen two Indian men in braids and high black hats walking on the other side of the road. He thought he might catch them and start up a conversation. The Shotz operation was underway.

Hoolie was getting bolder lately. Among his new Osage relatives, he had become an honored young man. Although no one would say anything out loud, the Osage people somehow knew that he had avenged the deaths of Ben Lookout and Tommy Ruffle, two widely respected Osage men. Ben, who was Hoolie's wife's father, and Tommy, the grandson of a revered Osage leader of the buffalo days, both had been murdered. Hoolie's newfound position as a warrior in the Osage way gave him a certain amount of confidence, and he seemed less nervous and shy when he talked to strangers.

He had approached to about five feet behind the two Indian men when a bullet smacked into the brick wall three feet from his skull. The sight of the bullet strike came at the same instant that Hoolie heard the gun go off. The round plowed into the wall and blew back reddish-colored dust and bits of brick. Everyone dropped to the sidewalk. Hoolie thought that the shooter must be very close—close enough not to miss again—but luckily no more shots were fired.

Lying prone with his hands covering his head, Hoolie could see nothing but the sidewalk. He cast his eyes up a bit and saw the feet of the two Indian men lying in front of him and the skirt bottom and lace-up shoes of a woman huddled in a door frame.

Since the shooting had stopped, Hoolie ventured a quick look in the direction of where the bullet had come from. He turned his head to the left. In the middle of the street was a white man standing with legs spread and a long-barreled .38 Colt revolver in his right hand. The man wore a neat brown fedora, a pair of black trousers with garish red suspenders, and a gleaming white shirt. His tie, like his sleeve garters, was royal blue. The blue tie and garters set off his eyes. Hoolie thought they were the meanest-looking pale blue he had ever seen. *Crazy eyes*, he thought.

The stillness of the moment was finally broken when the man with the .38 said in a low voice, "Get up, Indian—might as well take it like a man."

Hoolie's mind was in turmoil. He kept wondering who he had offended enough to take a shot at him after only a few hours in Anadarko.

The man with the gun raised his voice. "Get up, you sombitch gut eater —I'll kill you lyin' there like the snake you are. . . . Kick you into the street, by God."

Although Hoolie couldn't see which man answered, he heard one of the Indian men in front of him threaten in an unafraid voice, "Festus MacFarland, you let me get up, and we'll fight it out. No guns—just me and you. And I'll kill you with my bare hands."

Hoolie slowly raised his head once he heard that he was not the target of this MacFarland's rage. He saw another man in a blue jacket and a high-crowned cowboy hat slowly approaching MacFarland. This man held an old Colt .44. The gun's hammer was cocked and was pointed directly at MacFarland's head, and the man had a badge shaped like a star within a horseshoe. Hoolie thought that whoever he was, he was law. Through narrowing eyes, the lawman surveyed the sidewalk and the pistoleer, then said, "Put the pistol down, MacFarland. I'm placin' you under arrest. . . . Put it down or I'll blow a hole in you big enough for a locomotive to pass through."

MacFarland lowered the gun to his hip and eased the .38's hammer down on the cylinder. He dropped the pistol to the street.

The two Indian men quickly got to their feet and Hoolie came to one knee. The huddled woman rose and brushed off her skirt. She cast a haughty gaze toward the scene and stared straight at Hoolie as if he had done the shooting. She raised her chin and coolly walked away. Hoolie somehow got the notion from her demeanor that shootings occurred in Anadarko on a regular basis. At least to the woman it seemed more of a nuisance than a deliberate and deadly act. Hoolie pushed himself to a standing position, his leg wound from France hurting considerably.

One of the Indian men spoke up. "Deputy Albright," he said to the lawman, "take his gun and let me and him fight it out. Or let me borrow yours and give his back to him. One way or another, me and him is gonna kill the other."

Albright answered quickly but with a smile. "You keep still there, Chester. Festus here is a-goin' to the hoosegow. He's goin' outta the bootleggin' trade. And you might be in the can too, if'n you don't be still."

The deputy walked up to MacFarland, picked up the .38, and stuffed it into his belt. He kept his own pistol pointed at MacFarland's head and told him to turn around. In less than ten seconds, the deputy had MacFarland in handcuffs and in a kneeling position. Albright put his pistol back into a beautiful hand-worked holster on his right hip and withdrew from his back pocket a small blackjack. He looked at Hoolie. "You there," he called, "you see it happen?"

Hoolie looked around for a moment and said, "Yes, sir, sure did."

Albright narrowed his eyes and said flatly, "You ain't from around here, are you?" It was a question that white lawmen seemed to ask Hoolie nearly every place he went.

"No, sir," he answered. "I'm from Adair County, and now I live over in Osage County."

But as Hoolie opened his mouth to speak, the handcuffed shootist on his knees interrupted, "Now wait a minute, Albright— you ain't gonna listen to no redskin, are ya?"

Without warning, Albright slapped the blackjack across MacFarland's forehead. The man reeled backward and then pitched forward. He landed with his face down on the street. Hoolie grimaced. The man was hurt pretty bad; the cut on his forehead was bleeding profusely.

Without so much as blinking, Albright asked Hoolie to repeat himself. After doing so, the deputy demanded, "Well, what'd you see?"

"Well, Deputy, I was tryin' to catch up to these two men," Hoolie said while sweeping his right hand toward the two Indian men standing near him on the sidewalk. "Then a bullet hit the wall a couple of feet from my head. I went to the ground fast. Didn't see anything for a minute. Then I heard this man . . ."

Albright raised his chin to acknowledge Hoolie's explanation, the man on the ground groaned, and Hoolie nodded at MacFarland and continued, "He yelled out that he was gonna kill one of these men here. That's it. Then you showed up."

MacFarland began to stir and opened his mouth to protest again. Albright bent over and shook the blackjack in front of the man's eyes. "Shut your trap, Festus, or I'm gonna let this little fella give you another kiss on the head." MacFarland rolled his head away from the blackjack and fell silent.

The deputy raised himself to his full height, looked at Hoolie, and lightly tapped the blackjack in the palm of his left hand. "That all you have to say?" he asked.

"Yes, sir," Hoolie replied quickly.

"What's your business here?" the deputy added.

A crowd was gathering around the scene. Before Hoolie could answer, a gruff voice spoke out from Hoolie's right. It was J.D.

"Deputy, this man works with me."

Albright narrowed his eyes and stared straight at J.D. He said nothing, but everyone immediately knew that J.D. had some explaining to do.

"I was on my way to the courthouse," J.D. said evenly, "when I heard the ruckus. I'm J.D. Daugherty. I'm a detective out of Tulsa.

We'd like to go with you to the courthouse. My friend here will give you his full statement, and I'll talk to your sheriff. That'll get us all off the street. Fair enough?"

Deputy Albright was visibly taken aback. "Yeah, it's okay. Ah, well . . . we better go to the jailhouse."

Albright leaned down to help MacFarland back to his feet. He looked directly at the two Indian men now standing close to Hoolie. "You two," Albright said, pointing with the blackjack toward them, "can go now. We'll sort this out at the courtroom."

The man Albright had called Chester leaned toward the other man and whispered something in a language Hoolie took to be one of the several spoken in Anadarko—whether Caddo, Wichita, Delaware, or Kiowa, he didn't know. It might even be Comanche, Hoolie thought; they lived a bit farther south and west.

After Chester had whispered in his ear, the other man just nodded and folded his arms across his chest. Chester said, "Deputy, he took a shot at me and my brother. We better go too."

"No, you don't, Boyiddle. You and your brother just go on home now."

It was clearly a lawman's final dismissal, but the Boyiddles held their ground. Hoolie was the first to speak. He turned to look at the Boyiddle brothers, at J.D., and then back at Albright. "It was them that got shot at, Deputy Albright. Somebody should—"

J.D. finished, ". . . find out why this fella's taking potshots at people in the middle of town."

The growing crowd surrounding them began to murmur about taking them to jail at that moment. Albright felt the tension and started to open his mouth when another deputy in a suit coat with a badge pinned to the left label stepped from the sidewalk to Hoolie's right and said in a low voice, "Let's take 'em all in, Marty. We'll get some answers. Let's vamoose." His pistol, an even bigger Colt Army version .45, was still holstered.

The second deputy helped Albright get MacFarland moving in the right direction. Then he fell behind and scanned his eyes over J.D., Hoolie, and the Boyiddle brothers. "Okay, you all come with me." He turned his eyes to the crowd standing motionless on the sidewalk. "All right, you all go home. You're interferin' with county business. Go on now." The crowd began to disperse.

"Everybody follow me," Albright called over his shoulder. The strange-looking parade of two Anadarko deputy sheriffs, a handcuffed bootlegger with a bleeding head, three Indian men, and a heavyset white man with a thick moustache headed to the redbrick Caddo County Courthouse.

><

Along the way, Hoolie discovered that the Boyiddles, Chester and Harold, were Kiowas and that three days prior they had taken Clem MacFarland, brother of Festus and his partner in the illegal liquor business, and beaten him within an inch of his life. The Boyiddles had put Clem in what served Anadarko as a hospital with a smashed nose, a ripped ear, and a badly bruised hipbone. Chester justified the beating. "He was sellin' his whiskey—bad stuff too—to young peoples. Made us mad. So we took him out behind the lumberyard and whupped him. I wish I'da had a bullwhip on me. But I didn't, else old Clem would be in the infirmary permanent."

"How'd you hurt his hip?" asked Hoolie.

"Don't know," answered Harold, "coulda been that we throwed him down on some rocks. Didn't break it though."

They reached the courthouse and ascended the steps. Albright pushed MacFarland through the door into a main hall. On the other side of the little wooden railing were two desks. Behind one sat a woman with a long pencil in her hair. Hoolie presumed that the man sitting behind the other desk was a lawman, but since he was not in uniform or wearing a firearm, Hoolie didn't really know. But then again, the Anadarko lawmen he had seen all wore their own individual versions of uniforms. The thing to look for was the badge.

Without hesitation, Albright pushed MacFarland through the swinging gate in the railing and said, "Follow me." The other deputy who had come to Albright's aid said, "You can handle it from now on, Marty. I'll get back to work." He turned and exited the building, and Hoolie, J.D., and the Boyiddle brothers formed a column behind Deputy Albright.

They went through a door into an almost bare room with a single wooden desk and a jowly, bald green-eyed man in a khaki shirt with a gold badge pinned to it. He smiled widely when everyone crowded into the office, and then he leaned forward and put both hands on his green desk blotter. Still smiling, he said in an unexpectedly high voice, "Well, what have we got here, Marty?"

"Sheriff, Festus here thought he'd take a shot at the Boyiddles. Here's his gun. This fella here"—he indicated Hoolie with an arm sweep—"saw the whole thing." Then he looked directly at Festus. "I'm lockin' you up, boy," he said.

The sheriff raised his head, retaining his wide smile the entire time, and looked at J.D. "And who might you be?" he asked with a jovial, fraternal air.

Albright started to interject, but the sheriff raised his hand. The gesture stifled any and all commentary. "I think he can answer for hisself, Marty, thank you."

J.D. dragged a thumb across his moustache and coughed. Hoolie took off his hat at that moment and stroked the hollows in its crown. J.D. watched Hoolie's nervous fiddling with the hat, frowned, and looked pointedly at the smiling sheriff.

"Well?" the sheriff said, still grinning.

"Sheriff," J.D. began, "I was coming to see you when I heard a shot. I turned around, came back to my hotel, and found that my associate here was being questioned about the incident."

"Who are you?"

"My name is J.D. Daugherty. I'm a private investigator outta Tulsa. I have my office there. This is my operative, Mr. Hoolie Smith. I was hired to look into a missing persons case."

"Who's missing?"

"A man by the name of Shotz. He came here to look into the cattle business. He hasn't been heard from for a couple weeks."

"Never heard of him," the sheriff said. The grin left his face and was replaced by a grimace of malice. He pointed a chubby index finger at MacFarland. "Take that worthless so-and-so downstairs and lock him up."

"Yes, sir," Albright said with a grin. He jerked on MacFarland's cuffed hands hard enough to cause a yelp from the prisoner, grabbed MacFarland's shirt collar, and pushed him through the door.

"All right, Mr. Daugherty, Mr. Smith," the sheriff continued, "let me introduce myself. I'm sheriff of Caddo County. Name's Ferrell Wynn. Got reelected last year. This is my fifth term."

The office door opened and in walked another fat balding man in a blue suit, a badge pinned to his left label.

The smile left Sheriff Wynn's face once again. "It's gettin' crowded in here," he said. He looked at the man in the blue suit who had literally pushed his way between Hoolie and the Boyiddle brothers. "What can I do for you, Chief?" Wynn said. But before the man could speak, the sheriff held up his hand, once again bringing silence to the room. "Gentlemen," Wynn said, "this is city police chief George Collins."

"Sheriff," Chief Collins said, "I think you brought in Festus MacFarland on a shooting charge. That's city business, disturbing the peace."

Sheriff Wynn grinned even more brightly. "Well, George, I'm pretty sure that we have him on a more serious charge. It seems he tried to murder the Boyiddle brothers here. It's gonna end up as a 'state versus' charge, so we're justified in bringin' him in.

"Another thing is that the MacFarland brothers were runnin' liquor. There's Volstead and there's also laws against sellin' whiskey to kids. Might as well throw in the state laws and ordinances against sellin' liquor to Indians. The Boyiddle brothers took Clem MacFarland to task over it. Festus tried to kill Chester and would probably have gone after Harold as well. That's intent to kill, George. It's more than a misdemeanor disturbing charge."

"Wynn, these two beat up a white man, and Festus acted as a brother would. The real culprits are these two."

Collins pointed at the Boyiddle brothers and looked directly at Hoolie. "Who the hell are you?" he growled.

J.D. tried to step between Hoolie and Collins. He put out his hand and said, "Pleased to meet you, Chief, I'm—"

The sheriff cut in. "These men are *my* witnesses, Collins. I'll do the interrogating."

Collins turned and placed both balled fists on Wynn's desk. He leaned over, his face directly in front of the sheriff's. He whispered in a spine-tingling hiss, "You're gonna be sorry you crossed me."

Sheriff Wynn fairly leapt up from his chair. He closed the distance between his and the chief's face. "You tryin' to threaten me, Collins?"

"Call it anyway you want. The MacFarlands are important people in this town. If these savages are gonna beat up an upstanding white citizen and you don't do nothin' about it, then Festus was justified in takin' a shot at 'em."

"There ain't no justifyin' shootin' up the place and tryin' to kill somebody that's tryin' to keep these bootleggers from sellin' to kids. The goddam MacFarlands are scum, and you're on the take."

Collins stiffened and said through clenched teeth, "You're just lookin' for a payoff yourself, by God."

Wynn began to move from behind his desk. Both Hoolie and J.D. edged toward the door. Getting in between the two highest-ranking lawmen in Anadarko would have been a stupid move. The Boyiddles were thinking the same thing. They kept moving their eyes between each other and the door.

Suddenly the tension in the room broke. Deputy Albright entered the office saying, "Got him locked up like . . ." His voice trailed off as he realized the sheriff and the police chief were glaring at each other from a distance of only about two feet.

Collins backed down. Whether he was afraid of Albright or was feeling he was outnumbered for the first time, Hoolie couldn't really tell.

The chief chuckled deep in his throat and said, "Okay . . . okay, Ferrell, we'll work this out later." Gracefully done for a heavy man, he neatly pivoted on the ball of his left foot and brushed J.D. as he headed for the door. J.D.'s eyes briefly flashed anger at being touched by the chief, but he quickly resumed his normal thin-lipped, dour expression. Opening the door to Wynn's office and not glancing back, Collins said over his shoulder, "Good day, gentlemen," to no one in particular.

Hoolie stood stock-still waiting for someone to say or do something. The Boyiddles seemed to sway in unison to a rhythm locked in their own minds. Albright glared at the door. Sheriff Wynn simply clicked his tongue and sat down behind his desk. J.D. broke the silence. "Sheriff, if you'd like, my operative and I can give you full depositions and go. We do have some business to attend to."

The bright smile returned to Wynn's face. Hoolie immediately thought that it was the sheriff's "reelection smile" and could be put on at any given time. Wynn muttered, "No need . . . no need," and then checked himself. "Mr. . . . . ahh . . ."

"Daugherty," said J.D.

"Yes, Mr. Daugherty. I'd like to talk to you a bit. These boys," he said, indicating the Boyiddle brothers with a gesture of his right hand, "can go." Without saying another word, the Boyiddles slowly turned and disappeared through the office door. Hoolie stood there fumbling with his hat. "Deputy Albright," Wynn continued, "will take this man's deposition out front while we talk."

Hoolie began to ease himself toward the door in the same way that the Boyiddles made their exit. He still wanted to talk to them. Hoolie raised his eyebrows at J.D. in a silent way of asking if J.D. needed help. J.D. answered the unasked question: "I'll be right out. I'm gonna have a short conversation with Sheriff Wynn . . . that right, Sheriff?"

Wynn's bright smile stretched even further. "That'd be just fine, fine indeed."

Hoolie opened the door and exited, Albright following closely behind. The sheriff called out as they left, "Marty, now don't forget that deposition."

It only took Albright three strides to catch up with Hoolie. "Hold on a minute there, mister. What's your name again?"

Hoolie gave up on trying to catch up with the Boyiddle brothers. They were out the door of the courthouse so quick, it made Hoolie sigh in disbelief. He turned toward the deputy. "Name's Smith, Hoolie."

Albright coolly brought up his right hand to shake. Hoolie took it and gave it a quick pump, then took a step back.

Albright said, "Let's talk some. I gotta get a deposition. . . . Well, at least I gotta ask you some questions."

"All right, Deputy, we'll talk. But you know I'd like to talk to the Boyiddles. That'd be part of my job."

"How you get a job like that?"

"Just fell into it. J.D. had me talk to a old woman in Cherokee for him. He asks me to help out from time to time."

"You a Cherokee, huh?" He paused a beat. "Pretty good job?"

"Some ways. Get to travel."

"That might be good." Albright paused and looked down at his feet. "I reckon it beats hangin' around Anadarko all the time." He paused again and rubbed his hands together. "Let's go outside," he said finally.

"All right," Hoolie answered.

Once on the sidewalk, both men faced each other. Albright, smiling now, asked, "You in the war?"

"Yep. You?"

"Yeah. I was in the fight at Belleau Wood. I was a Marine. Took a bullet in the ribs and got shipped home."

"I was drivin' a French lorry near Château-Thierry. I was in the 42nd Division, Rainbow. I took some shrapnel in the leg on a wiring detail. I wasn't fightin', just workin'."

"That whole front was bad. Artillery. You could be twenty miles away and be killed with a bomb from a airplane."

"Yeah," Hoolie said, "I hope that it turns out like Mr. Wilson said, 'a war that ends makin' war.'"

"Sure hope so too. I got a baby boy. I'd sure hate to see him in the trenches."

Hoolie smiled, remembering Myrtle at home. "My wife . . . well, we got a baby on the way. From what her mama says, it's gonna be a boy. Her mama and her grandma can see things like that, in that way, you know?"

Albright probably didn't know much about medicine or being able to see things as yet unknown, but nevertheless he was smiling as if he'd discovered a kinship with Hoolie that he wanted to explore further. Hoolie was suspicious. There were only a few white men that he ever really trusted. J.D. was one, as was Mr. Sears, the owner of the automobile shop where Hoolie used to work; a sergeant in motor transport was another. On the other hand, Hoolie's experience with white people in general was limited. He had known very few while growing up in the hills. It seemed that in the army he got to know even fewer because they came and went so quickly. Afterward, most of the whites he dealt with were criminals, rich snobs, or lawmen—none of whom were particularly friendly. J.D. was a friend and so was Sam Berg, J.D.'s lawyer. Rose Chichester, the young woman he had helped rescue, visited Myrtle often and was seemingly just as excited about the baby as Myrtle's female relatives. She was a friend too.

Hoolie looked steadily at Albright and said, "How are you doin' since . . . ?"

"Well, still have dreams and such. I knew you was over there 'cause of your hat. How you doin'?"

"My relatives had ceremonies for me. Goin' to water, we call it. I do pretty well. The scars hurt sometimes, and I get jumpy at loud noises."

Albright laughed. "Me too. But my wife helps me out, and I go to church regular. They pray for me."

Hoolie nodded, knowing. "That's the best way. Prayin' sure helps."

"You know, nobody wears their campaign hats no more." Albright looked more closely at Hoolie's hat. "That a bullet hole in the brim?"

"Ahh, yeah. But it ain't from the war. Somebody took a shot at me a while ago when I was on a case. Lucky for me, he didn't shoot me in the eye."

"Dangerous work. Bein' a deputy in this town's pretty bad sometimes. Mostly it's the bootleggers. Like you saw today. They get a lot of money and think they can do just about anything. I'm temperance. Don't believe in drinkin'."

"Me neither."

Albright became serious once again. "I reckon we'd better talk about what happened. How 'bout havin' some coffee?"

"That sounds good." Hoolie extended his hand once again. "Name's Hoolie."

Albright shook hands again. "Mine's Martin. Call me Marty."

"Well, Marty, I better tell J.D. to meet up with us somewhere. We was goin' to a place called Violet's."

"Yeah, next street over."

Just as Hoolie turned back to the courthouse, J.D. walked out knuckling his moustache and looking self-satisfied. He greeted Hoolie and Albright. "Hool . . . Deputy Albright." He nodded in turn. "Had a good talk with Sheriff Wynn." He paused for a moment, still knuckling his moustache. "You boys wanna get somethin' to eat?"

"I'm ready," Hoolie said without hesitation.

"Well," Albright began after deliberating with himself, "I'd better finish up my shift and then get home to the wife."

"That'd be a good idea," J.D. quickly responded.

"See you around there, Marty," Hoolie said.

Albright turned and headed back into the courthouse.

"I break up something?" J.D. asked.

"Nope, don't think so. We was gonna get some coffee."

"Forget it for now. Let's go eat."

Chapter III

THE BOYIDDLE BROTHERS

The food at Violet's was reasonably good. Violet herself served and talked to the customers. Occasionally, a skinny white man in a not very clean white apron would step out of the kitchen to puff on a cigarette dangling from his mouth. Hoolie guessed he was the cook. A black busboy was everywhere at once, picking up dishes, wiping tables, bringing a pitcher of water to hand to Violet, and sweeping up the collection of food debris from the floor. Anadarko gourmets weren't all that neat.

Violet herself seemed to be interested in J.D. She kept drifting back to their table to check on how they were doing with their steaks, potatoes, and corn. She was probably around forty and very well dressed in a red-flowered dress, high-heeled shoes with straps across the instep, and a ruffled apron. Her dark curly hair was cut fairly short. She had two spit curls plastered to her cheeks. Those cheeks were heavily rouged and her lips were bright red. She had a soft, smoky voice and spoke with a smooth southern accent. To top it all off, Violet wore a red flower behind her left ear. Hoolie could tell that J.D. was flattered by his special treatment and taken with her looks and way of speaking.

"How're you gentlemen doin'?" Violet said for what Hoolie guessed was the fifth or sixth time during their meal.

"We're doin' just fine, miss," J.D. replied with as big a smile as he could muster. Hoolie thought he saw J.D.'s moustache quiver slightly in anticipation of Violet's attentions.

"Y'all new in town?" She smiled back.

"We are indeed," J.D. said with a slight clearing of his throat.

She put the pitcher of water she was holding down on their table and pulled out a chair. "All right if I sit down with y'all? I need to take a bit of a rest."

J.D. jumped to his feet and helped pull the chair out farther. It was as if he were a kid again, doing handsprings in the schoolyard to impress one of the giggling girls. He bowed as she lowered herself into the chair and crossed her legs, exposing a stockinged shin almost to the knee. J.D. nearly fell back into his own chair. Hoolie remained immobile and slightly amused.

"My name is Violet Comstock, and I own this place." She paused to let her name and proprietorship sink in. She held out her hand and said, "Well, where are you boys from?"

J.D. nodded and took her hand for a moment. "Tulsa, miss— the 'magic city.'" As he said that, he held up his left hand and spread his fingers before her eyes as if he were conjuring up a postcard of the place.

"I've been there," Violent said softly. "It's nice, but I like the friendliness of a small town. I believe Tulsa's just outgrown itself."

"Maybe so," J.D. said, "but I wouldn't be in business in a small town."

"Oooh, and what business are you in, sir?"

"I'm a private investigator. And Mr. Smith here's my associate and chief operative."

Hoolie had to put a hand over his mouth to hide his incredulous smile. J.D. always referred to him as his associate as if the private detective business actually supported the both of them. Hoolie thought of his way of making a living as being a mechanic with a wounded soldier's pension. Since he married Myrtle, he worked the horses and cattle at their home in Osage County. Myrtle, her sister Martha, her mother Lizzie, and Grandma Lookout handled all the family's money and dealt with their headrights and oil leases. Hoolie was happy with that arrangement; he didn't like to keep books. He worked for J.D. on a piecemeal basis and not for very good wages. He took on some mechanic jobs for family friends in Hominy, but nothing for money. J.D.'s insistence on calling him an associate put a shine on J.D.'s own sense of grandiosity.

"Name's J.D. Daugherty, miss. My associate's name is Hoolie Smith. You can call me J.D."

"Well now, J.D.," said Violet, "I would have guessed you were in the finance, oil, or mining business. Man as distinguished looking as yourself . . ."

J.D.'s grin was so wide that it looked like it hurt. He swallowed a bite of steak and had nearly choked when he stretched his mouth so wide. "No, miss, just a small businessman, like yourself . . . the difference being is you're a fine looking woman."

It was Hoolie's turn to nearly choke, but he hid it well. He was surprised by J.D.'s choice of words. J.D. was clearly playing the strutting rooster around Miss Violet. Hoolie wiped his mouth with the cloth napkin he had tucked in his shirt collar, laid it on the table, and pushed himself back. "I hate to interrupt," he said with a sheepish grin, "but I have to get back to associate business."

J.D. and Violet looked at Hoolie but made no protests about his leaving. "I'm gonna go look for the Boyiddles," he said.

Violet turned her head with a look of interest. It was as if she had a difficult time prying her eyes away from J.D. "You'll find the Boyiddle brothers out behind the feed store in the old corral. They still do some horse tradin' there. The Boyiddles know horses better'n anybody around."

"Sorry, ma'am, but it's sorta late for horse tradin'. They'd probably be somewheres else. I'll look around town, and if I can't find them, I guess I'll wait 'til mornin'."

"No, I don't think so. It's still light out, and besides, they put up a bunch of electric light bulbs out to the horse corral. Looks like a dance. Fact is they do put boards down and turn it into a dance floor. I'd bet those boys are still down there. They're horse-crazy, those two. 'Course, a lot of the men around here are horse-crazy. Beats me why a man would prefer a smelly old horse to a nice clean automobile." She turned to J.D. "You own an automobile, don't you?"

Hoolie spoke before J.D. could answer. "Well, thanks again, ma'am." Hoolie got up and headed for the door. J.D. would take care of the tab.

"I'm not very fond of horses myself, miss," J.D. said with his brightest smile.

》《

It took Hoolie all of five minutes to find the corral. He supposed it was located behind the feed store so ranchers and farmers would have a chance to look over the livestock for sale when they came into town to do business. Feed stores were always big meeting places in the country.

The brothers were sitting on the top rail of the corral and whispering to each other while looking at a couple of fine-looking horses. He walked up behind them and said, "Good lookin' mare, that one."

They turned in unison and recognized Hoolie immediately. The Boyiddle Hoolie remembered as Chester spoke first. "She is a good one. Eight-year-old, might be carryin' a colt."

Harold threw his leg over the rail and jumped down next to Hoolie. He took off his hat with one hand and brushed his hair with the other. After settling his hat on again, he said with a tilt to his head, "You lookin' for us? Or buyin' a horse?" Harold looked wary and not too pleased that Hoolie had come looking for him and his brother.

Chester landed on the ground next to Harold and brushed off his right sleeve. "Easy brother, this man's just tryin' to make a livin'. That so, innit?"

Hoolie smiled and adjusted his own hat. "That's so. I'd like to talk to you'ins for a while."

Both Boyiddles folded their arms in front of them. Hoolie recognized their posture as guarded. He proceeded with caution.

"You boys know a lot about what goes on around here, right?"

"No," Harold said with a lopsided smile, "we just know horses."

Chester chuckled while nodding his head. Hoolie knew he was being kidded and laughed along with them. The Boyiddles relaxed a bit, both dropping their arms and putting their hands in the pockets of their trousers.

"I've been in town for just a little while," Hoolie began, "and I've met a whole bunch of crazy people and watched a shootin'. I'd like to know about what I got myself into."

Harold answered, "You stepped into the middle of Anadarko. It's like that all the time."

Chester broke in. "Who you met?"

Hoolie tilted his head back in thought. "Well, there's Albright, Wynn, the police chief—what's his name? . . . Collins? . . . a rancher named Cooper, and the lady at the café. . . . And Cooper's boy."

"Yeah," Chester said, "you're meetin' the people in this town who run things. All you gotta do now is meet the mayor."

"And the rest of the bootleggers." This time Harold broke in with a knowing smile.

Hoolie's eyes narrowed. "Yep, I guess the MacFarland brothers take care of that part of city business?"

Harold answered, "They're just the catfish on the creek bed. The mayor and Collins run the town. The sheriff works for the county and says he's tryin' to clean things up around here, but the city police, the mayor's office, and the local Indian Office people go up agin him all the time. I think Wynn's runnin' his own business in liquor on the side."

It was a story Hoolie had heard before many times. As his friend John Tall Soldier always said, "It's all tied up together. Make enough money and everybody wants in on the deal."

Hoolie pulled off his hat and rubbed the brim with his finger-tips. "You think they're all together in the liquor business?"

Chester scowled. "Not just the whiskey, but they get together to make leases on our land and run cattle that ain't ours. The Indian Office people go around with all of them. That Cooper fella is leaseman for practically the whole tribe. Wichitas and Caddos too. He's pals with the Indian Office outfit that does the leases and with the police chief and the lawyers. And they all work with the bootleggers. It's all bound up together."

Hoolie stood for a moment with his hand over his mouth, con-templating what had been said. It was all too familiar, yet somehow different. He wanted to fix everything as his heart dictated, but he also knew that he was in Anadarko to investigate the disappear-ance of Frank Shotz. Hoolie decided to take an un-Cherokee-like direct approach. "You know anything about a fella named Frank Shotz?"

"Who?" said Chester.

"Shotz . . . a white man named Shotz."

"Sounds familiar," Harold answered. "He from around hereabouts?"

"No. He works outta Oklahoma City and Tulsa. He's some kin to a man who works for a lawyer that J.D. does business with. J.D.'s the white man who I work for."

"What's he doin' 'round here?" Harold made a circular gesture with his right index finger.

"Lookin' to get in the cattle business. That's why we went out to see the Cooper fella."

Chester broke in. "I worked cattle for Cooper oncest. He treats you good if you work hard. Pays good. I got too busy with the horses. We trade 'em and train 'em up too."

"What do you do with them?" asked Hoolie.

"We race 'em. Always got horse races at all the big doin's 'round here. The white people and the black people really like to bet on the horses. Indians like to bet too, but our people know horses better than them other peoples and win too much. We've had a good run of winners. We train 'em in the old way, just like they was in war or huntin' buffalo. They win a lot and we make some money here and there. Enough to keep us goin'." Chester puffed up his chest to punctuate his speech.

"Back to Shotz," Hoolie said, changing the subject. "He's been missin' for a time, and this lawyer sent J.D. and me out here to find him. So that's why we're askin' around about him."

Harold pointed with his lips toward the west and said, "There was a white man goin' around askin' about the cattle business. He was mostly talkin' to the white people, 'specially the Indian Office outfit and a few ranchers like Cooper. Coulda been him."

"Yellow hair. Tall . . . wore glasses. Wore a big straw hat," Chester put in.

"He talk to any Indians?"

"Not many," said Chester.

"He saw George Chargin' Horse. Talked to him in town, down on Main Street," said Harold.

"You know what about?"

"Well, George is a chief for the peyote church," Harold answered. "I help out. I talked to him and found out that this white man just wanted to look over his land. Camp for a few days."

"He didn't talk about range leases?"

"Nope. Just wanted to camp out."

"Mr. Chargin' Horse let him?"

"Yep," said Chester, "was out there for a day or two. But we ain't seen him since. I bet he's the man you're lookin' for . . . thinkin' about it."

"I think so, too," said Hoolie. "I'll have to talk to Chargin' Horse."

"That might be a good idea," said Harold. "We'll take you out there tomorrow if you want."

"That's good. I'll meet you here in the mornin'."

"You know how to ride?"

"Yeah, own a few horses myself."

"Good," said Harold. "We'll see you then."

>«

Hoolie went back to the hotel, sat in the room for a while, and then went downstairs. He went out in the cool evening air and sat down on a bench located on the walk in front of the hotel. At one point, a hotel employee came out and asked him what he was doing there. Hoolie held up his key and said, "I'm in 201." The hotel clerk left without saying a word.

Hoolie just sat on the bench and watched people go by. He heard what he guessed was a player piano at a café across the way. It was getting late, and J.D. hadn't shown up yet. Hoolie wondered if he was still sitting at the table, talking to Violet Comstock. In the back of his mind, he berated himself for not asking the Boyiddles about her—and the rest of Anadarko's denizens for that matter. He'd talk to them tomorrow while riding out to the Charging Horse place. Meanwhile, where was J.D.?

Hoolie went up to the room and rolled himself into a blanket on the floor. He had fallen asleep wondering about where J.D. was. Much later, he awoke to the opening of the door to his room. J.D. lurched in and sat on the bed. Hoolie rose up in the dark and said, "J.D., where you been?" He looked closely. J.D. was holding his right forearm close to his rib cage. "J.D., you all right? What's the matter?"

"Get the light," J.D. said, "and get a bandana or a washcloth. I got cut."

Hoolie eased J.D.'s coat off and finally got a look at the wound, or rather, wounds. The bleeding wasn't bad, and Hoolie could see that a knife had sliced through J.D.'s coat and had cut both his inner right arm and the side of his chest just below the armpit. Hoolie took his own knife and slit J.D.'s shirt and underwear, peeled the cloth away from the wounds, placed a folded bandana between arm and chest, and had J.D. press his arm hard against his side to staunch the bleeding.

"It ain't that bad, J.D. What the hell happened?"

J.D.'s lips were pressed together in pain. He took a deep breath and expelled the air from his lungs in a long whisper. It smelled of whiskey. He took another breath and said lowly, "Comin' back from Violet's place. Somebody came up from behind. I heard somethin' and started to turn. He stuck the knife between my arm and ribs then run off. Didn't see any more than the blade. Looked like a sword or long-bladed knife. Guess I'm lucky."

"Yeah, you are. Let's see." J.D. raised his arm, and the bandana fell away. "Not enough blood for the bandana to stick. You're okay."

"I gotta find out who did this and get him thrown in the can."

"We'll do that all right." Hoolie looked questioningly at J.D. "Just what were you doin' at Violet's place past midnight?"

"Long story, my friend . . . long story." Hoolie got a towel from the stack on the bureau and made an adequate bandage. He wrapped J.D.'s chest and upper arm. J.D.'s pain subsided, and he lay back on the bed. He was asleep in less than a minute, heavily exhaling whiskey fumes.

Hoolie sat up for a while. He made sure that J.D. was sleeping well and that he had stopped bleeding. It was a shallow scratch really, but painful because of where it was located. Worse was that J.D. had been attacked.

Hoolie rolled up in his blanket again. They'd been shot at and stabbed, and they had been in Anadarko for only one day. Hoolie was definitely in favor of abandoning the whole operation, but he knew J.D. well enough to realize that J.D. wouldn't give up the case until he found out who cut him. Hoolie dozed off wondering why J.D. had stayed so long at Violet's Café and whether or not he should go with the Boyiddles out to the Charging Horse place.

Chapter IV

VIOLET'S PLACE

After Hoolie had departed Violet's to look for the Boyiddle brothers, there were exactly six people left in the café: J.D., the cook, the busboy, a cowboy finishing a cup of coffee, an elderly man with no teeth and a bowl of soup, and Violet herself. She quickly hustled the cowboy and the elderly gentleman out, receiving from them cash and a signed note, respectively. When she returned to J.D.'s table, she sat down again and gave him a bright smile. "Drink?" she asked.

J.D. knuckled his moustache and rubbed his cheek. "What about Volstead?"

"Mr. Volstead can buy his own. You and me could have a couple, and we could talk. I'm pretty sure you'd like to find out more about this town—you being a detective and all on a case—and I'm the gal who can provide all the answers. How about it?"

"Miss Violet, you talked me into it."

"That's good. Now, how much is information worth? You all get expense accounts, don't you?"

J.D. pulled a face. Miss Violet was much greedier than he anticipated. "You're cagey all right, Violet. . . ."

"Call me Vi."

"Vi, I can offer cash for information. But it has to be good information. I'll let you know if it's good or not. We can just talk."

She smiled a knowing smile. "J.D., you're pretty cagey yourself. How 'bout some spirits?"

He nodded. Violet stood, walked slowly behind the lunch counter, bent over, and withdrew a pint flask of what was obviously whiskey. "This is good Irish whiskey. Picked it up for a song. I figured a good Irishman would come in sometime to drink with. Volstead's sure made it hard for a girl to have a good time."

J.D. had a gleam in his eye. "Girl such as yourself could have a good time at one of the honky-tonks I know they got set up around here."

"This gal ain't goin' to no smelly dirt-floor shack out in the hay-fields. These cowboys ain't gettin' their grubby hands on me. Better to stay at home, have a drink or two, and go to bed by myself. Ha, ha."

"Violet, you're the woman of my dreams."

"Now, Mr. Daugherty, don't get too forward. It's early."

J.D. chuckled and tipped his glass. He downed the whiskey in one gulp and put the glass down. She immediately tipped the flask over the glass to fill it again. "Damn, that's some fine liquor, Vi," J.D. said enthusiastically.

"It is good, ain't it?"

As J.D. was about to answer, the cook and the busboy peeked out of the kitchen. "All cleaned up, Vi—you gonna lock up?"

"I'll do it, boys. You two have a good night."

"Good night," they said, almost in unison.

She turned her attention to J.D. "Well, Mr. Daugherty, what do you want to know about my town?"

"Call me J.D. Now, you probably heard about the shootin' today. Well, Hoolie was real close to bein' killed."

"Oh?"

"Yeah, he was about a foot away from where the bullet struck."

"Poor man. Just come into town too."

"Well, he wanted to talk to the Boyiddles and, unfortunately, they were the targets. Anyway, the deputy came and arrested this MacFarland fella, and we all went down to the courthouse. Me, Hoolie, the Boyiddles, and a deputy named Albright. That's when we met up with the sheriff and the police chief."

"Lucky you," Violet said sarcastically.

J.D. chuckled and took a sip of his whiskey. "Okay, why 'lucky me'?"

"What's in it for me?"

"You got some good information?"

"I got some dirt."

"Now, what do I need with dirt?"

"You could use it to get these no account . . . say, listen, why are you in Anadarko anyway?"

"I'm lookin' for a guy. Name of Shotz. He's an oilman lookin' to get into the cattle business. Been missin' for a couple of weeks."

"He's a tall blond man, ain't he?"

"That's what I hear. Me and him haven't been formally introduced. I'm on a job."

"Well, he's sure been here. Came in for supper a time or two. Good lookin' man. He rich?"

"I imagine he's pretty well off. One of his relatives works for a lawyer in Tulsa. Readin' for the law. Mr. Shotz keeps the lawyer on retainer. He's got investments all over and needs legal services all the time. Don't see how it's worth it myself . . . spendin' that much money just to keep other people off your back."

Violet just kept looking at J.D., taking it all in. This was good material for gossip.

"Saaaay," J.D. said finally, "I was supposed to be askin' the questions."

"That's so, sweetie, why don't you do it?"

J.D. took another drink. "All right, here goes. Tell me all you know about those people. It's gotta be worth ten bucks."

"Oh, it's worth more'n that, hon. But I'll give you something, and we'll see if you want to spend more."

"That's a deal. Now, about the police chief—Collins is his name, right?"

"Right you are. And that's a man that shoulda been hung. But in Anadarko he gets to be chief of police. Beats all, don't it?"

"Now, why should he have got hung?"

"Oh, honey, that man's a killer, a rapist, and a real gangster. He runs the liquor business around here, and I know for a fact he killed Bobby Hensley."

"Who's Bobby Hensley?"

"He was a local boy. A good baseball player and real fine young man. His daddy was runnin' for sheriff and woulda won too. Bill, Bobby's daddy, made some pretty tough speeches against Collins. Bobby got into a scuffle with two or three of Collins's people and whipped 'em. He was a big, strong boy. The next day they found his body down near the train depot. He was cut up pretty bad. Somebody stabbed him and cut his throat—ripped him all up. Bobby's daddy dropped out of the run for sheriff. He said he was too grieved to go on. The family moved away, I think to Tulsa. . . . You every heard of 'em?"

"Nope. How do you know it was Collins?"

"If it wasn't him, it sure was one of his people. I'd bet he'd ordered it done, if nothin' else. Bobby woulda made trouble for the chief."

"Sounds like Collins helped Wynn get to be sheriff, right?"

"Well, in a roundabout way. He sure made it easier for Wynn. But—"

J.D. cut in, "It seems like Sheriff Wynn and Chief Collins don't get along too well either."

"That's so . . . that's so," Violet answered with pursed lips. "But that's a fallin' out betwixt two crooks. Wynn's a killer too, and he's tryin' to cut Collins outta the whiskey trade. I guess you could say that at least he ain't no rapist."

"Oh no?"

"No. He ain't that kinda fella, ol' Ferrell. He's mean as hell, but he ain't a lecher."

"Okay, but Collins is?"

"Sure is. He raped a young Indian girl, name of Botone. Felicia Botone. But Indians don't get justice 'round here. Some folks tried to get him locked up, but nobody'd do anything. Her family went to the Indian Office people, but they didn't do nothin' either. Finally, one of her brothers went after him. He stabbed George once, but the knife glanced off his ribs and didn't do much damage—just a few stitches. The iodine probably hurt the most. Anyway, Ferrell Wynn killed a man over in Oklahoma City a few years ago, they say. It was over a girl that he was seein' at the time. Now, he was for sure in on killin' a Negro ten years ago. It was a lynchin'."

"I heard about that one. We had a riot and a near lynchin' two years ago in Tulsa. Oklahoma's crazy over this. I hope the new governor does somethin' about it."

"Me too," Violet said, nodding her head. "This Klan stuff is runnin' the state into the ground."

"That's true. The Klan is changin' its tactics though. They're takin' people out and whippin' them. Or just beatin' 'em up. They pretty much stopped stringin' up the Negroes and the Jews . . . for now."

"Well, I'm pretty sure Ferrell's in with the Klan. Collins stays away from Klan doin's, but they're both crooks."

"Tulsa's pretty bad as well. Last year we had a Negro deputy sheriff kidnapped. The Klan left him on the street with his ear cut off. And then the coppers arrested a Jew named Hantaman for peddlin' narcotics. He wasn't, and the cops let him out and somebody let the Klan know. The Kluxers nabbed him front of a movie house on Greenwood—that's in the Negro section of town—and took him out of town to beat him up. They mangled his privates."

"Oh God, that's terrible." J.D. thought that Violet's look of disgust was genuine. Maybe she was indeed sympathetic to the idea of getting rid of the KKK.

"Well," J.D. said contemplatively, "the Klan has got to go. It leads to chaos. And chaos is a breakdown of law and order. You can't have any kind of peace with those fools runnin' around."

"That's right," Violet agreed, "startin' with gettin' shed of Wynn and Collins." She paused for a moment and bit her lower lip in thought. She nervously rubbed her hands together and fiddled with one of her spit curls. "You know somethin', hon, this town needs cleanin' up, just like in the old dime novels. A new lawman comes into town, locks up the crooks, and sweeps the streets clean of graft, grifters, and the yeggs who ply their trades in a place like that."

"Yeah, this place probably does need a crackdown. But that's somethin' that somebody from here has got to start." J.D. ran his thumb along his moustache and took another sip of his whiskey. He was feeling his blood heat up with the alcohol. "Somebody around here's got to get things movin'," he said. "How about a newspaper editor?"

"Nah, the paper's in Wynn's hands. It comes out for reform, but just goes after the bootleggers. Uphold Volstead and all that. Sometimes the editor—his name is Al Dupuy—writes an editorial about corruption in the city police. But nobody gets riled up. I think the mayor wants to get back in control. He's kinda shunted off to the side. Wynn and Collins are the ones holdin' all the marbles."

"Who's the mayor?"

"It's Archie Rohrbach. They was worried about him durin' the war on account of him bein' a Hun, but he proved hisself. He bought bonds and his oldest boy went off to France. Got his arm blowed off. Come to think on it, there's a lot of doughboys here in town. I bet they'd like to see some kinda clean sweep. They didn't fight to save the world for democracy when they ain't got it here."

"Why don't the mayor call the governor? Jack Walton ran on a reform ticket and promised to put the Klan outta business. I bet he'd help out if this Rohrbach put it the right way."

"What's the 'right way'?"

"I could talk to the mayor. I've been in on cleanin' up towns before. It ain't easy, but you gotta have the right backing and be able to call on higher authorities to back you up—like governors and the state troopers or guard. Sometimes these things get tough. If we could link up Wynn with the Klan, Governor Walton would be on Rohrbach's side in a heartbeat."

"Well, dearie, talkin' to the mayor is easier than you think. He lives in my boardinghouse and takes all his meals right here. It's only eight o'clock—let's go over there right now. He'll be in the parlor, sittin' and readin' a book."

"You own a rooming house?"

"Sure do. I'm the richest gal in town."

"You are?"

"Yep. I own three buildings down Main and got an interest in the Bryant Hotel. I'm part owner of a couple of cattle ranches around these parts, and the bank comes to me for advice."

"How'd you get so rich?" J.D. asked with a smile of incredulity.

"That's for me to know and you to find out. I'll get your hat, hon, and we'll go see the mayor."

》《

Violet and J.D. walked in dead silence to her rooming house. They didn't speak primarily because J.D. was in deep contemplation about why and how Violet Comstock had manipulated him into talking to Anadarko's mayor, Archie Rohrbach.

J.D. opened the door for her and stepped into an opulent parlor. Violet took his hat, took off hers, and laid them both on a richly carved table standing against a wall papered in what looked like velvet paisley designs. A stairway stood directly in front of him and to his right was a parlor done in purple chintz with two overstuffed chairs and an uncomfortable-looking love seat. In one of the chairs sat a skinny pinched-faced man in a high collar, reading a thick book with a brown cover. The man looked up, tilted his head to one side, closed his book, and said, "Welcome home, Miss Comstock. Who have we here?" His eyes had a glazed-over look as he stared unblinking at J.D.

"Arch, this is a new friend." She turned to J.D. and back to Rohrbach. "J.D., this is our mayor, Archie Rohrbach. Archie . . . J.D."

Rohrbach rose and stretched out his hand. J.D. stepped forward, shook the hand, and stood back. The man smiled, and J.D. smiled back. Everything was so cordial and proper. It made J.D. apprehensive.

"Pleased to meet you, Mayor," J.D. said in his most formal voice.

"And you," answered Rohrbach.

Violet went to the love seat, sat, crossed her legs, and scratched her right knee. She leaned over and pulled off her shoes. She kneaded the Persian rug with her toes and said, "Now that all the proper greetings are over, let's get down to business."

Rohrbach and J.D. sat in the chairs and looked at her. "Arch," she began, "J.D. here is a private detective from the big city. I'd bet he could help us get this town out from under—"

"Now wait, Vi," J.D. said, "I don't know what the situation is. And . . . and I'm on another case."

"J.D., I'm a pretty good judge of men," Violet said, "and you are the type of man that could help us out. Besides that, we'd pay a good fee."

Rohrbach put in, "J.D. . . . . I'm sorry I didn't get your last name."

"It's Daugherty," J.D. quickly answered.

"Good. Mr. Daugherty, we do need outside help. This town has been taken over by the worst element of society: the bootleggers and the crooks. The graft is . . . well, it's beyond anything I can explain. I can't go to the governor because the crooks in this case are elected officials. One of these officials is a member of the Ku Klux Klan. And you and I both know that the state legislature is filled with members of that obnoxious organization. Although the governor was elected on an anti-Klan platform, he's stymied by the legislative branch. And if he did act independently, it would open up a hornets' nest within the state. I daresay that he would be impeached. I know you're working on a case now, but if you just take a short time to look into the matter, I . . . we could pay you handsomely."

J.D. was intrigued. "What would you want me to do?"

"Simply investigate city corruption," Rohrbach said. "Look into the links between the sheriff, the police chief, and the bootleggers. General crime."

"Mr. Rohrbach, you just met me. You don't know anything about me or, for that matter, you don't know if I'm a real private investigator. I've just talked to Miss Comstock here for a couple of hours."

"Believe me, Mr. Daugherty, Miss Comstock is the finest judge of people I know of and the best businessman—woman—that I know of. She knows about people just by talking to them for five minutes. I trust her implicitly."

"Besides that," Violet interjected, "we're pretty damn desperate. We'd've had to hire some strong-arm boys from outta town if you hadn't come along."

"Yeah?"

"That's right," she said with a quick nod of her head. "But we knew you were comin' here, so we decided to talk to you."

J.D. looked at Rohrbach, who nodded his head in agreement. "Yes, Mr. Daugherty, we knew exactly who you were."

"Why'd you ask me my name?"

"Because I wanted to keep up the deceit for a bit. I hope you don't mind. I felt I had to sound you out first. Violet of course thinks that's idiotic, and I'm afraid she's right. She comes straight to the point."

"You bet I do," she said with a look of determination.

J.D. smiled his broadest and knuckled his moustache. "Well, well, I gotta hand it to you. You both know the routine of keepin' a man unbalanced. That's okay though—I'll listen and then decide if I can help or not."

"That's all I ask," said Violet.

"First," said J.D., "how'd you know about me?"

Violet touched a spit curl and answered, "Why, young Mr. Cooper—the one who picked you up at the depot this mornin'.

Can't say much for his daddy, but I know Eric pretty well. He told us you were comin' to look into this missin' person business. I told you before that I don't know nothin' about it, but probably some of the Indians around here do. He was campin' out at the Chargin' Horse place."

"That's right," Rohrbach broke in. "I never met him, but he went out there. At least that's what I heard."

"Who'd you hear it from?"

"I don't recollect."

"I heard it from the Boyiddle brothers," Violet said. "They do some horse tradin' for me."

"Horse tradin'?"

"Oh my, yes. I like to win at the horse races around here. I go every chance I get. Own a couple of good ponies too."

"You are quite a businesswoman," J.D. said with a wider smile.

"You don't know the half of it, hon. . . . You don't know the half of it."

"Well, Mr. Daugherty," Rohrbach said, "are you interested in helping us out?"

"Let's just talk for a while," J.D. answered with a straight face. "Let's just talk—I like to be thorough."

≫«

J.D. left Violet's place three hours later with a three-hundred-dollar cash retainer in his wallet and a plan of action. As he walked down Main Street toward the hotel, he caught the sound of fast-moving footsteps coming from an alley on his right. He turned to look but saw nothing. He proceeded on his walk, heard another footstep, turned, and caught a glimpse of a long blade as it rammed between his arm and his rib cage. He turned quickly, still on his feet. Whoever had assaulted him ran immediately away after thrusting the knife. J.D. didn't see his assailant. Painful as the wound was, J.D. knew it wasn't life threatening. He wouldn't go to the law because of what he had heard at Violet's place. Better to find Hoolie. He held his arm close to his side and increased his pace toward the hotel.

Chapter V

THE CHARGING HORSE PLACE

The voice sounded like the harsh whisper of a cooling steam locomotive. "Hoolie . . . Hoolie . . . wake up . . . wake up, man . . . wake up." Hoolie blinked his eyes open, rolled over, and looked up at J.D. sitting on the bed. J.D. was fully dressed. The bloody shirt, bandana, and washcloth he had slept in were piled on the floor in front of the nightstand. Hoolie sat up, still covered with his blanket. "You all right?" he asked while knuckling sleep out of his eyes.

"I'm better than worse," J.D. answered. He paused for a moment and rubbed his cheek. "You got any dirty shirts and drawers? I'm gonna take this stuff over to the Chinese laundry soon as we talk awhile."

"Okay, I'm listenin'."

"I think we're gonna divide up."

Hoolie looked incredulous. "How come?"

"It looks like we got a new job."

"Oh yeah? Miss Violet want you to wait tables or maybe cook?"

J.D. frowned and then leaned back his head and gave a hearty laugh. He bent to one side in pain and clutched his shoulder, pressing his injured arm to his gashed side. "It hurts to laugh, goddammit."

"I know. I had that happen. I could make a tobacco poultice?"

J.D. caught his breath, waited for the pain to subside, and continued, "No, I'll get better. What I am gonna do is a town cleanin', and you, my friend, are gonna find Shotz. I gotta line on him."

"If you're all right, I'm gonna follow up on some things I heard yesterday. The Boyiddle brothers want me to head out to see George Chargin' Horse. He's a medicine man or chief for the peyote religion. His family's got a place a couple miles outta town. We're goin' out on horseback."

J.D.'s moustache moved upward on both ends. He was visibly happy. "I got the same information from Violet Comstock. When are you goin'?"

"They said they'd meet me out at the feed store corral anytime this mornin'. I figured I'd eat somethin' first."

"That's good. We'll go over to Violet's and eat in a minute. I'll fill you in on the other operation here right now."

"Okay," Hoolie said with a puzzled look. "Now you gotta tell me how and why you're gonna clean up this place."

J.D. sat up straight and rubbed his hands together. He pursed his lips and rubbed his multicolored moustache. He looked as if he were going to deliver a lecture and then proceeded to do so.

"I've done this before. What usually happens is a couple of folks take over the town from the rightful authorities. They play their own parts down but have somebody runnin' things for them. Right now the mayor doesn't have any say in anything and the town is bein' run by county sheriff Wynn and police chief Collins. Now they're at war with each other, so it's kind of a mess around here."

"Wouldn't it be better for them if they joined up?" Hoolie asked.

"You'd think so, but neither one of them has the upper hand. That's why I think they're workin' for somebody else. Those boys don't have the brains to run things around here without help. I gotta find out who's really runnin' things. There's gotta be two or three people out there with some real money and real brains. The main thing is that these people—whoever they are—are layin' low."

"Why do they do that?"

"Don't want to be directly up front. I think Collins gets some money from the bootleggers."

"So the MacFarlands run things?"

"Nah, too dumb."

"Then who?"

"I don't know yet, but it's somebody who's makin' money off the booze and gets away without anybody knowin' it. Could be anybody."

"How about Cooper? He's rich."

"Maybe. 'Course, there's a few rich folks around here. Violet's loaded—at least as 'loaded' goes in Caddo County. She's got a roomin' house and a café and a few other things she's invested in."

Hoolie grinned. "She's diversified, huh?"

J.D. smirked. "Yeah, I guess so."

"So, who else is rich?"

"There's a few around. We'll just have to see who's who."

"Then you pit them against each other?"

"That's right. You stir up a cauldron and then let the real authorities call in the governor with the national guard. That's how it usually plays out. The mayor's the one that hired us. So he's got legal authority on his side. He just doesn't have real authority. And Violet's behind him. So I don't know who's callin' the shots for Wynn or Collins. It might be that we just stir up the bottom of the pond and see what kind of poison comes to the surface. You can bet that the bottom-feeders will be fightin' each other for what's left. We'll get them then."

"But you gotta find out who's callin' the shots, right?"

"Yep, but that shouldn't take too long."

"Why's that?"

"If I could get MacFarland busted out, see who he goes to get back at—the sheriff or Albright or whomsoever—then make the play that Collins is settin' MacFarland against Wynn, and see who takes a poke at city hall, I could get this burg scrubbed clean in a week."

"Sounds like a tall order."

"Could be. I'll have to go easy until I get a hold of MacFarland's brother."

"I ain't even gonna ask how or why. Right now I better get some food and meet the Boyiddles."

J.D. narrowed his eyes and nodded his head. "Yep," he said, "that's a start."

>«

Hoolie met the Boyiddle brothers at the corral. They greeted him with handshakes in the Indian way: touch and release. They looked amazed at what Hoolie had brought with him. He sported a blanket roll with the collar of a blue work shirt poking out from one end, and his old rifle. Chester just said, "We ain't goin' huntin' that I know."

Hoolie replied with a slight twist on his mouth, "No, but I don't like to be without it, particularly since what happened yesterday."

"Why the bedroll? You plan on stayin' outta town?"

"Might."

Harold nodded and pulled at the collar of his shirt. "You could be right. Let's mount up and get to goin'."

The brothers had fixed up Hoolie with a nice bay mare a little over fourteen hands high. She had three white feet, and Hoolie mentioned the saying about not buying a horse with white feet: "One white foot, buy him; two white feet, try him; three white feet, be on the sly; four white feet, pass him by."

Chester just laughed. Harold said, "That's just o'd white man tales. White hoofs are a little weaker, but you just take care of 'em. We never shod our horses, but we got medicine if the hoofs crack. And you lead 'em over bad ground. Out here on the grass, it don't make much difference 'bout the color of a horse's feet. It's when you ride 'em over rocks and such and not takin' care of their feet that they come up lame."

Hoolie looked around as they rode. They avoided the gravel roads and stayed on the grass. They followed fence for the most part, crossing the roads only when going in and out of barbed wire gates. The horses were well trained. A rider could sidestep the horse to the gate, reach over and raise the chain or rope fastener, and have the horse move away opening the entrance. The same rider could maneuver the horse into closing the gate without dismounting. The Boyiddles knew how to train horses.

The brothers didn't talk very much except to point out a few landmarks or tell Hoolie the medicinal properties of some of the bushes they passed and how they helped cure their horses of everything from thrush to worms. Hoolie decided that he'd comment on something that had to do with horseflesh in order to draw one or the other brother out and get him to talk in general.

"These are pretty good saddles," Hoolie said in an offhand way. "I grew up ridin' bareback."

"So did we," said Harold. "In the old days we always rode bareback or with a blanket or a pad. The women used to have fancy saddles. Not 'cause they needed 'em to ride, but they hanged things from the saddles. They'd do beadwork on 'em and all that."

Chester chuckled to himself and said, "I heard a story about how Sayn-day tricked White Man Sayn-day out of a silver saddle."

"Oh yeah?" Hoolie didn't know the name, but since Chester used the word "tricked," he knew that Chester was going to tell a kind of Rabbit story. Rabbit was the wily character in Cherokee stories who tricked the other animals and sometimes made them do what they didn't want to do in the first place. Rabbit fooled everybody, but sometimes he got punished for being a clown too.

"Yeah, one day Sayn-day saw White Man Sayn-day riding along on a saddle with these shiny silver plates all over it. White Man Sayn-day's bridle was coated in silver plate too. The sunshine just danced off all that silver. So Sayn-day told White Man Sayn-day that all that silver weighed down his horse so much that he wouldn't be able to hunt. Sayn-day noticed that White Man Sayn-day was wearing a silver belt and silver-toed boots and silver cuffs. Sayn-day told White Man Sayn-day that he couldn't hunt much of anything even if he left his horse behind and he tried to sneak up on the game. His boots and cuffs and belt would spook the animals.

"So Sayn-day made a deal with White Man Sayn-day. Sayn-day would give White Man Sayn-day his pad saddle and his hackamore and his aprons, leggin's, and shirt. In return, Sayn-day got the saddle, the bridle, the cuffs, and the belt.

"Now, when Sayn-day got home, his wife got really mad at him. She scolded him and said, 'That's the dumbest thing you ever did. How you gonna hunt with all that silver? Your huntin' horse is gonna be weighed down and them boots, bridle, belt, and cuffs are gonna spook all the buffalo, they're so shiny. That White Man Sayn-day sure tricked you. He always did want to be a Kiowa.'"

Chester chuckled again, Harold laughed out loud, and Hoolie clapped his hand over his mouth to keep the water he had just drunk from spewing out. He laughed so hard that he couldn't stop. He laughed for another half mile, barely catching his breath.

They headed into a stand of trees, crossed a small creek and came upon a clapboard house with a tipi on the left and an arbor on the right. It reminded Hoolie of some of the homes in Osage County. The tipi looked old and big. It had some horse figures painted on the outside.

The three men drew up their horses about fifty feet from the house. Harold called out something in Kiowa, and within the space of four heartbeats, the door opened. A big man with braids and a round, friendly face stepped out on the porch and eyed them carefully. "Harold . . . Chester, how you doin'?"

"Good, George, good," answered Chester. Harold waved his hand toward Hoolie. "Brought somebody out. He's a Indian from over in Osage County. But he ain't no Osage . . . he's a Cherokee. He wants to talk."

"Good. Come on in. Get some food." He looked up again and gestured with his chin toward the tipi. "Tie 'em up over there."

"All right," Chester said with a bright smile.

They dismounted and led the horses to a small bush next to the tipi and wrapped the reins around three twigs that jutted out from the deep green leaves. There was a bit of grass and the horses were tired. They wouldn't wander off.

Every time Hoolie rode a horse, even for a mile or so, his old wounds gave him fits. It wasn't so much that they gave him a great deal of pain—which they did—but they seemed to make all his joints stiff. His limp became even more pronounced. The blast and shrapnel from the German artillery round had taken its toll. Two years before, a bullet had grazed his side, and now and then the scar seemed to tighten. He had to flex and lift his arm painfully to stretch the skin around the scar back to normal.

As they walked to the front door, an elderly man in gray braids stepped out on the porch. He said a few words in Kiowa to the Boyiddles. Harold answered with a long speech. Hoolie heard "Hoolie" and "Smith" and "sheriff" and "Tulsa." So he thought that he was being introduced. He stepped forward with his hand out.

The old man's eyes narrowed. Harold quickly said, "Hoolie, he's a real old timer. Probably won't shake hands with you 'til he knows you better. Just say hello."

Hoolie did so and nodded. The old man stretched his cracked lips into a slight smile. The younger man on the porch introduced himself as George Charging Horse. He motioned with his left hand toward the arbor. "Let's sit over there. It's hot inside."

They all walked to the arbor and sat down on the ground. Hoolie had to ease himself down. George plucked a piece of grass and rubbed it gently between his thumb and index finger. He looked at the blade of grass and cocked his head to one side. "So, Mr. Hoolie Smith, you come a long way to talk. My relatives here"—he looked at the Boyiddles—"say you're a good man. You near got shot with them. My old dad here speaks some English. I learned most of mine out to Howard school. The same man that started that school held some of my relatives prisoner at a fort in Florida. My uncle died in that place. He was one that got locked up."

Hoolie let the little speech set for a while. He didn't want to talk out of place or say something that might be misinterpreted. Finally, he looked at the ground in front of his feet and said, "I'm sorry to hear about your uncle. He was a good man, I bet."

Although everyone remained silent for a moment, Hoolie somehow knew that he had said the correct thing.

The old man leaned toward George and said something in Kiowa, his hands moving all the time. Hoolie could almost make out what he was saying simply by watching the old man's gestures. George looked at Hoolie. "My dad said that we'll wait and eat somethin' first, then talk. My wife is gettin' some food together right now."

The Boyiddles nodded enthusiastically. Chester said, "That's good."

They heard a screen door bang shut and turned toward the house. A large woman in a green dress and high buckle shoes came toward the arbor with a plate of fry bread. In her wake was a boy with short hair and a tall teenaged girl. The boy carried a small black pot with a carrying handle; the girl cradled a stack of bowls and held several spoons in her left hand. She passed out the bowls and spoons, and the boy ladled out portions of beef stew with large chunks of meat, some carrots, and corn in it. The woman passed the plate of fry bread. When all the men had bowls of stew and a piece of bread in their hands, she motioned the children to stand back. George said with a smile, "This is my wife and our youngest boy and girl."

After George intoned a short prayer in Kiowa, Hoolie nodded to the woman and children, laid his piece of bread on one knee and scooped some stew into his mouth. He chewed on the meat, took a bite of bread, and said, "This is good, missus."

She just nodded once and led the children back into the house. She called over her shoulder as she retreated, "If you'ins want more, just call out."

They ate in silence. The stew and bread were eaten quickly and the bowls placed on the ground after every drop of the brown liquid had been drunk. Everybody wiped their hands on the grass. George Charging Horse got up, fetched a bucket of water, and passed it around. They all drank from the same dipper. It was time to open up the conversation.

"We passed through some good pastureland," Hoolie said in a low voice. "Raise horses?"

George answered after taking out a white handkerchief from his pocket to wipe his forehead. "Some horses and a few cows. We lease a lot of land to some folks. The Coopers and the Harts and the Wilkersons lease some; they got pretty big operations. We try to keep as much as we can in our hands. But the leasemen keep on tryin' to get all of it. A bunch of us try to get our agent to do somethin' to help us out. Mostly he sits around with the leasemen and makes deals with 'em. They keep comin' at us."

"My family in Osage County got cattle, and I been workin' the horses. Mine ain't as well trained as the ones we rode out here." Hoolie was trying to move the conversation from land to someplace—anyplace—else.

The Boyiddle brothers smiled slightly in acknowledgment of Hoolie's compliment. George turned to his father and said something in Kiowa. The older man nodded knowingly and said in English, "These boys good horse trainers. Use o'd ways. They ask all da o'd people 'round here. I teach 'em too." Charging Horse paused for a long time and breathed slowly in and out. Finally he asked, "Why you out here, boy?"

Hoolie looked at George. "I want everybody to understand, so should one of you'ins translate?"

George said something to his father, who answered quickly back. George then turned to Hoolie. "I think my dad here understands. His English is pretty good. He just likes to talk, ahhh, Indian."

"All right, then," Hoolie said, rubbing his hands together nervously. "My name's Hoolie Smith. 'Hoolie' is the word we use for 'drum' in my language. It really means 'big mouth' like a drum."

The elder Charging Horse emitted a sound that was more or less made in acknowledgment of Hoolie's words. The old man said lowly and slowly what sounded like "whuh" to Hoolie. He was encouraged to say more, which was precisely the effect Charging Horse wanted to make.

Hoolie prepared himself for a long speech. He wanted to make himself clearly understood, so he coughed once to get their attention and began, "I traveled out here with a friend. He's a white man, and I work for him sometimes. I live in Osage County now, but the man I work for is in Tulsa. A lawyer hired us to find a man. His name was Frank Shotz, and I understand he lived out here in a tent for a time."

Charging Horse, George, and the Boyiddles all nodded their heads in the affirmative. George said, "That's so," and leaned forward, his hands on the grass. He leaned back again, this time resting his hand on the knees of his crossed legs. His discomfort was plain to see. Hoolie didn't know if it was due to sitting on the ground or because of something he had said about Shotz.

"The man disappeared a while ago," Hoolie continued, "and his people haven't heard a word. Do you know anything about it?"

George's eyes went quickly to the ground. "We knew the man," he said quietly. "He asked if he could camp out over the hill yonder. And we said yes."

"What'd he want?" Hoolie asked.

"Said he was lookin' around for good grazing land. Wanted to get into the cattle business. Asked about leases and such."

"He mention oil or drillin'?"

"No," George said with a slight smile, "but we all knew that he was out there lookin' into the land. Had a strong feelin' that he was doin' somethin' more than lookin' at the grass."

"I think you're right," said Hoolie. "When was the last time you saw him?"

"Right about a week or so."

"Nothin' since?"

"Can't say no more."

"How come?"

"There's a lot of things goin' on round about here. The white people are tryin' to steal our land again, and they're all the time puttin' their noses into our ways. I'm a leader, and we follow Grandfather Peyote's road. Now the white people are tryin' to stop our meetin's and take away the peyote we use. I'm just afraid they're gonna make somethin' out of Mr. Shotz campin' here and then come and take our things away. They done it before."

"What do you mean?"

"Well, one time somebody said that we rustled some of Mr. Cooper's cows, and Sheriff Wynn come with some deputies and a few posse members. They just tore up the place. Took the tipi down, threw the peyote buttons on the ground, stomped on the altar, and just did everything they could to stop us from holdin' meetin's. They wasn't lookin' for cattle at all. They was just tryin' to take away our religion. All of 'em is in on it, local Indian Office, Cooper—everybody. They can't shut us down because we got federal law that favors our church."

"When I was in town, Sheriff Wynn helped us out. He even put the man who took a shot at Chester and Harold here in jail."

"Let me tell you about Sheriff Wynn," Chester said. "He's a o'd rascal. He ain't no friend. He's just usin' us to get in with the Indian Office people. I think he's runnin' a liquor business his own self and is tryin' to cut out the police chief and the bootleggers who work for him. He ain't no friend. He's just in it for hisself. And he'd look to throw us in jail so's he can get land. The land's the main thing. Out here he can get all the liquor he wants. Out here he can bring in the whiskey and store it. He needs it for his business."

"His business pretty big?"

"Oh boy, yeah," Chester said. "I heard that Collins's 'leggers sometimes gotta buy from Wynn's people. See, Wynn ships in the good stuff from up north, while o'd Collins sells bathtub gin, a little bit of beer, and some bottled rotgut whiskey they sneaked in from Texas. Some of the white people make moonshine and sell it themselves. I think Collins'd like to put 'em outta business."

"You sure know your liquor," Hoolie said, wiping a grin from his face with the back of his right hand.

Harold shook his head but nevertheless had a smile on his face. "It's pretty bad 'round here. Wynn has to have places to set up sheds with guards to keep the liquor he gets from bootleggers that bring it down from Canada, they say. So he's gotta have money to pay them people. He sells all over western Oklahoma, down in Texas, and in the panhandle. It's pretty safe from the federal agents way out here. Collins buys and sells the liquor he gets from hereabouts. He don't make that much money, but he don't pay anythin' out. His 'leggers just get it, sell it, and split up the money with Collins. Wynn's the big time. Collins is just keepin' his head above water."

"Who buys this stuff?"

George coughed once. "I hate to say, but it's our people. And the Caddos, Delawares, Wichitas, and some Kiowa Apaches. The Comanches buy it in Lawton, and the Cheyennes and Arapahos get it around El Reno. But they say that Wynn is the one who gets the stuff to sell in Lawton and Fort Sill, El Reno, and Texas."

"I thought the Indian Office people kept close watch over the liquor."

"No . . . no," George replied. "Those folks are all in on it, like Chester says. They make the leases for our land and see to it that the leasemen pay out. And the bootleggers are standin' right there. The leasemen sometimes even buy a round for everybody."

"Ain't nothin' for our boys to do," Charging Horse said, "so they drink that whiskey. My boy George here, along with these boys . . ." —he pointed with his lips to the Boyiddles—"They try to stop it. These two whipped one of them white men."

"I heard," Hoolie said. He paused in the deep silence under the arbor. He played with the grass for a moment, then looked up at George. "I'm pretty mixed up about this. Can't seem to get a handle on who's doin' what to who."

George shook his head. He had a serious look on his face. His black braids seemed to shine. He looked at the grass and took a deep breath. "Well, let me see if I can straighten it out some. Bringin' in and hidin' the stuff is the tough part. The federal marshals can't do anything 'cause they don't know the territory and they depend on the Indian Office to let them know who's sellin' it to us. The marshals can't enforce prohibition out here. Wynn has good connections up north and has the money to get the stuff down here. There's only two things standin' in his way. That's o'd Collins, who's doin' his own business in alcohol, and us."

"Who's us?" asked Hoolie.

"Young man," George said, "do you know about the Peyote Road?"

"Some. Some of my wife's relatives follow that way. They say it's hard."

"It's hard . . . it's a narrow road. Only a few can stay on it. But we always say that you got to keep tryin' to get back on it and stick on it. One of the things it does is get our people off the whiskey. We teach our people just how bad the liquor is, and when they follow the way of Grandfather Peyote, they stay away from it. Like these boys here." George looked pointedly at the Boyiddles.

Harold rubbed his chin in thought and said, "George is right. See, we was sent up to Pennsylvania to the boardin' school at Carlisle. They closed it down durin' the war and didn't open it up again."

Chester nodded and smiled. "One good thing the white people done," he interjected.

Harold continued, "Now there's a lot of Indians 'round here that went and thought it was good for 'em. Don't believe it. We were there, and the only good thing was findin' ways to do somethin' against the rules, like stealin' food or sneakin' out at night or seein' the girls. Me and Chester used to do things to the schoolmaster's horse. We knew 'bout medicine even when we was little, and every time that mean o'd man went for a ride, we made that horse sick. Later on, we even had the horse trained to hobble itself when o'd Pratt'd go for a ride. That was a little over twenty years ago now."

Amusement creased Hoolie's face. He could picture an old white man out somewhere in the woods with a diarrheic horse or, even better, being miles away from home and having to walk back leading a limping animal that was no more lame than the man himself.

Harold looked pleased with himself and said, "Yep, nobody liked that man. They got shed of him when I was ten. Chester was eleven."

George gestured that he wanted to speak, and so Harold immediately turned to him and nodded. "You know," said George, "that same man, Pratt, was the jailer for some of our relatives. One man, my mother's uncle, died right over in that house. He was a prisoner in Florida under that man."

"That's too bad," Hoolie said.

Harold's eyes narrowed. "Another bad thing we learned at Carlisle was drinkin'. That was one more thing we did just to do somethin' against the rules. The bad thing is that it took us in. Made us slaves."

Chester's mouth was a slash. "We hate that liquor," he growled.

"And we fight it," Harold said, finishing his brother's thought.

Charging Horse had sat listening and sometimes asking questions in Kiowa. George, Harold, or Chester would answer in a polite whisper whenever one of them wasn't talking. The elder drew in a deep breath. "We should smoke on this. I'll get the pipe when we finish up. But I want to say somethin'. To get it right, George, speak in white man talk."

Charging Horse launched into a long speech during which Chester and Harold make sounds of agreement. George interpreted almost simultaneously. "My father says he's seen many years go by. I was one of the people who put aside the Sun Dance and took up Grandfather Peyote. We did it to put an end to the young men dyin' because they drank whiskey.

"My father says that the whiskey is a power like many other powers. It can be good. It can clean wounds. It's also bad for us. We drink it and die. If it wasn't for Grandfather Peyote, we'd all be dead now.

"We all have to fight against the liquor people. My nephews, the Boyiddle boys, taught that man MacFarland a lesson. He was sellin' whiskey to children. Five of my grandsons have even torn down a storage shed or two. We have to fight against this sickness. That's what is needed. . . ."

The old man stopped himself. George's skilled interpretation halted just as suddenly. They both thought that they had confessed too much. Hoolie was an Indian and probably sympathized with their rage against the liquor trade, but he was still a stranger, an unknown quantity. He might tell someone about the vandalized storage sheds or turn on the Boyiddles.

Hoolie immediately knew what they were thinking. A large number of Indians, particularly those from the eastern part of Oklahoma, did not like or feared the peyote religion. They were just as likely to work against it as they were to help other Indians eradicate problems like alcohol. Trusting an outsider like himself was difficult at best. At worst, Hoolie could go back to town and tell the sheriff who had vandalized the liquor storage sheds. Hoolie thought for a long moment and addressed the elder Charging Horse. "Mr. Charging Horse, I'm lookin' for Mr. Shotz. That's the only thing I gotta do. I'd like to look at his camp and maybe stay there for a couple of days. That is, if Chester and Harold could tell my boss back in town that I'm still workin' on the case."

"I can take care of that," Chester said.

The Charging Horses sat for a long time without speaking a word. Then the old man began a long speech while George sat rock-still, just listening.

When the old man finished, George took in some air and said quietly, "My father says that it's all right for you to stay here for a while. You could go out to the man's camp and look around. He thinks you should go ahead and camp closer to the house. He says maybe you should sleep in the tipi. He likes to sleep in there, but lately his back has been hurtin' and he seems to sleep better on the feather bed.

"He says that you should look for signs of other people out there. He hasn't been out there, and I was out there just once to see Mr. Shotz."

George took a deep breath before he began again. "My father says that we will tell you something tomorrow. He also says that the man you're lookin' for is dead."

Hoolie was taken aback and sucked in air so hard that he choked. As he was coughing, Chester Boyiddle hit him with an open hand right between the shoulder blades. It forced Hoolie to stop coughing and try to regain his breath. "Learned that trick at Carlisle," said Chester.

When Hoolie regained his composure, he asked, "How do you know he's dead?"

George answered, "He just knows. I know it too. You just take your bedroll over to the tipi and have these two show you where the camp is. We'll talk about things later. Now Khōn wants to smoke."

≫≪

The late afternoon ride to the Shotz campsite was relatively short, but hot and tiring. The windy heat of a western Oklahoma summer was almost like standing in front of a blast furnace. Hoolie turned in the saddle to Chester. "It's almost like a sweat bath except that the wind's blowin'."

"Yeah, it gets that way," Chester said as he pulled a handkerchief from his back pocket and wiped his face.

They topped a small hogback and saw the tent. Even from a distance, it looked as if it had been abandoned for years. The tent stakes were still holding down the corners, but its poles were leaning heavily to one side, the result of steady winds and animals rooting around inside. The ash of the cooking fire had been blown away, leaving only the rocks encircling the fire pit. The cooking rack was pushed over, and a couple of pots and a frying pan were lined up in a trail from tent to fire. The wind kept a flap moving in a steady beat against one side of the lopsided tent. It was a lonely, ghostly place.

Hoolie, Chester, and Harold hadn't spoken much during the ride out to Shotz's campsite. They dismounted and stood looking intently around the horizon for a moment, as if Shotz might appear from a clump of trees or walk over a swell in the prairie. The horses stood stock-still when the three men dropped their reins to the ground. The constant rush of the wind made the horses turn away. The look of the deserted area made Hoolie shiver despite the fact that it was a hot late July afternoon. Hoolie walked to the tent alone; Chester and Harold took a few tentative steps forward but got no farther than the cooking rack and the old campfire.

Hoolie raised the tent flap, got down on his knees stiffly, and looked in. There wasn't much there except for some folded-up blankets, a few shirts, a couple pairs of trousers, and some canned goods. A kerosene lamp hung from the lopsided tent pole. Hoolie thought that the lamp indicated that Shotz was reading or writing something down, and indeed there were a few pencils and a pen and ink bottle placed neatly on top of one folded blanket. There were no notebooks or papers of any kind lying around, and no books either. Shotz was a learned man. He must have wanted to read or write or something out here in the loneliest bit of prairie Hoolie had seen in a long time. Somebody must have walked off with the man's papers or books or both. He'd work on that puzzle later.

Then he saw a few scraps of paper scattered here and there where the tent canvas touched the ground. Somebody tore up Shotz's papers. He crawled around and picked them up. A few had writing on them. Hoolie was sure that they came from a notebook that had been ripped apart. Most of the strips had probably been carried away on the wind; the ones he held in his hand had evidently blown back in the tent without being noticed by whoever tore the notebook apart in the first place. He found three strips with writing. One said: "pest place to dri." The second said: "al sandst." The final read: "ost sh." Hoolie slightly smiled. The Cherokee word for good is *osda* and usually pronounced "ost." Shotz probably wasn't writing in Cherokee, so the word could be "lost" or "most" or even "frost." Didn't make sense. Hoolie guessed that "al sandst" had something to do with sandstone, but he couldn't tease out any further meaning. The longest piece of writing, "pest place to dri" could have been connected to finding a place to drill, since Hoolie didn't figure that Shotz, an educated man, would spell "dry" with an "i." The word "pest" was more than mystifying.

He put the paper strips in his pocket and backed out of the tent on hands and knees. He stood up and looked off to a stand of trees about five hundred yards in the distance. "There water over there?" he asked the Boyiddle brothers, pointing with his lips.

"Yeah," Harold answered, "that's a little spring. It makes a creek that runs off west. Not much of a stream though. Kinda slow."

"Wonder why Shotz camped here and not close by the water. Don't make much sense."

Chester chuckled a little and said, "He's not even on a rise so's he can see who's comin'."

Hoolie nodded his head and decided he'd bring up Shotz's supposed death. "I have to ask you boys why Mr. Charging Horse let it out that Shotz was dead. How's he know?"

Chester took off his hat and brushed back his hair with his free hand. Harold rubbed his hand over his mouth. Finally, Chester said, "They know he's dead 'cause they buried him."

Hoolie stared at Chester in disbelief, sighed, and said, "Let's go down and look around the creek bed for a while."

Chapter VI

THE ANADARKO OPERATION

J.D. stood in the doorway of Violet's Café for a few moments, shifting his eyes in every direction and glowering menacingly at a couple of the younger customers. He knew that he could be intimidating and often used his lined facial features, big moustache, scarred countenance, and heft to threaten a single person or an unprepared large group of people. He had learned and used that glower when he was a copper in Chicago. It still worked. Every eye in Violet's Café stared at him for a moment then switched quickly to the breakfast plates in front of them. J.D. could see that most of them tried to keep him in their peripheral vision.

One of the customers did not shift his eyes. It was the mayor, who smiled and waved J.D. over to his own table. J.D. strolled over and said in a gravely whisper, "Good morning to you, Mayor Rohrbach."

"Please sit down, Mr. Daugherty," the mayor said with a kind of triumphant smile. "How are you?"

J.D. knuckled his moustache and frowned. "We've gotta talk, Mr. Rohrbach, but not here. Where's Miss Comstock?"

"Oh, sometimes Violet sleeps in. She had quite a night."

"Well, so did I. Let's talk after breakfast in your office. Would that be okay?"

Rohrbach's face fell. He was wary now. "I think that would be fine. Let me order for you—the bacon and eggs are perfect for starting your day." He turned toward the black man who was cleaning up at the next table. "Leonard, tell cook that my friend here needs a good bacon-and-egg breakfast. Hurry along now."

"Yes, sir," he said and practically ran to the kitchen.

Rohrbach turned to J.D. and put the smile back on his face. "Mr. Daugherty, have you seen the morning news?"

"No."

"Well, the headline is of some interest to you." He turned the paper lying to the right of his plate around so that J.D. could see it. It read: GOVERNOR DECLARES MARTIAL LAW IN OKLAHOMA, OKMULGEE, AND TULSA COUNTIES.

J.D. picked it up and read it intently. The 1921 race riot in Tulsa had not satisfied the Klansmen, despite the loss of buildings and businesses, and the cost of cleaning up the Greenwood area and covering up the extent of the horror. No one knew exactly how many lives were lost. J.D. told him that the official estimate of the dead was about ninety. But J.D. was sure that the number was at least triple that. Evidently the Klan bosses had decided that instead of using murder, arson, rape, and theft to rid the city of Little Africa—as they called the Negro section of Tulsa—they took up kidnapping, flogging, and mutilation. Lynching and mob violence became a secondary method for terrorizing the black population. Instead, a group of hooded figures would show up at someone's house in the middle of the night, drag them out to the countryside, and torture them, amputating ears, fingers, noses, and genitalia. The police had become ineffectual; the numbers of people who had been taken from their homes and beaten and tortured nearly to death had been on the rise in Tulsa, and the governor had finally acted to restore some semblance of order.

"Jack Walton's finally done something about this lawlessness," Rohrbach stated without emotion. "Now we've got to go after the bootleggers and criminals who prey on the helpless. They're as bad as the Klan. Maybe worse."

"Don't see how they can be much worse," said J.D.

"The corruption comes from all angles, Mr. Daugherty—time to weed it out."

"I guess you're right, but I still think Volstead's a pretty dumb law. Unenforceable."

"That may be right . . . but for now let me buy your breakfast."

≫«

Rohrbach's office was much larger and grander than the sheriff's. J.D. and the mayor entered the room and removed their hats, and

Rohrbach waved J.D. into a soft visitor's chair that fronted a magnificent mahogany desk with scrollwork and gilt trim. Nobody did much writing on the desk; it was more for show.

Rohrbach rubbed the highly polished wood of the desktop and calmly looked at J.D. "Well, Mr. Daugherty, how can I be of service?"

"Mayor, how far do you want me to go in cleaning up this town?"

"What do you mean?"

"I mean that there could be blood spilled. The hold they got on this town is tight, and it might take some doin' to pry their fingers off. Somethin's up. Goin' back to the hotel last night, somebody tried to stab me. Now, tryin' to kill me this early in the game means somethin'. Maybe somebody out there already knows that you and Miss Comstock hired me. Have you or her been braggin' about cleanin' up around here before we talked?"

The mayor was clearly taken aback. "You . . . you . . . were . . . attacked?" he stuttered. "Did you see your assailant? This is terrible."

"Don't panic, Mayor. We'll get to the bottom of this. Now, did you—either of you—say anything to anybody about hiring me? That is . . . before you did it last night?"

"No . . . no, we didn't."

"But it was Eric Cooper that told you about us comin' to town?"

"In a way, yes," Rohrbach said warily. "He just mentioned that his father was asked to talk to a Tulsa detective."

"Okay," J.D. said. "We'll have to work from there. Are you willing to go to the governor after I've started the snowball rolling, so to speak? This could easily turn into a war. The stakes are pretty high from what I understand."

Rohrbach hesitated. "I think we'd better."

"All right. What I need from you is a letter on official paper stating that you, as the senior elected official in this town, have hired me to investigate political corruption in the city of Anadarko. Is that still the idea?"

"Yes."

"Next, I need to get Festus MacFarland out of jail."

"I understand. It will be done. The chief of police, the sheriff, and I"—Rohrbach grinned—"will have a heart-to-heart talk this very morning."

"Do you want to know why?" asked J.D.

"Not at all. I'm sure letting Mr. MacFarland go will help you help me."

"Good, Mr. Mayor. Let's get it done then."

>«

J.D. folded up the mayor's letter and put it in his inside coat pocket. As he walked down Main Street, he patted the jacket once or twice over his heart, heard the muffled crinkle of the paper, and set a deep frown on his face. The letter was simple. It authorized him to uncover any and all corruption in the town and report it to the senior Anadarko official—in this case, Mayor Rohrbach. If things got rough, the mayor could call on the governor to declare martial law. Governor Walton had sure enough done it already, and there would be nothing wrong with putting Caddo County on the martial law list. The problem would be the state legislature. It was dominated by the Klan, and Walton's declaration just might not be legal according to the state constitution. That would give the Kluxers an opening. J.D. shrugged. He would just open the can of worms and see what crawled out. Better yet, he'd open the can and watch all the worms pull each other back into the can.

As a detective for Great Western Investigations, J.D. had been a part of the reactionary violence against suspected anarchists and communists. He had left the agency precisely because of his particular idea that radicalism simply begat radicalism. Five years before, a friend of his had left Great Western to take a job with the Baldwin-Felts Detective Agency, a notorious outfit that took part in the massacre of miners and their families in Ludlow, Colorado, in 1914. In 1920 the friend had been sent to Matewan, West Virginia, to evict striking miners from their company-owned homes. A gun battle had ensued with the town's chief of police over the attempt to arrest the Baldwin-Felts agents. Seven Baldwin-Felts operatives were killed, including J.D.'s friend and former colleague, along with two miners and the Matewan mayor. Police Chief Sid Hatfield had gunned down Albert and Lee Felts, Baldwin-Felts owner Tom Felts's own relatives. The next year, Baldwin-Felts operatives assassinated Hatfield and another man on the courthouse steps. J.D. hoped that his own operation in Anadarko would not escalate to such extremes, but he was also prepared for it. The letter was his license to get the job done, and Mayor Rohrbach had assured him that Governor Walton would come to his aid in order to quell any kind of violence.

J.D. rounded a corner and spotted two men coming toward him. One of them looked very familiar. He looked like Festus MacFarland but with a pinched mouth and close-set eyes. The man walked with a cane and held one arm limply. Since he clearly resembled Festus, J.D. guessed that he was the beat-up brother, Clem. J.D. put on his most disarming smile and stopped in front of him.

"Hello, Mr. MacFarland," J.D. said politely. "I don't mean to be rude, but could I have a word?"

The man stopped and lifted his cane, ready for a fight. He turned slightly to his right, dropping his right foot backward about six inches. He was set to throw the first blow with his cane. His companion reached for his back pocket, probably to pull out a knife. J.D. recognized exactly what was going on and put his hands up, palms forward. The men relaxed a bit, and the one with the cane said, "You're the man who was with the ones that threw my brother in the can. I oughta belt you one."

"You might, but I've got a better deal for you."

"Just who the hell are you, anyway?"

"I'm a private investigator. From up Tulsa way. I'd guess you're Clem MacFarland."

"That's right. What do you want?"

J.D. looked at him, raised his bowler, and brushed back his hair. He eased the hat down on his head and said, "I'm here to find a man. But I'll tell you right now that Sheriff Wynn didn't want me around here to do my job. Sorry I looked like I was with him when your brother got taken in, but I was tryin' to keep my own man from gettin' thrown in too." J.D. paused for a moment, looking at the man.

Clem rubbed his cheek and looked agitated. "Yeah, keep goin'," he said warily.

"I heard you got hurt pretty bad, but you look pretty fair now. What do you think of Sheriff Wynn?"

"I get around all right, some stitches and a busted up hip. Wynn? . . . Well, he's a no-good varmint," Clem said. A snarl curled his stitched-up upper lip. "A skunk," he added.

J.D. knew at once that he wasn't dealing with a mental giant. "I'm not a vindictive man myself, but I don't like bein' treated the way Wynn treated me. He gave me the high hat."

Clem nodded his head vigorously in agreement.

"Well," J.D. continued, "even though I don't like to do such things, I'd sure like to find out how I could get back at him. I know you and him are in competition."

MacFarland drew back and looked away as if to deny the conclusion J.D. reached.

"Now, I know you're in the liquor trade. Don't get me wrong. I think Volstead's a dumb law, and there's nothin' wrong with makin' a buck. The government's just tryin' to tell us what to do."

J.D. read MacFarland easily enough. The brothers thought of themselves as a new breed of outlaws like the Dalton Gang, Jesse James, and the Younger brothers. The trouble was that most of them ended up dead or in prison. Flaunting a "bad" law like Volstead and providing for themselves and their families was better than robbing banks and trains, especially in a small town in Oklahoma—provided, of course, that they had the protection of the town police. Most of all, the MacFarlands thought of themselves as fully independent men who neither needed nor wanted government interference in what they considered their business. The law only counted when it let them alone or stopped someone else from interfering with their business. They really could not comprehend why Festus should be arrested for attempting to murder the Boyiddle brothers. They had beat up Clem. Justice—real justice—demanded that Festus retaliate. It was nobody else's business—especially not the sheriff's, whose own business was at odds with the MacFarlands'.

J.D. nodded at Clem in a way that said he fully understood his ideas and situation. MacFarland stretched his lips in a tight, moronic smile. "I'd like to help you boys out," J.D. began, "crackin' down on Wynn's politics. He favors the big cheeses around here, doesn't he?"

"Yeah," Clem said enthusiastically, "he's always lockin' up the poor folks. The swells in this burg always get off clean."

"How come Chief Collins don't take over?"

Clem scratched his head, wrinkled his forehead in contemplation, and said, "I don't think he's got enough people with money backin' him up. It's like a war, and Collins don't have a big enough army." He paused for a few long seconds and said, "Wynn's got some pretty tough fellas workin' for him."

"Who's that?" asked J.D.

"Marty Albright is one. Moe Tucker is the other," Clem answered, looking over his shoulder. He was now clearly worried that he might have said too much to J.D. or that he might be reported to the sheriff. Albright and Tucker were names that certainly inspired fear.

"I met this Albright. Who's the other boy?"

"I heard you was there. Friend of mine told me that Moe's the guy who told Marty Albright to haul Festus in for takin' a potshot at Chester and Harold. He don't say much, but he's meaner than a pissed-on rattlesnake."

J.D. tried to remember him but could only think of a tall man in a suit coat with a .45 Colt revolver strapped on the outside of his jacket. Normally pistols were worn under the coat. The holster and belt were nicely tooled leather.

"Moe Tucker, huh?" said J.D.

"Yep," Clem replied immediately. "Moe makes Marty Albright look soft as mush. He uses that big .45 to put dents in people's hats. Meaner than a stepped-on snake. You gotta watch yourself 'round him."

"You like the chief, right?"

Clem nodded vigorously. "He's better'n Wynn."

"Now, he's supposed to uphold Volstead, ain't he?"

Clem answered, "That's right, but he's for the poor folks. You can't do nothin' to help out the regular folks 'round here without no money. 'Sides, regular folks hereabouts like to have a beer or two every night. Tastes good and helps out when you're workin' in the hot sun all day long. Now, Wynn's booze goes to the richies in town and the redskins."

"Where does he get his hooch?"

"Oklahoma City, Tulsa—probably by way of Canada. They truck it in and then stash it outta town. I don't know where."

"What would you do if I found it?"

Clem smiled widely and answered, "We'd get it, or get rid of it."

"But you don't have the authority. Chief Collins can't raid any- thing outside of town."

Clem slowly moved his head from side to side. "Nope, but we ain't coppers. Man's gotta take care of his own business, don't he? Well, if there's somebody out there wreckin' business, then we gotta do somethin' about it."

"What about Wynn, Albright, and Tucker?"

MacFarland laughed a sly laugh. "We just blame it on the redskins. See, boys like the Boyiddles use that peyote and are a-tryin' to get rid of the liquor around here. Now, Wynn knows this, but he keeps things quiet around 'em. Indians is the best cus- tomers. They get lease money from the ranchers that use their land for cattle. Wynn sells to them on the cheap. Chief Collins says that Wynn keeps the redskins happy to cut our business off at the ankles. Then he won't have no competition. He'll be sellin' his hooch to our Indians."

He smiled at his analysis of the Wynn-Collins feud and rewarded himself by rolling a fat cigarette. After he lit up, he blew smoke in the air and said to J.D., "Now, I done told you our busi- ness, what's your'in?"

"Well, sir," J.D. said, brandishing another toothy smile under his heavy moustache, "I think I could help you out. See, Wynn didn't do me any favors. And he's playin' things close to the vest. I used to be a copper in Chicago, and I worked for the Great Western Investigations."

"What's in it for you?" asked Clem. "Ain't nobody gonna go agin Wynn, Tucker, and Albright for nothin'. That's just crazy."

"You're right, Mr. MacFarland," J.D. said, his smile fading slightly. "I've got the experience as a copper and a private dick. I'll get your man on top and you all back in business." J.D. paused just long enough for what he was saying to sink in. "For a price, mind you, I'll have this place and your business hummin' along like a new Buick sedan. Just let me talk to Collins alone. You set it up, and I'll be there."

"You wanna sit down with Chief Collins?" asked Clem.

"That's the deal—take it or leave it."

"I ain't sure you can get past Albright . . . let alone Tucker and Wynn," Clem said with a sneer.

"I can do it, Mr. MacFarland. I play in the big city. A hick town with hayseed deputies is nothin'."

Clem scratched his chin, pursed his lips, and stared at the ground. Finally he said, "I'll set it up. Somebody will come by the hotel."

J.D. tipped his hat, said "Good-bye, Mr. MacFarland," and turned. He stopped at once, looked around, and said quietly, "I worked a deal . . . go to the courthouse this afternoon. They're gonna let your brother out. Maybe in time for supper."

At first Clem didn't understand, but after a few seconds, it sunk in. "Ahh . . . thanks, mister. I'll do that."

»«

J.D. practically ran to Violet's. He stuck his head inside the door, saw her standing with an elbow on the counter, smiled at her, and went in. She smiled back and gestured toward a table in the back. J.D. walked slowly through the practically empty café and sat down at the indicated table. Violet sauntered to the table, sat, crossed her legs, and said simply, "How's tricks?"

"Depends on who's doin' the trickin'."

"Ha! Very good. What can I do for you, handsome?"

J.D. dropped his voice to a whisper. "The MacFarlands are gonna get me a sit-down with Collins. I'm gonna have to give him somethin' so's that he'll trust me a little bit. What I want to give him is a way to go after Wynn in a big way. When that happens, it'll be open war between the two. And I got a strong Irish feelin' that when war breaks out, it won't take long before we can get the troops in and get Rohrbach in power again."

She put on a sly grin and said, "Now, what in the world could a girl like me give you that could start an open fight between those two bumpkins?"

"I'll tell you straight out. Give me one place where Wynn stashes his goods. Come on, now. This is personal—I got knifed after I left you and Rohrbach."

Her smile left. "I heard, sweetie, and I'm sorry. But hold on a minute," she whispered harshly. "If you let Collins know about that, he'll raid the place, and I'll lose money. Honey, I do other kinds of business besides run this café. And Wynn gets the good stuff. If I have to do business with Collins, all I'll get is rotgut."

J.D. was surprised. "I knew you had property and sold a bit of good whiskey outta here." His arm swept across the café interior. "But you don't do that big a business in the food trade, do you?"

"Honey, I also own the best speakeasy and cleanest bordello in the county. Probably the best in the state outside of Tulsa and Oklahoma City."

"I didn't know that."

"It wouldn'a took you long to find out, I'd bet."

J.D. shook his head in disbelief. He'd gotten himself into a threefold struggle to run the world of crime in Anadarko.

"Okay, Violet. Let me lay this out for myself. You and Rohrbach don't really want me to clean things up around here so much as you want to take over all the dirty business in this town. That right?"

"In a way, yes. Now, you said yourself that you know Volstead is a law that everybody's gonna break anyway. And I'll tell you another thing: Ain't nobody gonna stop men from gettin' relief in a carnal way, right? Why not give people what they want so long as nobody gets hurt?

"Listen, I just wanna run my businesses without problems and real quiet-like to boot. Collins and Wynn are lettin' things get outta hand. You know there's been a couple of killin's around here. And I'll tell you, they got nothin' to do with the liquor and honky-tonk business. It's got somethin' to do with the land. Wynn and Collins are just gettin' too loud about their feud. The Holy Joes around here want everything shut down, but you know that ain't gonna happen. Me and the mayor could keep business goin' on the quiet, and the Jesus people could go around with smiles on their faces, pretendin' everything's hunky-dory. The deacons and preachers can get a quiet drink and visit the girls, and nobody's the wiser. We like things quiet around here. Collins and Wynn are gonna go too far."

J.D. knuckled his moustache to hide the outright shock on his face. After he let Violet's quiet speech sink in for a few minutes, he said, "Let me get this straight. What you really want is to get both of them out of the way but to stay connected in some way with Wynn's and Collins's suppliers. That right?"

"I could make my own contacts, but right now Wynn and Collins are the ones that got 'em—Wynn gets the good stuff and Collins gets the dregs. I wanna do away with the rotgut in this county and run my business. Wynn would be all right to keep around for a while, but the man's just too damn greedy and violent. I know he's behind some rough stuff, and his boys—Moe and Marty—are plenty bad actors."

"Okay, but let me tell you somethin' else—somebody always gets hurt runnin' liquor and whores. I spent too many years as a lawman to know any different. I don't like it. You don't really want to stop corruption. You just want it in your own hands."

Violet put on a kind, sad smile. Either she was a consummate actress or she was genuinely sorry that things had to be the way they were. "I hate the way you put it, but I guess you're right, J.D. If we get the businesses, we—me and Rohrbach—can calm everybody down and make it so nobody does get hurt. I know we can. But listen, I'll buy you a drink later on, and we'll talk about what kind of world it is that we're forced to choose between two evils. Right now, I have to find a way to keep myself alive and well. Wynn likes my business, but I don't like him. He'd like to take over everything that I have. Collins is just dirty, and he'd like to run me out 'cause I don't do business with him. They don't mind hurtin' folks. I do."

"I feel like I've been conned," J.D. said with an equally sad smile under his multicolored moustache.

"You haven't really," she said. "It woulda come out. But you'da seen my side well enough. I reckon if you want to back out, you can. I'll square it with Rohrbach."

"Damn, Violet. You got me in a rough place. I'm an old-time lawman, and I like to keep the law. And I've done some pretty rough things to do it. The law is what keeps us protected from the people who wanna steal our lives and property. But I understand everything you've told me. I know you're right. My mother, good woman that she was, believed in day and night, good and bad, black and white. Rest her sweet soul, she just wouldn't have understood the gray. One of the reasons I quit bein' a copper and a dick for Great Western is that we were doin' bad things to uphold bad laws. Beatin' up guys to stop unions from gettin' organized was bad."

J.D. paused and looked out the glass window that had "Violet's Café" painted on it and said quietly, "I don't guess I'll back outta the deal I have with you and the mayor. I'll start things in motion and try my best to protect you. But you gotta keep some kind of control over the liquor and the girls. You gotta promise me that young people and poor people don't get hurt or lose all their money to vice. You gotta promise."

Violet looked intently at J.D. She was actually trying to gauge the depth of his feelings. "I promise," she said in a whisper, "I promise."

He turned and looked straight into her eyes. "Good," he said, "now you have to tell me where Wynn has a stash of liquor hid away. I'm gonna put Collins on to it, and I'm tellin' you right now, he'll try to smash it up. You might lose some, but you'll gain in the end."

"Sorry, J.D., but that's not a good play. These boys can be rough. Moe Tucker—"

"Hold on just a minute. Didn't you just promise me?"

"I promise to keep stuff away from the kids and the poor boys. That's it. You took the deal. Now clean this place up without . . . without bringin' me into it. Or Rohrbach."

J.D.'s chivalric ideals and sense of propriety faded out. "You'd better give. I can't get things rollin' without that one piece of information. You want to win this game, you'll have to play. I've heard enough about how tough Moe Tucker is. Fish or cut bait. Now give. Or else we'll play another angle, and you'll end up bein' in worse shape."

Violet dropped her eyes to the table. "All right, all right. Come back around six thirty. I'll have something then."

Chapter VII

MARTY AND MOE

As soon as Hoolie heard that the Charging Horse men had buried Shotz, he turned on the Boyiddles. "I gotta get back to town. You knew about Shotz and didn't tell me in town. Why?"

Chester dropped his eyes to the ground. "Well, we wanted to find out if you was gonna get the laws on us. They're always tryin' to break up our meetin's or throw us in the jail."

"Why'd they just bury him?"

"He was killed in a bad way. Gutted. Cut off his nose."

"What?"

Harold said, "Somebody dressed him out like you would a deer."

Chester added, "No blood—and his guts was missin'."

"Who found him?"

"O'd Khōn. The grandpa. He got up in the mornin' to pray. He sometimes sleeps in the tipi. He found him under a blackjack."

"But why didn't you get the laws out here?"

The brothers exchanged looks as if confused by Hoolie's mention of bringing the law into the problem. "I don't know what it's like for you'ins where you live," Harold said, "but 'round here you don't wanna get mixed up with the law. Me and Chester push our luck sometimes. But bein' a Indian 'round here is like standin' on a tree stump with a thousand rattlesnakes crawlin' 'round. You can't get down, you can't jump far enough, and you can't fly away. You just hope you don't get 'em to notice you. So you just keep still 'til they leave."

Hoolie shook his head. He knew instantly that Harold was right, that calling out the sheriff would probably lead to more problems. "Where'd they bury him?"

"Don't know," Chester answered. "They ain't sayin', and I don't want to know."

"Yeah, I can see why. I need to get back to town."

"It'll be nightfall soon," Harold said with a frown. "We can go back in, but it'll be real late. I guess we can get one or two lanterns."

"That's good with me. Let's get goin'."

"We'll go back to the Chargin' Horse place first . . . to get the lanterns." Chester was thinking out loud.

They mounted their horses and set out at an easy lope. It wasn't too long until the Charging Horse place came into view. Hoolie immediately saw that things were different: a Packard automobile was parked near where they had earlier tethered their horses, and a white man in a ten-gallon hat was sitting on a chair under the arbor talking to George Charging Horse and his father. The Indian men had brought chairs out for themselves as well.

As the three men walked their horses slowly toward the arbor, Hoolie saw that a man was leaning on the Packard's front bumper. It was the Cooper boy, Eric. So the man in the big hat who still had his back to them was his father. The men under the arbor and the boy noticed them coming and stood to face the three riders. George Charging Horse raised his hand in greeting. Old Charging Horse lifted his chin in a signal of recognition. The senior Cooper scowled, and his son just smiled a smile that looked somewhat simpleminded.

Hoolie and the Boyiddles walked their horses to the same tree and came back to the arbor. Hoolie reminded Cooper that he had met him before at his house. Cooper, in turn, tightened his mouth slightly and acknowledged that he knew Hoolie. Cooper looked sharply at the Boyiddles, who narrowed their eyes menacingly at Cooper. It was at once clear that a bad relationship of some kind or another had brewed between Cooper and the brothers.

Hoolie broke the tension, addressing George Charging Horse directly. "Mr. Chargin' Horse, I've got to get to town as soon as I can." He scanned the men around him and continued, "I'd like to borrow a lamp, and if you'd point me in the direction of town, I'll be a-takin' my leave."

Cooper spoke up. "Smith . . . right?"

"Yes, sir."

"If you'd give me a few minutes with Mr. Chargin' Horse and his father, me and my boy will take you into town."

"Well, thanks. I'll just go over by the automobile then and pass the time with your son."

"That'd be fine." Cooper looked pointedly at the Boyiddles, and they reluctantly followed Hoolie to the car.

As they approached the automobile, Eric Cooper pulled himself up from his slouching position on the bumper and stood almost at attention. Hoolie came closer and asked, "You're Eric, ain't you?"

"Yeah," the young man replied. As he had done upon their first meeting, Eric Cooper maintained his air of superiority and disdain for Hoolie.

"I'll be hitchin' a ride with you and your daddy back to town." Hoolie was doing his best to put a damper on his urgent need to get back to town and tell J.D. about Shotz.

Eric showed his surprise. "We ain't goin' back to town. Don't wanna go back. . . . It's a long drive goin' to town and then back out to our place."

"I know, and I'll be beholdin' to you and your daddy."

Eric pulled a deep frown and muttered under his breath, "He don't know. He don't drive no how. I do all the work—"

"Eric, how old are you?" Hoolie interrupted.

The young man looked up and said, "Seventeen. Why?"

"No reason—just wondered. You know a lot about automobiles?"

"Sure. I learned from a man from Oklahoma City. I can fix 'em up with the best. Got me a whole set of tools too."

The boy's pride in being a mechanic showed clearly on his face. His eyes seemed to have widened, and his mouth curved upward slightly.

"That's good," Hoolie said, "I'm a mechanic too. Learned when I was young and drove trucks in the army. I worked at an automobile repair place in Tulsa. Pretty good pay too."

Harold turned his head to look at Hoolie. He looked astonished. "More money than you get as a detective?"

"Some, yeah. Mechanic work is good to get into."

Eric looked down at his feet. "I just fix up my pa's cars. Wish I could set up a business though."

"Well, maybe you should," said Chester.

"I don't think pa would like that. He don't drive and that's pretty much my job around the place." Eric had lost his snooty manner.

"Your Packard looks in good shape. Mind if I take a look?" Hoolie asked.

The young man's sense of pride rose again. "Go ahead. She's in perfect condition."

Hoolie slowly walked around the automobile. He brushed his hand over the fenders and mounted spare tire in the back and carefully inspected the interior leather seats. "A Packard Sport Touring," Hoolie said with an enthusiastic smile. "Can I take a look at the engine?"

"Yeah, go on."

Hoolie twisted the latch on the right louvered panel of the hood, lifted it, and stared intently at the big engine. "You take good care of her."

"Thanks. You know how she rides." Eric Cooper gestured toward the arbor. His father was walking toward where they stood with a frown on his face. Evidently whatever business he'd had with the Charging Horse family had gone sour.

Cooper strode past them and jerked open the passenger door. He sat and with a quick movement pointed with his thumb to the rear. "Get in the back," he said to Hoolie. To his son, all he said was "Drive to town."

As the vehicle pulled away, Harold called out, "We'll catch up with you in a day or so, Hoolie."

>«

Silence marked the trip back to town, and the Coopers let Hoolie out of the car in front of his hotel without a word. It was just as well. Hoolie was so anxious to get a hold of J.D. that he was out of the Packard before it came to a full stop. "Thanks for the ride," Hoolie said to the rear end of the departing automobile.

Hoolie entered the hotel lobby and walked over to the front desk. He asked the man behind it if J.D. had come in. The desk clerk's negative reply prompted Hoolie to ask the time of day and walk back out to the street without going up to his and J.D.'s room. Since it was well past dark, Hoolie decided to walk to Violet's Café in the hope that J.D. would be eating supper there.

Hoolie turned left onto the sidewalk that would take him past Violet's and saw J.D.'s bulky silhouette talking to Deputy Marty

Albright and another man in front of a haberdasher's store across the street. Hoolie's news about Shotz would have to wait. Hoolie crossed and approached the men quietly. "Hello, gentlemen," he said as he came within speaking distance. J.D. and Albright both lifted one side of their mouths in friendly, lopsided smiles. The third man slowly positioned his hand over his holstered Colt pistol. His frown contrasted markedly with the friendly grins of the other two. Marty Albright spoke first. "How do, Mr. Smith?"

J.D. raised his right hand slightly and said, "Good to see you, Hool. We were just talkin' politics."

The third man eased his wary facial expression and dropped his hand to his side. Albright looked from him to Hoolie. "Mr. Smith, this here is my partner, Moe Tucker. Moe's a deputy too."

"I could tell by the badge," Hoolie said as he stuck out his right hand. Moe's hand closed on Hoolie's like a vice. Tucker was so obviously trying to intimidate Hoolie that J.D. broke the tension deliberately, saying, "Hoolie, Mr. Tucker was in the war too. I think you three ought to get together and reminisce about France."

"Nothin' to reminisce about," Moe Tucker said, relaxing his grip. "We just killed Germans." He withdrew his hand and clutched his lapel.

"Well," J.D. began, "how about we go and have some supper? On me."

Marty and Moe exchanged looks that seemed to say "why not?" Marty said quickly, "Sure, Mr. Daugherty, sounds good."

Hoolie nodded and pointed his chin at Violet's place down the street.

Moe tilted his head as if to question Hoolie's idea. "I think we could go over to the Jew's place down near the hotel. Cooks a good steak."

J.D. hesitated for a moment. "I've gotta do somethin' real quick. I'll meet you boys over at the restaurant in just a few minutes." He saw that Moe Tucker had a look on his face that implied J.D. was going back on his promise to buy supper. J.D. smiled and ran a thumb across his moustache. "Don't worry, boys—I'll be there in time to pay the tab."

Moe led Hoolie and Marty back toward Main. J.D. watched them go, and as soon as they turned the corner, he walked to Violet's place.

Violet was sitting by the counter. "Hi, good-lookin'," she said as J.D. approached.

J.D. looked straight into her eyes, knuckled his moustache, put his chin against his chest, and said nothing.

Violet pursed her lips and then put on a crooked smile. "Nothin' yet, sweetie. My friends ain't givin' up the information as quick as I thought. Give me more time."

All J.D. could do was frown, nod once, turn on his heel, and walk out of the café. Violet called after him, "Don't be so damn difficult. I'll get it." And after the door banged shut, she muttered, "Better stop givin' me the high hat, mister."

»«

Hoolie knew as soon as he walked into the place that the "New York" restaurant was once a fairly nice saloon. Back before the war, it probably did a rich business in selling beer and whiskey to local cattlemen and wranglers and setting up a "free lunch" counter spread with meats and bread. Hoolie had seen one of these once when he and his family had gone into the small city of Muskogee. Hoolie and one of his cousins had gone exploring on their own and had found a saloon where they were welcomed with open arms until it was discovered that neither one of them had any money to spend. The "free lunch" sign at the door didn't really mean "free lunch."

They hung their hats on a rack inside the door, and a waiter in a white linen apron and a celluloid collar seated them at a table with a red cloth cover. As they stared at the bill of fare, Hoolie heard J.D.'s voice directly behind him. "Well, boys," J.D. said quietly, "what's good?"

"The steak," said Moe Tucker.

They all put down their menus, and J.D. took the remaining seat at the table. The waiter came over, and they all ordered steak and fried potatoes. Hoolie was the only one who ordered his steak well-done; the white men all wanted their beef blood rare.

The sounds of cutting meat, chewing, and slurping coffee overtook any and all conversation. After the busboy picked up their squeaky-clean plates, J.D. produced four long cigars, passed out three, and leaned back in his chair. J.D.'s vest had visibly tightened over his full stomach. All four withdrew penknives from their pockets, trimmed their cigars, pulled out matchboxes, and carefully lit up. Soon a cloud of blue smoke enveloped their table, making it seem as if they were in a very private enclosed space.

"I wanted to talk business with you boys," J.D. said, looking back and forth between Albright and Tucker.

Moe Tucker spoke first. "What about?"

"Well, I think I have a way that you and the sheriff can do well by yourselves and lessen the competition, so to speak."

"I don't know what you're talkin' about," Marty Albright interjected. "I'm a sheriff's deputy. I ain't in no business deals."

"Oh, I guess I was misinformed," J.D. casually replied. "Sorry. I reckon I'll take my information elsewhere."

"What information?" asked Moe.

"Well, if you two ain't in business, then my information can't do you any good. So I'll just keep it to myself."

"Now, just a minute," Marty said. "You ain't been in town long enough to know about things that we don't know about."

"What?"

"What Marty's tryin' to say," Moe began, "is that us and Sheriff Wynn know about what's goin' on 'round here. We keep close tabs on our town. You just got here."

"That may be, but you forget that I'm a private detective, and when I get somewhere, I collect all the information—all the dirt—that I can turn up. In the detective business, you gotta be thorough."

The word "thorough" was so much a part of J.D.'s business philosophy and everyday business lectures that Hoolie had to put his hand over his mouth to hide the tight smile that leapt to his face when J.D. said it.

The two deputies were obviously impressed with J.D.'s confidence. But they narrowed their eyes and looked at one another. In unison they turned their eyes to J.D., who had just expelled a narrow stream of smoke from his lips.

Moe Tucker smacked his lips. His eyes couldn't have gotten narrower. "I don't think I like you knowin' my business, friend. Maybe you're tryin' to cut in on us. Maybe we should take care of business by takin' care of you."

"Steady, boys," J.D. said. "I'm just tryin' to help you out. It's no skin off my neck if you don't wanna know what I know. I'll tell you now that the sheriff would like to get this information, even if you don't."

J.D. paused to let the idea sink into the rocks that Marty and Moe called their heads. J.D. frowned and shook his head.

"You boys," J.D. finally said, "are gonna need help in this—and I know something. . . . Listen, I'm just tryin' to be friendly. I'm on a job. I need all the friends I can get. It's the only way I can do a good job for whoever is payin' me. Maybe if I let you in on this, you'll turn out to be a friend. Maybe so will Sheriff Wynn. And he's a man I'd like to have as a friend."

"Okay," Marty said, "what have you got?"

"All right. Now, part of your business involves stashing away your goods after you get a shipment, right? And you don't squirrel it away in town, do you? Can't get around Chief Collins and Volstead in some town warehouse, right?"

"No," Moe said grudgingly.

"I didn't think so. So you boys got a barn somewhere out in the country, right? Anyway, I got a good tip that the MacFarland brothers are either gonna hijack your shipment or smash up your stockpile. I'm guessing they'll hit the shipment at your hidey-hole."

"They don't know when it's comin' in or where it is," Moe whispered fiercely. "How'd they know?"

"I don't know. I just got here. We found out that much, and me and Hoolie here could help out."

"Yeah, how?" said Marty.

"Well, you know there's bad blood between the Boyiddle brothers, me and Hoolie, and the MacFarlands, right?"

"Yeah."

"What we do is start settin' up right before the shipment comes in. Maybe land them in the can right before they get their goods. Or we get them and the Boyiddles to fightin' so me and Hoolie can help guard the place. You got guards out there, don't you?"

"Nah," Marty said despite Moe's look that said to keep his mouth shut.

Moe was angry. "What this fool means is that we don't usually look after the place 'cause it's pretty safe right where it is."

"That means it's well hidden or in a place that nobody would even suspect," J.D. stated emphatically.

"You might say that," said Marty.

Hoolie took up J.D.'s line of thought. "Listen, I know there's bad blood between the MacFarlands and the Boyiddles. Now that means just about all the Kiowas around here are gonna go against the MacFarlands."

J.D. continued the idea. "You boys know that the sheriff sells pretty high-class goods, and the MacFarlands and Chief Collins sell the cheap stuff. We know that bad blood between the MacFarlands and the Indians around here means that the MacFarlands are gonna lose money because they won't be able to sell their goods. That means they'll want to cut in on your business. Up until now your businesses haven't met head-on. It's the marketplace, boys. The brothers MacFarland have to cut you and Sheriff Wynn off at the ankles. If they don't, they might as well move to Alaska. I'm bettin' you they're lookin' to hit you hard somewhere."

The cigars were almost gone and the conversation among the men had tapered off to mild pleasantries about the steaks, smokes, and quality of service in the only real restaurant in Anadarko.

"What about Vi's place?" asked Hoolie.

"That whore?" Moe replied sharply.

Hoolie and J.D. were taken aback by the venom in his voice.

Marty tried to ease the tension. "They wasn't askin' about what she does on her back, Moe—they was askin' about how she cooks. Heh, heh. Well, she don't even do that, heh, heh."

J.D. practically tipped over his chair as he got up, pulling out his watch and checking it with a frown on his face. "Well, fellas, we got to go now. Time is money, you know."

Hoolie stood, and all shook hands. The deputies remained seated as J.D. threw down a wad of cash that more than covered the bill and the tip. He and Hoolie exited the place without saying a further word.

Outside, J.D. turned on Hoolie underneath a streetlamp. "How come you're back here so quick? I thought you were gonna spend some time nosin' around."

"I got back as soon as I could 'cause I got somethin' to tell you that you ain't gonna like."

"Damn, don't tell me that. Things are goin' pretty well here. I'm gonna set up a hijacking or a fight between Wynn and Collins. All's

I gotta do is find out where. I'll pass that information along to the MacFarlands, and then it'll just be a matter of time. I wanted to be in on what's gonna happen."

"Sorry, Jimmy," Hoolie said with a slight smile. J.D. hated being called by the diminutive of his first name. Hoolie usually did it as a joke, but now it was used to get J.D.'s full attention. "I gotta tell you that Shotz is dead."

"Dead! How? What happened?"

"I don't know exactly, but from what Harold and Chester said, he was gutted and had his face pretty well carved up."

"Where's the body?"

"Buried somewhere. The Chargin' Horse family took care of it."

"Why didn't they get some law to take care of it?"

"Come on, J.D. That's Wynn's territory, and as much as Wynn is nice to Indians around town, they're scared as hell of him out in the country. They're scared of the white people no matter what or who. They know somethin' else, I think. Wynn and Collins both are dealin' in liquor. The peyote people are dead set against it, and Wynn and Collins know it. They know that both of 'em won't stop tryin' to sell their poison either. And that might mean murder, 'cause down the line, all the white people are gonna get together to try and bump off the peyote people. We got to find out who killed Shotz. I think he was left at the Chargin' Horse place to scare them. Shotz was pretty friendly with the family. George Chargin' Horse is the top peyote man 'round here. And his daddy is probably the most respected o'd grandpa of the Kiowas. Like my friend John Tall Soldier always says—it's all connected."

J.D. stared pensively at his friend. His hand came up to knuckle his moustache, and he hooked his other thumb in his vest pocket. The silence between them lengthened. Hoolie looked at the ground and shoved his hands in his pockets.

Finally, J.D. spoke. "Well, hell. You're right we gotta find out who done it and get the body back to his relatives. I guess they'd want him back. But now I have to look into this town-cleanin' operation. It shouldn't take too much to set these boys off so that the mayor can call on the governor to send in the state militia like they did in Tulsa."

"Yep. And then what? Shotz was out lookin' over the country. I'd bet all the money I got that he was lookin' for oil."

"I think so too," J.D. said. "I've had that Irish feelin' up and down my back for the last twenty-four hours. My mother—rest her soul—told me to trust those feelin's too."

J.D. paused to collect his thoughts. He looked at Hoolie, who in turn looked directly into J.D.'s eyes.

"Did I ever tell you about the time I almost got shot in the back of the head?" J.D. asked casually.

"No."

J.D. actually smiled at the recollection. "I was a young man on the beat that day. My mama was makin' a soup and some new bread at home, and I was headin' that way for the noontime break. I was walkin' along with my billy and I thought I heard my mother's sweet voice tellin' me to turn around. Well, sure enough, I turned around and there was a man who I put in the pokey three days before, pointin' a pistol at my head. We used to wear those tall helmets in those days, and when I turned, somehow the helmet tilted. He saw the movement and fired at the helmet. The bullet hits it and it flies off. While he's still lookin' at the hat, I club him down. That's what I mean by listenin' to your feelin's."

Hoolie scrunched up his face in disagreement. "Nope, J.D., that's what comes from listenin' to your mama."

J.D. slowly nodded his head. "Maybe you're right," he said, still in deep thought. J.D. looked left and right and then took a step closer to Hoolie. "Here's what we'll do," he whispered. "You get back out to the Chargin' Horse place. I'll get some information about the liquor comin' in for Wynn. Let's just keep on track. Only now we're lookin' for a killer."

"I was thinkin' the same thing. . . . But speakin' of killers," Hoolie said in low voice, "what about the fella who tried to knife you?"

"Never mind that. I'd bet whoever he was, he was tied up in the business with Violet, Rohrbach, Collins, and Wynn."

"Think so?"

"Yep. Pretty sure. He stuck me just as I was leaving Vi and the mayor."

"Looks like it, huh?"

"Got to be somethin' there."

"This is gettin' complicated," Hoolie said with a frown.

"That it is, me boy," J.D. said. "When you do a thorough investigation, things always get complicated. But I'm on my way to Vi's joint now. I'll see you later. And don't take any wooden nickels."

"Right. And don't get stuck like a o'd hog again."

They parted, J.D. with a jaunty smile on his face, and Hoolie looking as if he had seen a bad spirit stalking J.D. Hoolie felt that J.D. pushed his luck too far and relied on his "Irish feeling" beyond what was sensible. Hoolie decided to walk around town in the cool night air and think things over. He often had a hard time dealing with the twists and turns of J.D.'s personality. J.D. could be very serious about seemingly trivial details of a case and casual about the dangers involved in poking into people's private lives. Hoolie grew up with stories about how Rabbit, the trickster of Cherokee history, got in trouble doing exactly that. Rabbit also got other animals hurt when he pushed the rules beyond the boundaries of normal behavior and common decency. In Hoolie's mind, the white people that hired him and J.D. didn't really care about getting along with each other; they typically cared only about themselves personally or about the property they owned. When it came to getting what they wanted, common decency might very well be chucked out the back door like so many bones for the dogs.

It was about time for Hoolie to cleanse himself in the old way and get ready for the coming strife. J.D.'s plucky habit of calling out trouble to do battle face-to-face always led to some kind of fight, and Hoolie had to be ready. He turned on his heel and headed back to the hotel. There, he bedded down on the floor with the thought that he would go back to the Charging Horse place and ask George or his father for some help. He needed to quiet his nerves, rest his soul, and get into a kind of equilibrium with Anadarko's environs, including its land, spirits, men, and women. Anadarko had become a living being with a heart, liver, soul, skeleton, stomach, nerves, and muscles all working in concert with each other. Knowing now what he was going to do and how he was going to do it, Hoolie fell into a deep sleep.

Chapter VIII

THE TULSA OPERATION

Whoever it was knocked three times. Then the wailing began. The terrible high-pitched keening was both piteous and hellish. But even though he knew what the knocking meant, he was still drawn to it. He had to see. He took seven steps, grasped the doorknob, and, with his eyes held tightly shut, threw open the door. He opened his eyes and gazed with horror upon the beautiful naked woman with white hair streaming over her shoulders and covering her breasts. Her jaw dropped and her mouth gaped; now she looked cadaverous. She screamed and he knew she was the banshee of legend, knocking on the door to let those inside know that death was approaching. He slammed the door shut. She knocked again. . . .

J.D. woke with a start. Someone was knocking on the door to their room, and the barely audible tapping had been melded into a part of his terrible dream. Hoolie was scrambling up from the floor. Clad only in his sleeveless athletic union suit, Hoolie strode across the room and, embarrassed, slightly cracked open the door to their room. A boy in knickers and a Western Union cap said, "Telegram for Mr. Daugherty."

Hoolie signed the boy's sheet, closed the door, and handed the telegram to J.D., who had just thrown off the covers and sat up on the bed. He touched his feet to the floor, winced, and said, "Floor's cold." He held the telegram at arm's length and read it aloud. Hoolie had returned to sit on his bedroll.

POLICE HAVE ARRESTED T. WELBOURNE STOP
LOUISA ABDUCTED STOP PLEASE RETURN STOP
ROSE SHELBY

J.D. angrily tossed the telegram on the nightstand. "Goddammit," he said flatly. "I knew somethin' was wrong. Had a bad dream. A banshee dream."

"What's that?" Hoolie asked curiously.

"Some people call her the wailing woman. She knocks on your door when terrible things—like a death in the family—happen."

"Damn, that's bad. Cherokees have those kinds of bad signs too. You don't wanna know—believe me." Hoolie paused and looked away, contemplating all the bad things that could happen. "What's the telegram about? Mrs. Shelby want you to come back to Tulsa?"

"Yep." J.D. knuckled his moustache and pursed his lips. "You remember Minnie," he said slowly. Hoolie knew that Minerva Whitwell's murder two years before had hit J.D. hard. When Hoolie frowned deeply and nodded his head, J.D. continued. "The girl Louisa is the one who saved Minnie and Little Bill's boy. Theodore is her daddy's name. He was in the fight at the courthouse during the riot of '21. The Shelbys have been helpin' them out. Evidently he got locked up and the girl got kidnapped. Somethin's goin' on. And I'd bet a hundred dollars to your old campaign hat that the Klan is in the middle of it."

"I reckon you gotta go back. But what about the shipment of liquor? You're gonna leave me here to handle this, ain't ya?"

"For now. I better get back. It's more than Mrs. Shelby callin' me back. It's kinda personal."

"All right then, what's goin' on?"

"Gimme a minute. I got in late. Not enough sleep."

"I heard you come in."

"You did? Why didn't you say somethin'?"

"Didn't want to talk. I could smell you. You was drinkin' hard last night."

"Okay, you're right. I was tryin' to hold my own with Vi. I swear she could drink plenty of men under the table. Rohrbach passed out before midnight."

"So, you find out anything?"

"Shipment's comin' in a day or so. Big one too. Wynn's got good contacts. Most of it'll go to the two speakeasies in town, the whorehouse, and a big roadside gamblin' joint ten miles outside town goin' east. This is gonna be a distribution point to northwest Texas and all of western Oklahoma."

"Collins got any buyers?"

"Some. See, Wynn's hooch is good stuff, and he's buyin' it cheaper now. He's got the good buyers, and he'll break into the hayseed and Indian—sorry Hool—markets real quick. He'll undercut Collins's prices and cut his throat. I don't think Collins has got a prayer."

"Okay, so you're gonna spill it to the MacFarlands about the shipment. There's gonna be big trouble. Maybe some killin's. That what you want?"

"That's the way to play it right now. This is a city-cleanin' job." J.D. paused and smiled slightly to himself. "That's if you call this a city." He paused for another moment, then added, "I'll have to send a telegram to Mrs. Shelby that I'll be on the first train outta here . . . well, after I tip off the MacFarlands."

"What about Marty Albright and Moe Tucker?"

"I don't like that Tucker fella. He's the kind who'd shoot a boy's dog for laughs."

"He acts like he's a *sgini*—a devil, an evil spirit. He's just a real bad man." Hoolie gathered his thoughts. "Where they gonna store their . . . goods?"

"Place called Owl Creek. There's supposed to be an old tin shed up there. Anyway, it's about five miles outside town, almost due west."

"Owl Creek . . . it would be. Owls ain't usually good signs, J.D. I had a uncle that had a big owl 'bout four foot tall land out front of his house. He told it to get on out of there and then he run into the cabin to get his gun. My uncle came running out and tripped on the step down. He blew off his big toe. That owl just laughed and flew off."

"Don't try to make me believe that, boyo," J.D. said, shaking his head. "I've heard that about owls before. Maybe they are bad luck or bad omens or just plain bad—I don't care. I want you to go out there, but I want you hiding out. Don't get into a fight with any of these hicks, hear me?"

"How do I get there?"

"I don't know. You'll find a way. You got a couple of days. I only got one. I'm gonna go to the depot and find out how I can get back to Tulsa quick."

"All right, I'm packed up. I want to go out and see the Chargin' Horses. I'd like to find out why Cooper was there," said Hoolie.

"That's fine." J.D. looked up suddenly. "I wonder why Cooper was out there myself. Hmmmm." He paused again and said, "I'll check out as soon as I find out about the train and find one of the MacFarlands. You'd better find a horse or a car or a mule or somethin' to ride out there."

"I'll do that, but how am I gonna pay for it? I only got around three dollars."

J.D. frowned his usual penny-pinching frown and reached in his pocket for his money clip. He stripped off five ten-dollar bills, replaced the money clip, and reached in the other trouser pocket and pulled out a five-dollar gold piece and a silver dollar. "There, that oughta do you. But now you gotta pick up the laundry. Hold mine, and I'll get it when I come back."

Hoolie took the money and stuffed it into his trouser pockets. "Fifty-six dollars is a lot of money. I could buy an old heap with it. Or a real good horse." He looked at J.D. "You gonna pack up now?"

"Yep, let's get outta here."

"Just a minute, now. What's so personal about Mrs. Shelby's telegram?"

J.D. fidgeted for a moment, brushing off his coat sleeve, knuckling his moustache, and rubbing his hands together. "Well . . . okay . . . I'll tell you. Me and that little girl saw the worst of that riot. I'll tell you that she's a smart girl. I talked to her a little less than a year ago. She remembers things that I don't about that day. I got knocked silly, remember? I've got to get her back, and I've got to put them low-life thugs that took her in the can. That'll be the hard part."

"What do you mean?"

"I'll find them . . . and her. You mark my words on that. But I'm pretty sure the law ain't gonna want to put them away. I'll have to count on Mrs. Shelby to use her pull to get the law to work on mine and Louisa's side."

Hoolie smiled at J.D. "I see. Yeah, you'll get the job done. Even if you are an o'd-timer."

"You watch. I'll show you 'old-timer.'"

"I just bet you will, J.D. We should get goin'. And you're comin' back here too?"

"That's right. I'll get the Tulsa job done as soon as I can. You just do the same here. When I get done in Tulsa, I'll get the next train back here," J.D. said. He bent to pick up his grip. "Let's go . . . and use the telegraph."

>«

After some discussion with the hotel clerk, J.D. grudgingly paid the bill. He argued that the hotel should give him a business rate, but the young man behind the front desk was just as adamant—or just as cheap—as J.D. and won out.

Outside, J.D. took out his watch and looked at Hoolie from the corner of his eye. "You know what you're gonna do?"

Hoolie put his bedroll, rifle, and tow sack full of clothes down by J.D.'s cardboard suitcase. "Yeah, sure do. Soon as you get through with tippin' off the MacFarlands, I'm gonna find a horse or an auto and go out to the Chargin' Horse place. I'll look around again."

J.D. nodded and took out his cigarette case. He offered a pre-rolled cigarette to Hoolie, who took it with a smile. They lit up and smoked for a few seconds. Then Hoolie broke the silence. "When you get back to Tulsa, you gonna find out what to do about Shotz?"

"I'll do that and wire you back here. You gotta check in with the telegraph office, so don't get yourself hurt agin. You find out who killed him, and I bet the family will want to dig him up and take him somewhere else to get buried."

"Damn," Hoolie said with a grimace. "Why dig him up? I think just leave him be."

"You afraid of spooks?"

Hoolie looked at his feet then raised his head and pointed with his lips in the direction of the depot. "You better get goin'. Lot to do in a short time."

J.D. stared at Hoolie. "You are afraid of spooks, ain't you?"

Hoolie twisted his mouth. "In the o'd way, you put 'em in the ground and cover 'em up. If you don't, the bad spirits will get out. It's just smart to leave the dead alone. You clean their graves and you pay them respect, but you leave them be."

J.D. knuckled his moustache, took off his hat, and resettled it on his head. Hoolie could tell it was a nervous gesture. "Maybe you're right," he said in an almost inaudible whisper. "Maybe you're right."

The paper he had purchased at the Oklahoma City train station had been read, folded, and reread at least thirty times before J.D. stepped out on the platform at the Tulsa depot. The main problem J.D. had with riding the train was the lack of activity—that, and the fact that he had to spend nearly all night in the Oklahoma City depot before boarding the Tulsa train. Whenever he had a problem to think through, he either pulled files and read through them in his office, or he took a stroll to the courthouse to talk with city cops or the sheriff's deputies. Sitting in a depot or on a train folding and refolding the paper was driving him nuts.

Still, J.D. had thought through a couple of issues. Before he had caught the train out of Anadarko, he had talked to the MacFarlands outside the pool hall. He smiled as he pictured them in his mind. To J.D., the brothers had been dressed in hicksville splendor. Clem was wearing bright red braces, a red bow tie, and red sleeve garters all on top of a red pin-striped shirt with a pure white high celluloid collar. To ease the pressure on his Boyiddle-induced hip wound, he had a purchased an expensive-looking silver-capped cane. Festus had on a blue shirt, a red string tie, and white celluloid collar. He wore no sleeve garters, but his suspenders, which matched his brother's, were attached to the most outlandish pair of plaid trousers J.D. had ever seen.

The brothers had been standing next to the pool hall door when J.D. approached. "Hi, boys," he'd said. "You goin' to a dance?"

Clem smiled an empty-headed smile and said, "Naw, we goin' out to have us a time tonight."

"Well, you boys behave now." J.D. sidled up and said in a low whisper, "Wynn's gotta shipment comin' in to Owl Creek in two days, maybe sooner. Better tell Collins."

J.D. stepped back to look at the brothers. Festus raised his hand to rub his cheek. Clem pursed his lips and spoke softly, "We'll do just that."

J.D. turned to go.

"Where you goin'?" asked Festus.

"To the train depot. Gotta get back to Tulsa. Business."

The brothers nodded in unison. J.D. knuckled his moustache, smiled to himself, and kept walking.

As he was boarding the train in Anadarko, Hoolie came running up to give him the news that he had rented a horse and saddle from the Boyiddle brothers and was going with them to the Charging Horse place in the morning. The Boyiddles and Hoolie were going to camp outside of town for the night.

"Have a good trip, Jimmy," Hoolie said, teasing J.D.

J.D. gave him a disgusted look and said, "You take care of yourself. Don't get shot at again. Stay safe. I don't want to have to tell Myrtle you're hurt. She'd shoot me dead."

"Somebody meetin' you in Tulsa?" Hoolie called over the noise of the steam engine.

J.D. jumped on the Pullman coach step and cupped his hand around his mouth megaphone-style. "Yeah, just got a telegram off to Mrs. Shelby. She'll be there."

Hoolie smiled and held up his hand in more of a salute than a wave good-bye, and called out over the puffing engine gathering steam, "You take care of yourself. Don't you get beat up or shot again." The case they'd worked on two years ago had left both physical and emotional scars.

On the train J.D. kept thinking about how the Anadarko operation would play out. He was sure that Collins would try to ambush and hijack Wynn's hooch. How Wynn would handle things was more problematic. Would he be able to defend his shipment and destroy the Collins operation?

An image of Louisa Welbourne kept intruding in J.D.'s mind. He had never considered that anyone would do anything wrong to her. She was sweet, shy, and, despite the horrors she had witnessed two years prior, always smiling. As much as J.D. knew about the seamy side of criminality and unmitigated violence of the Klan, he still wouldn't have suspected that a little girl like Louisa would become a miscreant's target. In a way, J.D.'s own sense of justice and propriety made him somewhat naïve. For someone to be cowardly enough to kidnap a little girl was almost beyond his imagination. Up until the riot, when Minerva Whitwell had been murdered and burned, he'd still held the notion that a certain degree of what he considered masculinity existed in criminals. Unfortunately, J.D. was always being pulled back from thinking that there might be some level of gallantry among human beings, even bandits and gunmen. To J.D., the new century had ushered in a new sort of lawbreaker. Unlike many of the bandits he'd helped track down as a young man, these new felons had no sense of chivalry or manliness. They killed without provocation or remorse, whereas the old bandits like "Flatnose" Curry and Butch Cassidy only killed when their lives were threatened. The new outlaw, J.D. thought with conviction, was a completely new type of unredeemable degenerate. And to J.D., the Klan seemed to be an organization of, by, and for criminal reprobates of the lowest sort. The worst criminal gang couldn't match the KKK in terms of malevolent behavior.

As J.D. stepped from the train onto the platform, he could see that although lovely as her namesake, Mrs. Shelby had her thorns prominently on display.

J.D. was always glad to see Rose Shelby even when she was annoyed. Not only was she an attractive woman, but she also had an air of confident dignity about her. J.D. thought of her as a person who absolutely befitted her namesake: beautiful, but if you went too far, you were bound to be cut by a hidden thorn.

She extended a black-gloved hand as he walked toward her. He barely touched the ends of her fingers and quickly snapped off his bowler. "Mrs. Shelby, I'm so pleased to see you."

"Ah, Mr. Daugherty, I hope your trip to Anadarko was . . . profitable. It could hardly have been enjoyable." She paused and said, "Please walk with me to the automobile. I can tell you what's happened. And we'll take you to your flat."

≫≪

The ride had been relatively short. J.D. entered his room, set down his case, and sat down in his overstuffed easy chair. The case was simple. In his head, J.D. gave it the title of "The Tulsa Operation." And although the focus of the operation was on a little girl and her father, the whole of what Tulsa had become under Klan terror characterized the case.

As Mrs. Shelby had outlined it, one of the leaders of the local Klan had been brutally murdered with his own pick as he sat in his car. The case had stalled for quite some time. Then someone claiming to be an eyewitness to the crime came forward to say that he saw Theodore Welbourne fleeing the scene, and that he had recognized Welbourne from a picture in the paper. The police had arrested Welbourne and a neighbor took Louisa in.

Mrs. Shelby's daughter, Elizabeth, had been the one who'd found Louisa and the baby Thomas at one of the ballparks where a large number of black people had been collected during and immediately after the riot of 1921. Elizabeth had taken Louisa in, visited her often, took her and some of her girlfriends shopping, and had become like an older sister to the girl. As the only Shelby grandchild, even though half black—and much to the dismay of Big Bill Shelby—Thomas was being raised in the Shelby household. After Big Bill's own moral failings, he could hardly have countered Rose and Little Bill's principled and loving need to keep the boy close. Louisa's father had found employment through Shelby contacts, and Little Bill Shelby had helped him rebuild his home. It was only two doors away from where Little Bill's de facto wife Minerva and his son Thomas had lived and where she had been shot and burned to death. The murderers then burned her house down. The Welbourne home had also been burned down during the general conflagration that followed.

Louisa had been abducted on her route home from Booker T. Washington High School. As soon as it had happened, the girls Louisa was with ran back to school to tell the principal. He knew Elizabeth because she had done some fundraising for the school as a result of her connection with Louisa. The principal, being a smart man who had a strong feeling that the Tulsa police or sheriff's department wouldn't make the kidnapping of a black girl a high priority, called Elizabeth. Mrs. Shelby and her daughter then went to the police and were able to visit Theodore in the county jail.

Mr. Welbourne had been sure that the Klan had abducted his daughter and that the police were also somehow involved in the crime. Police interrogators had made a veiled threat that something might happen to Louisa if he did not confess to the murder of the Klansman.

When J.D. had asked about how Welbourne had been identified as fleeing killer in the first place, Mrs. Shelby said, "I'm afraid it was because of me." It seemed that Theodore Welbourne had had his picture in the paper with Mrs. Shelby. Because of her philanthropic work, she had been asked to ceremonially break ground for a Negro veterans' home. Welbourne was not only a veteran but had also become one of the new leaders in the attempt to rebuild the gutted Greenwood district and surrounding thirty-five square blocks of charred neighborhood. Mrs. Shelby thought that he had been recognized as a participant in the effort to protect a black prisoner from being lynched, the confrontation that led to the race riot of two years before. "Mr. Welbourne's arrest came on the heels of the appearance of that picture in the paper," said Mrs. Shelby. "I'm positive that these people in the Ku Klux Klan made a conscious decision to remove him from doing good works and rebuilding Greenwood. They are truly evil."

The whole story sounded plausible to J.D. All J.D. could say to her was, "Mrs. Shelby, I doubt that those men can think that logically or clearly." In his mind, however, the murder of a local Klan leader might just as well have been the result of a power struggle within the organization. The new governor had promised to control them and perhaps even rid the state of their diabolical influence. The Klan indeed had launched a new kind of reign of terror. Rather than relying on older methods like lynching and arson to keep black people "in their place," the Klan was kidnapping, beating, and torturing individual victims and letting them live to pass along the fear by word of mouth. If he was able to discover that Klan members themselves had been involved in the murder of this local leader, then people might stop thinking of these dolts as heroic knights when they were really dangerous criminals far worse than the Bolsheviks or any other group in the world. J.D. would have loved to pin a murder on a Klansman.

He rolled his neck to relieve the stiffness, took off his hat, laid it on the end table next to him, and rubbed his eyes and face. He was tired, but he knew he had to get something done quickly and get back to Anadarko. Hoolie might be out enjoying the scenery without a concern over the timing involved in cleaning up a town and simultaneously keeping the threads of finding Shotz's murderer together in one bundle. Or Hoolie might get into trouble. Or worse, shot again. Despite the fact that it was before noon, the train ride had fatigued J.D. to the very bone. The cut under his arm even hurt for the first time since the night the stranger had stabbed him. It irked him that he had not yet brought his attacker to justice. J.D.

was sure that it was more of a warning than an attempted homicide. The attacker could just as well have shot him after he left the meeting with Vi and Rohrbach; it was just one more thing that was strange about the Anadarko operation. As he had done many times before while thinking through his cases, he fell asleep in his familiar overstuffed easy chair.

Chapter IX

OWL CREEK

Two cans of beans, some jerked beef, five ears of dried corn, a sliced onion, and a couple of chopped turnips had gone into the water in the cook pot. Chester Boyiddle squatted by the fire stirring the mixture. He sampled a bit of the liquid, grimaced, spat it out, and muttered something in Kiowa. He rose and took a few steps to his bedroll, reached into a gunnysack and extracted a small white bag. He nodded once to Hoolie, who was sitting cross-legged near the fire, returned to the pot, reached into the small sack, and drew out some salt. He added pinch after pinch to the stew. "Needs salt," he said.

"Why don't you dump the whole sack in?" Hoolie teased.

Chester smiled and said, "Bad as this stew is, I might just do that." He squatted once again, stirred the mixture, tasted it, and declared, "This'll do. Ain't real good, but it'll do."

Harold walked into the firelight and sat down beside Hoolie. "Horses are all brushed down. I put hobbles on 'em, but they don't look to go far anyways. They're takin' in some good grass. . . . That's what horses should eat. Too much grain, and they get colic."

"I never thought of that," Hoolie said. "They do?"

"Sure do," Chester replied. "Horse was made to eat grass. Just look at their teeth."

"Thinkin' about it," Hoolie began, "horses are made to do just what horses do. They're strong and fast, and they get along with human bein's."

"The horses came out of the big lake—at least that's what my mama told me," Chester said. "Look at their heads. Their eyes are set way up so's they can see over grass, and their ears twist around to hear in all directions. Eyes are big . . . see plenty . . . plenty good." He chuckled to himself.

"I was thinkin' about somethin' you'ins could help me with."

"What?" said Harold.

"I'm not sure if it's your way or not, but when we ask a medicine man to do somethin', we bring somethin' like tobacco or a gift of some kind or another."

Harold smiled, nodded in agreement, and laughed a bit. "We give stuff away all the time. Yeah, that's what you do if you want a medicine man to help you out."

"Well, I want to ask Mr. Chargin' Horse, maybe George, to give me a good blessin'. Trouble is, I don't have somethin' to give out."

"What for? What do you need a blessin' for?" asked Harold.

"There's a shipment of whiskey for the bootleggers comin' in at a place on Owl Creek."

"How much money you got?" asked Chester.

"Fifty-some dollars."

"Whooooah . . . lot of money," Harold said, looking shocked.

"Tell you what," Chester said, "you give us twenty of them dollars, and you can have that horse to give to o'd Khōn, Grandpa Chargin' Horse."

Hoolie stood. "That's a deal," he said and shook hands with the brothers. He paused and asked, "Then what am I gonna do to get around?"

Harold looked puzzled. "Give it to him and borrow it back. He knows the horse is his."

Hoolie now looked puzzled. So Harold said, "Let me tell you about how it worked in the o'd days. See, a man rich in horses used to give 'em out to the younger mens who didn't have none. Then the young man would go get some horses from the enemies. He'd come back and have a giveaway of his own. The rich man would probably get two, three horses back. See?"

"Okay," Hoolie said, "the young man would steal the horses, right?"

"Well . . . yeah. You might call it stealin'. But they were enemies that'd use their own horses on you anyways. So you take from them, and then without no horses—if you take the good ones— they have a hard time comin' after you. You gotta look at takin' horses from the enemies as just bein' smart."

"I guess I understand."

Chester added, "That's why the Great Man who created all things gave us horses. We hunted from horses and kept our enemies away. Kiowas were a strong people because we had horses."

"All right, how do I do this?"

"I'm a relative," said Chester, "so I'll talk to o'd Khōn for you. You don't even have to give me nothing." He smiled, paused, and said, "Then say, 'I want to give this horse and ask you to help me out.' Then you just tell him what you want. What *do* you want?"

"I'd just like to have a sweat bath or a prayer or some medicine. I'd sweat my own self, except we're in your part of the country, and I wanna be right with the spirits here."

"That's just bein' smart too," Harold said with a nod and a crooked smile.

Chester looked up and said in a serious tone, "You know that you're lucky in a way. We was goin' out to the Chargin' Horse place 'cause there's a meetin' tomorrow night. That's why we're campin' out—leave 'em to get things ready."

"A meetin'?" asked Hoolie.

"One of the Coomsas' granddaughters is sick and asked for a meetin'. George is a chief, and Chester here pokes fire for him."

"Oh, it's a peyote meetin'?"

"Yep, you ever been?" asked Chester.

"No. Some of my wife's family is peyote people. But they don't ask me to go. They don't guess I'd want to 'cause I wasn't brought up in that way. I think my wife tells 'em to leave me be."

"They should ask you," Harold said judgmentally. "Chief Peyote is the way for all Indian peoples. You come into the tipi with us. You'll see."

"After morning water," Chester said, "you ask Khōn for a blessing. He might not sweat you, but he'll do one thing or another."

"That's good. I need some help."

》《

When Hoolie emerged from the tipi, he was exhausted but happier, unencumbered, closer to the spirit world, and just a bit wiser than before he had smoked the corn-husk cigarette, heard the prayers and songs, and drank some of the peyote tea. They had told him that it would probably taste terrible to him at first. "Try and keep it down," Harold said. "Mrs. Chargin' Horse makes the tea with a good and strong heart, and that makes it sweeter." But Hoolie didn't actually think the medicine was bitter. At one point during the meeting, he felt nauseated, but he wouldn't allow himself to throw up. Chester had said that he might want to upchuck, but that was just the bad things leaving his insides. The nausea quickly passed though, and Hoolie began to enjoy the singing. It was just like going to an Indian Baptist church—at first he was uncomfortable, but when the singing started, he began to enjoy himself more than at any other time. It was as if the power was built into the songs.

He thought about that. George Charging Horse had conducted a wonderful ceremony, even from Hoolie's limited point of view. And though Hoolie had not understood a single word of the Kiowa peyote songs and prayers, he'd felt an almost overwhelming sense of tranquility and, most of all, power.

It wasn't power in the same way that white men look at it. In their world—in his friend J.D.'s world—power was control, supremacy, muscle, and command. In the Cherokee way, and, from what he had seen of the Kiowa way and had observed among his wife's Osage people, power was spiritual wellness and the ability to do well the often mundane things connected with simply living life to its fullest. Power was also happiness. Power was the ability to fight, but it was also the ability of a medicine man to find the correct plant that could heal illness or close wounds.

The power of the peyote songs came through to Hoolie even if he didn't understand the words. The elder Charging Horse's voice wasn't strong in itself, but the songs were. Certainly the words had power, but the songs themselves were even more powerful. The water drum moved counterclockwise in the tipi, and each of the men there sang. Chester undoubtedly had the most beautiful voice, but George's was certainly more powerful. The medicine and the songs purified and healed not only Hoolie's soul but also the things around him. He had seen no visions in this meeting, but he had gained confidence and wisdom.

The Boyiddle brothers, George, Hoolie, George's sixteen-year-old son, Grandpa Charging Horse, and several other men had participated in the prayers before they entered the tipi. About halfway through the night, they had a drink of water out of a bucket. In the morning, George's wife brought in the morning water. When they came out of the lodge, they shook hands all the way around and exchanged pleasantries. The Boyiddles, George and his father, and the elder Charging Horse all expressed their pride in Hoolie. For his first time in a meeting, he had conducted himself well. According to Harold, he would no doubt receive a blessing. They all returned to the Charging Horse arbor for a large breakfast of fried eggs, smoked beef, boiled potatoes, and the inevitable fry bread.

When they had finished eating and Mrs. Charging Horse had directed the cleanup, George looked pointedly at Hoolie. "So you're goin' out to Owl Creek?"

"Well, later this evening. Yes, sir."

"Why so soon?"

"I want to get set up before morning. I want to be there hidin' out when the whiskey comes in."

"You gonna surprise 'em?"

"I don't think so. I don't want them to know I'm there. I have to look things over and tell J.D. He's my boss."

George Charging Horse pointed with his lips at the Boyiddles. "These two goin' with you?"

"Only if they want to."

George looked at the brothers. "You'ins goin'?"

Both Chester and Harold nodded in unison. Harold spoke. "I think so. Our friend here..."—he gestured toward Hoolie—"Well... he'll probably get in trouble and need some help."

Hoolie's eyes crinkled, and he put his hand over his mouth to prevent himself from laughing. He said matter-of-factly, "You two are the ones that got shot at in town. I ain't been in as much trouble since bein' taken to the jailhouse with you two."

"They let us go, didn't they?" Harold asked with a wry look in his eyes.

"Yes, they did," Hoolie said, "but that was because they had that Festus fella with a gun in his hand and o'd J.D. doin' some smooth talkin'."

"Don't forget that the sheriff hates the MacFarlands," said Chester.

The elder Charging Horse spoke rapidly in Kiowa. George quickly interpreted to Hoolie. "Thau—that's my father—wants to know who J.D. is. He also says that you have something to ask him."

Taken aback, Hoolie looked at Chester and Harold, who shook their heads in unison. The old man knew something without being told.

"Yes, sir," Hoolie began. "I wanted to ask Mr. Charging Horse to help me out in a matter. And I want to give him that horse I been ridin'."

The old man spoke in Kiowa once again. They all listened intently, and George interpreted for Hoolie. "He'll take the horse and knows that you'll have to use it to go after the evil men who are stealin' our brains and our hearts and our livers with that whiskey. He's asking that you destroy it. . . . He would like to say a prayer for you and say one over your weapons. He also wants to give you some medicine as in the o'd days."

"Thanks," Hoolie said simply. "I appreciate what he's doin'. I'll need the help. But I'm supposed to leave things alone and let those men quarrel among themselves."

"We should get rid of that whiskey," Harold said with conviction. "We can stop it."

Hoolie grimaced. "Look, I'll do what can be done. J.D. don't want me to get into trouble. He wants me to watch and listen." He paused for nearly a minute, looking at the ground. Finally, he looked up, grimaced again, and said, "Well, if we get a chance, we'll take care of it. I promise."

"Good," said George. He looked at his father and moved his chin up in the old man's direction. "He'll take care of things before you leave. But right now he'd like to know about this J.D."

"Not much to tell, sir. He was a policeman in Chicago. Then he went with a detective company called Great Western. He helped chase down murderers and train and bank robbers—some really bad men. He also worked for the oil companies against the workers. But he quit that and set up a business. He mostly works for the white people. Oil people. He finds runaways."

George's translation was halting, but he finally got through the whole message. The elder Charging Horse spoke in rapid Kiowa. Hoolie liked the singsong language, which contained totally new sounds to him. There were hard consonants and soft vowels. But what was most fascinating about the Kiowa language to an outsider like Hoolie was the resonance that seemingly came from deep in the speaker's chest. Hoolie called them "heart sounds" in his own mind. It sounded difficult but really beautiful.

"Thau would like to know about this J.D.'s heart," said George.

Hoolie had to think for a moment. He looked down at the ground and rubbed his chin with his right hand. Finally, he looked up. "J.D.'s got a good heart. He believes in doin' the right thing, but sometimes he can't see the right thing to do. . . . He tells stories about his people, the Irish, but he doesn't often listen to what they're sayin'. I've heard some of them. He tells a story about being warned the path he's walkin' on is dangerous . . . but instead of bein' careful when he's on that road, he just charges ahead . . . and laughs about it."

"Sounds like one of the o'd-timey warriors that staked themselves out in front of the enemy. He knows he's gonna die, but he's livin' life all the way. He's doin' what he does best," Harold said with a knowing look in his eyes.

Hoolie contemplated Harold's short speech. "I reckon," he began, "that's one way to look at it. But there's a difference between bein' brave and bein' crazy."

George held up his hand and said, "That depends on if the warrior is doin' what's right for the people. If he has to die for them, then that's what he has to do. It has to be done in a good way, like that. He'll be remembered and songs will be sung about how he thought of his relatives first."

Hoolie nodded. "Yes, sir, you're probably right. I just wasn't thinkin' right."

George squinted hard at Hoolie and said, "My father didn't really understand the business about runaways. Oil people runnin' away? From what? Why would you run away from it? They got rich pullin' it from the ground."

"I had a hard time understandin' that my own self," Hoolie said with a slight smile. "I think it comes down to feelin' bad 'cause you ain't doin' a whole lotta good with it. It's mostly the girls and young wives that run away. Seems like they get fed up with doin' nothin' and havin' their husbands thinkin' more about drillin' for oil than about them. I just don't know."

The elder Charging Horse shook his head slowly, then spoke directly to Hoolie. He raised one finger in front of Hoolie's chest and said, "Now, you."

George quickly said, "Thau wants to know about you."

"Not much to say about me."

The elder man gave a fairly long speech in Kiowa. George translated smoothly. "Thau says that you wear the hat of the white soldiers. You've seen war. You know fear and you know death. You also know of the good things like bein' with your relatives. You know happiness as well. Anybody who's seen war knows the bad and the good things about the world. You're a wiser man because you've seen all these things. You also carry wounds. You limp slightly and you live with your pain well. Warriors have to do that in that way. So what about you?"

Hoolie looked at his feet and began to speak haltingly. "Your father can look deep into a man. . . . Yeah, I was in France and I got wounded. Put me out cold. But I'll tell you that no one else was alive or able to move because of the shell that exploded among us. The spirits took me to an aid station. That's why I limp. But the white doctors saved my leg."

"Go on," said George.

"I guess I'm just tryin' fit in a world that's a takin' off in all kinds of different directions. My own *edudu*—that's grandpa—tells me that things were hard when he was young, but then you didn't have that many paths that you had to walk all at oncest. You can't hardly make a livin' without doin' a bunch of different things. Like now: I fix automobiles, do some detective work for J.D., help out my wife and her mother and grandmother with the garden, tend our horses and cattle, keep up the hogs, and try hard to pray and do the right things with the spirits of this land."

"That's all good," Chester said.

"Well, you gotta keep tryin' anyway."

"I think that my father is glad you ain't forgot where you came from," said George. "You might have to get along in the white man's way, but you gotta keep up with the man above. That's the tough part."

Hoolie frowned and wiped his hands on his trouser legs. "Mr. Chargin' Horse, I try hard to keep up with that. I always wanna be right with the spirit world. But I have to get to Owl Creek and finish up a job. Now J.D. is countin' on me, and I'll do all I can for him. I have to ask you about somethin' when I get back."

George nodded. "You want to know about Mr. Shotz?"

"Yes, sir, I do. But that'll keep 'til later."

>«

They tethered the horses nearly a mile from the big metal shed where they thought the delivery was to be made. Chester and Harold were sure that no one else was around. The Sheriff Wynn outfit—as Hoolie thought of them in his head—were obviously so confident in their hideout that they didn't even post a guard, unless the guard was off in the bushes somewhere. And surely the Chief Collins outfit, with the brothers MacFarland at its head, would have set up an ambush on the shipment well in advance. They're pretty dumb though, Hoolie thought. Maybe they were just scared of Marty and Moe. Moe was genuinely and outwardly a mean killer. From Hoolie's point of view, Moe was one of those people who would take gruesome pleasure in torturing and finally rubbing out a human being. Marty was one of those seemingly happy-go-lucky fellows who might kill somebody as if he were swatting a fly. Hoolie had known and seen both types and couldn't decide on which one was worse. In reality they probably both were. One of them pulled the wings off the flies before he mashed them, and the other just killed them outright without any sort of emotion. One was simply cruel without expressing anger, lust, greed, or joy; the other took pleasure in cruelty.

They lay with their rifles in the brush next to the creek. The morning was dark, but if the sun had been out, Hoolie would have been staring up at an overcast sky; there were no stars, and the moon was a hazy, dim silver color. Harold whispered something. It startled Hoolie, who had thought that both Boyiddles were sleeping—at least they hadn't moved a muscle since they all got settled in. "What?" Hoolie said under his breath.

"Listen," Harold said in a low growl. "I can hear movement off in the direction of the shed. I should go scout it out."

Hoolie breathed in through his teeth. "Maybe—but don't get caught or even let 'em hear you. I don't know what to do."

Chester made a *sssssss* sound. "I hear somethin' too," he said. "I can't tell, but it might be off in that direction."

"What direction?" asked Harold. "It's dark—I can't see you a-pointin'."

"Over to the shed but off to the right."

"Yeah, that's where I thought."

"I can't hear nothin'," whispered Hoolie. "You sure you boys ain't just hearin' things?"

"I reckon it could be a coyote or a deer or somethin'," said Harold. "I'll go look. And I'll be quiet."

"Okay," Hoolie said with caution. "Don't get caught or get into trouble."

Hoolie caught a glimpse of Harold's smile as he silently crawled backward to the creek bed.

"Just like a crawfish," said Chester.

Hoolie smiled to himself. He knew that Harold would use the brush and tree stand next the creek to work his way over to the shed. Hopefully he wouldn't meet up with either Collins's or Wynn's boys along the way.

Chester and Hoolie waited for perhaps twenty minutes without saying a word between them. Then, as Hoolie was about to open his mouth, a flash of light and a loud *whump* almost broke their eardrums.

"That's a grenade," growled Hoolie.

"Harold . . . ?" whispered Chester. Muzzle flashes were seemingly everywhere. There were pistol shots and the cracks of modern high-velocity rifles. To the right of where the shed was supposed to be, an automatic weapon rattled. Hoolie guessed it was a Thompson submachine gun. The military wasn't buying them anymore, and so they were being bought up by the cops, crooks, and detective agencies to use against strikers. Hoolie had only heard of the Thompson; it was known as the "trench broom" because its inventor's intention was to counter the trench warfare stalemate that had developed during the Great War. The gun in the distance sounded as though it was spitting out bullets at a much greater rate than any other automatic weapon that Hoolie had ever heard— even the BAR. Hoolie wondered which of the cops were using the weapon: Wynn's sheriff's department or Collins's city police.

"Harold!" Chester said with greater emphasis. "We got to do somethin'."

"I don't know what," Hoolie said through clenched teeth.

"Do somethin', dammit!"

Hoolie shook his head, jumped up, and ran as fast as he could on his bad leg toward the muzzle flashes. As he went, he cocked and fired his old Winchester as fast as he could. Chester followed and then forged slightly ahead of Hoolie.

Hoolie halfway expected to die in this charge, but when he and Chester both tripped and fell into the same shallow rut in the ground, they both whispered at the same time, "I'm all right . . . I'm all right," as if to reassure themselves personally rather than each other. Except for a few stray rounds, the shots weren't being fired in their direction, yet the firing was unceasing. This was a true gunfight with all the stops pulled out. Strangely, Hoolie had not heard any cries of pain. The Thompson rattled, and rifle, shotgun, and pistol shots were blazing away. That much gunfire surely should have hit somebody.

On the other hand, Hoolie recalled a gunfight he saw in Tahlequah once. Bobby Crittenden and Arch Alberty faced each other in the middle of a dusty street near the courthouse, drew their pistols, and let fly. They both emptied their firearms at each other at a distance of no more than ten feet, but neither hit the other. When their six-shooters ran out of bullets, both men put their guns back in their belts, turned their backs on each other, and walked away satisfied, perhaps, that they had protected their honor as men, even if they failed as expert pistol shots.

The thought of the Crittenden-Alberty gunfight amused Hoolie. What might have happened was that Bobby and Arch were mad, but since they were kinfolks, neither wanted to kill the other. So they shot it out in public but deliberately missed each other. It was the only way to explain what had gone on. Hoolie's thoughts perplexed him. The memory of a crazy gunfight in the middle of another crazy gunfight must be crazy, he thought. It sure wasn't like the trenches in France.

Now Hoolie and Chester were both feeling relatively safe lying in their rut while bullets were flying everywhere else. They heard no cracks or buzzes of rounds being shot in their direction. The Thompson rattled steadily, and the reports of the other weapons continued.

Finally, somebody yelled, "You boys better give up! We'll find you in the end. You're gonna be sorry."

"That you, Moe Tucker?" someone near the shed yelled back. "Who's that?"

"Just yell one more time," came the voice near the shed, "and I'll put a hole in you big enough to drive a team of mules through."

"Well, come on then! Shoot!"

The guns sounded again. This time a painful scream came from near the shed. Somebody was finally hit. The gunfire died down, with only one or two straggling pops coming from weapons farther away from the shed. The Thompson ceased fire completely.

There was another cry of pain, and a man yelled at the top of his voice, "Goddam you, Moe—you done shot Dick!"

Moe, far to the right where the shed lay, shouted back, "Serves him right, and I'll get you in the end too, by God!"

No gunfire erupted after the exchange of words. Hoolie whispered to Chester, "Let's move back before sunup, or we'll get caught in the open."

"Yeah, what about Harold?"

"I don't know where he is. Maybe if we go back to where we started, he'll find us."

"Yeah, I guess so."

"I shouldn'a come down here," Hoolie said through his teeth. "That was dumb. Now we're stuck in a rut in the road in the open. They'll kill us for sure if we don't get back to the trees."

"All right," Chester said, "but let's go slow."

They crawled along the rut for about twenty paces and then got to their feet slowly. Without a sound, Hoolie and Chester crouched low and walked to the tree line along the creek. Just as they were about to settle in the brush, a bright light flared and a loud whooshing sound hit their ears. A bright ball of fire engulfed the shed. Someone had ignited the alcohol seeping from the whiskey cases that had been shot through. Hoolie likened the fire to the quick red-and-black explosions of natural gas that occasionally lit up the oil fields across the Arkansas River, but on a much smaller scale. The angry shouts began and the gunfire increased. Suddenly, a call originating some distance from the fire came: "Let's get on outta here, boys! Job's done!"

A few pops from the smaller caliber firearms went off and the Thompson emitted a last burst of five or six rounds. A voice near the shed and fire called out, "I'll get you yet, Festus, you bastard!" But that half of the gunfight seemed to have fled the scene. The blaze in the shed had died down to several separate smallish fires burning what was left of the whiskey crates. It was still hot enough to shatter some of the bottles though.

Hoolie and Chester waited, secure in their brush hideaway. The darkness held for a while and then the gloom of early dawn started creeping in. A long way off, a Ford coughed to life. Hoolie could tell what it was. He saw that the brush in different places around the burning shed was also coming to life. Men were moving and talking, but he couldn't hear what they were saying. Without much concern over whether or not they might be ambushed, several men carrying buckets went to the creek, filled them, and walked to the shed to sling water on the various fires. Pretty soon the men were sitting or lying on the ground, looking from this distance worn out and ready to fall asleep. Then one man stood—he looked like Marty—said something, and motioned to his right. Two men stood and walked over to the shed. They picked up rifles and walked over to the trees. A car engine started and a Ford touring car emerged from the cover of the trees and rolled down a deeply rutted path back toward the main road. Hoolie guessed it was the road that he and Chester had hidden in not an hour before.

"I see Marty and Moe down there," whispered Chester. "I hope Harold is okay." And then, "Listen. . . . Truck headed this way."

Hoolie cocked his head, trying to pick up the sound. Then he heard it. The sound was heavy rumbling. "Lay low—they're comin' back," he whispered harshly.

A bush rustled behind them, and Hoolie and Chester swiveled around, aiming their rifles.

"Don't shoot. It's me, Harold. Looks like the MacFarlands missed the shipment." Harold crawled forward and squeezed in between them. He had a smile on his face. "Marty and Moe are gonna be happy the trucks is a-comin'. Their whiskey got blowed up."

"Saw that," said Chester. "Who did it? You see?"

"I did," Harold replied with a tight smile. "Got close, lit a match. Went up like kerosene."

Chester could hardly control his excitement. Hoolie could tell even in the grayish just-before-dawn light that he was going to shout out in a victory celebration. Indeed, Chester opened his mouth and started to cry out but muted himself so that the sound emitted from his lungs was a kind of strained, undertoned "ahhhhhhhh."

Hoolie wanted to laugh out loud but stopped himself as well. Harold silenced them both. "Sssssssss. Listen. . . ."

Loud noises and a single gunshot came from the direction from which the trucks were coming in. Hoolie guessed that the MacFarlands were hijacking the incoming shipment. Then two rifle reports echoed over the low swells of the prairie.

The men by the burnt-out shed got to their feet. One of them—Hoolie thought it was Moe—yelled a loud "Goddam" then started pushing the men, muttering something that neither he nor the Boyiddles could understand. The men went into the brush and cranked two automobiles, then roared off in the direction of the rifle shots and the trucks bringing in the whiskey.

"I'd like to see this," said Chester.

"Bad idea," Hoolie replied through his teeth. "There's gonna be more killin' out there."

In less than five minutes, another shootout began, presumably at the sight of the hijacked trucks. The Thompson rattled again, and this time two hand grenades exploded. The MacFarlands had probably destroyed the shipment by now—if it wasn't destroyed, it was very likely shot to pieces and just about worthless. Very little good whiskey could be sopped up from the red dirt of the Anadarko basin.

"Let's get outta here," Hoolie said as he stood up. "Whoever it was that started the shootin' waylaid that liquor shipment. My bet is that it's the MacFarlands. And that means it's Collins against Wynn. There's gonna be a war in this county—you can bet on that. The good thing is that they didn't find out we was around here."

Chapter X

THEODORE WELBOURNE

In his blue overalls, high brown shoes, light blue work shirt, and billed workman's cap, Danny Ryan looked much different than he did when he was a young pimple-faced and not very adept pickpocket. Gone were the plaid knickers, the red, white, and blue striped calluses, and the open-necked white shirt. As an apprentice mechanic at Sears's automobile repair and refueling station, Danny was earning a fair and, best of all, honest living. He brought money home to his large family and had even gotten his da a steady job at the machine shop down the block from Sears's. Danny and his old man walked to work together six days a week and had gotten to be very close. Every time J.D. saw the boy, he got a surge of pride and a genuine feeling of gratitude to Mr. Sears, who had put Danny on at J.D.'s request. Hoolie had put in a good word too, but since Hoolie was married and living in Osage County, he hadn't been around to keep tabs on the boy. The Ryan family was J.D.'s project.

The elder Ryan was a union man to his very core, and J.D. had helped him out of a jam that arose as a result of company goons busting up a union meeting. John Ryan had been run up on charges of assault and battery because he had allegedly punched a Great Western detective. That was back when J.D. worked for Great Western busting up union meetings and undermining union strikes. Ryan really had been arrested because he was a member of the Wobblies, or Industrial Workers of the World. The IWW actually had a meeting hall in downtown Tulsa. J.D. was sick of his own involvement in the anti-Red and anti-union crackdown and had given John Ryan's defense an alibi for his whereabouts during the melee between the union men and the union busters.

The Ryan family was grateful to J.D. Danny, the eldest son, had helped on some of J.D.'s cases, and John was always ready to have a beer or swap stories about the old country. The Ryans had come from a different part of Ireland than J.D.'s folks, but both were Irishmen nonetheless and somehow connected in story and song about the old sod.

J.D. had come to see Danny at Sears's place. He found the young man under a Chevrolet, fixing a broken shifting mechanism. J.D. grunted, and Danny scooted out from under the Chevy. Not seeing anything of J.D. except his pant legs, Danny offered a cordial "Can I help you?"

J.D. smiled crookedly and knuckled his moustache. "Good to see you, boyo."

Danny recognized J.D.'s voice and raised his head to see out from under the bill of his grimy cap. "How's things?" he said through a grease-stained grin.

"Look's like you're doin' well," said J.D. "How's the family?"

"Good. Yes, sir, we're doin' real good. The old man's workin' steady, and Ma's happy as she can be. Are you doin' well?"

"Tolerable . . . tolerable," J.D. said while rubbing his cheek. "I need a favor . . . from your old man."

"My old man?"

"Yeah. I know he's still got friends with the Wobblies. You think he'd ask a few things for me?"

"You know the old man's pretty touchy about stuff like that. That was pretty bad a few years back. And he don't wanna get any of his pals in Dutch with the law."

"I know what he means," J.D. said. He ran his right thumb along his moustache. "But you know me and your da knows me. I'm not after the IWW—I'm lookin' into the KKK."

"J.D., they're about as far apart as night and day. Why do you think that the old man might know about the Kluxers?"

"I don't think he does. But remember there's dusk between day and night. Some of the guys who're in the IWW have still got jobs in the oil fields. And I know for a fact that a bunch of the boys who parade around in their bedsheets at night also work in the business. I just want your da to ask his friends if they've picked up on a few things goin' 'round."

"I get it," Danny said. "Those boys mighta let somethin' slip?"

"That's right. And I'm just seein' if your da can help me out."

"Sounds jake to me, J.D. How about meetin' me and the old man 'round six at Boston and Fourth?"

"I'll be there." J.D. tipped his hat and left.

>«

J.D. walked into the courthouse, said hello to the desk sergeant, and meandered his way up the stairs and into the large squad room. Two uniformed officers were sitting at the large table painstakingly writing out reports on pads. After nearly every word they printed, they would pause and lick the ends of their pencils. They looked like two burly blue-clad schoolboys writing "I will not bring firecrackers to school again." They did not look up from their labors until J.D. spoke. "Hiya, boys. Lieutenant Finch around?"

The copper with the fiery red ears lifted his head. A smile of recognition lit his eyes and he said, "Howdy, J.D. Yeah, he's down in the basement, checkin' up on the boys in the can. He'll be up in a few. Just take a chair and cool yer heels."

"Sure, Mac. I can dangle for a few minutes. But if he don't get back in a couple of minutes, I'll have to check out. If I have to go, I'll leave a message with you."

"That's okay, J.D." The officer paused. "Well, gotta get back to the paperwork."

"Sure thing. Didn't want to interrupt."

J.D. sat, knuckled his moustache, and played with his hat. He had dusted the brim twice before Marv Finch walked in the door. The burly officer with the craggy face looked down at J.D. and said, "'Lo, old man. Thought you was in Anadarky or somewhere out in the hayfields. Got tired of the hicks?"

J.D. chuckled. "Hiya, Marv, how's things?"

"Could be better."

"I hear you boys got some backup from the state militia. . . . How's that goin'?"

"Damn pain in the neck, J.D. They patrol the streets, but I think they're spendin' too much time in the speaks to do much good."

"Have they quieted things down with the Klan?"

"Some. There's been a few snatchin's, but no mobs bustin' up the town. We still gotta catch the outlaws." Finch looked over his shoulder at the two officers painstakingly writing with their pencils. "And do the paperwork," he added sadly.

"Sorry to hear that. . . . Say, Marv," J.D. said, changing the subject, "I hear you got a man named Theodore Welbourne locked up. Can I talk to him for a while?"

"You know the boy?"

"Yeah, sure do. You know about the scrape I had a couple of years back?"

"Yeah, you shouldn'a been in colored town, that's for damn sure."

"Now, you know I was workin' on a case. Couldn't be helped."

"Okay," the beefy police lieutenant said, "so how do you know Welbourne?"

"Marv, you've heard of Mrs. William Shelby, right?"

"Oh, you're gonna pull her outta your hat again, huh?"

"She's been here, ain't she?"

"About a hundred times. I been gettin' hell for not cooperatin' with her."

"Why?"

"Well, I let her in the jail. She tries to talk to him. But he don't say nothin'. Then she says that he won't say anything 'cause we have to be there when he's got visitors. But that's the by-God rules."

"Okay. So?"

"She wants to talk to him alone. I say 'you can't,' and she walks out and complains to the mayor. Jesus, I can't change the rules down there. Not even for Mrs. Shelby and the mayor."

"I understand, Marv," J.D. said quietly, "but she swings a lot a weight around here. Now, she asked me to talk to Welbourne. She's payin' me to look for his daughter. We figure the Klan snatched her."

"See . . . now I didn't even know that. That's tough about the girl. But what the hell you gotta talk to him for? He can't get out. We gotta lock him up tight, so's the Klan don't stir up a mob to lynch him. The militia boys pull night duty around the courthouse. And he's gonna swing for this one—got an eyewitness says he knocked off an out-of-work oil-rig roustabout a while back. Cut and dry."

"Well, Mrs. Shelby thinks there might be somethin' else to it. She thinks the Klan is tryin' to pin this one on him because he's a leader with the black people. If he gets hung, then he's outta the picture. And he got his picture in the paper with Mrs. Shelby. If you want to pin something on a Negro in this town, you might as well go after the one you think has the most pull with the oil people and the politicians."

"I see what you mean. I know for a fact that the guy whose word got the boy thrown in the pokey and charged with murder is a member of the Klan. . . . Okay. I'll take care of things. But you gotta follow the rules. I'll be down there with you."

"That's sounds good to me. When can we go?"

"Right now, if it suits you."

"I'll follow you, my friend."

Finch turned and opened the door.

≫≪

"Mr. Welbourne, I came to talk to you because of your daughter. Whatever is going on with your case has nothing to do with me. I understand that you've retained Mr. Berg as your counsel. He's mine as well, and I can tell you that he'll do everything in his power to help you."

Welbourne sat stock-still on the metal bench inside his cell. J.D. sat on a wooden chair about three feet from the bars, with Lieutenant Finch standing directly behind him. Welbourne hadn't spoken a single word. All he did, in fact, was nod his head in recognition when J.D. came into the cellblock.

"Mr. Welbourne," J.D. continued, "I want to find your daughter. She means a great deal to Elizabeth and Mrs. Shelby . . . and to me."

Welbourne looked down to the floor and compressed his eyelids together very hard in an effort not to spill tears. He looked into J.D.'s eyes and said, "I'll take care of my own."

"Welbourne, you can't, for God's sake," J.D. said angrily. "This is about finding her before those thugs do something bad. By God, I was with her when Minnie Whitwell was killed. Your daughter did somethin' I wasn't able to do . . . save that child. Now I've gotta save her."

Welbourne pursed his lips together. "Don't worry," he said, "I'll take care of her." He turned his head and rubbed his chin. He stood and said, "I don't wanna talk about it anymore."

It was a dismissal. J.D. knew it and stood up. "Welbourne," he said in a parting shot, "you're behind bars. What the hell can you do?"

"Just wait, Mr. Daugherty, just you wait."

»«

J.D. saw John and Danny Ryan walking up Boston on the other side of the street. He waved at them, and they returned the gesture. They walked into the middle of the street, avoided the northbound trolley, and crossed to where J.D. was waiting.

"Greetings, Danny boy . . . and Sean, how's by you?" J.D. sometimes called John Ryan Sean, as "John" was said in the old country.

John Ryan laughed and shook J.D.'s hand. "Haven't seen you in a while, old man," he said. "We've been good, and you look in the pink."

"I could be better," answered J.D.

Ryan got to the point. "Me boy says you wanted to talk?"

"That's right. How 'bout we talk over a beer?"

"Can't do that right now. The woman's got a stew on. How about comin' home with us? You could use some home cookin', and I got a bottle of rye we could tip. Talk then."

"Tell you what," J.D. said, "I'll do it—if we can stop and I'll buy us some good cigars. What could I bring your wife?"

John thought for a minute, but Danny answered, "I think Ma would like some fresh tobacco her own self. She likes her pipe after supper."

"Good idea. Pipe tobacco it is," declared J.D.

»«

John Ryan had been right. J.D. relished the supper that Margaret Ryan had put before him. The savory stew had celery, carrots, red potatoes, onion, and a beefy broth that was rich and thick. The chunks of beef that were in the stew actually melted in his mouth, and the crusty homemade bread was simply perfection. J.D. slathered butter on the bread like a kid. Mrs. Ryan also brought out some johnnycakes and strawberry preserves.

J.D. thanked her profusely.

"J.D.," she said in return, "thank you for the pipe tobacco, and you're welcome here anytime you need a meal or a good sit-down to talk."

After the meal, the men went into the front room. The fact that Danny was included signaled to J.D. that, as one of the bread-winners in the family, he was now entitled to be treated as a man. And that was all thanks to J.D. Mrs. Ryan retired to the kitchen to smoke her pipe and supervise the Ryan daughters in the clean up. The two other boys played with their wooden horses in the hallway.

John Ryan ritualistically passed a penknife around to J.D. and Danny to cut the tips off their cigars. He also passed the kitchen matches to light them up. After each man had had a few puffs, John, as was his privilege as head of the household, began the conversation. "So, J.D., Danny tells me that you wanna talk some about my ol' pals in the oil fields."

"Indeed, my friend. I'd just like to know what's goin' on around the IWW, and especially what's goin' on with the jokers in the KKK. Thought somebody might've spilled the beans on what the fools in the bedsheets are doin'."

"Why you askin'?" Danny put in. John nodded in agreement with his son.

"Well, boys, I'll tell you. You know a couple of years ago, those boys put me in the hospital durin' the riot. Now the girl that I was talkin' to at the time was colored, and she got killed and burnt up. Another young girl was there and helped me. She carried off the dead girl's baby. She's a brave girl. Anyways, the Klan kidnapped her, and I gotta find her." J.D. looked directly at John. "I have to tell you that Rose Shelby is payin' me to look into this." He glanced at Danny and quickly returned his eyes to John. "But you know it's more about my own principles than the money."

John was nodding his head. If there was anything in the world that John Ryan fully understood, it was honor. "I understand," he said. "I'll help out as much as I can."

"Thank you, my friend. I'd like to ask about what's goin' on with the IWW nowadays?"

"Well, you pretty much know. After we got attacked six years ago, everybody got pretty quiet. The local was still around as the

Oil Workers Union. The IWW was completely closed down some-time after the '21 riot. Nobody was goin' down there anyway, and most of the guys went up to Kansas. There's some guys around, but you gotta be pretty scared after everything that's gone on around here."

"I know. Seems like Tulsa has a gift for mob rule."

"Don't I know it," said John.

"Da, you think all that stuff that happened to the IWW and the Negroes is tied together?" asked Danny.

"Appears so. They was bustin' our heads together. . . ." John looked at J.D. with a lopsided smile. Back then J.D. had been part of the private detective organization that broke apart Wobblie meet-ings. "But that," John continued, "was what we expected. I think it was the principles that put everything over the edge. The IWW was the only union that let the black folks in. Then the fight started among the workers. The oilmen started it. They started hirin' the Negroes on the cheap. They needed the work and took it. That's when the roughnecks got riled up over them stealin' work from white men. You know how they work. The guys who got canned were all IWW, and the guys who kept their jobs were all KKK. Then those guys hired the coloreds and started spreadin' the word that the blacks were takin' white jobs on the cheap. The guys who got canned blamed the colored boys and joined up with the Kluxers. It's a way of bustin' up the unions and pointin' the finger at some-body else. Bad business all around. Then the Kluxers got involved with the Legion boys, and both of them went after the IWW and the Negroes. The fight was on then, boyo!"

"I saw all that goin' on. That's one of the reasons I quit Great Western," said J.D. He paused, took a pull on his cigar, and contin-ued. "So you think that the roughnecks in the oil fields are pretty much KKK now?"

"Some. Some of 'em are Reds. God, we got some anarchists too. But I think most of them just wanna make a livin'. All my old friends just wanna stay clear of all of 'em."

"You think anybody knows anything about the Kluxers from the inside out?"

"Oh, I get some rumors down to Spellman's speakeasy."

"Anything lately?"

Danny was on the edge of his seat. "I heard some stuff at Sears's. Couple of the boys was talkin' about bustin' that Negro outta jail and stringin' him up."

"I heard the like my own self," said John. "That's about it. Heard he killed a KKK boss of some sort or another. Ike's joint is another hangout."

J.D. nodded enthusiastically. "That's just the sort of news I need. You know the man who the Klan is after is the girl's pa. I think the Klan boys snatched her to get some kind of confession outta him. But he hasn't done it yet. He won't talk to anybody. I'da talked my head off to get my daughter let go."

"Yeah," Danny began, "but you gotta be sure that they let her go before you said anything. I don't think I'd trust the Klan."

"That's right, J.D.," said John. "I wouldn't sign nothin' 'less my girl was let go. More'n anything, that colored boy knows what the Kluxers do. He might be thinkin' that the girl is dead right now. He needs to get outta jail to get back at 'em. Leastways that's what I'd do."

"You're probably right. But if they've done somethin' to that girl, I'm goin' after them too. Hope you boys will help me out."

John put his cigar in the holder of a cigar stand and ashtray and said, "For you, J.D., this family would walk off a cliff. You just give us a lead, and we'll find somethin' out."

"Just anything you hear about this case—what happened to the girl, what the Klan is doin'. Just any of that kind of thing."

"You got it," said Danny.

John took his cigar from the stand, drew in a great deal of smoke, and released it with a sigh. "You wanna do somethin' about them tryin' to lynch the daddy?"

J.D. looked at the floor and took a draw on his own cigar. "Nah, I don't think anything's gonna happen. With the martial law, the militia boys have got the jail pretty well covered. I don't think the Klan will lynch anybody with that kind of guard around the courthouse."

"Maybe not," Danny said, "but the Klan's got people on the inside."

"You may be right Danny, me boy," said J.D., "but I'd like for you to keep an eye peeled. John, I hate to ask this, but could you help me out if I need somebody to watch my back?"

"Why sure, J.D.—you know I'll help out. I don't mind skinnin' a knuckle or two on some two-bit punk. Anytime."

"Thanks, gents. I reckon I'll be takin' my leave now."

John and Danny saw J.D. to the door. Mrs. Ryan waved from the kitchen. J.D. turned and said, "I'll be in touch soon."

"Right you are, J.D.," John said. "Right you are."

≫≪

Six men dressed in old-fashioned horseless carriage slickers, driving gauntlets, white feed-sack masks, and roadster goggles darted quickly and quietly across the alley to the side door of the courthouse. The national guard private saw them and turned his back. The guardsman was only nineteen, and he didn't want a confrontation with men who had the look of evil all about them. He wasn't going to get killed fighting it out with a bunch of murdering Klansmen. All he wanted to do was get back to Oklahoma City, his new wife, and his job.

The first of the men to reach the metal door softly knocked on it with his gloved hand. The door opened and the six moved in. They spread out in a shadow along the inner wall. The police officer who let them in stood in front of them with a frown on his face. He couldn't see their faces—even their eyes were hidden behind the tinted goggles. He looked at the leader and whispered, "Got my money?"

"You Fred?" the leader asked quietly.

"Yep," came the reply.

The leader reached in a pocket and took out a roll of bills. He handed it to the officer and said in a scratchy, breathy voice, "How about taking care of that militiaman out there?" The leader's sleeve caught on a bulge under his slicker and pulled it above his gauntlet's cuff. The officer glimpsed light skin and blond hair on the man's forearm. Just as he had thought, the sergeant who had told him to let these boys in for a bit of cash had to be Klan. *That's okay by me*, he thought.

"Yeah, sure," he murmured. He would go out, talk to the soldier boy, maybe offer him a drink from his flask. He'd get him to walk with him to the other end of the alley. "I'll do that right now," he said with a sigh. He turned and went out through the door.

As soon as the door was shut, the men pulled out their weapons from underneath their slickers. Following the leader, they turned a corner and rushed toward the jail guard who was reading at a desk placed in front of the outer steel cage that blocked the cells. The leader of the six men ran toward the guard and pushed a Colt Army .45 automatic in his face. The guard was taken completely by surprise. He raised his hands. "How many guards?" the leader whispered.

"Three more. They're walking their rounds."

"Get 'em over here. We're takin' the nigger."

"Okay . . . okay," the guard said in a frightened voice. The other masked men were holding guns—one of them had a Thompson, another a sawed-off shotgun. The officer at the front desk called out, and in a few seconds, two more officers were glaring down the barrels of an assortment of very lethal firearms. "Where's Fred?" asked the desk guard.

"Never mind," the leader rasped. Fred was the one who let them in.

The man with the shotgun pointed the weapon directly at one of the officers. "Keys," he said. The officer showed a ring on his belt.

Two men armed with pistols stepped forward and pushed the officer with the key ring to the door. He opened it and led them to the cells. They all came back in less than five minutes with Theodore Welbourne in their midst. "Let's go," the leader said. He pointed at the guards with his .45. "We know what you look like . . . who you are. Give us an hour before you raise the alarm, or we'll find you and slit your throats. Got it?"

The man at the desk said, "Yes, sir."

The six men disappeared down the corridor with a handcuffed Welbourne in tow.

In unison, the three guards breathed a heavy sigh of relief. "By God," the one who had unlocked Welbourne's cell said. "That's about as scared as I ever been."

"Did you see the nigger? He knew he was gonna die," the man at the desk said. "He kinda looked like he was dead already."

"Damn," the third guard said. "The Klan is good at snatchin' 'em."

"Wonder what happened to Fred?" the desk officer said. "You think they killed him?"

"Nah," the guard said, "they was probably Klan—they wouldn't kill no white man, 'less he was a Jew or a Red or maybe a mackerel snapper. Fred'll turn up."

As they were all taking deep breaths, the fourth guard walked toward them down the corridor.

"Fred," the desk man said, "where you been? The Klan just took our prisoner."

"What! I was in the commode. What the hell happened?"

"Those fellas just came in, stuck guns in our faces, and marched me back to that boy's cell. I thought the Klan did things different. I saw the mob two years ago."

"No, not no more," said Fred. "We, ahh, *they* work just like in the old days. Those boys musta been real night riders. Looks like they slipped in, grabbed the boy, and were out again, slick as a road in a ice storm. None of 'em been caught snatchin' the uppity ones . . . and they never will. Mark my words, boys, the Klan's bigger than ever. And it's more ready to fight this war against the Reds, niggers, Jews, and Cath'lics that's tryin' to take over this country. We better call out the night force and get the guard boys on it anyway. Make us look like we doin' what we supposed to do. Now let's get movin'."

The men just nodded their heads in agreement. They knew Fred was a member of the "invisible empire." Then the desk guard raised his hand. "Listen, Fred, they got a good look at us and said they knowed who we was. The head guy said they'd kill us if we turned in the alarm too soon. Let's hold off a while. They mean business."

Fred scratched his chin and said, "Yeah, I reckon we better wait. Don't want to get you boys killed."

"Thanks, Fred, you're a pal. You didn't see those fellas. They scared the bejesus outta us for a little while."

Fred was smiling on the inside.

≫≪

The ringing of his telephone awoke J.D. He rolled over, scrambled for his pocket watch that he'd left on the nightstand, grabbed it, and turned on the light. Five o'clock in the morning. *By God!*

The telephone rang again, and he lifted the earpiece. "Hello?"

"Mr. Daugherty, this is Rose Shelby. Can you come to our house as soon as possible? Mr. Welbourne has been kidnapped from the courthouse."

J.D. groggily shook his head. He coughed once and said, "Sorry, Mrs. Shelby, you want me to come to your home now?"

"Yes, please."

"I'll have to get dressed and get my automobile."

"I'll send a car if you wish."

"No . . . no, that's fine. I'll be there as soon as I can."

"Thank you so much. Until then. . . ."

J.D. put the earpiece back in place and sat for a moment on the edge of his bed, his thoughts coming in rapid but disconnected succession. *Goddam Klan snatched Welbourne . . . damn shame . . . he's got to be dead by now. But this might be a break in the case . . . the cops might be embarrassed enough to help me find the girl—if she's alive. I'll talk Finch into raiding Klan meetings. If they can get him out of jail, then the police failed. This whole business about martial law failed. The guard failed . . . if the police looked the other way, then the Shelbys can go to the mayor or maybe even the governor. I know damn good and well that the Shelbys and the governor are peas in the same pod. The mayor and the governor aren't going to stand for this . . . politicians hate to fail. This has got to be a break . . . I'll turn it in to one. The Shelbys have enough pull to get the papers involved . . . that will do it. Got to get ready.*

J.D. knew that snatching Welbourne wasn't really a break in the case. Welbourne was surely dead by now, and Louisa had probably been killed days ago. Nevertheless J.D. got up, brushed his teeth, lathered up, shaved, and dressed in his best suit. He was going to force the Shelbys, with all their influence and wealth, into action. Now he wanted vengeance on the Klan itself.

≫≪

As on a couple of previous visits to the Shelby mansion, J.D. was led past several fake portraits of Shelby men going back to the Crusades, and into the library smoking room. He walked past the butler who announced his arrival straight onto the thick Persian rug. Rose and Elizabeth Shelby occupied the couch, Big Bill the armchair. Rose Chichester was seated in a stiff-backed wooden chair, looking as lovely as ever. William Jr. was, for a change, in a business suit like his father's—somber gray, with a striped blue tie and diamond stick pin. As usual, the women were dressed in the latest Paris fashions: sleeveless flounce dresses in different soft colors, beaded scarves, and hardly any jewelry. J.D. thought that the skirts were getting shorter by the minute, but that was nothing more or less than his conservative, practical, and rather stiff-necked upbringing coming out in his opinions regarding how women should dress.

"Good morning, Mr. Daugherty," Big Bill said. He was very nervous around J.D. As a result of the Chichester case, Big Bill had been exposed as a philandering husband. The family had more or less forgiven him, but it was just as perceptible that he wasn't entirely comfortable with the rest of the household yet. Little Bill looked far more serious than he ever had been, and his demeanor was businesslike but friendly. Elizabeth Shelby was equally sober. Mrs. Shelby appeared tired and melancholy, as was her namesake, Miss Chichester.

"Good morning, everyone," J.D. said with a slight bow to the women. "It looks like we've got another problem. I just hope I can do something before it ends in tragedy."

Rose Shelby spoke first. "Mr. Daugherty, I'm very worried. If those terrible men have kidnapped both father and daughter, then I'm afraid they'll be killed. Mr. Welbourne has become a friend and a civic-minded leader who has been like a beacon of hope to the people who had been uprooted, impoverished, and terrified during the riot. The colored people of Greenwood are rebuilding, and Mr. Welbourne is in the forefront of that undertaking."

William Jr. broke in. "I think Mother simply wants you to do your best in finding both Mr. Welbourne and Louisa, and in bringing the perpetrators of this crime to justice."

"Yes," Elizabeth said loudly, "I want them to hang."

"My dear," Big Bill said with all the fatherly concern he could muster, "I'm not sure that a capital offense has occurred as yet. Mr. Daugherty here is a very fine investigator. If anyone can help, he can."

"Well, thank you, sir," J.D. said, "but I have to ask you to use all your influence with the mayor and the governor to crack down on this criminal activity. Jack Walton ran against the Klan, sir, and I think he's willing to crack the whip, so to speak, on the militia. Since martial law is in effect, they should have the ultimate responsibility in letting Mr. Welbourne get taken from the county jail. Both the police and the guard should take the blame. Now we have to have them on the job. Really on the job."

J.D. paused and looked around the room. "I'll do my best to find both of them. But I must have your support. I would say that the mayor and the governor should tell the police and the sheriff's office and the guard commander specifically to find Mr. Welbourne and Louisa. They can't be given a general order to stop the Klan or to tighten the guard around the businesses and the courthouse. Unless they're told exactly what is wanted from them, they'll do a little here and a little there. They won't concentrate their efforts."

"I see what you mean, Mr. Daugherty, and I'll place a telephone call to Jack Walton," Big Bill said with a determined look. J.D. read Shelby's concerned expression as a bit of a show for his wife, but hopefully he would carry through with his promise. After a few moments, Big Bill offered a caveat to his agreement to convince Jack Walton to do something about the situation. "To tell you the truth, Mr. Daugherty, Walton will say that he's already called in the guard and is doing his best to control the Klan. What I'm worried about, however, is the fact that the legislature might very well get the votes to impeach him for overstepping his constitutional boundaries by imposing martial law so—as they see it—arbitrarily."

"I understand, Mr. Shelby," J.D. said, "but all I ask for is for you to do your best."

"I'll do that, certainly."

≫≪

J.D. drove back to his rooming house, parked the flivver on the street, and took the trolley to the courthouse. He found Lieutenant Finch sitting at the big table, staring with vacant eyes across the room. J.D. followed his gaze and saw nothing but a wall with various kinds of notices—even one for the circus—pinned to a corkboard. Finch suddenly realized that someone had walked in. He turned and looked at J.D. "Oh, hiya, J.D., what's cookin'?" he said in a single breath.

"Not much, Marv," J.D. replied. "Somethin' wrong?"

"Oh, I guess this business is gettin' to me. You was a copper—why can't we get a handle on all the tomfoolery 'round here?"

"I reckon there's just a bunch of bad people out there, and they can't stop. Dealin' with criminals ain't like the rubes goin' to a Billy Sunday or an Aimee Semple McPherson tent show. No professional yegg or killer is goin' to sign a pledge not to open somebody's safe or shoot somebody in the head. Some poor sap who don't have a pot to piss in ain't gonna shy away from holdin' up a store if he needs the dough just because the local preacher says you'll go to glory if you don't.

"I'm really sorry, Marv. When I was on the force in Chicago and then with the agency, I'd get forlorn all the time just thinkin' about all the bad that's in the world. About how we can't control it. About how we can't stop it. That's why I went on my own. I figure if I'm on my own, it's all on me. If things look bad, I can take control."

"I got four more years to my pension, J.D. I hope I can last that long."

"What's got you down now?"

"The Klan takin' my prisoner. I coulda strangled those dopes that let this happen. And we had the state guard outside the courthouse. By God, that's bad. Somebody had to get paid off."

"Klan, huh?"

"That's right. Had to be. Nobody else woulda pulled off somethin' like this."

"Got any leads?"

"They got clean away. Nothin'. Not even a decent description. The fools downstairs say they was all covered up and they was all around five eight to six foot."

"Taller than average."

"Yeah, so what? The Imperial Wizard or whatever he's called this year coulda just said to his monkeys that they have to be that tall to pull off the job. Probably had their outfits lying around the meetin' hall. They was slick too. In and out just like that!" Finch snapped his fingers.

"What'd they wear?"

"Had light cotton flour sacks with the eyes cut out and clothes like they used to wear drivin' horseless carriages. You know—long slicker, long-cuffed gloves, cap. Had the old sun-goggles on over the masks. I wonder if they was soldiers?"

"Why?"

"'Cause they knew what they was doin'. They operated like they was on a raid of some kind. No monkey business. No foolin' around. And they had the right kind of guns that would stop you cold. They just pulled off this caper slick as ice. They musta been soldier boys."

"Maybe, maybe not."

"If so, maybe the Legion was in on it."

"Probably not, Marv, unless these boys belonged to both the Legion and the Klan."

"Yeah, I guess."

J.D. had heard enough. "Well, I gotta go. I want to let you know that the Shelbys themselves are gonna pressure the mayor to get somethin' done on this one. They're gonna call the governor too."

"Thanks, J.D. That's all I need right now. You think it'll all roll down pretty fast?"

"Yep, 'fraid so. So get ready for the heat to come down from the top."

"Gotcha, J.D. Maybe I should go downstairs and question those guys with this." Finch pulled a blackjack out of his coat pocket and tapped it hard on the table. It sounded almost like a pistol shot.

"Maybe you oughta save it. . . . Well, take it easy, Marv."

"Bye, J.D. Look out for yourself."

≫≪

J.D. unlocked and opened the door of his office and immediately caught sight of a neatly folded piece of paper at his feet. He picked it up, unfolded it, and read:

> *My dear Mr. Daugherty,*
> *You would be wise to meet a green-painted Buick automobile at the northwest corner of Main and 2nd at 4 p.m. today. The man driving has a name, but it is of no concern to you. Call him Bob. He will take you to meet a person who will help recover a certain girl from her captors.*
> *S., A Veteran of the Great War*

J.D. quietly shut the door and went to his desk. This was a really odd summons. Maybe it was from the Klan. Maybe they'd already killed Welbourne—now maybe they were ready to collect a ransom for Louisa. A glimmer of hope passed through J.D.'s mind. They would probably know that he was working with the Shelbys, and they knew for certain that Mrs. Shelby and Elizabeth were willing to pay for the girl.

He pulled his watch out of his pocket and saw that it was half past three. He thought he would lock up the office, grab a newspaper from one of the boys on the street, and slowly make his way to Main and Second.

J.D. had been on the corner less than five minutes when the described automobile pulled up. The driver looked at him and said in a pleasant voice, "Get in, friend."

J.D. opened the door, got in, and looked at the driver. "You Bob?"

"That's me," was the answer.

The driver was fairly dark complexioned with pasted-down brown wavy hair. J.D. guessed that he was part Indian or maybe part Negro, but his features resembled the Mediterranean types— Greeks, Italians—that he'd seen in the flickers: aquiline nose, square jaw, deep-set dark eyes. *That Valentino fella*, thought J.D.

"Where we goin', Bob?" J.D. inquired.

"We're headin' across the river, Mr. Daugherty. It'll be some time. Out in the country. In the meantime, have a drink. It's under the seat."

J.D. pulled out a small flask and took a pull. It was a good-tasting rye whiskey. He put the flask down beside him and settled in for a long drive. He wasn't frightened in the least. The note offered help, and the driver was young, pleasant, and not threatening. And he sure didn't look like Klan.

After passing through a green countryside with large oaks and cattle dotting the pastures, they finally rolled up to a farmhouse. The house had been freshly painted and the grass in front had been mowed. Nice place.

Bob set the brake and said, "Mr. Daugherty, go ahead and go to the front door. Knock three times. They'll answer with two knocks. You give two back, and they'll let you in. It's gonna be fine. I'll be back in an hour to take you back to Tulsa."

J.D. looked apprehensive now. "It's okay," the driver reassured him. "Nothin's gonna happen. Go on ahead."

J.D. walked to the door, knocked the requisite number of times, and was answered. He returned the knocks, and the door swung open. A black man in a dark suit with a high, tight collar stood there. "Let me take your hat, Mr. Daugherty. And please follow me to the dining room."

It didn't add up. A black butler dressed in a suit at a lonesome country farmhouse? The man led J.D. through the parlor. He ushered J.D. through a door and into the dining area with a large table. Six black men were sitting at the table, and at its head sat Theodore Welbourne with a triumphant smile on his face. The man who answered the door wasn't a butler at all. He was part of a bodyguard.

"Good day to you, Mr. Daugherty," Welbourne said. "We're about to have supper. I hope you'll join us."

J.D. took the empty chair to Welbourne's right. In front of him was a delicious-looking pot roast with potatoes and gravy, a bowl of peas, and a loaf of freshly baked bread. Without a word, the men around the table all dug in.

When everyone had finished, cigars were passed around and one of the men went to the kitchen to get a pot of fresh-brewed coffee. With everyone relaxed and smoking, Welbourne looked at J.D. and said, "I suppose you're wondering what you're doing here, Mr. Daugherty."

"Yes, indeed, Mr. Welbourne. But call me J.D. I'm overwhelmed by seein' you again."

"I would imagine so. But first let me introduce my comrades-in-arms. We all served in the Great War." He went around the room, naming names and telling a little story about each of the men. Most worked for white families and one was the owner of the farmhouse in which they had partaken of the meal. All were veterans and all bore the scars of battles in both their homeland and abroad. J.D. was reminded of the fact that they had seen the horrors not only of the trenches but also the horrors of the worst race riot in America's relatively short history. A thought of Hoolie crossed his mind.

"Now that you know their names and what they've done in their lives," said Welbourne, "I'd like for you to forget what I've told you. From now on, we are all named Smith."

"Nice meeting all of you," J.D. said. "Smith, eh—my associate is also named Smith, so the name will be easy to remember." He turned to Welbourne. "But I thought you'd been abducted by the Klan. I honestly thought you were dead."

Welbourne grew very serious and replied, "Not yet, sir. I have a few things to do before I die." He sat back and puffed on his cigar for a moment. He stretched his lips into a forced smile and said, "This is *my* klan, J.D., and it wasn't kidnapping—it was a jail break, pure and simple. I'll probably have to square it with the law someday, but not just now. I might not even bother, considering that the law was framing me, and the boys in blue probably thought they were aiding the Klan in my so-called abduction. I know the KKK was going to try and lynch me and that the police were in on it. I had to get out to get Louisa."

"I'd like to know how you did it. Did you pay somebody off? How'd you get past the militia boys?"

"All in good time, sir. I want to talk about getting my daughter back. I'm sure you can help. In fact, no one else I know of can provide me with the information that is needed to find her. When you do, we . . ."—he paused to look around the room—". . . will take care of the rest."

J.D. stiffened. "You mean you're planning to get her back by force? That's gonna be more than difficult. If the Klan's got her . . . well, they're dangerous. Why not let the law handle it? I can bring 'em in."

"J.D., thanks for the offer, but the police and the sheriff haven't much interest in helping Negroes, and certainly not me. That was proven during the riot two years ago. Martial law hasn't done anything either. We got past the sentries at the courthouse with ease. And, to tell you the truth, we're more dangerous in our own right than the boys in the Klan.

"I would like to hire you to find Louisa, and I'll gladly pay you twice your usual fee. In fact, I'll give you a retainer now." He leaned over and extracted a large roll of bills from a valise under the table.

J.D. looked at the money. "That's very generous," he said. "And all you want me to do is find Louisa?"

"Yes."

"Well, Mr. Welbourne, I won't take your money. Mrs. Shelby has already commissioned me to do the same thing. Besides,

Louisa is an extremely brave girl, and I would do all I could to find her without a fee." J.D. paused a very long moment. "If you make contact with Mrs. Shelby, you'll be putting her in danger of being prosecuted as your accomplice. She's my client, and I have to protect her interests."

"I understand that, Mr. Daugherty. I do not deal with her directly."

"What does that mean?"

"Just that."

"Do you have indirect contact with her?"

"Very indirectly—perhaps not at all at this point. We worked together, but now I'm a fugitive from the law."

"All right. I can get into trouble as well. I can't treat you as a client. You'd have to get any information I get from another source. . . . Your indirect contact."

"That's good, Mr. Daugherty. Please, remember that the police are not your clients."

"I only bring them in when I need them."

Welbourne nodded, leaned forward in his chair, and said seriously, "I think we have an understanding. I'm going to give you a telephone number." Welbourne handed J.D. a plain sheet of paper with "8375" printed on it. "If you need help in any way, have the operator ring it. When someone answers, say 'In the trenches,' and our friend Bob will contact you on the same day either by note or by telephone."

At that, J.D. figured he'd better see his lawyer first thing in the morning.

>«

Sam Berg's secretary was a small bespectacled woman of about thirty, with a cleft chin and down-turned blue eyes. She also had a warm smile that she gave to J.D. as he peeked through the door leading to her desk.

"Hiya, Marlene," J.D. said, removing his derby. "Sam in?"

"He is . . . and he ain't busy. Too early in the morning."

"Good, I'll just go in."

"Suit yourself, J.D. He's in a good mood."

Sam Berg sat behind his desk with his feet propped on an extended drawer. He saw J.D., took the fat Cuban cigar from his mouth, and waved happily. "Hiya, J.D. How's tricks?"

J.D. shook his head, took the client's chair in front of Sam's desk, and said, "Nothin' you're gonna like, Sam."

Berg pulled a frown, dropped his feet to the floor, and leaned toward J.D. He put the cigar in a big amber-colored glass ashtray. "What's up?" he asked stiffly.

"I'll get the bad news outta the way first," J.D. said. He drew in a deep breath, held it, and let it expire slowly. He, too, leaned forward. "Listen, Sam—I'm afraid that Shotz is dead. Looks like he was murdered. Don't know who yet, but Hoolie's in Anadarko and is in contact with the people who found your man. They buried him. He was cut up bad."

"What do you mean, 'cut up'?"

"Well, apparently he was gutted."

"Oh, damn. That's bad. Bad enough he was killed, but why would anybody do that? I met him—he was a fine young man, smart and a good head for business."

"I'm sure he was. We don't know the why of it yet, but we'll find out. You gonna tell your boy about his brother?"

"I'll do that, but I'm not going to tell him about the way he got killed. I guess the Anadarko authorities took over the case?"

"Not exactly, Sam. In fact, there's a kind of war going on between the city police and the county sheriff's office. Also—and I don't know yet what this might mean—he was found on Indian land."

"What? What the hell's going on down there?"

"I'll tell you a little bit. Nothing complicated. The police chief and the county sheriff are fightin' over who's gonna control the liquor trade. Your boy's brother was found out in the country, so the murder should be under the sheriff's jurisdiction. But the sheriff doesn't know anything about the murder yet. But since it might be on Indian property, that'll bring in the U.S. Marshals. And I'm cleanin' up the town for the mayor—that is, until I got a telegram from Mrs. Shelby."

"The Shelbys? Again?"

"Yep. I'm tryin' to find Theodore Welbourne's daughter."

"Hold on, J.D., this is getting complicated. I've heard of Welbourne, but I can't place him off the top of my head. How does he fit in with the Shelbys?"

"The reason you've heard of him is that he was arrested for killin' a Klansman downtown. Welbourne's a leader in the Negro community on the north side. He's been involved with the Shelbys' community projects and things."

"Okay. What else?"

"Well . . . the Klan took his daughter. Now, she's the one who rescued Little Bill Shelby's kid by the girl Minnie when Minnie was murdered during the riot. Mrs. Shelby is tryin' to get her back, and she hired me."

"Okay . . . okay."

"Now, everybody thinks that the Klan took Welbourne outta jail. You know how they been operatin' lately. They don't riot or lynch too many folks anymore. But they kidnap 'em and cut 'em up or whip 'em and leave 'em alive as a warning to the rest of the Negroes."

"Believe me, J.D., I know what the Klan does. So has the Klan let Welbourne go? Did they kill him? And what does all this have to do with the murder in Anadarko and cleaning up a town?"

"Listen, Sam, how bad can I get into trouble for helpin' a guy who broke outta jail? I mean, without turning him in?"

Sam's eyes widened considerably. "What?" he said emphatically. "Yeah!" The lawyer tried to lower the pitch in his voice to a kind of more reasonable baritone. "J.D., that's aiding and abetting a felony. That's accomplice liability. You'd be an accomplice after the fact. Is it Welbourne? The Klan didn't get him?"

"'Fraid so, Sam."

"Damn, J.D. Why?"

"Well, he sent for me, but I didn't know that it was actually him doin' the sendin'. Know what I mean?"

"Sort of."

"I got a note signed by a veteran of the war settin' up a meetin' to give me some information about the girl."

"Okay. You can get off the hook by saying that, but legally, you should go to the police and tell them that you saw Welbourne. If you don't and he's recaptured, you're damn sure an accomplice. It's my job as your lawyer to tell you to go to the cops."

"Can't do it, Sam. You know that."

"Okay, J.D. I'm going to treat this conversation as if it never took place. Keep mum."

"I'll do that, Sam, and you too. Now about the other. Hoolie's in Anadarko. He's stirrin' up trouble and at the same time tryin' to find Shotz's killer. I'm gonna send him a telegram as soon as I leave here. I can trust Hoolie to get the job done. Do you know if Shotz was lookin' for oil leases?"

"No, not that I know of. His brother told me he was looking into the cattle business."

"Yeah, but why? He made money off oil. Ranchin' is a hard business."

"I asked his brother the same question. The young man said that he'd been out there before and liked the place. Beats me why."

J.D. sat rubbing his forehead for an extended minute. "Well, I guess I'll go now, Sam. You take care of yourself."

"I'll do that. And J.D. . . . ."

"Yeah?"

"Just keep mum."

"All right. Bye."

J.D. stepped out onto the street and watched people and the trolleys go by. He kept thinking that he had to find a way to organize these particular operations. It was getting more than a bit daffy. Keeping all the loose ends together might be hard. And although he never would have admitted it, Sam was right. Conducting these disconnected operations was confusing, contradictory, and plain old complex. J.D. also knew that, in the detective business, you had to conduct several investigations all at once. If you weren't able to do so, you'd be out of business quickly. He trusted Hoolie to hold up his end in Anadarko, but he also knew that Hoolie always did things on a kind of catch-as-catch-can basis. Organization, planning, control, and thoroughness were not Hoolie's stock and trade. J.D.'s associate operative—as he always referred to Hoolie—just threw himself into things and worked his way out. The bad thing about that was a person could get killed doing so. And Hoolie had been shot, beat up, and thrown into jail on a few occasions while working for J.D. Hopefully, though, Hoolie would at least go to the telegraph office. But then again, J.D. realized that he, too, had been shot, beat up, and thrown into jail even when he did everything in a thorough, controlled, and thought-out method.

Chapter XI

THE MACFARLAND BROTHERS

That same morning, Hoolie was sitting in the Charging Horse arbor talking about the fight at Owl Creek and the subsequent hijacking and burning of the whiskey trucks. Hoolie, Chester, and Harold had stealthily visited the scene after the sheriff's men had dashed out to save the shipment. They were not witnesses to the gunfight. When they got to the scene, they watched from the brush. The trucks had been set on fire and Marty and Moe were loudly cursing and gesticulating wildly as they tried to get their men to put out the fires and perhaps save some of the shipment. The MacFarlands and their men were gone. They and Chief Collins had won the first round.

The elder Mr. Charging Horse was smiling brightly as the Boyiddles told about the fight at the liquor storage shed in a mixture of Kiowa and English. George Charging Horse interrupted, "All that whiskey got burned up?"

"It did," Hoolie said. "And the MacFarlands burned up the rest of it . . . what was on the trucks." He paused. "At least, I think so. We got there after the fightin' was over. The trucks was burnin', and we saw them fellas Marty Albright and Moe Tucker yellin' at everybody and then drivin' off. The MacFarlands were long gone. There's gonna be hell to pay back in town."

"We oughta go into town and see what's gonna go on," said Chester.

"I gotta go back too. I have to get to the telegraph office and wire J.D. about what happened."

>«

Harold, Chester, and Hoolie tethered the horses inside the corral at the feedlot and walked the short five blocks to the center of town.

It was fairly quiet. Families walked slowly down the sidewalks and kids gazed into the windows of a couple of stores. No drunks were on the street and no automobile noise corrupted the sound of murmuring talk on the walkways or the music of a hurdy-gurdy coming from one of the city's eateries. It was just a pleasant, quiet summer evening. Only the cafés were open. The haberdasheries, dry goods stores, banks, and most other businesses were closed.

They entered Vi's diner and sat down. She came by their table looking a bit haggard, agitated, and unfriendly. "What you boys want?"

"Just some meat and bread," said Chester. "We're pretty hungry."

"We got steaks we can fry up," she said blandly. "That suit you?"

"Potatoes?" asked Hoolie.

"Sure. Take off your hats."

"Okay," Hoolie said as he and the Boyiddles pulled off their headgear. "The steaks'll do. I'll buy."

Chester and Harold just smiled at the prospect of a free meal. They chorused, "Wi-ahhh." Hoolie didn't know what it meant; he guessed it was a kind of sound of approval. In any case, they both said, once again in unison, "Aho." Hoolie had found out over the course of being in their presence the last couple of days that "aho" meant "thanks."

When Violet came back with the steaks, she pulled up a chair, sat, and asked, "Heard anything from your boss?"

Hoolie looked at his plate, wishing he could finish without engaging in a conversation with the restaurant's proprietor. "No, ma'm. I have to check the telegraph office. If anything's goin' on, J.D. will send me a wire."

"I guess that's okay. But you'll have to wait 'til mornin'." She leaned forward and whispered to Hoolie, trying hard to ignore Chester and Harold. "How about steppin' out back with me for a minute or two?"

Hoolie rose and looked at Chester, who nodded slightly. Vi Comstock beckoned, and Hoolie followed her back to the kitchen. The cook looked up from the stove for just a second and quickly bent over his frying pan. Hoolie followed the woman out the back door. As soon as she heard the screen door spring back, she turned on Hoolie.

"Listen, things are heatin' up in town. Marty and Moe are lookin' for the MacFarland brothers right now. I think they'll shoot 'em down on the street. The whole arrangement with Mr. Daugherty went too far. They're bringin' the fight into town, and that will make it bad for business."

Hoolie spoke in a whisper. "Excuse me, ma'am, but the way J.D. talked to me, it just took the mayor to call in the governor when it got this way. And then the state militia boys would take over."

"The mayor won't do nothin' yet, the spineless so-and-so," Violet snapped. "If he'd had any grit in his craw, he might be a decent guy." She stopped, composed herself, and went on in a breathy voice, "Rohrbach's about to crawfish on callin' in the governor. He hired Collins, and Wynn is an elected county official. Now he's scared to do anything. They've got strong backing from a few folks around here—real rich folks. You got to get a telegram to your boss. Since Rohrbach won't do nothin', he's got to call on his friends back in Tulsa to get the governor to send in the guard. Certain people have gotten to him, so he's not gonna call in the governor. You get what I'm sayin'?"

"I get it, Miss Comstock. But what people? You mean like Cooper? He's the richest man around, ain't he?"

Violet drew back with a hiss and quickly went back into the café. Hoolie followed.

Hoolie got back to the table and looked at his plate; the meat and potatoes were calling him. He and Vi took their seats once again. Harold and Chester both darted their eyes back and forth between Vi and Hoolie. There was dead silence for at least a full minute. Then Hoolie spoke. "Well, Miss Comstock, what about Cooper?"

Chester looked astonished. "Where does he come into all this?"

Hoolie smiled. "Just a thought. He's a real rich man. Got leases all over, runs cattle, he's in with the Indian Office bunch, right? Why not get into the liquor business?"

Violet narrowed her eyes. "He's out of this. He's temperance and don't wanna get involved in the liquor trade. Too complicated."

"Marty Albright's temperance. That's what he told me. Why would he shoot it out with the MacFarlands for all that hooch?"

"To keep his job," Harold said bluntly and emphatically. "Lot of money too. And Albright's a mean man. He just don't show it like Moe does."

"I still think Cooper might be involved somehow."

"You keep thinkin' like that, dearie," Violet said, "and everything will slip through our fingers. I know him and his boy well. I knew the brother before he got killed too. You can't tell about them. Just leave 'em be."

"I reckon," Hoolie said thoughtfully.

"Damn right you reckon," she retorted. "Cooper don't have anything to do with the problems at hand."

Chester stared blankly at the far wall, then turned to Hoolie. "I think you just don't like him 'cause he's rich."

"Okay, I'll let Cooper go . . . for now. J.D. always says to be thorough. If that's so, I gotta keep Cooper and his boy within sight." Hoolie looked at Violet. "How about you? Who's side are you on?"

"I'm on my own side," she hissed, "and don't forget it."

≫≪

He could look down at his own bare feet as he ran as hard as he could to keep the bigger boys from running into him and stealing the deer hide–covered ball. He planted his right foot, cut to his left, and dodged one boy who swung his ball-stick at his head. He jumped as high as he could and nearly missed having his legs taken out from under him as he landed. He was so quick and agile that he became the bat of the old story. But then he watched as a big boar hog rooted in the ground, digging up whatever it could found to eat. The hog's forefeet would scrape the dirt, and his snout would sniff and push the earth around. The hog rooted deeper and deeper, and Hoolie saw that it had unearthed a human hand. The hand was gray and shrunken. The hog nosed it out of the ground and left it there. It moved.

Hoolie sat straight up, looked around, and then adjusted his blankets. The Boyiddle brothers were asleep. They had all bedded down near the corrals behind the feed store. The grass was soft under his bedroll. He lay back down, rolled to one side, and tried to sleep again. He hated dreams like that. They switched from a good feeling at a ball game to something horrible. He understood so little about dreams. Sometimes they helped; other times they scared the hell out of people for no good reason. His grandfathers both put great store in dreams. To them, dreams were messages from the spirit world. They should never be discounted as being meaningless. But a hog digging up a human hand that moved? That was nothing more or less than a nightmare. And Hoolie had had his share of nightmares, especially since the war.

He couldn't sleep. He finally put his shoes on, stood, and got a drink of water from the pump at the water trough. Although it was still dark, he began to walk downtown. The streetlights were still on and all was quiet. The bad dream was fading from his memory.

His walk led him to the courthouse. He saw a bench on the lawn near a large bush and decided to sit and rest. He sat waiting for the sun to come up and cast its light on the slowly awakening city of Anadarko.

As first light broke, a car drove up and parked in front of the courthouse. It was a Ford touring car with the top up. Hoolie squinted his eyes to see inside the automobile, but it was still too dark. Hoolie ducked behind the bush. Whoever was in the car didn't stir, and it was several minutes before the doors opened and four men got out. Hoolie had not seen the driver before, but although they all had their hats pulled low, he immediately recognized Chief Collins and the MacFarland brothers. When they all emerged, they gathered in a tight circle and went through a strange ritual on the front lawn. They shook hands all around and the MacFarlands held their hands up in the air in mock surrender. The driver took their hands down one by one and handcuffed them behind each brother's back. Clem smiled and winked; Festus threw his head back and chuckled. Collins patted Clem on the shoulder. Then they all turned and followed Chief Collins up the front stairs into the courthouse. None of them seemed to notice Hoolie. It was one of the most curious arrests he had ever witnessed. Maybe it wasn't even an arrest; maybe it was a way of safeguarding the MacFarlands and mocking Sheriff Wynn. J.D. had sure enough turned the town upside down. And it looked like all the poisons were going to spill out.

Hoolie walked back to where the Boyiddles were still asleep. He sat down on the ground with his back against a corral post, eased his pack of tobacco out of the pocket of his trousers, and rolled and lit a cigarette. The arrest of the MacFarland brothers could only mean that Collins was trying to keep them safe from the sheriff's deputies. The problem was that they were going to be locked up in the county jail. Wynn and the others had access to them. Hoolie was beginning to think that this whole turn of events was something like a ball game back home. Everybody was running and twisting and turning and stealing the ball and hitting each other with their ball-sticks and dodging around the open field. In the old days the people called the ball game "little war." And it was. It was a kind of controlled mayhem that often led to bloody noses and broken bones. Some ballplayers used bad medicine to make them quick and agile enough to jump, change direction at full speed, and make their opponents think they were going one way when they were really going another. That was old-time war medicine too. His grandfathers had fought in the Civil War and told him that many of the men used the medicine that made them appear in one place when they were really in another. Hoolie half smiled, thinking he could have used that medicine in France. Maybe then he wouldn't have the limp and the stiffness that would now go with him to his grave.

Hoolie pulled out his watch. It would be a while before the telegraph office was open. He hated to sit around doing nothing. One of the horses in the corral was tossing his head and acting up. Hoolie had a horse at home that was like that. A certain smell or the glint of the sun on water might set him off. The horse could shake his head, paw the ground, and get riled up over seemingly nothing. Hoolie went over to talk to the horse and maybe calm him down.

"Shhhaaah, *soquili* . . . shhhaaah." A slight breeze, or perhaps something not even as substantial as the wind, raised the hair on the back of Hoolie's neck. The horse was reacting to something—maybe a scent clinging to the gentle current of air. Hoolie went to his bedroll, bent, and rummaged through the tow sack in which he carried his supplies. He found a bruised apple and took it back to the shying and fidgeting horse. The horse ate, calmed himself for a moment, then went back to tossing his head and snorting. "There's somethin' botherin' you, ain't there, horse?" Hoolie asked.

Hoolie decided he'd take a walk into the breeze. Maybe there was something out there. Anyway, taking a walk sure enough beat sitting around an old corral waiting for the Boyiddles to get up or continuing a conversation with a crazy horse. He began to slowly walk in the direction of a couple of blackjack trees.

He had walked a hundred feet or so before he picked up a trace of alcohol on the slight wind. He noticed that the trees to his front were swaying a bit. The wind was picking up. He found no whiskey bottles, but the smell of liquor was blowing straight at him. Hoolie walked on. He thought to himself that he was probably walking in the direction of a hidden-away speakeasy or juke joint. He heard voices in the direction of a stand of trees near a creek bed. He walked forward and squatted down behind a bush. Four men were in the creek up to their chests in the water. They were working hard, pulling up rocks and tossing them over their shoulders. One man said, "Okay, boys, let's pull her up."

The men lowered themselves into the water and groped toward the bottom of the stream, trying hard not to get their faces under water. They tugged in unison, and one man pulled a grayish-white human hand and arm to the surface.

Hoolie felt the gun barrel press against the back of his campaign hat. He closed his eyes and missed the sight of the men in the creek pulling the body of Violet Comstock out of the water and onto the far bank.

"Stand up real slow, Indian, or I swear I'll plug ya," the voice behind him said.

Hoolie rose to his feet, not daring to say a word. The voice said, "Turn around." Hoolie complied just as slowly as he had stood. He turned and faced Deputy Moe Tucker. "I thought that was you," said Moe. He holstered his pistol, smiled, and in one swift motion whipped out a blackjack from his back pocket and hit Hoolie hard in the left temple.

The pain was blinding; it was as if he had been hit with a white-hot ball of iron. Hoolie caved in on himself and dropped to the ground. Moe Tucker kicked him in the right shoulder. "Gotcha, you dumb redskin," the deputy sheriff muttered.

》《

Hoolie sat on a high four-legged stool in a room that had a single light bulb hanging from the ceiling. It was a dank cellar of some kind. Moe Tucker and a couple of other men had dragged him from the creek to a car. Hoolie kept going in and out of consciousness the whole time. Tucker and the men had walked Hoolie into the courthouse and straight downstairs. They sat him on the stool and Tucker punched him a couple of times, telling Hoolie to confess to something he didn't know anything about. Hoolie had been unable to answer, so Tucker hit him a few more times and left him sitting there.

The smell in the room was almost overpowering. It was mixture of vomit, mold, blood, sweat, fear, and hatred. This was a dungeon, and at first Hoolie couldn't understand why or how he had been taken back to the stories of medieval castles, evil princes, the Spanish Inquisition, and the unspeakable torment he had read about in the white man's school. His mind wandered, and he thought for a moment that Moe Tucker might produce some kind of torture machine or, worse yet, a branding iron.

Hoolie suddenly realized that his ankles were connected to two legs of the stool with leg irons. His wrists were locked behind his back in handcuffs. He actually smiled at his predicament and the diabolical thinking of those who had locked him to the stool. If he tried to move from his precarious position, he would pitch forward or backward without his arms to help break the fall. So he would land either on the back of his head or flat on his face. If he fell sideways, he would probably separate his shoulder. From all of what he had heard and what the man had done to him at the creek, Hoolie knew this was all the doings of Moe Tucker and Sheriff Ferrell Wynn. He had an urge to scratch his blood-smeared nose, but he knew he had to sit very still in order to keep from toppling over onto the cement floor. He'd been beat up a time or two, but this was about as scary a situation as he'd ever been in before.

The pain shot back into his face, temple, back, and bruised shoulder all at once. He gritted his teeth, sat perfectly still, and tried to overcome the agony by thinking of something else. It didn't work. Hoolie smirked to himself—at least his nose didn't itch anymore.

He didn't know how long he'd been sitting unmoving and tight-lipped. Finally, the door opened, and five men crowded into the room. Sheriff Wynn led Marty and Moe and two other grim-faced official-looking men in dark suits. One of them had what looked like a U.S. Marshal's badge pinned to his lapel. Except for Wynn, all were wearing their fedoras low, shading their eyes.

"Smith," the sheriff began in loud voice, "you're gonna be charged with Violet Comstock's murder. Might even have you on another killin', or at least aidin' and abettin'. I think you know my deputies. And I'll introduce you to United States Marshal Cleveland Peeler." Wynn paid no attention to the other man.

Peeler stepped a foot forward and nodded gravely. He looked Hoolie up and down as if he were studying Hoolie's size and weight in preparation for a stew. Hoolie shuddered in pain and apprehension. Peeler was a frightening man who looked as if he had nothing better to do in life but accuse, judge, and execute criminals. Peeler suddenly broke into a smile and turned to Sheriff Wynn. "You caught him at the scene of the crime?"

"Sure did," Wynn said brightly. "Well . . . Deputy Tucker did anyhow. And he was talkin' to Miss Comstock the very same evenin' she got killed."

"Might be open and shut then," Peeler declared. "What about the other two Indians?"

"They're locked up. Pretty near got the whole criminal element of Anadarko in the hoosegow."

The other man spoke up. "Sheriff, Marshal, it seems like you're locking up a good number of Indians . . . and that's my interest in this . . . shall we call it a roundup?"

Peeler stared narrowly at the man and said, "Listen, Hughes, the Major Crimes Act gives jurisdiction to the federal government when Indians commit murder, arson, and the like—"

"On federal or trust land, Mr. Peeler . . . on trust land."

"That ain't how I interpret it, Mr. Hughes. You're the Indian agent here—I recognize that—but the district court will have to decide about whether or not the marshal's office will handle the case."

"Now listen, boys," Wynn interrupted. "Maybe we should take it to my office. I think my boys Marty and Moe should get the credit for the arrests in these foul crimes."

Peeler and Hughes nodded in agreement, and Wynn ushered them out the door. Tucker and Albright remained until the door reopened and Wynn stuck his head back in. "Moe, you come with me. Marty, you stay here with the redskin."

Moe exited and slammed the door behind him.

Deputy Albright stepped forward and looked into Hoolie's eyes. He pushed his hat to the back of his head and pursed his lips. Digging out a bag of tobacco and some papers, he said with a slight smile, "Want a smoke, Smith?"

Hoolie nodded his head slowly, hoping the pain wouldn't increase. Marty Albright rolled a cigarette, put it between Hoolie's lips, struck a match, and lit it. He took two steps backward and casually rolled another for himself.

When Albright had finished the cigarette-smoking ritual, he took a puff and said, "Man, you and the Boyiddles and George Chargin' Horse are in a big heap of trouble." He paused for a moment and then added, "Y'all might get the chair."

Hoolie shook his head slightly and, around the cigarette, replied, "Could you take this outta my mouth or uncuff me?"

"Can't take the cuffs off." Albright reached over and took the cigarette from Hoolie's swollen lips. "Moe handled you pretty rough. But you should know that he liked Violet a lot. Ate at her place all the time. That makes a man do things he oughtn't."

"Tucker called her a whore."

"So what?"

"Why would he say that if he thought highly of her? Don't make sense."

"You can think well of somebody and still not like what she does."

"You people think I killed Miss Comstock?"

"We don't think it—we know you done it."

"How do you figure?"

"Lots o' ways."

"Gimme one."

"She took a .44 bullet in the chest. Now, we know that you carry a ol' .44-40 Winchester. We got you cold."

"Wait a minute. Lots of people carry .44s. You got a Colt .44 your own self. I've seen a dozen .44s around this town. Chief Collins carries one. So does Sheriff Wynn. About the only ones I ain't seen carry a .44 is Moe Tucker and Festus MacFarland. And Tucker's is a .45. That's close."

"Well, we got you, don't we?"

"I didn't kill her, Deputy Albright. I wouldn't lie about it."

Marty Albright grew sullen. "That's what anybody'd say. But you're gonna pay for killin' her, even though she's a dirty whore anyways."

"Why the hell'd you say somethin' like that? You even said your pal Moe liked her. You hated her, didn't you? Why else would you call her a whore?"

"'Cause she was. And this town is better off with her dead." He put on a crooked grin. "She traded in liquor and ran whores. You did a good thing there, Mr. Smith, but you're still gonna fry for it. Too bad. And you was in the war too. We both saw some misery there. You just did a bad thing. All we got to do is find out who put you up to it. Who you takin' orders from?"

Albright stopped, tilted his head, and stared intently at Hoolie's battered nose and swollen temple. "Guess you're gonna try to hold out. But Moe and the sheriff they know how to get people talkin'. In the end, they're gonna get the answers."

Hoolie ground his teeth together. His eyes shifted from one point on the wall to another. He couldn't see a way of escaping the beating and the agony he was sure to suffer at the hands of Moe Tucker. He might as well take a chance on bluffing.

"Marty," Hoolie said through clamped teeth and swollen mouth, "you're gonna have to kill me. I don't know what you're talkin' about. I didn't kill that woman. Now, you think beatin' me is gonna do the job . . . but I'll tell you right now that if you ain't willin' to rub me out, then why should I be scared? I'm already hurtin', and your friend probably can't do much more than what he's already done. But remember, if you'ins kill me without takin' me to court first, then Chief Collins will put a murder charge over your heads. You know he will. And the mayor will have to back him up."

"The mayor," Albright spat. "He's scart of his own shadow. He won't do nothin'."

"He will, Marty. My boss's gone on and made him promise to call the governor and send in the national guard troopers if things get outta hand. Killin' me without a trial won't set. My boss'll pull out all the guns he's got, and he knows the biggest oilmen in the state. Rohrbach'll call in the guard to keep his job and get over on Wynn. Believe me."

Hoolie could see that his desperate argument was taking effect. Albright's eyes were moving back and forth, he pursed and relaxed his lips, he opened and closed his hands rhythmically. Albright threw his and Hoolie's cigarettes to the floor and stamped them out. He took a step forward, put a steely look into his eyes, and said, "All right, boy, but you and the Boyiddles and ol' George Chargin' Horse got to answer for the body they dug up at George's place."

Hoolie was struck dumb. "Wha . . . what b-b-body?" he stammered. "What the hell are you talkin' about?"

Albright put on his best alligator grin. His eyes narrowed. "We think it's that guy you and your boss was lookin' for. 'Course, he was pretty much just dried-up skin and bones. But his hair was still on his skull. Face all bashed in though. Buried on the Chargin' Horse place."

"Marty, I came here lookin' for him. I didn't kill him."

"We know that. But you knew he was dead and didn't tell the law. That means you're one of them accessories. You might not hang for it, but you're gonna get it for the Comstock whore's killin'."

"Marty, you gotta listen to me. Who told you about the dead man? I know that the Chargin' Horses buried him. But whoever told you that knew he was dead. The Chargin' Horses didn't tell anybody else. The guy who told you about it had to know it beforehand. He might be the killer."

"Smith, you're pretty sly. But it was ol' George hisself who showed us where the dead guy was. So you just persuaded me that George done it."

"That can't be. Why'd he show you? Somebody had to tell somebody else for you all to go out to the Chargin' Horse place!" Hoolie felt his voice rising in fear for his life.

Marty gave a short derisive laugh. "Now, wouldn't you like to know? Just say that we had somethin' else to go on."

The door to the cellar opened. Tucker, Wynn, Hughes, and Peeler squeezed into the small room again. They joined Albright in staring at Hoolie sitting on his precarious perch.

Wynn was the first to speak. "Well, well. Looks like you and the Boyiddle brothers are a county problem. But then again, you all might just come under the jurisdiction of the United States government. Shotz was found on the Chargin' Horse allotment. That's trust land. We might have us two hangin's"—he chuckled—"one state and one federal."

He stopped and looked back and forth between Peeler and Hughes for a few moments. "Now, Mr. Hughes—Alonzo Hughes— is from the agency hereabouts. You don't fall under him. You a Cherokee Indian, right? Somebody told me that, Mr. Smith. I think it was Chester Boyiddle. Don't make no nevermind anyway. Mr. Hughes called over to Muscogee for your agent. But you know there's a bunch of redskins they got to take care of over there, and so if the crime didn't occur on your land, then they ain't gonna do nothin' about it. So, boy, you is stuck with the local law. You'll have to be tried just like a white man if he done them murders."

Albright interjected, "Sorry, Sheriff, but I don't think we can charge him with murderin' Shotz. He came with his boss to look for him."

"That's right, Marty. He was an accessory after the fact. So they'll try him on that count in the federal court, and then we get to try him for the Comstock murder right here. We got the Boyiddles on that one as well as the Shotz killin', so their gooses are cooked either way. George Chargin' Horse is goin' to the can or he's gonna fry for murder.

Hoolie was nearly in a panic. These people had what was left of his life planned out. The end was in the electric chair. That single gruesome thought spurred him to speak loudly and clearly. "Sheriff, you know damn good and well I'm bein' framed for this. Somebody else killed Shotz and left him on the Chargin' Horse land. And I didn't kill Violet Comstock, and you know it."

Hoolie paused and drew in a deep breath. "I saw Chief Collins take the MacFarlands into the courthouse. Why would he do that? Maybe one of them killed the woman, and Collins is lockin' them up to keep them safe. When was she killed? If it was last night, the MacFarlands or even Collins coulda done it. You gotta look into it."

Wynn rubbed his chin in thought. Hoolie looked at Tucker and could tell that Moe liked the idea of pinning Violet's death on the MacFarlands. The problem was finding proof. It was much easier to railroad Indians. He had to get a hold of J.D. "Sheriff," he said thickly, "you think I could wire my boss? I know good and well that he'd be here on the next train. He could solve this."

"Nah, Mr. Smith"—Wynn smirked—"I don't think we need anybody elst on this case. We got you dead to rights."

Hoolie's head sunk to his chest. He gave up. Hughes spoke. "You have to be defended in court, Mr. Smith. That's the law." Hughes looked around the room defiantly, turned, and walked out.

Peeler laughed and said, "Glad to get shed of that chucklehead. He walked over and put his fingertips under Hoolie's chin. Hoolie opened his eyes and looked directly at Peeler. "I didn't do it, Marshal. You gotta believe me."

Peeler turned to the rest of the group. "Well, I'm done here. Seems like you got 'em. I'll file a report to the district judge, and he'll issue warrants. Good work." He tipped his hat and said, "Sheriff . . . Deputies," and walked out.

Wynn went to the door. "Marty," he said, "take this boy down to the cell with the Boyiddles. And put Chargin' Horse in there too."

Tucker turned and said quietly, "Cells only got two bunks in 'em."

"Well, throw in two extra blankets. They's Indians . . . used to sleepin' on the floor. We'll get 'em charged by the judge tomorrow."

Tucker and Albright unlocked Hoolie and took him down from the stool. He walked unsteadily. The deputies half dragged him out of the room and down a short hallway to the cells. Anadarko's jail cells didn't have bars. They were cages of steel slats, welded and bolted together so that you could barely see anyone inside except through the checkerboard light pattern made by the ceiling globes. Formidable lockups, they.

They shoved Hoolie into the cell with Chester and Harold, locked the door, and went to get George Charging Horse. Soon the three Kiowa men were sitting cross-legged on the floor of the cell. Chester, Harold, and George were speaking in rapid Kiowa. Hoolie, lying on one of the bunks, listened for a while, then pulled the blanket over himself and closed his eyes. George leaned over and patted Hoolie on the shoulder. "They sure beat you up, brother. But things will get better in the mornin'. They will."

"You look bad, Hoolie," said Chester.

Harold nodded. "Yeah, they beat you pretty good. But we're gonna get outta here. George has got a good feelin' about things."

Hoolie looked skeptically at the three Kiowa men. "You guys must be crazy," he mumbled. "These white men are out for our blood. How'd they find Shotz's grave?"

"Sheriff Wynn showed up at the place," George said. "It wasn't too long after you all left yesterday. He was with Agent Hughes and Mr. Cooper and four other mens."

"Cooper?"

"Yes. He's our leaseman for about forty acres."

"What happened?" Hoolie could barely form his words, but he pushed ahead anyway.

"Well," said George, "they asked to see where Mr. Shotz was buried, so I showed them. They made out like they knew he'd been killed and left at our place. They talked like they knew we treated him right and buried him proper."

"Then?"

"They started diggin' that poor white man up. We wrapped him in a blanket when we buried him. They brought him up and unwrapped him. He looked pretty bad. Then they put the handcuffs on me. Said they was gonna bring me in for killin' him. I said I didn't to it, but they didn't want to listen."

"I wonder how they knew it was Shotz."

"Couldn't tell you," George said with finality.

Hoolie slowly turned his head and looked at Harold. "When did they get you?"

"I don't know. We was sleepin' and Chester got kicked. It was Moe Tucker and Marty Albright. They walked us over here and locked us up. Didn't say nothin' about nothin'."

"That musta been after they took me in."

"Your bedroll was still down," Chester replied. "We didn't get to put away anythin' though. So it's all still layin' out at the corral."

Hoolie looked at George. "You been in here since yesterday?"

"Yep, they brought me in here a little after dark."

"I'd like to know more about Violet Comstock." Hoolie pointed with his bruised and split lips toward Chester and Harold. "We ate at her place last evenin'. She looked like she was worried about somethin' or other."

Hoolie lightly touched his throbbing temple and took a deep breath. "I gotta tell you all somethin'. . . . I was up walkin' around this mornin' and saw Collins bringin' in the MacFarlands."

"You mean lockin' 'em up?" asked Harold.

"Yeah, right out front. Four of 'em drove up, and the MacFarlands and Collins and another fella shook hands and then handcuffed Festus and Clem. Then they walked into the courthouse. I saw that and then walked back to the corral. That's when I saw that the roan was upset. I walked toward the creek, hid myself, and got a pistol stuck at the back of my head."

"Busy mornin'," said Chester.

Harold looked dubious. "You reckon they woulda let us be if that horse didn't act up?"

"No," Hoolie began, narrowing his eyes, "they woulda come after us anyways."

"How do you figure?" asked Chester.

"That's hard to say. I think that somebody decided to bring everything together. The killer was the one who told somebody that the white man was buried out to your place, George. And somebody killed the woman and decided that they'd just pin it on us. Maybe somebody knew that we was out to the creek the night of the fight, and they guessed that Miss Comstock tipped somebody off that the shipment was comin' in. Or maybe it was just Moe that killed her. That Marty told me that he liked her. He mighta got mad at her for runnin' a cathouse. Somebody could be runnin' this whole thing. He could be tryin' to calm things down by takin' us in and hangin' it all on us. But blamin' us ain't gonna stop some of these boys from doin' somethin' bad. Meanness and bein' greedy is in their blood. Born to it. Maybe a bad wind took 'em. I don't know."

George looked downcast and shook his head sadly. "Terrible how some men just fall in to it. And they say they follow the Jesus road. That ain't the way I heard about the Jesus road."

"I know, but they keep doin' bad things—I mean real bad things—anyways." Hoolie paused for a moment, rubbed his cheek, and began again. "You know, that horse put me in mind of one of my relatives' horses. It happened about forty years ago. He was the high sheriff of Goin'snake District when it was the Cherokee Nation. He had a horse that shied at the smell of blood. Well, one day he was sittin' on the courthouse porch when a woman come up and told him that two white men was passin' through in a covered wagon. It was a two-horse team and small wagon. She didn't much care for the way they looked. Kinda like they was gonna do bad things.

"Well, my relative thought that they might be into some meanness, so he followed them at a distance. They made camp, and my relative thought he'd go home and look in on them early in the mornin'.

"So before sunup, he says his prayers and goes out to see what the white men were doin'. He thought they'd be gone. He's ridin' toward the camp, and his horse starts shyin' away. He knew somethin' was wrong because the horse only shied at the smell of blood. Now, we always treat blood with care 'cause it carries power. So everybody thought that horse had a special kind of way about him. He had a power that needed takin' care of, and my relative always paid attention to that horse."

George and the Boyiddles nodded their heads in unison. They knew about taking care of that kind of medicine. That horse had a sacred power that they had seen before.

Hoolie continued, "As soon as that horse shied, my relative tied him to a bush and went about on foot. He creeped up on the white men and found that one of them had gone on and killed the other. The man was covered in blood. He had hung the other man up like a hog, cut his throat, and rolled his innards out. He was startin' to butcher him, so my relative pulled out his pistol, tied the man up, and took him in. The marshals from Fort Smith took the man, and they hung him a week or so later. The medicine men had to work on my relative for a whole season. He'd been around too much blood, and they had to get him cleaned up before he got real sick. Took him to water seven times, and he still had the evil spirits callin' to him in his sleep. The medicine man had to take care of everythin' 'cause my relative had caused lots of problems with the things around him as well.

"He fought with the Union side during the war and had been in a few fights and had seen a lot of blood. They took him to water after the war, and he did fine. But seein' the evil that that white man had done to the other and bein' around all that blood was more than he could handle. So the medicine man had to do a lot for him. All of this was told to me when I was a boy. My relative was o'd by then and wasn't sheriff no more. He didn't talk about it."

George looked down at Hoolie and said, "That was bad. It makes me think about the white man we buried. He was done just like that other white man. Gutted, cut throat, face pushed in. Terrible things. I don't know what makes 'em so evil."

"Well," Hoolie concluded, "that was why I paid attention to that horse. Because of my relative's horse. That's why I started walkin' into the wind. That horse smelled evil—it was on that wind. Sure as I'm lyin' here."

Hoolie paused for a moment, moved his head slowly back and forth, and added, "I still can't figure out how they knew it was Shotz and how they knew he was at your place."

"That troubles me too," George said.

They all sat in silence, thinking about the bad things men did to each other. They uttered not a single word to each other until two guards came along and distributed bowls of beans to each cell. Hoolie couldn't eat, but his cellmates ate their not very tasty supper, made small talk until after sundown, and rolled themselves up in their blankets. All four fell into a profoundly disturbed sleep.

>«

Hoolie heard the commotion first and shook Chester awake. "Wha . . . wha?" he said, rolling over and rubbing his eyes.

"Quiet," Hoolie snapped. "Wake everybody up."

George and Harold were already responding to the voices and the growing noise. A shot was fired.

"What the hell!" a voice from the next cell exclaimed.

"What's goin' on? By God!" answered another.

A door burst open, and a man dressed in a slicker and wearing a bandana over his nose and mouth stepped into the cell room holding a lantern. "Fes . . . Clem . . . where you at, boys?" he called in a gravelly voice.

"Over here," a voice called back.

The man in the slicker turned and barked an order. "Bring 'em in here!"

Three men with bandanas on their faces and pistols in their hands pushed two jailers through the door and handcuffed them to the nearest set of iron slats. One of them threw a set of keys to the man in the slicker. He strode to a cell four away from where Hoolie, the Boyiddles, and George stood trying to see what was going on. Suddenly, a door clanged open, and the MacFarland brothers came out and began slapping the men with the bandanas on their backs. "Glad to see you boys!" one of them shouted.

Festus took the keys and led the way around the cells, freeing every one of the ten other prisoners being held in the jail. He got to Hoolie's cell and declared loudly, "Well, if it ain't the redskins!" Festus looked into each of their faces and said through his teeth, "You boys is stayin' here, and ol' Sheriff Wynn's gonna do more than skin the four of ya. And I'll tell ya, that's good enough for me. I won't even have to dirty my hands on ya. I'll just see you in hell!" He turned to leave, but his brother put a hand to his chest.

"Hold up a minute, Fes," Clem said evenly. "It might be better to unlock these boys."

"You crazy?" asked Festus. "I want to see these red niggers fry."

"No, think about it. Wynn's gonna come after us pronto. If we let these boys out, they'll be the ones Marty and Moe will come after. It'll give us some time to get the rest of the boys ready, come to a fight. Wynn's gonna get in trouble—that's why we're gettin' busted out. If we let them go too, he's gonna catch even more hell. He let some uppity redskins get away."

"All right," Festus declared. He dropped his voice to a deadly whisper and looked into Hoolie's eyes. "I'm gonna let you boys out 'cause I want a clean breakout. Everybody goes."

Clem backed his brother up. "That's right, everybody goes so that Wynn and his boys are gonna have a hard time huntin' all of you down." Clem stared intently at the Boyiddle brothers. "Don't have time to fiddle with you boys just now, but just you wait," he said with a hiss, "I'll get you in the end. You're still gonna pay."

Festus tossed the keys back to the man in the slicker. "Let 'em out," he said as he ran out of the cell room. The man in the slicker raised his pistol and said, "Step to the back of the cell, you shit eaters." When they complied, he tried four keys before opening the door. He pointed his pistol at the four men once again and said, "Stay right where you are until I get clear. Then you better head to the hills. Wynn's gonna come after you first. That's the only reason we don't shoot y'all down right now." He turned and fled.

Hoolie waited for a couple of moments then pushed the door open. The Boyiddles and George followed him out. The guards started yelling at them. "Get the keys over there. By God, unlock us," one of them said. "Unlock us, or things are gonna get tough on you," the other said. Hoolie shut his ears to the jailers' threats and led his three companions out the door and out a back entrance. Even though he had been beaten up, Hoolie was thankful that he at least had remembered the courthouse layout. They went out the back door, ran for a while toward the north, then doubled back to the corral. In the dark, they saddled horses, stole one for George, and rode off. Hoolie thought that if he ever saw Anadarko again, it would be too soon. Things were going to get tough enough anyway. The notion that both Wynn and Collins would add horse stealing and jailbreak to the murder charges against him crept grimly into his brain. "Tough enough" might not be strong enough words for what was to come. Now everyone in Anadarko law enforcement was after him.

Chapter XII

LOUISA

It was lucky that J.D. knew just about everyone in law enforcement in Tulsa. Were it otherwise, he wouldn't have been able to move about asking questions like he did. Dealing with other lawmen seemed to come naturally to him. He was a comrade-in-arms so to speak, and law enforcement was a true community in the sense that cops did almost everything together. They had baseball teams, they drank together, they lived in the same neighborhoods, they hunted and fished with each other, and they often went to the same churches. Every once in a while, J.D. would go to church—more in honor of his late mother than as a true believer—and invariably he'd see half a dozen or so cops with their large families squeezing into the pews for Mass.

J.D. found Lieutenant Finch, the circus strong man with the old man's countenance, sitting as usual at the large table in the squad room grumbling about the elementary school reports his officers turned in.

"Hiya, Finch boy! How's tricks?"

"Ho, J.D., what's cookin'?"

"Not too much, Marv. Still on the Shelby case."

Mention of the Shelbys always made Tulsa law enforcement from the lowest beat cop to the chief of police—especially him—prick up their ears. Finch was no exception. When he last encountered Mrs. Shelby, Finch was forced against his will to give in to her demand that she talk to Theodore Welbourne. He was very wary of Mrs. Shelby, but he had to acknowledge that she was easily the most politically powerful woman in the city. One word to her husband about even a minor lack of cooperation and heads would roll. Not only that, but Mrs. Shelby was a staunch suffragette, and since the Nineteenth Amendment had been passed, she, her daughter, and Rose Chichester were working to put together a women's voting association. On the other hand, Mrs. Shelby ended up graciously thanking the lieutenant for his help. Finch feared and yet was charmed by Rose Shelby.

Without being asked to do so, J.D. sat down at the table, unbuttoned his coat, and reached for his cigarette case. He tilted his bowler to the back of his head, offered Finch a cigarette, and said, "Lieutenant, my friend, I gotta ask a few questions about your coppers around here."

Finch looked surprised. "You know 'em all," he replied. "Go ahead." He looked dubiously at J.D. "Why ask me anyways?"

"Marv, I think some coppers are in on the Welbourne kidnapping."

"You mean the girl?"

"Yeah, sounds like a setup."

"Sure it was. They wanted to make sure Welbourne talked." Finch paused. "You don't think so, do you?"

"Well . . . yes and no."

"What's that supposed to mean? Spill." It was a command.

"I'll spill if you'll help out."

"Okay, that's a deal."

"All I want is if I find out that a copper helped the Klan take the kid and her daddy, you'll do everything you can to lock them up and throw away the key."

Finch's eyes narrowed. His face turned ashen. "I'll break their heads and laugh about it." Finch rubbed his hands together and placed them flat on the table. "I know that some cops are Klan and that this was a Klan deal. If you find out somebody under me is breakin' the law, I'll do everything I can to put 'em behind bars . . . or crack their heads open."

"Okay, Marv, that's all I needed." J.D. pulled out his cigarette case and went through the ritual of offering Finch another smoke. He lit up, blew out a smoke ring, and whispered, "Let me set this up. You had Welbourne on a murder charge. He don't talk. So his daughter gets snatched to make him talk. That sound about right?"

"Yeah."

"All right. Then Welbourne hisself gets snatched. All of this under the eyes of the militia. Martial law's in effect. I hate to say this, but it was under the eyes of you all here at the courthouse."

"I know . . . I know . . . but since the riot, the Klan has been snatchin' Negroes right and left. They're good at it. Martial law don't seem to stop anything. The guard boys are addin' to the revenue of the speaks and the whorehouses though. The boys downstairs are ignoramuses, but they're county. The police force comes out of all this okay. But I have this bad feelin' up and down my spine about what's goin' on."

"What's that, Marv?" J.D. inquired with concern. He was completely in the dark.

"Well, it's just a feelin', but I'm pretty sure the mayor wants to keep the guard boys around 'cause it's good for business. The city turns a profit with them here, and I know damn good and well that a bunch of my boys and probably the whole sheriff's office is on the take. I'm pretty sure that the Klan, no matter what they say about bein' Christians, is runnin' a protection racket."

"You think so?" J.D. asked.

"Pretty sure. How else they get the money to operate?"

"Dues?"

"Naw, most of the members are just poor white trash and couldn't afford to pay a nickel a year to join up. The Klan's got a national organization. . . ." Finch sneered and chuckled under his breath. "How'd you think they afford them sheets and pointy hats?"

"That don't say much for Tulsa's government."

"No, it don't. That's one of the reasons I'd like to see the Klan booted out of town. I been on the force more'n half my life, J.D. I joined up to enforce the law, by God. And now it seems like the law is somethin' that these boys—the mayor included—just dance around. This city's gonna lose control again, and I swore to stop that. As God is my witness, I'll do everything I can to get the city back. Now, the politicians say that less than fifty people got killed in the riot. I know that's plain bunkum. It's been two years, and little boys goin' fishin' still find bones washed outta the bank of the river. That ain't right. My youngest boy found a skull. Near scared him outta his wits."

J.D. saw the passion in Finch's eyes and decided to take his leave. "Well, Marv, I'm gonna do all I can. And if I find the Klan did somethin' illegal, we'll put 'em outta business together."

"I'm good for that, old man. I believe in law and order."

"Marv, take care of yourself. I gotta get back to the office."

"Yeah, J.D., you do the same. Let me know what's goin' on."

"Will do."

≫≪

Two hours later J.D. was behind his desk locked in a thought-induced trance. Theodore Welbourne was free, but J.D. wasn't going to tell Finch that Welbourne broke out of jail rather than was snatched. Finch wouldn't understand not telling him about Welbourne and why J.D. failed to bring the fugitive in. Louisa must be still alive simply because she had not turned up—alive or dead. J.D. shook his head. He didn't want to contemplate Louisa's death. He had to find her. But why would they keep her, especially if Welbourne was out of jail? They must know that by now. She'd be useless as a way of extracting a confession from her father. Everybody thinks that the Klan snatched both Welbourne and Louisa. And they expect that both of them will turn up dead at any time. The whole point of the Klan abductions was to instill terror among the black people. Their brutalized bodies, alive or dead, should have been left on the streets somewhere. The Klan has to be holding Louisa somewhere because the leaders know that snatching Welbourne wasn't a Klan job. They might be keeping her as insurance just in case Welbourne shows up again. Or maybe Welbourne would turn himself over to them to set the girl free. But to keep her would be to risk being found out. Kidnappers could only hold somebody for just so long. So where was she?

Then there's Anadarko. J.D. had sent two telegrams to Hoolie, but neither had been answered. Where was Hoolie? He had to wrap up the Welbourne operation fast and get back to Anadarko. No telling what kind of trouble his associate operative was in.

A knock on his office door broke the spell. J.D. snapped out of the mind-boggling and confusing crush of possibilities surrounding Louisa, her father, the Shelbys, Hoolie, and Anadarko. He quickly got up from his chair, crossed the room, and opened the door. Waiting to be let in were Elizabeth Shelby and Rose Chichester.

J.D.'s eyes widened in surprise and delight. While Elizabeth Shelby reminded him of a spoiled princess, he knew Rose

162

Chichester to be an exceedingly brave, resourceful, and smart young woman. Even though both women were very attractive, J.D. felt positively light-headed around Rose. J.D. stepped aside and ushered them through the door. He quickly grabbed the spare chair, placed it beside the never-moved custom's seat, and beckoned the two women to sit. He took his chair, put his hands on the desk, and looked at both women with what passed for a businesslike frown. He changed his expression to a pleasant smile and spoke. "Well, it is indeed good to see you both. And may I say you both look lovely today? How can I be of service?"

Elizabeth put on her most charming smile and said, "Rose and I were downtown this morning, and we wanted to drop in and perhaps ask about the hunt for Louisa."

J.D.'s smile left him. "I've only been back in town for a few days, ladies. I'm working on it."

Elizabeth too dropped the smile from her face. "I'm sorry, Mr. Daugherty. I know you've been doing your best. But I'd like to perhaps offer some added incentive. . . ." She broke the sentence short.

Rose picked it up. "Mr. Daugherty, Elizabeth came here with the idea that you might be working on other cases and wanted to promise you more money so that you would drop other business in favor of concentrating on Louisa."

J.D. knuckled his moustache and rubbed his embarrassed, burning cheek. Somehow the notion that he needed extra monetary motivation to complete the operation hurt his considerable pride. His mouth became a straight line. "Ladies, I want you to know that at this moment Louisa is my first concern. True, I have other worries, but rest assured that I've already put them aside to look for the girl. I will find her . . . and very soon."

Elizabeth looked at and straightened her right sleeve cuff in a gesture more pensive than fastidious. She met J.D.'s eyes and replied, "I'm sure you're working hard, but you may as well know that we've been doing some detective work ourselves."

"What? I don't get you—what do you mean, you're doing detective work?" J.D. was taken aback—severely aback.

"Yes," Elizabeth said with her head held up and a serious expression on her face. She looked at Rose and back to J.D. with the slightest of knowing smiles. In a whisper, she spoke conspiritorially and with a haughty look on her face. "Mr. Daugherty, we decided that the men who might have taken Louisa belong to the lowest class of reprobates in Tulsa. As you may know, a while ago I frequented some of the city's better speakeasies. . . ." She paused, looked down at her dress, brushed an exposed curl back under her chic cloche hat, and pursed her lips.

J.D. suppressed a knowing and sanctimonious smile.

"In any case," she resumed, "I thought that we . . ." She cocked her head and smiled curiously at Rose. Embarrassed, she then whispered, "I thought that we could dress like . . ." She paused, smiled, giggled like a schoolgirl, and said, "You know, all dolled up like a couple of floozies, and go slumming around some of the juice joints in town. Maybe one of these lowlifes could have a slip of the tongue, and we'd find out something."

Rose raised her hand and waved in a kind of excited gesture that a teacher might see in a classroom full of kids. "Mr. Daugherty," she began, "I was more of a homebody and often looked down upon Elizabeth's antics. Since we discovered we are indeed sisters, we've become quite close. My . . . my . . . adventure . . . let's say . . . two years ago taught us both that we have to be more responsible. Elizabeth brought up the idea, and we worked everything out."

J.D. sat for a moment with his mouth gaped open. Finally, he shook his head in disbelief, knuckled his moustache, and said sternly, "You both should know better. You could get hurt. These places are not for young women such as yourselves." He paused and then raised his voice, "Just what the hell are you thinking? What's your mother and father gonna say? You get involved in this kind of sordid work, and you could land in trouble or maybe even get yourselves killed."

Both women put on contrite frowns. Rose spoke first. "Mr. Daugherty . . . J.D. . . . you and I are quite familiar with each other. You know more of our family secrets than anyone outside the family itself. You know me. I've survived buckshot in the back and some days' worth of beatings and humiliation from two of the worst scoundrels ever." Her voice began to rise, but she stopped, caught herself, and continued, "What I'm trying to say is that I'm strong. I can handle myself."

"And so can I," Elizabeth said as she reached into the bag she held on her lap. She withdrew a small caliber automatic and showed it to J.D. "Mr. Daugherty, do you know what this is?"

"It's a pistol, miss. And I'd like for you to put it away."

"Mr. Daugherty," she repeated, "this is a Savage .32 automatic. I use it very well. My brother and I learned to shoot long ago. One of the family secrets that you may not know is that I'm an excellent shot. With this, I can hit a playing card at ten paces."

"That's very well, Miss Shelby, and I'm sure that if he was alive, Buffalo Bill would hire you on at a top salary. And I'm sure that you both know how to take care of yourselves. But you young women have to be careful. Knowing how to take care of yourself doesn't always translate into actually taking care of yourself. Know what I mean?"

Elizabeth's lips went straight and she paled considerably within seconds. J.D. knew from her expression that she was becoming even angrier, more tense, and more desperate than ever. He held up his hands as if being robbed and said, "Miss Shelby, please, I'm only trying to save myself from getting plugged." He forced a joking laugh, and the tension in Elizabeth's face eased somewhat. She caught the joke, relaxed, and put the pistol back in her small bag. "Don't worry," she said with a slight smile, "I won't shoot."

Rose Chichester sat calmly, as through Elizabeth pulling a gun out of her purse was as innocuous as filing her nails. J.D. began knuckling his moustache nervously. Rose re-creased a pleat in her skirt and said as politely as if she were talking to a guest in her home, "Mr. Daugherty, we have already been to some of the seedier dance halls and speakeasies in town. We came through unharmed, but we appreciate your concern. And we have something to tell you that might be of help."

"Okay, pray tell me, but please don't do this again."

"Fine," Elizabeth said testily. "I won't . . . we won't. But listen."

Rose took a deep breath and stroked the front of her long neck. "We were at Deke Pepper's place. . . ."

J.D. winced and groaned audibly. "What?" he breathed. "You didn't?" He quickly caught himself. "All right, I'm sorry, please go on."

Rose smiled defiantly at J.D. "Mr. Daugherty," she began again, "Deke's joint is filled with the worst sort of people in the city."

"And his hooch is nothing but rotgut," Elizabeth interrupted.

"That's true," Rose said, "but to continue—at Deke's we were able to attract some attention, if you know what I mean."

"I'm afraid so," J.D. answered with a sigh.

"Two men sat with us at one of the cleaner tables in the place. One was named Ozzie and the other was a Frank or Fred or Farrin, something. . . ."

"It was Fred," Elizabeth reminded.

"Yes, Fred. Fred said they were off-duty jailers. I asked why they didn't close this place down when they were on duty. He said that Deke had protection from the highest officials of the county and the city on up to the mayor. Besides, that was a job for the coppers, both county and city."

Elizabeth was on the edge of her seat, opening her mouth again and again, trying put in her own two cents' worth. J.D. gave her an encouraging smile and said, "I'm sorry, Miss Shelby, but you look like you're gonna bust if you don't let it out. What is it?"

"I almost forgot. This Fred started saying something about the national guard in town . . . that the soldiers brought money into town and that was the only reason the mayor and the rest of the city and county people want them around. He said the KKK is really in charge." She paused to let the weight of her observations sink in.

"That's when I asked him why he thought the Klan was running things," she began again. "He said that it wasn't necessarily running the mayor's office or the coppers, but it was able to do anything it pleases despite the governor calling out the militia."

"Miss Shelby," J.D. interjected, "that's pretty much all common knowledge. I even had a police lieutenant tell me the same thing this very day."

Rose raised her hand again and said, "Yes, sir, I'm sure that it is, but this Fred went on to say that he is a member of the Klan. And that even if the mayor and the police wanted to do something about those people, they couldn't. Many of the city officials are Klan."

"And so is half the police force," Elizabeth said with disdain.

"True," Rose said, looking at her half sister, "but remember what he said about the Klan abducting Mr. Welbourne. He said that the Klan was so powerful, smart, and slick that it could snatch

Mr. Welbourne from under the eyes of the guard, the police, and the mayor's office. He said it was like fifty years ago when the Klan put the fear of God into everybody."

J.D. sat forward and put an elbow on the desk. He knuckled his moustache. "What else did he say?"

"He knew it was the Klan because he helped them get in."

Rose broke in. "He opened the door to let the kidnappers in. That's what he said. He thought he was impressing us. He also said that he got some money out of the deal, but he said that he would have helped anyway."

"The next thing he said," Elizabeth interjected, "was that he was pretty sure that Mr. Welbourne was taken to a place in Collinsville."

"Why'd he say Collinsville? What the hell's—excuse the language—in Collinsville, anyway?"

"Who knows?" said Rose. "The Klan might have a place there . . . where they take people to beat them up."

"Why do you think that this guy would know about Klan hideouts or whatever they are?"

"Because," Rose said, "this Fred said that he was not only in on abducting Mr. Welbourne from jail, but that he'd had a hand in taking Louisa as well."

"I guess I'd better find this Fred, huh?" J.D. smiled. "He sounds like he could answer a few of my questions."

"Given the right incentive, Mr. Daugherty," Elizabeth replied. "Given the right incentive."

"Just what do you mean by that, Miss Shelby?"

"I mean that he spoke to us because we're women."

"I understand. Please continue."

"Well, I think that we would be able to get more information in our way than in yours."

"You mean that I would be threatening and that he'd keep quiet because of the threat."

"Yes," Rose said. "You always get more with honey than with vinegar. Isn't that the old saying?"

"I think it's 'you catch more flies with honey,' miss."

"Then it's exactly what we're talking about."

J.D. looked sternly at each of them in turn. "Catching flies is one thing, ladies. Being around these kinds of people is another."

Elizabeth thought for a moment. "Can we cooperate, Mr. Daugherty?"

"What do you mean?"

"See," Rose said, "we can at least identify this Fred person—put the finger on him. . . . Isn't that the cops and robbers expression?"

"I'll go along with that," J.D. said quietly, "but let me put some things in order first. I'll give you a telephone call. Then together we'll find this Mr. Fred."

"We'll expect your call, Mr. Daugherty," Elizabeth said.

≫«

After he showed Misses Elizabeth and Rose to the door, J.D. sat down to ponder his next play. There was something very wrong with the Fred story. Had the county jail guard really helped the Klan snatch Theodore Welbourne? But Welbourne himself told J.D. that, with the help of several of his own men, he had broken out of jail. The Klan had nothing to do with Welbourne's escape. If Fred was a Kluxer, why would he help a Negro escape? Welbourne and his friends tricked good old Fred, J.D. thought with sudden delight. If the typical Klansman is this goddam dumb, they couldn't last long. On the other hand, it might become an ongoing organization precisely because dumb people joined its ranks. But what the Klan lacked in brainpower, it made up for in ruthless and appalling viciousness in addition to its simplistic message of hatred.

The problem at hand was to get a hold of Fred and find out just how much he really knew about Louisa. He had to make contact with Welbourne's go-between, the guy called Bob. J.D. had the telephone number and a plan in mind.

J.D. decided to initiate his plan immediately. He gave the operator the number, and Bob—if that really was his name—answered after a few rings. His voice was easily recognizable and as pleasant as it had been when he had spoken to J.D. in the car driving out to meet Welbourne.

"In the trenches," J.D. said. The telephone went dead.

In less than ten minutes, J.D.'s own telephone jingled. He picked up the earpiece and said, "This is Daugherty."

The same voice asked, "How can I be of assistance?"

"There's a man who might know where the daughter of our mutual friend might be," said J.D.

"Is that so? Well, I think I should come by Fourth and Boston at five. That's fifteen minutes. Can you be there?"

"I'll be there," J.D. answered. He replaced the earphone on the receiver, got his derby from the hat rack, and locked up. He was at Fourth and Boston with time to spare.

Bob had changed automobiles. He was driving a very nice Cadillac with plush leather seats and an armrest on the door. Once again, he steered the car west and crossed the river. The drive was of a shorter distance this time, and Bob pulled the automobile into the front yard of a small white house with a green roof. As on his last visit to Welbourne, J.D. got out of the car alone, walked to the door, and knocked.

He was let in immediately. Welbourne was sitting with three other men in the parlor.

"Welcome, Mr. Daugherty. I hear you have news?"

"I do indeed, Mr. Welbourne. This might be a break. We need to kidnap a jailer named Fred, and you and your people can do it. Your jailbreak proved that you can pull off this kind of operation as well my old employer Great Western could. Besides, I'm pretty sure your motivation is on a higher level than anything we did with the company."

"Well, I don't know if that's a compliment or not. I'll take it as one though. . . . So, Mr. Daugherty, what's the plan?"

≫≪

It took a few days to put everything together and to sort out Fred's habits and haunts. John Ryan discovered that Fred only had a tenuous tie to the Klan as a beer-drinking sometime member with no rank or say-so in Klan operations. His name was Frederick Krendle, and for the time being, he was working the graveyard shift from midnight to eight. He was thirty-three, unmarried, and had been a county employee for six years. He lived in a one-room flat on Cincinnati. Krendle owned a two-year-old Ford but walked to work, only taking his automobile out when he made his visits to the speakeasies. Danny Ryan found that Krendle was one of the best customers at Deke's. He always came into Deke's precisely at ten o'clock and had at least two drinks before returning home to park his car, change clothes, and walk to the courthouse. His staggered nights off were usually spent at Deke's. If ever there was a creature of habit, it was Fred Krendle.

Elizabeth and Rose were brought into the "Krendle Operation," as J.D. had dubbed it, but only to the extent of identifying the intended target. After they pointed out the man, J.D. and Danny followed him closely. Two people on a tail—so J.D. had learned in his years as an investigator—could leapfrog a subject and be less quick to lose him in a crowd. J.D. spent one night standing under his umbrella in the rain outside the courthouse waiting for Krendle to get off work. The next evening he attended a not-so-secret Klan meeting west of Sapulpa. No crosses were burned, no one wore their robes and masks, and no one made a big speech. From what J.D. could make out while hidden in the woods nearby, the Klansmen just stood around, joked with each other, drank some bottled beer, got back in their automobiles, and drove home.

J.D. recruited John and Danny Ryan at five dollars a day to help him keep an eye on Fred Krendle. It was a lot of money, but J.D. could charge the cost to Big Bill Shelby as part of his expenses. They planned the snatch to take place late at night when Krendle was walking to work. John would stand watch across the street from an alley that Krendle had to pass. Welbourne himself would be stationed in the alley. When John saw Krendle, he would approach him for a light for a fat Cuban cigar. Welbourne's men would emerge from the shadows and toss a blanket over the man's head, throw him into a waiting car, and drive him to the small white house west of the Arkansas River. Timing was important. J.D. would be waiting there to question a blindfolded Krendle and extract any and all information about Louisa. J.D. was an expert interrogator and was sure that his plan for getting information was infallible. Fred was not only about to miss work, but he was also about to have the fear of the Almighty put into him. J.D. was not the kind of interrogator to skin his knuckles on a guy in the hot seat, but he used a combination of fear and kindness to get what he wanted.

And the plan worked to a T, except that John got a bit nervous or angry or anxious for some action. As soon as Krendle pulled out a match for John's cigar, John whipped out a blackjack from his back pocket and smacked Krendle on the forehead. Welbourne and his men emerged with the blanket. Welbourne asked John why he had hit Krendle. "It was nothin' but a bit of a love tap," John said. "The man looked at me funny. Reminded me of me days as a boy in the old country and the Anglish coppers."

J.D. was sitting in the front room of the little white house when he heard Bob's purring Cadillac drive into the yard. The door opened slowly, and a walking army blanket was pushed into the parlor.

"Put him in the back room," said J.D. "And turn out all the lights. I'll take the blanket off myself."

Krendle was hustled through the hallway and thrown onto the bed. The blinds were drawn and the kerosene lamps were blown out. Everyone and everything went silent. Only Krendle made muffled noises, making the bedsprings squeak while he attempted to loosen the rope around his arms and body.

Back in the front room, Welbourne removed his flour-sack mask. The three men with him stood silent. Welbourne sat, crossed his legs, and asked, "What now, Mr. Daugherty?"

"First, Mr. Welbourne, you're gonna put the fear of God into him. I want you to accompany me back into the room with one lantern. I'll pull the blanket off him, and all you'll need to do is hold up the lamp so Krendle can see your face." J.D. paused for a moment. "Is that all right with you? I'll stand behind Krendle and throw the blanket over him real fast so's he'll only get a glimpse of you and won't see me at all."

"Certainly. I don't think I'll see him again, and my face is presumably already plastered all over the county post offices anyway."

"I haven't been to one lately, but I guess you'd be right."

"When do we start asking questions?"

"I'll do the asking, Mr. Welbourne. Right now we'll let him stew for a while. He doesn't know what's happenin' to him. Tell me what happened at the snatch."

Welbourne smiled broadly and smoothed a crease in his trousers. "Everything went like clockwork. Mr. Ryan got his cigar lit but decided he'd pop Mr. Krendle on the head with his blackjack. We threw a blanket over his head. He squirmed a bit, but Mr. Smith, an ex–bare-knuckle fighter, hit him in the stomach and he stopped.

Another Mr. Smith hog-tied him in a few seconds. The man you know as Bob turned the corner and stopped in the alley, and all three Mr. Smiths loaded Mr. Krendle into the automobile. Mr. Krendle was very quiet during the entire trip. I saw Mr. Ryan walk off smoking the cigar with a satisfied look on his face."

"John's a good man, but he does like to get into a scuffle every once in a while. . . . I take it I'm not trusted enough yet to know who the three Mr. Smiths really are?" J.D. said with a twisted smile.

"I'm afraid that Mr. Smith, Mr. Smith, and Mr. Smith do not wish to reveal their names to you. It's not that they don't trust you. It's that they're worried about slip-ups here and there. Better to be masked at this point in time."

"I can well understand that. But you . . . you've got to be worried as well?"

"I'm a marked man, Mr. Daugherty. When I get my daughter back, we're heading west to a new life. At least I hope it'll mean a new life. Oklahoma was once considered a place where a Negro man could live a good life. As you know, the Greenwood area was a thriving community. Now it's a burnt-out wreck and—seeing as how it's in Oklahoma—maybe not worth rebuilding."

"But you were working to rebuild it. Mrs. Shelby was involved in it, and she's the most prominent woman in Tulsa."

"I realize that, Mr. Daugherty, but Tulsa might as well be Alabama or Mississippi or anywhere else in the Old South. Mr. Crow is alive and well there as well as here. They're not going to let us rebuild."

"Mr. Welbourne, you're a very brave man. I would think that you would want to continue . . . to stick to a goal . . . to rebuild."

"I only wish I could. But my arrest, the abduction of my daughter . . ." Welbourne put a hand to his forehead as if he were in deep pain. "I don't think I can stay in a place where even the attempt to rise up from bondage and degradation is met with hatred, more degradation, fire, cold steel, and murder."

J.D. wanted to change the subject. Clearly Welbourne was angry and, at the same time, melancholy to the point of surrendering to hopelessness. "I'm sorry, Mr. Welbourne, but we should begin questioning our friend Mr. Krendle."

Welbourne quietly stood and picked up a kerosene lantern, scratched a match on his thumbnail, lit the wick, and looked at J.D. for guidance. J.D. took the lead, and they walked to the bedroom where Krendle lay on his back, still tied up, with his head covered. J.D. motioned to Welbourne to stay outside. Krendle was struggling when J.D. entered. "Mr. Krendle," J.D. said in a low voice, "now settle down and listen to me. I want to show you something. The lights are off and it's very dark. I want to pull the blanket off and show you somethin'." J.D. took the blanket off slowly. He let Krendle have a few breaths before he said to the door, "Come on in now, Mr. Krendle is ready." J.D. stood in a corner out of Krendle's view.

Welbourne walked into the room with the lantern raised, the wick low. The light cast a shadowy glow. J.D. could see that Krendle was adjusting to the light. Then Krendle's eyes flew open, and, almost instinctively, he bared his teeth. "What the hell is this?" he growled.

"This," said J.D., "is Mr. Theodore Welbourne. The man you helped escape." J.D. quickly threw the blanket over Krendle's head and pulled him back onto the bed.

Krendle squirmed against his bonds and the blanket and gave up. The blanket muffled his voice. "That's a damn lie. I helped the knights. They came in. This nigger should be dead now."

J.D. saw that Welbourne was on the verge of killing Krendle with his bare hands. "Mr. Welbourne, please," J.D. whispered, "I'll handle it from here."

Welbourne set the lantern on the night table, turned it down completely, and quickly walked out of the room. J.D. took a chair in the corner and stared at the lumpy blanket-covered figure. After about only ten seconds, Krendle started raving under the blanket. "Who says I helped that nigger?! I'll kill 'em! Let me up, by God! Who the hell are you?! I'll get you, by God, I'll get you!"

J.D. smiled briefly; the muffled threats were ludicrous. J.D. had him. "Quiet down now, Mr. Krendle. I'll tell you what happened."

"I'm gonna kill you bastards! All of you!"

"I don't think you're in a position to harm anybody, Mr. Krendle. And Mr. Welbourne and his friends aren't likely to forget that you're a Kluxer."

The thought that he may be in grave danger finally penetrated Krendle's thick skull. He took a deep breath and whispered, "Who are you? You sound like a white man—why you helpin' these niggers?"

"I wouldn't use that word anymore, Krendle. These men are just as likely to skin you alive as to listen to you yell threats at 'em, especially since you're tied up with a blanket over your head. Now simmer down and answer my questions peacefully. I'll get them to let you go, and you can go back to work and tell them that you were kidnapped but that you escaped. You know Lieutenant Finch, don't you?"

"Yeah, I know him."

"Do you know who I am?"

"No. But you're a white man, ain't ya?"

"You'll never know, Mr. Krendle. But you do know Lieutenant Finch?"

"Yeah, so what?"

"Well, I know him as well. And I'll pass the word to him that you were indeed nabbed by a group of Negroes and that someone was tailing them. We'll set you loose, and you can go back to work. If you keep your mouth shut about what has and will happen, then my friends won't come and pay you a visit again. That way you won't lose your job, and you'll be a hero. On the other hand, if we let you go and you talk, I can guarantee that you're a dead man." J.D. paused for a moment. "Listen, Krendle, if you don't like this deal, I'll just turn you over to them now. Or, better yet, I'll leak the word that you helped Welbourne break outta the can. That'll put you in real good with your chums in the bedsheets."

"You can't to that. I know it was the Klan that snatched him."

"Sorry, pal, but you're dead wrong. And that might be taken in two ways. Mr. Welbourne's friends helped him and bought you off."

"No, they didn't. Clyde McSimmons hisself told me the plan. And they gave me the dough when I let 'em in. And I saw that they was white. Now let me up outta here. Them Negroes or whatever you wanna call 'em didn't snatch Welbourne. It was the Klan. Please take this blanket off my face."

"Nope, I'm not gonna do it. You're wrong again. You just saw Mr. Welbourne. His accomplices are all colored. I don't doubt that somebody paid you off. But believe me, whatever you think you saw when you let those fellas in the jailhouse, they were all black."

"I saw a white man's wrist, plain as day."

"Sorry, friend, but you can't always believe your lyin' eyes."

"I ain't your damned friend."

"You should be. The Klan ain't gonna like you for helpin' Mr. Welbourne break out of the hoosegow. I can spread that notion around real easy. And the fellas out in the hallway don't like the fact that you're Klan and that you might know where—or at least what happened to—Mr. Welbourne's daughter. Yep, you could be dead wrong or just plain dead."

Krendle was struggling to get the blanket off. J.D. knew instinctively that he was frightened and desperate. All of a sudden, the struggling stopped. Krendle had given up.

J.D. smiled benevolently. "Now, Mr. Krendle, it doesn't have to be either the Klan kills you or my friends in the next room kill you. Like I said before, we can come up with a story that'll make you into a hero all around. Now, how about it?"

There was a long pause. "Okay. I don't have much of a choice elseways."

"Nope. You sure don't."

"So, what you want me to do?"

"Well, first I'm gonna let you up so's you can sit on the bed. Then we'll talk turkey. You're gonna keep the blanket on, and I'm not gonna untie your hands and ankles. That all right by you?"

"Sure, I got no choice."

With J.D.'s help, Krendle sat up on the edge of the bed.

"Krendle, you know the consequences if you don't cooperate with me, right?"

"Yeah, I guess."

"Well, here's the deal. You know where Mr. Welbourne's daughter is. You've told people. That's right, ain't it?"

"Yeah."

"It's in Collinsville, correct?"

"Yeah."

"That's good. Now tell me why you know she's there."

Krendle hesitated. J.D. said, "Don't hold out on me now, Krendle. I can call in somebody with a pair of pliers and a sharp butcher's knife."

Krendle threw himself back and started to struggle once again. The blanket stayed in place and his bonds didn't let him move very far. He gave up once again. "Okay . . . okay, don't let them in. I'll do what I can."

"Okay. Now tell me how you know the girl is in Collinsville."

"I heard it at a meetin'. She was comin' from school. It was two of 'em. One of the boys had a touring car. They threw her in back and skedaddled."

"Who were they?"

The blanket moved from side to side. Krendle was trying not to speak their names.

"Don't stop now, Krendle. You might as well name 'em."

Krendle started to pant like a dog. J.D. thought he was about to have a breakdown.

"Krendle," J.D. whispered, "you serve in the war?"

"No."

"Oh. I thought you might be havin' some shell shock."

"No. I just swore I'd never tell."

"Well, you've already come over halfway, so you might as well spill it all."

"All right . . . all right. It was Jess Poindexter and Ralph Cunningham."

"Cunningham—sounds familiar."

"It should. Ralph's brother was the one that got killed."

"Welbourne didn't do it. You know that, don't you?"

"Don't make no difference. Bryant was a good man. He was workin' to keep the white race pure. He was a hero too. He led some men down into Greenwood durin' the riot. The niggers started that, and he burnt 'em out."

"And killed some innocent people," added J.D.

"Ain't none of 'em innocent. They started it."

"Yeah, and the Klan didn't show up at the courthouse to lynch Dick Rowland, did it?"

"Well . . . they started shootin' anyways."

"Enough of this. Tell me about Louisa."

"They drove her to Sapulpa first and then over to Collinsville."

"Why Collinsville?"

"Klan's got a house there. It's pretty much a pure white town. That's where the fellas take the niggers they snatch. That's the place where we put the fear of God into 'em. Then they take 'em back to the north side of Tulsa and let 'em go. They ain't so uppity no more after the boys get through with 'em."

"Probably because they can't walk, talk, or work anymore, you lame brain."

"You don't have to get sassy with me. You're a white man."

"Keep that up, and I might just turn you over to Welbourne and his men right now."

"You wouldn't do that."

"Try me again. Now I want you to tell me the exact spot where they're keepin' the girl."

"All right. But we got a deal about you goin' to get the word to Lieutenant Finch. You keep these people off my back. I'm only trustin' you 'cause I know you're a white man."

"Well, let's put it in a different way. You'd better trust me, because I'm the only one around here who doesn't want you dead right now. But I want to know a couple of things before I let you off. Right now give me the way to get to the house."

"Okay . . . okay. It's easy to get to. You go west on Main, then turn right, then left on Center Street, and you just keep headin' west. The house is out near a river or a big creek. It's got new brown siding, looks like brick."

"Good. I'm gonna step out for a minute to tell my compatriots."

J.D. left Krendle sitting on the bed and closed the door to the bedroom. Welbourne was in the hallway. J.D. filled him in on the Collinsville house.

"Soon as the men get ready," Welbourne said, "I'll send somebody out to look over things in Collinsville. You sit with Krendle until we have my daughter. Then we'll come back here, relieve you, and toss Krendle out near where we nabbed him."

"What then?"

"We leave. I still feel like blowin' his brains out, but I know you made a deal. If Louisa is harmed in any way, we'll get these bastards back. And I'm gonna start with him." He casually pointed toward the bedroom. "But I'll hold up my end of the deal if she's all right."

J.D. could only agree. "Listen," he said to Welbourne, "I'll kill him myself." He waved a hand toward his face. "Those bastards shot me and gave me these scars. They murdered Minnie Whitwell

. . . a beautiful young mother. They almost killed your daughter and the only reason she ran away was because I made her. She was ready to protect young Thomas with her life and she did. You can rely on me to do right."

"I think I can, Mr. Daugherty, but now we've got to see about getting my Louisa back."

"You're right. I'm gonna go back and babysit Krendle. When you've scouted out the place in Collinsville, I'd like to know how you're gonna pull off gettin' her back. When do you think you all are gonna go?"

Welbourne smiled for the first time since they nabbed Krendle. "It'll have to be at night, Mr. Daugherty—we'll have to ride at night."

J.D. caught his little joke about night, skin color, and just being in Collinsville after dark. Many Oklahoma towns had sundown laws whereby black people had to be in their houses or outside the town limits after dark. But Welbourne's joke was even more nuanced: Klan members often called themselves night riders.

J.D. went back into the bedroom with Krendle. "Krendle, we're gonna keep you here until they get back with the girl. I just spoke to Welbourne. I think you better spend your time in prayer, beggin' the Almighty that she's still there and we get her out safely."

"We made a deal," Krendle pleaded.

"True," J.D. said quietly, "and I hope I can live up to my end of the bargain."

"What do you mean, 'hope'?"

"I mean that if something has happened to the girl and one of the men comes back here and shoots you dead, I'll be sorry that I couldn't uphold my end of the deal."

Krendle started to struggle again. "Goddammit, let me go! You promised." He wrestled with the rope for a while, threw himself backward on the bed, and gave up again. He began to weep under the blanket.

"Get a hold of yourself, Krendle. I'll do my best not to let them kill you . . . but first I have to know something." J.D. pulled him back into a sitting position on the bed.

After a few moments Krendle asked, "What do you want to know?"

"Tell me something. At some point the morons that run the Klan must have discovered that Welbourne wasn't in Klan hands. Why did they keep the girl? Why didn't they just kill her? Or cut her up or whip her? Or have they already done it?"

"We didn't know nothin' about Welbourne. Like I said, they took the girl because they thought they could get Welbourne to confess to Bryant's killin'. Nobody elst knew about it. Since McSimmons asked me to let the boys into the jail to snatch Welbourne, I thought it was gonna be some knights a-comin'. And I saw a white man's wrist—I swear I did! I figured that some of the boys were doin' the same with McSimmons runnin' things. See, McSimmons is a muckety-muck in the KKK. And everybody kept mum. The boys thought that Welbourne might have been hid away or that he got lynched and nobody left his carcass out. I ain't seen nobody in a while to ask. Nothin's been goin' on in a long time. I thought they snatched Welbourne to beat him up a bit and let him know that the Klan was in charge. Maybe even let him see the girl. Maybe show him that the Klan can get to her anytime it wanted. I just thought the boys who nabbed the girl lost touch with the guys who grabbed Welbourne. McSimmons might have been handling one outfit with the left hand and the other with the right. Get what I mean? McSimmons betrayed everybody, and he's gonna pay."

"Hell with McSimmons. Are you sayin' that one outfit in the Klan doesn't know what another might be doin'?"

"Yeah. It sometimes works like that."

"So, this has been goin' on for nearly a couple weeks without the right hand knowin' what the left hand is doin'?"

"Yeah, it's like that. We're a secret organization."

"You're a deaf, dumb, and blind organization. Well, Krendle, that's right up there with the dumbest thing I ever heard. You keep secrets from each other?"

"Have to. Somebody might spill their guts on the activities. Or somebody might be a stool pigeon. You gotta be careful."

"It seems like you people are workin' against each other. I'm glad to hear that the Klan ain't as all-powerful as you fellas say it is." J.D. stopped the flow of conversation to light a cigarette from his gold case. He took a deep drag and expelled the smoke slowly. "You ever see the girl?"

"No."

"How many you think are still with her?"

"Probably just one guy. From what I hear, they been takin' turns. And she keeps real quiet."

"How are you treatin' her?"

"I hear that she's okay. She eats regular. They bought her some dresses. Nothin' very pricey, but good enough. She cleans up and keeps herself up."

"I have to warn you, Krendle, if anyone of them has—"

"No," Krendle interrupted. "Nobody touched that girl in a carnal way. They want her happy so's to get her daddy to confess."

"Why was a confession so important?"

"Good reason to finally move the niggers out. See, our goal is to keep 'em boxed in or move 'em out of the country. Who was that fella a few years back who wanted to take all of 'em back to Africa?"

"Garvey."

"Yeah. He had the right idea. He even met with our Imperial Wizard, Ed Clarke, last year. That was before he stepped down. They should want to keep to their own places. And we just want to help 'em do it."

"Clarke didn't step down, he was thrown in the can for fraud. Besides, Oklahoma's already got laws keepin' Negroes in their own areas. Oklahoma's even got all-Negro towns."

"Well, the Klan don't think that's enough. Land is the most important thing, and they been takin' up too much. Injuns take up a lot of land too. And this is a white man's country. Won it fair and square. Besides, the jigs been takin' up jobs that white men could have. They're tenant farmers too."

"You know that's all bunkum. Tenant farmin' is bad news, and damn few Negroes make any kind of good wages. And Indians have had their land stolen out from under them. The Klan's crazy. You people are crazy."

"Well, ain't none of 'em real Americans. This land was made for the white man."

"The Indians were here first. Tulsa's a Creek word. This whole area was Creek land."

"They lost it to white men. This is white man's country."

"What about Catholics and Jews?"

"They ain't exactly white."

"Well," J.D. said with finality, "I'm Catholic, and you can go to hell." He got up and walked out. He saw Welbourne in the front room.

"I've had about enough of talkin' to that idiot. Can you have one of your men tie him to the nightstand and gag him while he's at it?"

"I think, Mr. Daugherty, any one of my men would take pleasure in doing so."

»«

Welbourne's men had parked their two automobiles fifty yards down the road from the house. Dressed in their usual old-fashioned driving slickers, sack masks, gauntlets, and goggles, each man gingerly climbed over the white rail fence and quietly made his way to the front porch. Welbourne himself walked boldly through the gate and went directly to the door; his men would stand against the wall while he pretended to call on those inside the house with a message.

He rapped on the door lightly, figuring that whoever was inside would be on the alert for intruders of any kind. The door wasn't opened, but a man behind it whispered gruffly, "What you need?"

"Got a message from Fred," Welbourne said in a low voice. "Jess here?"

"Naw," came the answer, "he's out for a walk."

Welbourne quickly drew his Colt .45 service automatic and simultaneously kicked in the door with his left foot. In a rush, he and his men came through the door, threw the guard to the floor, and spread out. Welbourne called out, "Louisa . . . Louisa!"

The answer came quickly. "Daddy!"

Welbourne rushed into one of the back rooms. He emerged seconds later with his arm around his daughter's shoulder. She was crying, and he probably was too, albeit under the flour-sack mask.

The man on the floor ceased struggling immediately. One of Welbourne's men had his knee in the man's back and his free hand pushing the guard's face into the wood floor. His other hand held a .45 automatic to the back of the guard's head. "Name?" he said.

The guard said in a muffled voice, "Sooles . . . Phil Sooles."

"Who else is here?"

"Nobody."

"All right, Mr. Sooles, you're goin' for a ride."

Two men quickly pulled Sooles to his feet, bound his hands, blindfolded him, and led him out the door.

Welbourne and his men searched the house and found a cache of rifles, shotguns, pistols, and boxes of ammunition. He even found three sets of Klan robes. Since there were only four of them and Welbourne stayed with his daughter and the bound Sooles, it took four trips to move everything out to the automobiles. The cars were overloaded with loot and two extra passengers, but they rolled steadily south toward Tulsa. The whole rescue only took about ten minutes; they had taken a longer time loading up the automobiles with the Klan's weapons and robes. Everybody involved in the raid was exhilarated. The raid had cost the Klan a great deal in weapons and prestige. Its two most important prisoners were free.

>«

J.D. was sitting on the porch swing, nervously waiting for news from the rescue party and, as was his wont, knuckling his moustache. Four men had gone in the automobiles. Before leaving, Welbourne had explained that they'd all learned how to conduct these kinds of small raids in France. Welbourne had taken part in a number of flying raids to take prisoners, knock out machine gun positions, and toss explosives in the wire. "Our captain was a white man." Welbourne chuckled to himself. "He didn't know much about us and would send us out at night because he thought the Huns wouldn't see us coming. 'Course we sweat and have skin oil so we had to cover our faces in mud anyway." He chuckled again and added, "The Germans didn't know what hit them." Welbourne's face grew serious. "That's the way we're gonna get my daughter back. Hit 'em fast and hard enough, and it only takes four or five men."

The two automobiles pulled into the front yard. The men began to quickly unload both Sooles and the cache of weapons. Two Mr. Smiths came out to help. Welbourne and Louisa stepped up on the porch to greet J.D.

"Hello, Mr. Daugherty," Louisa said with a bright smile. Her father, his mask pulled up, was simply beaming. "Well, J.D.," he said, "everything worked like a Swiss watch. No trouble, and my baby's fine."

"Let's get inside," J.D. said, following the two men carrying Sooles through the front door. Welbourne's prisoner said nothing. J.D. could see that Sooles was literally stiff with fear.

As soon as Welbourne showed Louisa to the kitchen where a stew was cooking, he returned to the parlor, pulled off his hat, goggles, and mask, and looked into J.D.'s eyes. "We took the Klan's rifles and a couple of pistols from the house. I don't know if we'll need them or not, but it's good that the Klan doesn't have them anymore."

"I saw. That's what I thought too," J.D. said. "I might keep one of them. I saw a .38 police special that I think I'll keep at the office."

"Sure, J.D. Take what you want. I'm sure my men will divide up the spoils, so to speak."

"Yep, I guess. I see you collected a few of their robes or whatever they're called."

Welbourne chuckled a bit. "Yes, yes," he said, "we might have a bit of fun and burn them. Like they burn their crosses."

"That's a good idea," J.D. said with a smile. Then J.D.'s mood turned serious. "Is Louisa going to be okay?"

"I think so. She told me they treated her well." He paused. "Mr. Daugherty, I want to thank you for all you've done."

"Don't think twice about it," J.D. replied. "What will you do now?"

"I plan to leave Oklahoma. This place has turned into a hell on earth for our people. I have to find a place where Louisa can grow up without having to fear walking down the street. Up north somewhere or maybe in California, I suppose. They'll be looking for me here. What about you? Fred and Mr. Sooles back there . . ." Welbourne gestured toward the back rooms. "They might identify you to their comrades."

"You've taken enough precautions to make sure they haven't seen my face. I'm not scared of their hooligan friends. Krendle is still under the blanket, so he can't identify me. Your new prisoner is presently gonna have the fear of God put into him. What's his name?"

"Sooles."

J.D. smoothed his moustache and said, "I plan to have a short conversation with both of them before I leave. I'll simply tell them that your men will come for them in the middle of the night if they so much as breathe a word of this incident. I'll give them a story to tell. They'll go back to Tulsa and be Klan heroes. They'll tell about how they were attacked and fought off your men. They'd rather tell that tale than say that they were outsmarted and overpowered by us."

"I see what you mean. When you get done, sit down with me and my daughter. She'll want to thank you."

"I will. Now let me get back to see our two captives."

J.D. walked toward the back of the house. Once in the hallway, he opened the first bedroom door he came to. He looked in and saw two of Welbourne's men with their masks pulled up above their faces. He recognized one of the men from that meeting with Welbourne in his first hideout. But as soon as J.D. had opened the door, the other man had quickly pulled the flour sack back over his face. "Sorry," J.D. said as he shut the door. J.D. had inadvertently seen that the man who pulled the flour sack down to cover his face was white. And the white man was none other than Little Bill Shelby.

Chapter XIII

DEAF BOB

Hoolie was poking at the meager fire George Charging Horse had built. He'd told George that he didn't think making a fire was a good thing to do. After all, George, Harold, Chester, and Hoolie had busted out of jail and stolen a good horse. Additionally, they had been named as murderers or accessories to murder. Hoolie was more concerned with the jailbreak and horse theft charges; he knew that he had not committed murder and, given time and the right circumstances, could prove it. Hoolie was sure that all of Anadarko—if not all of Caddo County—was looking for them. And they had made some pretty powerful enemies.

George and the Boyiddle brothers appeared unconcerned about what Hoolie perceived as a dangerous, even deadly, situation. "Take it easy," Chester had said when they'd picketed the horses. "We're in sight of our mountain—Rainy Mountain. This place is real important, and the white people mostly leave us be here. It's where we ended our long journey from the far north where we were with our friends the Crows. They put up a Kiowa boarding school pretty close by and the Baptist mission church. They tried to change us into white people here, but most of the folks roundabouts followed Big Tree, one of the first deacons in the church. So they didn't really make us into white people. Lots of Kiowas are Baptists, but they're still Kiowas. We're the ones that followed Grandfather Peyote. There's still lots of medicine to protect us here."

Maybe if it was Cherokee medicine, Hoolie thought, *it would feel better.* But as it was, they were still on the run after several days now and still had no reason to feel secure. George had prayed and made a tobacco offering. Harold and Chester went looking around for firewood and even set a couple of rabbit snares with some loose barbed wire they'd found. They were camped on a small creek bed where they could look out over a nearly flat meadow and see the gentle slope of the mountain. It sure enough was a beautiful place.

The serenity of the place made Hoolie much more contemplative. He thought about his situation—the already filed murder and accessory charges as well as the soon-to-be-filed horse theft and jailbreak allegations—and what he could do about it. He found that he was completely at a loss for solutions. Obviously the real killers of Vi Comstock and Frank Shotz had to be discovered. But that might not be enough. The whole system and structure of city and county government was after him and his newfound Kiowa friends and fellow fugitives. J.D. was right. Anadarko itself needed a thorough cleaning from the top down. That was indeed the only way to get them off the hook.

George came and sat down by Hoolie, looked off toward the mountain, and began a muted conversation. "My friend," George said in a low voice, "I know you're worried, but we'll find a way outta this whole mess. You know the blue soldiers been comin' after us for a long time now. We fought for a time, but they had the guns, the horses, and the numbers of men that moved across our land like a wildfire. My father and uncles fought them, and many Kiowas was sent off to prison in Florida for a while. My father decided to take that step toward a new way of livin'. We took up the Peyote Way knowin' it would be hard. You have to live right even when all them white people want to kill and bury Grandfather Peyote. All's I know is that we gotta keep strong in our ways and strong when the white people come to take everything away from us." He spoke as if these things had happened yesterday.

"I see what you mean," Hoolie said. "It's like us. We try our best to keep away from the white men, but they keep on a-comin'."

"And they always will. I remember one of my uncles tellin' me that the white people are like rabbits, there's so many of them."

"Rabbits. That's like so many of our stories. Rabbit—we call him Chisdu—is always trickin' 'Possum or Wildcat or Deer or whatever and causin' mischief."

George laughed. "Causin' mischief. Maybe 'rabbit' is a good name for white men."

Harold walked over, leaned down, and spoke in Kiowa to George. In turn, George translated for Hoolie. "We should probably find some place to hide better. Being out in the open might not sit well with some of the people out here."

"Where to?" Hoolie asked. He was becoming weary of being on the run and staying with his friends' Kiowa relatives or hiding out in tree stands or hay barns.

Chester raised his eyebrows. "Why don't we go over to Deaf Bob's cabin?"

"Might be a good idea," said George. "Cover that fire and get the saddles on."

"Who's Deaf Bob?" Hoolie asked.

Harold answered while kicking dirt on the tiny fire. "He's a o'd white man who married a Comanche lady. She died on him a ways back. He used to be in the cavalry. He fought us and the Comanches and the Cheyennes. Then he got married and got out of the army. He took to prospecting. Says there's gold out here somewheres. He's kinda crazy now, but he's always ready to help out the Indians around here. Give us a place to go easy for a spell."

"Why 'Deaf Bob'?"

"Well, he got in a fight down in Texas with some white men, and four of 'em held him down and cut off both ears. Those Texas white people are pretty harsh. Anyways, all the Indians around here took to callin' him Deaf Bob 'cause he ain't got no ears. He still hears pretty good, but the old folks liked to joke people."

Hoolie chuckled and shook his head. "I see. You think he'll help us out?"

"Sure will," Chester answered. "Deaf Bob hates lawmen, and he hates all the white people. Said white men killed his wife and took his children. . . . I don't know about his wife—I think she passed away with the smallpox. But his boys—he had three boys—were took off to Carlisle like me and Harold. They didn't come back. I know two of 'em passed away there. Graves are there too. Gotta feel sorry for o'd Deaf Bob. He's had a bad run of luck all his life. He hates the white people 'cause of his wife and sons and 'cause they cut off his ears."

When the horses were saddled, they all mounted and followed Harold in a southeasterly direction. It wasn't long before they came to a creek. They followed the stream for a mile or so and turned into the setting sun. Then they came to a shabby cabin located on a small rise. The sun was down, but there was light enough to see figures and shadows. Harold whispered to his brother, "You better holler—if he can't make out who we are, he might start shootin'."

Chester called out, "Wooooo-ahhh, Deaf Bob, woooo-ahhh."

The rickety cabin door opened and a skinny, bent, unshaven white man walked out into the dim light. Hoolie squinted his eyes to see better. Deaf Bob was dressed in trousers, old brogans, and suspenders. He wasn't wearing a shirt, and he held an old gray wide-brimmed felt hat in his left hand. The man was practically bald, and he had a big gray moustache that drooped down both sides of his mouth. He had no ears, only holes where they should have been. In his right hand was a Colt .45 Single Action Army revolver. "State your business," he said loudly.

"It's George Chargin' Horse, the Boyiddle brothers, and a man—Indian man—name o' Hoolie. Can we talk?"

"Yeah, git down and come inside. Got coffee?"

"No."

"Well . . . I reckon I'll make up some of my own. How 'bout some tobaccy?"

"Got some," Harold said.

"Come on in, then."

They dismounted and tied the horses to a weather-beaten corral that enclosed an equally weather-beaten dun gelding and a tall bay mare. Deaf Bob turned, went into the cabin, and lit a kerosene lamp on a table. Deaf Bob and George occupied the only two chairs in the place, leaving Harold, Chester, and Hoolie to sit on the dirt floor. Harold passed a bag of tobacco to Deaf Bob, who rolled a cigarette. They passed around the sack, and soon everyone was comfortably smoking. Bob got up and started a pan of cowboy coffee on a wood stove in the corner. Hoolie looked around the single room. Deaf Bob evidently lived a sparse life. There were a few blankets in a corner, an old saddle, and a shelf stacked with canned goods. What took Hoolie aback was the number of guns that were hanging on the walls. And there were five pistols lying on the table excluding the one Deaf Bob stuffed into his belt.

After what seemed a long time, Deaf Bob began the conversation. "Ol' Man Nevaquayah was over this mornin'. Told me about you boys." He looked at Hoolie and said, "I talk good Comanche. He told me that you boys broke outta jail and shot up Anadarko. That true?"

"No, sir," said Hoolie. "We didn't shoot up the town. We wasn't even armed."

"How'd you get out with no shootin'? Damn, I wished you'da kilt some of them white men on the way."

"The MacFarland brothers—Clem and Festus—broke out and left us the keys," replied George.

"Why? I thought them two boys was a-gunnin' for you'ins."

"That's right," Harold said, "but they figured that the law would come after us first and leave them alone for a time. They called us murderers, and the MacFarlands was only bootleggers."

"I reckon. You boys better watch your backs—you're dealin' with some pretty bad people. Just as soon kill you as look at you. To tell the truth, I don't know which of them people is the worstest. Them MacFarlands wouldn't stop at killin' their own mama."

"Ol' Man Nevaquayah said that all y'all was on the outs with the sheriff and the police. Tryin' to pin the killin' of that Comstock woman on ya. And Wynn and Collins is cut from the same dirty cloth as the MacFarlands, and that goes for Albright and Tucker too. I know all of 'em. They's lice. But I think the one you boys gotta watch out for is that man from the Indian Office—what's his name? Hughes?"

"That's him," Harold said matter-of-factly.

Hoolie's eyes opened wide with interest. "Sir, I met this Mr. Hughes. He acted like he was tryin' to help out me and my brothers here. I don't understand."

Deaf Bob smirked. "This here Hughes has been workin' with Paul Cooper for years gettin' Indian leases. You know about that business?"

Hoolie nodded. He knew about the leasing business very well. Most Indians who received allotments held them in trust. The federal government had declared Indians who were half-blood or more incompetent to handle their own affairs. So the Indian agents negotiated the deals that leased allotted lands for use by cattlemen and, most recently, by the oil and natural gas industries. "So you think that Hughes is gettin' somethin' outta this leasing business?" Hoolie asked, looking at Deaf Bob.

Deaf Bob chuckled and gave Hoolie a patronizing smile. "There ain't a white man in all of western Oklahoma who ain't as foul as an outhouse in mid-July. 'Cept me."

He paused for a few seconds and added, "Listen. I been out here for years. I got no love for the white people. What I been doin' since my wife passed on is lookin' for Spanish treasure. If I find it, I'm a gonna buy back the land and give it back to the Indians. Lotta people think I'm nuts. But I tell ya, I ain't as nuts as the crazy white men lookin' for the treasure that God put in the ground. It's the oil that makes 'em crazy. And now they's in the business of sellin' hooch to people and makin' them crazy too. But it's all comin' from the same thing. They got to have the land so's they can pull oil and gas from the ground and to hide their damn whiskey and to run their cows. So they lie and cheat and even kill people to keep their hold on the land."

Deaf Bob is beginning to sound like John Tall Soldier, Hoolie thought as he gently rubbed the bruise on his left cheek. Hoolie's good friend John was fond of railing against the white people and purposely picked fights with some of the young white cowboys that hung around the streets of Hominy. Hoolie's mind wandered back to John and especially to thoughts of his wife Myrtle and his soon-to-be-born baby. He needed to get home, and he was afraid that because of all the trouble he'd gotten into, he'd never see his family again. His mind snapped back to the here and now as fast as he fell into the daydreams of his family and friends.

" . . . Even that man that stayed in the tent out to your place was prospectin'," Deaf Bob was saying. He stopped and shook his head with a sad look on his face. "Sorry to hear about that boy," he said.

"Prospecting for what?" Hoolie asked in a soft voice.

"Natural gas. I met the boy—well, I reckon he weren't no boy— but he took coffee with me one day and told me. I came near to shootin' him 'cause he's a white man. But he stood his ground and called out to me. I took him in. I told him that I was lookin' for gold. He kinda laughed and said that's probably easier than grindin' down through the rock out here. He finally said that he'd probably go back home. Yep, natural gas—what else?"

"Why do you say 'what else,' sir?"

"Why, that's the onlyest thing out here to get rich on, 'ceptin' gold. I find some gold and silver every oncest in a while. Go trade it in for a shootin' iron or two. If'n I find a big payoff, I'll give the land back. But right now gotta stay armed to keep the white men away from me. They say I'm touched. Wanna keep it that way. They think I'll kill 'em if'n they git too close. I will too."

Deaf Bob stopped speaking and placed his hand on his cheek. He looked at Hoolie. "What was I talkin' about? Oh yeah. How to get rich out here. . . . Well, cows take up so much room and grass that the ranchers got a hard time just keepin' 'em fed, much less keepin' 'em from wanderin' off to hell and gone. Cost 'em too much in keepin' wranglers around. Besides, them cowboys always seem to get drunk and go bad. Buffalo was better suited to this place. But they killed them off just like everythin' elst."

Deaf Bob paused, took a few puffs off his cigarette, and added, "Oil's gonna play out soon, the rate they're a-pumpin' it. But that young man told me that the gas down there ain't gonna give out for hundreds of years. All you gotta do is git down there, and they say that drillin' through is the tough part and that it'd cost a bunch of money. He did say that your place would be the best place to drill. But the profit would be a long time comin'." Deaf Bob paused for a moment and said, "I'll stick to lookin' for gold."

"You found any lately?" asked George.

"Nope, but I had some good finds a while ago."

"How's that? Where's the mine?"

"I ain't talkin' about diggin' it outta the ground. Well . . . maybe I am in a way. I'm talkin' about gold and silver and such that was hauled betwixt St. Louie and Santa Fe, New Mexico. Big trade route that ran through these parts. I hear tell that your people and the Comanches used to waylay them wagon trains to get the horses. Now, I also heard tell of Spaniards carryin' gold clear from Old Mexico to take part in the trade along the Arkansas, Mississippi, and Missouri Rivers. And they got themselves waylaid on the way. Now, that gold and silver went somewheres. I figure the Indians didn't have much to do with it. Too much to carry, and they was consentratin' on the horses and useful stuff like cloth and guns and such. So they either left it out there somewheres, or the Spaniards hid it out afore they got kilt. I just know that it's out here."

"You got quite a bit?" Hoolie asked, looking around at the number of guns in Deaf Bob's cabin.

"Yeah, but it ain't easy. I recollect one time ol' Ten Bears hisself showed me where him and a bunch of braves took one wagon years ago when he was just a boy. I dug around there and got a small box of silver Mexican pesos. That was a long time ago too. Little bit here and there. Keeps me goin'."

Hoolie looked up at the ceiling deep in thought. After a few seconds, he looked at Deaf Bob and said, "What can you tell me about Hughes?"

"Well, I don't like him much. He's a white man. He came out here about six, seven years ago ready to do some good. But like everybody else, he got caught up in makin' money offin' the Indians. Him and Cooper and Rohrbach."

"What about Violet Comstock?"

Deaf Bob smiled and snorted contemptuously. "Violet Comstock," he began, "well, she's kind of in the middle of this whole mess." He thought for a moment. "Well . . . she *was* anyway. Any of you boys see her body?"

They all shook their heads.

"Well, it'd help to find out just how she got killed. One of 'em plugged her."

Chester spoke. "The laws told Hoolie that she got killed with a .44-40 like the rifle he used to carry."

"Those fools don't know nothin'. They was tryin' to pin it on you. When was she killed?"

"Late at night, 'bout four, five days ago. They threw her in the creek near the livery," Hoolie said.

"Did you boys hear any shootin' in town that night?"

"No," answered Harold.

"That might tell you somethin'," Bob said with a sneer. "The Comstock woman always carried a piece. And her cook does too. I think there'd have been some shootin'."

Deaf Bob stood and walked over to a corner and sat on a pile of blankets. "I'm gonna hit the hay now. You boys can spread your blankets out on the floor and sleep with a roof over your heads for a while. The laws ain't gonna bother you here. They know what I'll do. And don't worry 'bout gettin' caught. I got plenty of places to hide you all out. And if'n they find us, we'll take a stand together. Stake ourselves out like in the ol' days."

The old man looked up at the wall as if contemplating what he was going to say next. After about a minute, he said with a focused look cast directly at Hoolie, "You boys oughtta think about goin' after each one of them scum one or two at a time. 'Cause if'n you go after all of 'em at oncest, they's liable to gang up and kill ya. The white people always come after you'ins in a bunch. Now, Ol' Man Nevaquayah tol' me that the MacFarlands gone to ground 'bout a mile north of that ol' sweat bath ya'll used to run on Hog Creek. Ya'll could sneak up on 'em and rub 'em out. That'd be a couple less shootin' irons aimed at your heads anyways." He chuckled to himself and unceremoniously lay down on his side, pulled a blanket over his head, and was soon snoring.

Hoolie wasn't ready for sleep. His swollen face still hurt, and he didn't want to go through another fight with the likes of Festus, Clem, Marty, and Moe. He had already seen too much gunplay in this investigation. And he sure didn't want to get into a gunfight with the MacFarlands on their own ground, wherever that might be.

Hoolie's mind wandered. He began to picture in his mind a number of interconnected threads of deceit, strife, greed, stupidity, and cruelty woven together in a spider's web of politics, racial hatred, and criminality. All at once, he stopped thinking about the intricacies of the mystery, and a slight smile came to his face. As he lay in the dark on the dirt floor of Deaf Bob's cabin, an old story came to him. This wasn't a dream, but it was a reminder of how things, as John always said, came together—like how Deaf Bob related all the seemingly disconnected threads of Anadarko's turbulent politics and crookedness. Hoolie thought of his grandma's story about how Spider stole some of the sun's fire and brought it back to earth so that everyone could benefit from its warmth in so many ways. The story itself was intricate. Many animals tried to get a part of the sun. They all failed and, unfortunately, were burned in their attempts. When Buzzard tried carrying back the part of the sun he had captured on his head, he was burned. That's why Buzzard has a naked red-colored head. Robin burnt his breast in the attempt to obtain a bit of the sun's warmth. Only Grandma Spider was able to capture part of the sun by using her web.

Hoolie would have to think of a way to net in his own web some of the principal characters in this complicated tale of lies, murder, and corruption. Cooper would have to be confronted. But the rest of them—the MacFarlands, Wynn, Albright, Tucker, Collins, Hughes, even U.S. Marshal Peeler—would have to be sorted out. Hoolie simply didn't have an Indian army big enough to do the job of capturing every one of them. Hoolie smiled to himself. He was actually thinking about kidnapping Hughes and Peeler, two government men. That would really start another Indian war. But that had happened not too long ago when Chitto Harjo and the traditional Creek people at the Old Hickory grounds got into a gun battle with the marshals over some meat stolen from a white man's smokehouse. Everyone knew that the Creeks didn't steal the meat, but the whites wanted to break up the encampment at Old Hickory. The wounded Chitto Harjo eventually had to flee for his life.

Hoolie had only the Boyiddles and George to count on. And maybe Deaf Bob. Something Deaf Bob had said got him to thinking about Violet Comstock. Deaf Bob was probably right about the way she had been killed. Digging up her body was not going to happen. The dream he'd had about the moving dead hand came back to haunt him. He would not live out that nightmare. Perhaps he could find someone who had actually seen her body. A wound from a .44 or .45 is easy to recognize, and Hoolie had seen plenty of wounds that had been inflicted by other caliber bullets fired from Mausers, Lugers, Springfields, .22s, .38s, .45s, .32s, Enfields, and everything in between. The war, terrible as it was, taught him many things.

Hoolie had to think of a way to get J.D. back to Anadarko again. As a white man, J.D. could ask questions and look into things that would get an Indian thrown in jail or even killed. Maybe J.D. could bring in the prohibition agents. And J.D.'s contacts with the Shelbys could force Oklahoma state authorities to bring some law and order back to southwestern Oklahoma. But what happened to J.D.? Why wasn't he in Anadarko? And what happened in Tulsa? J.D. was supposed to be getting Jack Walton to send in the troops to clean up Anadarko. Hoolie had to get a hold of J.D. at any cost. He began to think about how Grandma Spider had captured part of the sun. It would take him another three days to pull a plan of action together.

Chapter XIV

GRANDMA SPIDER'S WEB

Telegrapher Eugene Johnson had opened the station just in time to look out the window and see one of the oddest sights he had seen in his two years working at Gotebo Junction. At first he thought that the Oklahoma August morning heat had gotten to him, but no, it was a real rider mounted bareback on a nice-looking tall bay mare. The rider wore blue trousers with yellow stripes, beaded Indian moccasins with long leather fringe at the heels, a chambray work shirt, beaded suspenders, and a big gray Mexican sombrero pulled down over his ears, with a tall eagle feather sticking upright from the beaded hatband. He had two pistols hanging from his waist and a double-barrel coach gun across his lap. Johnson quickly looked around his office. If the rider intended to rob him, he had nothing in the office with which to defend himself. He had the cash left from yesterday's receipts in a desk drawer. It only amounted to about five dollars. But then again, people had been robbed and killed for far less money.

The rider pulled up his horse, dismounted, dropped the hackamore rope to the ground, and walked casually into the telegraph office. The well-trained horse stood quiet and still. Eugene Johnson grew more and more apprehensive.

When the rider pulled off his sombrero, Eugene immediately recognized the man as Deaf Bob, a local legend known as a hermit, treasure hunter, and crank. Bob propped the shotgun against the wall and dug into a shirt pocket, extracting a wrinkled piece of paper. He attempted to straighten out the folded paper, gave up, and handed the note to Eugene. "I want you to send this to Tulsa," Deaf Bob growled.

"Okay," Eugene said with a big smile intended to disarm Deaf Bob both emotionally and physically.

"Got the name and place on the paper," Deaf Bob said. His eyes narrowed as if the telegrapher were about to reject the job.

"All right, sir. The name's Daugherty, that right?"

"Reckon so."

"Yes, sir. Long message. I'll get to it after I've straigtened things out here first." He looked around the room as if to find something missing or untidy in the already neatly appointed office.

"Get to it now, boy," Deaf Bob said menacingly, "I ain't got all day."

Eugene caught Bob's threat and said, "Yes, sir. I'll send it now." He turned to the desk with the telegraph key.

"Just a minute," Deaf Bob said. "How much?"

"It's pretty detailed—I think this'll be two bits."

"That's a lot of money for some words." And under his breath, Deaf Bob said, "Don't let your finger get tired with all that hard work," as he counted out twenty-five cents in nickels and laid them on the counter. He then dug into his other pocket and pulled out another piece of paper. "Got another telegram for ya," he said.

"What's that one, mister?"

"This'un goes to Anadarko. To Marty Albright at the court-house. Can you do that?"

"Sure can," the telegrapher answered.

"That another two bits?"

"No, I'll do it for another nickel."

"That'll be good," Deaf Bob said as he laid another nickel on the counter.

As Eugene turned to tapping out the messages, Deaf Bob opened the door to leave. Eugene called after him, "Thank you, sir." He finished sending the first message and, with a smile, added the name of the sender: "Deaf Bob."

The sender himself had picked up the hackamore rope and mounted the mare, turning her head toward Rainy Mountain.

≫«

Alone in his flat that same evening, J.D. sat with a telegram in his hand, staring at the cheap small commemorative plaster bust of

Abraham Lincoln he'd bought in Chicago on the one hundredth anniversary of the great emancipator's birthday. The telegram was from Gotebo Junction, of all places. The message itself was almost as indecipherable as the name of the town, crossroads, depot, train switch, or whatever it was. Not only that, but who the hell was Deaf Bob? It had to be from Hoolie because the message asked him to get to Anadarko at once and bring federal reinforcements. That could only mean that Hoolie was in serious trouble with local law enforcement. Hoolie had a propensity for jumping into the middle of trouble. Instead of looking for weak spots to exploit or singling out one thing to work on, Hoolie took on everything all at once. Hoolie had once said to J.D. that a mechanic had to listen to what the whole car was telling you; fixing one thing at a time would only mean that the automobile's owner would just keep coming back again and again. J.D. had shaken his head in disbelief. The whole idea of running a business was to keep customers on the hook. Hoolie just replied that keeping a fish on a hook meant that you couldn't ever eat it. The two men had a way of communicating that was indefinable. Rarely did they agree on anything philosophically. In fact, just about everything one said didn't make sense to the other.

As soon as J.D. received the telegram, he started making telephone calls. He called Mrs. Shelby, Sam Berg, and Lieutenant Finch at the police station. They all agreed to get in touch with various people in the Prohibition Unit, the U.S. Marshals Service, and an obscure agency within the Justice Department known as the Bureau of Investigation. Heading that particular office was, unbelievably, an old friend. J.D. had known William J. Burns as a no-nonsense investigator with a competing detective agency. Bill Burns eventually became the director of the agency and was asked by the Harding administration to lead the Bureau of Investigation. J.D. put in a personal telephone call to Burns and got immediate action. Burns's young underling named Hoover set up meetings in Oklahoma City with his own agent, a U.S. marshal, and a prohibition agent. J.D.'s immediate reaction was to ask if Hoover was related to Herbert Hoover, who had arranged relief efforts in Europe after the war, or to the people who made the vacuum sweepers. Burns had laughed and said that his assistant was not related to either one of them.

Mrs. Shelby arranged, through her own and her husband's contacts, to talk to Governor Jack Walton. Walton refused to send guard troops to Anadarko because it sounded to him as if the trouble there had to do with Indians, and that was a federal problem. J.D. thought that Governor Walton had committed a serious political mistake by bucking Mrs. Shelby. The Shelbys were just too big to say no to. If he ever got into trouble, having Big Bill Shelby as an ally would be invaluable. If Big Bill was an enemy or even simply indifferent, it could cost Jack Walton his entire political career. J.D. wouldn't bet two cents on Walton's reelection.

Lieutenant Finch had contacted both the Caddo County sheriff's department and the Anadarko city police only to find out that Hoolie and a group of Indians had broken out of jail and were "on the warpath." Sam Berg turned up nothing except that prohibition agents were looking into a liquor hijacking that had occurred recently near a place called Owl Creek just outside Anadarko. Hoolie was right in telling J.D. to bring in federal officials; state and local law enforcement agencies weren't going to help.

J.D. was going to catch the evening train for Oklahoma City and then go on to Anadarko the next afternoon. He would, with Bill Burns's influence, pick up a couple of federal agents along the way. He stopped staring at the Lincoln bust and started packing for the trip. As he was throwing a few pairs of socks into his cardboard suitcase, someone lightly tapped on his apartment door.

J.D. pulled open the door, and, to his surprise, Elizabeth and Little Bill Shelby and their half sister Rose Chichester were standing in the hallway. All were flawlessly groomed and businesslike, and all wore their most solemn expressions. With a dubious look on his creased face, J.D. asked them in, gave them seats, and asked if they needed drinks. Little Bill wanted nothing; Rose and Elizabeth asked for water.

"To what do I owe this visit?" J.D. began. "You took me by surprise."

Little Bill spoke first. "Mr. Daugherty, I want to give you my personal check for two hundred dollars. It is, of course, a token of my and my sisters' personal thanks for helping Theodore and his daughter. Our father will pay your regular fees plus a more substantial bonus."

Elizabeth reached into her purse and pulled out a gold cigarette case. She took a cigarette out, stuffed it into a three-inch gold cigarette holder, and asked for a light. "Mr. Daugherty," she said after taking a puff off the newly lit cigarette, "I also want to thank you. You were most patient with us." She paused and looked at Rose. "Rose and I wanted to see Louisa alive, and you made that happen."

Rose followed Elizabeth in expressing her thanks and added, "I see you're getting ready to travel, is that right?" Since her terrible ordeal two years before, she was much more familiar with J.D. than either Elizabeth or Little Bill.

"Yes, miss, I'm heading to Oklahoma City tonight to meet with some federal investigators. Then I'll head to Anadarko."

"The federal offices might be closed down," Little Bill said offhandedly.

"Oh, why is that?"

"You haven't heard?" Little Bill commented. "President Harding died today."

"No, I haven't heard. But I'm sure these men will meet with me anyway. It pertains to a case of great importance."

Rose asked, "Is Mr. Smith involved?"

"Yes, he is."

"I suppose it has something to do with Indian people, no? Why can't they be allowed to live without constant meddling in their lives?"

"I agree with you, miss, and that's exactly what Mr. Smith and I are trying to stop. It has to do with the liquor trade."

Bill looked anxiously at J.D. "Mr. Daugherty, I wonder if I could speak to you alone?"

"Certainly. If you'll excuse us, ladies."

J.D. led Bill into the small kitchen and made sure the swinging door was still before he spoke. "What can I do for you?"

"Mr. Daugherty . . . J.D. . . . I know you saw me the other night. I've been helping Mr. Welbourne for quite some time. I was with the party that aided in his escape. That's why Krendle thought the KKK had kidnapped Theodore from the jail. He must've seen something that made him assume that I and my partners were white."

"After I saw you with the sack off your head, I assumed the same thing." J.D. paused, took a deep breath, and continued, "It's a dangerous business you've gotten yourself into. Now that Mr. Welbourne is free, I hope that you'll give up breaking folks out of jail and raiding the Klan."

"I hate to say this, J.D., but dealing with the Ku Klux Klan in this way gives me a great deal of satisfaction. I firmly believe they killed my Minnie, or at least provoked those murderers to take her life. I loved her, and taking some kind of revenge on the Klan is something I feel very good about."

"Bill, why don't you use your money and your contacts to put them out of business."

"Believe me, I've been trying—if only for my son's sake. But they're getting stronger. Right now they're influencing our state legislature into impeaching Jack Walton because he dared to go against them."

"I've heard that. Hopefully that won't happen."

"Well, whatever happens, I'm going to fight this scourge. And that's what it is." Bill looked down and said in a whisper, "I don't think anyone knows how much I loved Minerva. Thomas is hers and mine, and I intend to open every door that I can for him. It's been two years, and I still haven't been able to move ahead. So I'll fight the Klan and the hatred it inspires as long as I live. And I'll find those men who killed her and bring them to justice."

"Son," J.D. said with sadness in his voice, "I think I fell a little bit in love with Minnie myself. But maybe we should go after those men who killed her. With all my heart, I wish that I could have done somethin'—"

"J.D., stop right there. You tried to save her, and you and Louisa saved Thomas . . . and I know that you nearly lost your life in doing so. We'll go after them together."

J.D. turned to leave the kitchen and said under his breath, "That we will, my friend. That we will."

The two men came back into J.D.'s living area to find Elizabeth and Rose sitting in silence. Rose spoke to them. "Are you two harboring secrets? I think we've earned the right to be let in on the ins and outs of this business. I've seen it all, and we have certainly had a part in getting Louisa back. I don't think we should be kept in the dark. If you're keeping secrets to protect us, you'd better find somebody who needs protecting—because we don't."

J.D. knuckled his moustache in embarrassment. He looked at the two women and put a crooked grin on his red face. "Ladies, I do apologize. You're absolutely right. You have a right to be let in on this—"

Bill cut in, "J.D., I don't think—"

J.D. turned. "Yep, the cat's comin' out of the bag. Sorry, son, but they have to know—especially if you and me are gonna try and find Minnie's murderers. It isn't so much a matter of fighting the Klan, it's a matter of finding the slime who killed her. We can't possibly fight the whole organization by ourselves. But I'm a detective first and foremost. I should be able to find out who these people are."

Elizabeth interjected, "Listen, William, I support you. We'll find those bastards."

J.D. nodded. "Ladies, you might not know this, but your brother has been clandestinely working with and joining Theodore Welbourne's . . . what would you call them? Maybe raiders? Whatever they are or were, now that Mr. Welbourne and Louisa are safe, Bill isn't going to participate in raiding the Klan anymore. I want to join in a pact with you three. Keep everything secret, and we'll all concentrate on finding Minnie's killers. Is that agreeable?"

Elizabeth, Rose, and Bill all nodded. Elizabeth spoke up first. "The only thing I'm concerned about, Mr. Daugherty, is what do we do with them once we find out who and where these murderers are? Unfortunately, we live in a state that seems to have been overrun by the Klan. Can we bring them to justice in Oklahoma? I'm not so sure that we can."

"We'll find a way," said Bill. "Oklahoma is the oil industry. We're calling our city the oil capital, aren't we? Well, Shelby Oil has both the resources and the influence to get things done here."

"That's true only to a certain extent," Rose said. "It all depends on how Shelby Oil applies its influence. We support Jack Walton in trying to eradicate the Klan, but it looks as if the legislature might very well impeach him."

J.D. looked with admiration at the three. They were very astute young people with their eyes on the future. "That's very true, Miss Chichester. The fanaticism is at this point outweighing reason. Right now they're making the argument that Governor Walton has overstepped his constitutional bounds. But he's overstepping to make sure justice will be done and people can be safe. I truly believe that the Klan represents chaos and anarchy. I just hope that reason will prevail. . . ."

J.D. looked at his watch and announced, "Ladies and gentleman, I've got to get ready to go. I have to meet a young man at the train depot in Anadarko tomorrow. In fact, I've got to catch the late train to Oklahoma City tonight. So, I wonder if I could impose on you to wait while I finish packing and take me to the depot?"

Bill answered, "Of course."

»«

George Charging Horse and Hoolie rode on horseback to one of George's relatives' house near Mountain View. They were greeted with warmth and offered a much-appreciated meal of fry bread, pinto beans, and boiled meat. After the meal—which was a feast compared to the fare they'd been eating for the past few days— George and Hoolie went with George's cousin Richard for a smoke near the well. Most of the conversation took place in Kiowa, and so Hoolie sat on the ground, contented to smoke and relax for a change.

After a while, George turned to Hoolie. "Everythin's settled. Dickie's gonna let us have his automobile for a time. We'll go into Anadarko and take care of things we gotta take care of. Then we get out quick."

Hoolie looked around for an automobile and saw nothing.

George pointed with his lips to a shed that Hoolie guessed was a smokehouse. "It's in there," said George. "You know how to drive it?"

Hoolie smiled. "Yep, I'm a mechanic. Been drivin' for years. I can drive anything."

"Good. Let's go."

The drive to Anadarko was relatively pleasant with the Ford's top down. The afternoon heat was dying, and the sun was low in the western sky. Hoolie turned the Model T down the main road and into the long driveway of the funeral home just outside of town.

Hoolie killed the motor and said to George, "I hope the undertaker don't shoot us before we get to talk to him."

"No, Mr. Merriot's a good man. He's been puttin' on Indian funerals for some time now. He's got a cousin married to a Caddo lady. They go to a lot of Indian doin's 'round here."

They exited the car, walked to the front porch, and pulled the bell. The door was pushed open by a woman dressed in a severe black dress. She pinched her lips together and then spoke. "May I help you?"

"Yes, Mrs. Merriot," George replied with his hat held centered on his chest. "Can we talk to your husband?"

"Yes, please come." The two men moved toward the door. Mrs. Merriot looked at them and said, "And wipe your feet. Don't want dirt tracks on my clean floor."

"Yes, ma'am," they said in unison as they followed her into a parlor.

"Please sit," she said. "I'll get my husband."

It wasn't long before a portly man with heavily oiled dark hair and a pencil-thin moustache entered the parlor and sat down in a cushioned rocking chair.

"Boys, how are you?" he began. "I haven't seen you, George, in quite some time. Have things been cleared up between you and the sheriff's office? I suppose so, or else you wouldn't be sitting in my parlor." Mr. Merriot gave a slight chuckle and turned serious. "I reckon you're here to view Mr. Poolaw. He fixed up quite nicely and is in the viewing room. He was quite a character and so widely recognized as one of the old chiefs."

George looked surprised. "I didn't know. Was it Crawford?"

"No, Mr. Charging Horse, it was Crawford's older brother Ezra."

"I see," said George, "but we're here to ask you about something else. This is my friend, Hoolie Smith from over near Arkansas. . . . You see, we haven't straightened out everything with the sheriff. We need to find the people who killed Miss Comstock, and Mr. Smith here thinks you can help us."

"Are you boys wanted still?"

Hoolie butted in. "Yes, sir, we are. But my boss is a detective outta Tulsa, and we're being railroaded because we found out about the liquor trade here and about the crime that's tearin' this city apart."

"Well, Mr. Smith, you're right about the corruption, but our city is still based on a solid tradition of faith and community spirit. As a man who sees death on a daily basis, I know that all of us—red and white—are but corruptible flesh. All our souls are together united under the everlasting love of God."

Hoolie didn't want to hear a sermon, but he held his peace and smiled evenly. "Yes, sir, I believe that too. But I'd really like to ask you a question about what you've seen as an undertaker."

"Mortician, if you please, Mr. Smith."

"Yes, sir, mortician. Mr. Merriot, did you bury Violet Comstock?"

"Yes, I did. Poor woman . . . although 'fallen,' you might say . . . she was killed most brutally."

"How was that, sir?"

"I was told that you, Mr. Smith, shot her with a .44 caliber rifle." He paused and pulled a deep frown. "But I'm inclined to think differently. Otherwise I would have had my wife call the sheriff's office. That is, since you've told me that you haven't cleared this up with Sheriff Wynn."

"Thank you for that, Mr. Merriot. But why don't you think she was killed by a .44?"

"Well, for one thing, the hole in her chest was smaller than a large-caliber bullet. There was no exit wound in her back. Also, the hole wasn't exactly round as I've seen bullet holes before. Close, but not exactly."

"Did it enter at an angle?"

"No, that isn't what I mean. I mean that the wound itself wasn't caused by a bullet. It was a puncture, sure enough, but something different. I've never seen a wound like it."

Hoolie bore in. "You didn't retrieve the bullet, did you?"

"No. I was told to embalm and bury the body."

"Could the wound have been made by a knife or a tool of some kind?"

"I thought so at the time. But I couldn't have told what kind of tool. It wasn't a knife because it would have made a slit in the skin. It could have been something like a large ice pick, but I've never seen an outsized ice pick like this had to have been. It was big for an ice pick."

"No, sir, but I think I know what it was. That's all I needed to know. You've been a great help. And when this whole mess is cleared up, I'm coming back to thank you personally. When we leave, I would appreciate it if you'd wait 'til after sundown or so, call up the sheriff, and tell them that we were here and were heading to the train depot." Hoolie rose from his chair, paused for a moment, and extracted a piece of paper from his shirt pocket. "I'd like to ask another favor," he said. "Please take this." He handed the mortician the paper.

Mr. Merriot looked at it carefully, gave Hoolie a puzzled look, and put the note in his suit coat pocket. "I'll do it," he said, "but I won't abet a crime."

Hoolie turned to George. "We gotta go."

Both George and Merriot looked stunned. Hoolie cocked his head to one side and said in a low voice, "Don't worry. I know what I'm doin'."

George asked Mr. Merriot to take him to see Mr. Poolaw. When they returned, Hoolie thanked the mortician once again and walked to the door. George followed, and they walked to the Model T, cranked it up, got in, and drove off. Driving away, George asked, "What was in the note, brother?"

"Not much," Hoolie replied. "I just asked him to make another telephone call for me."

≫«

Harold and Chester watched the courthouse from the shadows of an alley across the street. They had tethered four horses to a picket rope stretched between a drain pipe and a wooden rail located in the back of the pool hall a short distance down the alley. Hopefully they would do what they came to do in a big hurry. Hoolie had said that, at some point during the early evening, the courthouse would empty itself, and the Boyiddles would be free to take one or two people captive. The brothers were actually smiling in anticipation of carrying out the assignment of kidnapping Sheriff Wynn, Marty Albright, Moe Tucker, or all three.

Chester yawned, took off his hat, and rubbed his face with his free hand. It had been a long day. Just as he placed his hat on his head once again, the front door of the courthouse burst open. Out ran several officers. They ran to a couple of parked automobiles and roared off toward the other end of town—toward the funeral home. Harold looked at Chester. They pulled Deaf Bob's pistols out of their belts and walked calmly to the courthouse front entrance. From there, they met no opposition and ended up in front of Sheriff Wynn's office door. Harold whispered, "This is it." He kicked the doorknob with the flat of his foot, slamming it open. Wynn sat with a look on his face as if he were looking at Jonah's great fish getting ready to swallow him whole. Chester put the muzzle of his Colt .45 against Wynn's head and said, "Let's go, sheriff, you're a-comin' with us."

Wynn's face turned bloodred. He growled through tight lips, "You're gonna regret this, you goddam blanket-ass gut eaters. I'll get you for this."

Harold put an evil grin on his face. "Wynn, you'll be lucky to get through tonight alive. You better just pray we don't tie you to a spit and hang you over a low fire."

Wynn started to scream, but Chester shoved a dirty bandana in his mouth. Harold took a short bit of rope that had been tied around his waist, pushed Wynn face first over the desk, and bound his hands behind him. The Boyiddles took Wynn by his arms and walked him out the front door. No one stopped them. Nor did they even see anyone about. When they got to the horses, they lifted Wynn into a saddle, tied his feet in the stirrups and his waist to the saddle horn, mounted themselves, and rode off. The capture was timed perfectly. Most of the deputies and the police were off somewhere, and the most dangerous of the sheriff's men, Marty and Moe, were chasing the shadows of Hoolie and George Charging Horse. They couldn't believe their luck.

>«

Khōn Charging Horse hadn't entertained a white man in his tipi in years. The last time was two summers after the Kiowas had put away the Sun Dance in favor of Chief Peyote. He was then a man of strength and knowledge, and the white man was gathering information about his people so that he could write books about them. Charging Horse liked the idea of recording Kiowa history and especially of recording Kiowa ways and knowledge. It seemed that very few young people wanted to learn about the old ways. How to hunt buffalo. How to look at the stars in order to determine when the old ceremonies were to take place. How a person could conclude when the buffalo hides and wool were ready by looking at certain plants on the prairie. How the Sun Dance was done properly and how the Tia Piah had been the village police during those summer months when all the Kiowas and the Apaches camped together and when the Sun Dance and the great buffalo hunts took place. That white man wanted to hear the songs and see the things in the medicine bundles.

Now the white man in his tipi was a captive. George sat by the door flap with a pistol in his lap, not saying a word. The white man was equally silent, even after George had untied him and pulled the bandana from his mouth. Still, Charging Horse offered him the pipe. The white man refused and looked more sullen than ever. George's wife and eldest daughter came to give the captive soup and fry bread. But he looked scared—as if a piece of fry bread would choke him and the soup drown him.

After some time, the white man began to speak to George. "Charging Horse," the man said angrily, "I'm the goddam sheriff of this county. You kidnapped me and are holding me at gunpoint. You're gonna fry for this. Now everybody knows you're a criminal and that you killed and buried that young man. You cut him up, by God, and I'll see you executed for it. That's not to mention that your friends killed Violet Comstock. If I could throw the switch on the electric chair twice on you, it wouldn't be enough to pay for what you did."

George sat patiently through this diatribe, and after the white man finished, he translated the speech into Kiowa for his father. Khōn Charging Horse was impressed. The white man spoke that harshly in a tipi while his hands were tied and two of his enemies were present. Making those threats when he clearly was in no position to do so meant that he was either exceedingly brave or just plain crazy. Maybe Harold and Chester should have beaten him up a little to make him more docile. As it was, the white man continued to make threats. It came to the old man that this white man at least thought he could command others without ever earning that respect or position. In the old days, a man had to be generous, truthful, courageous, and, at the same time, humble to be a leader. Apparently, in the white man's world, a person didn't have to be any of those. The white man in Khōn Charging Horse's tipi was so obviously greedy, deceitful, cowardly, and arrogant that it was inconceivable to him that the man could be in a position of prominence among people. Strange . . . very strange indeed.

Finally George spoke to the man in English. Khōn Charging Horse made out some of what he said.

"Sheriff Wynn, by tomorrow we'll really know who killed both Mr. Shotz and Miss Comstock. And you yourself might be in the jail for sellin' liquor to Indians and to the white people. I reckon you know that that's against the law too.

"We're gonna do this kind of like in the old days. I'm a peyote chief and my father here is an old-time chief. We're gonna bring everybody here in this sacred place, this tipi where Grandfather Peyote's ceremonies are done, and we'll have some high-placed white lawmen to help us figure out what to do with you'ins. You'd better get used to the notion that we—me, Harold, Chester, and Hoolie Smith—didn't kill nobody.

"Now you better keep still and get some rest. Harold, Chester, and Mr. Smith are gonna round up some more white men that we gotta talk to."

≫≪

The Boyiddle brothers were happily carrying out another kidnapping. But this was not really a kidnapping by their lights. They were going to Alonzo Hughes's house, located within the city of Anadarko, to ask him politely to come to the Charging Horse allotment. As the local Indian agent, he should be more than willing to come at any time to hear about the misery that plagued those whose care had been entrusted to him. If he didn't want to come, Harold and Chester were prepared to force the issue. They had been disappointed that they'd missed taking either Marty or Moe. And so they didn't want Hughes to escape their grasp.

The pair sauntered up to the front door and pulled the bell cord. The door was answered in seconds. It was Hughes himself. Chester spoke for the brothers. "Mr. Hughes, we've got a problem out to the Chargin' Horse place. You've got to come."

Hughes was actually horrified to recognize the Boyiddle brothers. "But . . . but . . . you . . ." he spluttered.

Harold quickly said, "Don't worry, Mr. Hughes. The sheriff is out there waitin' on our agent. That's you." Chester put on a knowing smile because Wynn was indeed tied up in Khōn's tipi on the Charging Horse land.

"Does this have to do with you two being charged with murder? If so, your case cannot involve my office. So please go away. I have no jurisdiction."

But Hoolie had armed the brothers with a legalistic argument that, because of what had occurred among his wife's people, he knew well. "Mr. Hughes," Chester began, "you've heard of the Major Crimes Act, haven't you?"

"Of course, but what has the law got to do with me? If you're trying to bluff me into going, you'd better think again."

"It's not a bluff, sir," said Harold. "The murder happened on Indian land that's held in trust by the government . . . the federal government. And you're our agent."

Hughes broke in. "Violet Comstock was killed in town."

"Is that so?" Harold said. "How do you know?"

"Don't try to bully me. Now go away before I call the law."

"Can't do it," said Chester. "By law, the federals come first. And there's another U.S. marshal, a federal prohibition agent, and an investigator from the Department of Justice there."

"How do you know all this?"

"We're Indians," Chester said defiantly. "We better know the laws you'ins threw at us. Now you gotta to come."

Hughes reluctantly turned inside. "You wait here," he commanded. "I'm gonna go, but this better be good. It'll go in my report that you threatened me."

"We didn't threaten you, Mr. Hughes," said Harold.

Hughes turned back and said, "Maybe not physically, but by threatening me with the law and intimidating me."

"The law's the law," said Chester. "The law shouldn't scare you if you've done right by it."

"No more double-talk. I'll get my hat and coat."

Hughes went inside for a few minutes. When he reappeared in the doorway, he had bent a fresh collar around his neck and had put on a coat and a straw boater. "I'll drive my car," he said. "That way I won't have to stay long."

"Good," said Harold. "Give the horses a rest."

"I didn't invite you to ride with me."

"It'd be nice if you did," Harold replied.

They rode in silence toward the Charging Horse allotment—Chester sitting next to Hughes, Harold in the backseat of the new Chevrolet. Suddenly, about a mile outside Anadarko, Hughes threw on the brakes. "I'm turning around. I don't have to do this. Get out of my automobile!"

Harold sighed. "Didn't want to have to do this." He pulled out a small .32 caliber pistol—another gun from Deaf Bob's arsenal—and put it to the back of Hughes's neck. "Drive on ahead," he said quietly.

Hughes started to bluster. "You . . . savage . . . by God . . . you'll pay."

"Simmer down, Mr. Hughes," said Chester. "You'll either be a hero to all us poor o'd Indians, or you're gonna be in jail. We'll know pretty soon."

Hughes pulled the Chevrolet into the Charging Horse front yard next to the arbor. George came out of the tipi to greet them. "Good evenin', Mr. Hughes. Be good enough to come inside the tipi. We raised the bottom to get fresh air in and cool things down. Right now it's real nice in there."

Hughes went to the tipi, bent low, and stepped in. When he saw Wynn, his eyes grew large, and he took a deep breath. "What's going on?" he said with a raised voice. "Why is the sheriff tied up? By God, you'd better—"

George, who had followed him inside, cut Hughes short. "Don't start, Mr. Hughes. We can treat you like a guest or like an enemy—there ain't no other way. You can sit with my dad and talk, or you can be hog-tied and gagged. You choose."

Hughes quickly sat down. First, he frowned in his discomfort, then he changed his mask and smiled at Grandpa Charging Horse. "Mr. Charging Horse," he said politely, "how are you?"

Khōn nodded and said simply, "Good, *aho.*"

George sat cross-legged, wiped his hands on his trousers, and said, "Mr. Hughes, my wife is gonna bring you somethin' to eat and drink in a few minutes. We should have everything in place by mornin'. If not, you and Sheriff Wynn will be let go, and the rest of us will go on and go to jail. When a few people get here from Oklahoma City, we'll take care of things."

George got up and exited the tipi. He met with the Boyiddles in the arbor. He looked at them as a father would in sending off his sons to perform some great deed. He had never experienced—nor would he ever experience—what his grandfather had felt when he sent George's father, the young Charging Horse, off to defend Kiowa land and ways, but readying Harold and Chester for this next step in Hoolie's plan to restore some semblance of justice might be as close to that emotion as he was ever going to feel.

"You two ready to go again?"

Harold nodded. George could see fatigue in the brothers, but he could also detect a willingness to get the job done and even excitement in the way they were carrying it out. He was proud, as was his father, to see that being a warrior in the old way was not dead.

"All right," George said, "you'ins go meet Hoolie at the old sweat bath lodge near Hog Creek. I showed him where yesterday. He'll tell you what you're gonna do. Take Mr. Hughes's automobile. We'll keep him company."

Chester got behind the wheel and set the spark. Harold gave the Chevrolet a crank, and the engine sparked to life. He got in, and off they rattled, leaving behind a dust cloud that hurt George's eyes.

>«

The bent willow framework of the sweat lodge was centered in an open hard-packed piece of ground near the creek itself. Close by was a big fire pit and several stacks of rocks. Hoolie felt as if he could use a sweat and the peace it brought to his mind and body before doing what he had to do on that day. The brothers were telling him about the place and about the old days before warriors set out on raids or to fight in the great pitched battles. The members of the warrior societies would thrust their lances through a ring in a cloth bandolier worn across their bodies and stake the lances into the ground. The warrior would be staked out like that until he was killed in battle, or until the battle was won and the enemy driven off, or only if another member of the same society came and physically pulled the lance from the ground, releasing him. Hoolie could hardly imagine having that kind of courage. But he had also heard about the things his own ancestors did on the battlefield, not to mention the valor he had witnessed in the trenches. What they were going to do today took a great deal of bravery. Because he and the Boyiddle brothers were facing danger not only from the people they were going to take captive but also from local law enforcement should they fail to do what they had to do with those caught in the spider web he'd woven. The white people would think of what he started as an Indian uprising, and they always dealt harshly with Indian uprisings.

All that Chester, Harold, and Hoolie were hoping for was that Mr. Merriot at the funeral home had placed the other telephone call Hoolie had requested. If he did, then their intended prisoner would be motoring along a predictable route. The three would place themselves in a position to intercept the vehicle and take the captives back to the Charging Horse place. After that, they would wait until the final strand in their intricate web had spun out.

They took one car—Richard Charging Horse's—and left Hughes's Chevrolet behind to be retrieved later. Hoolie had scouted the place where he thought they might set up their ambush. It was a rocky red dirt road bordered on one side with a brush-covered ditch and on the other by a barbed-wire fence and more heavy brush and high grass. One man would stand in the middle of the road to stop the automobile while the other two would spring from the brush alongside the road and puncture the vehicle's tires so that the target of their ambush could not drive away or run somebody down. It had to be done swiftly, with no gunfire or bloodshed.

They piled up a few sticks of firewood and a few layers of brush over the road. Rather than a roadblock, it made it look like the dirt road simply ended in a pile of brush. Hoolie was to take his station on the other side of the brush with one of Deaf Bob's Springfield '03 rifles cradled in his left arm. Chester would crouch in the ditch while Harold lay in the high grass close to the fence. The darkness would hide them anyway.

Hoolie heard the big black Packard first. "Get ready!" he called. As the automobile approached, he saw Eric Cooper driving while his father Paul was sitting in the touring car's rear seat.

Things began to happen almost all at once. Eric Cooper braked the Packard just as Hoolie raised his rifle. Before either

Cooper could act, the Boyiddles rushed from either side of the road to puncture a tire on each side with their hunting knives. As soon as they stabbed the tires, they let go, dropped, and rolled themselves back into the brush and the ditch. Eric threw the car into reverse and stepped on the accelerator pedal. The flat tires couldn't get good traction in the dirt and rocks of the old road. The Packard stopped. Paul Cooper appeared to reach for something. Hoolie fired a bullet into the air and yelled, "Cooper, I'll shoot you dead if you try anything!" Cooper sat back and raised his hands in the air.

Eric Cooper was putting the car into first gear and back into reverse, trying to get better purchase on the road to turn the car around. Hoolie yelled again, "Stop it, Eric! Stop the car!"

He wouldn't stop. Finally, he jerked the car into first gear, popped the clutch, and pressed hard on the accelerator. The car lurched into the brush pile, and one of the logs jammed itself into the front axle. Eric tried to put the car in reverse again, but all he did was grind the gears. Hoolie immediately suspected that he had wrecked the clutch assembly and disconnected part of the transmission linkage.

"Stop it, Eric!" yelled Hoolie. "You're not goin' anywheres."

Paul Cooper reached and picked up a pistol that was evidently lying in the backseat. That's when Harold popped up beside the car again and put his own pistol to Cooper's head. "Put it down . . . put it down," Harold whispered. By that time, Chester had pulled a gun on Eric, who put his head against the steering wheel and shouted, "You win, goddammit! You win."

"Okay, get out of the car," Harold commanded.

The Coopers, father and son, had looks of unadulterated hatred in their eyes. Eric was carrying a long bayonet that Hoolie knew belonged to a Springfield '03 of the type he had been issued before going to France. "Still carryin' the army's surplus?" he asked Eric.

"No, this was my brother's," Eric said. They found nothing on the elder Cooper, but the gun that he'd tried to pull while in the backseat was a Smith & Wesson revolver that was probably thirty or forty years old if it was a day. While going through the Coopers' Packard, they found a sawed-off pump shotgun that Hoolie called a "trench gun" and a Colt .45 automatic pistol, also army issued.

"Looks like you boys done cleaned out an arsenal," Hoolie said flatly. "How come you didn't bring along a machine gun or a Browning Automatic?" He was only half joking.

Harold pushed Eric and said, "Let's get movin'." The Coopers sullenly trudged ahead of Harold and Hoolie, with Chester leading the way back to the car they'd borrowed from Richard Charging Horse. When they got to the car, Chester took out a lariat and began to truss the Coopers up. They put Eric in the middle of the backseat between Hoolie and Harold. Chester drove with Paul Cooper in the seat beside him. Hoolie held the .45 on the back of the front seat nearly touching Paul Cooper's head. They drove in silence over the bumpy, rocky red roads all the way to the Charging Horse home.

》《

The afternoon of the next day, J.D. and his traveling companions—a U.S. marshal, a Bureau of Investigation agent, and a prohibition officer—all stood on the Anadarko platform waiting for someone to contact them. The four men looked somewhat alike. All wore celluloid collars and bright ties with stickpins, all were portly, all wore straw boaters, and all of them had light-colored linen or cotton suits on. They all were surprised when an Indian boy about thirteen years old approached them asking specifically for "Mr. Dartee."

"That's me, young man," said J.D. "And who might you be?"

"I'm Benson Tsotigh," he said, fingering one of the straps on his bib overalls. "I'm here to drive you'ins back to my Uncle George's place. They're all there waitin' for you. Who's these men?"

"Well, Mr. Tsotigh—I hope I pronounced your name correctly?"

"Close enough."

J.D. smiled broadly and began again, "Well, Mr. Tsotigh, this is Mr. Adam Shuler, the finest prohibition officer in the state, and this is Mr. Bill Hess of the U.S. Marshals' office." J.D. paused for effect and swept his hand to the last man to the boy's right. "And this is Mr. Horace MacGregor who works for the Bureau of Investigation in the Justice Department."

"Okay," Benson said, "but we're gonna need two cars to get us out there."

"Why's that, son?"

"Well, Mr. Smith and my Uncle George say that you gotta bring the mayor out too. So, with all your cases and things, we'll need two cars."

"You're right, young man. You got it figured out. We'll get the other automobile—think no more about it."

Benson turned and walked toward a parked black Model T touring car. He got to the automobile, reached in by the steering wheel, set the spark, and cranked up the motor. He got behind the wheel and raised his chin as if to say "let's go." J.D., Shuler, Hess, and MacGregor practically ran to the automobile and squeezed in. Benson took off with his full load of cardboard suitcases, suits, hidden pistols, and sweaty, beefy men.

"Where we headed, Mr. Tsotigh?" asked J.D.

"Courthouse, get the mayor," replied Benson. "I heard he always works late. I reckon we'll take the mayor's car when we get him, that right?"

"That's a good guess."

"He won't go easy."

"That's why I brought some federal lawmen, Mr. Tsotigh. We'll ask the mayor to come nice and polite like."

Benson Tsotigh expertly parked the Ford in a space in front of the courthouse. The four men walked in the front double doors and asked the officer at the front desk for the mayor's office.

"He's upstairs, can't miss it."

J.D. led his companions upstairs and walked through the glass-paned door clearly marked "Mayor's Office."

J.D. turned to his companions and said facetiously, "This must be the mayor's office!"

The men laughed and crowded through the door. They stood before a middle-aged woman, her red hair piled high. She had a pencil roosted on her ear and a pair of pince-nez perched on her nose. The woman looked and acted like an overworked secretary-receptionist who clearly should have been allowed to go home hours ago. She looked over the nose pinchers, removed them slowly, and let their chain retract into the round pin she wore on her chest. After scrutinizing the men for a few seconds, she said, "Gentlemen, may I help you?"

"You sure may, miss," J.D. said. "We need to see the mayor."

"I believe he's busy right now."

"That's fine," Marshal Hess said, showing his badge. "We'll see him right now."

"But you can't—"

"Looks like we can," J.D. said as the four walked into Mayor Rohrbach's chambers.

Rohrbach's eyes widened considerably when they entered and closed the door. "Who are you? Is that you, Daugherty? What does this mean?" he blustered.

"Well, Mr. Mayor," Hess said, flipping out his badge once again, "we'd like you to come with us, please. We have to iron out a few things regarding certain business practices that take place in this city. We're going to Mr. George Charging Horse's house."

"Am I being arrested?"

"No," MacGregor answered. "We just want to talk about a few things."

Agent Shuler rubbed his hands together and said, "Mr. Mayor, I'm a prohibition officer, and there are a few things that have gone on in the past few days that have come to the attention of my unit and Internal Revenue."

≫≪

Moe Tucker and Marty Albright recruited three youngsters who had helped them load and store booze to form a posse to go against the MacFarlands. They knew exactly where to go. At least the telegram to Marty said that Clem and Festus would be at the site of an old moonshine still. The shed that had protected both the equipment and the product from the elements yet stood and could be expected to provide sleeping quarters for men on the lam. It was no fortress, and so Marty and Moe could expect to level the entire structure with the firepower they had brought. They fully expected to sneak up on the building, riddle it with bullets from the two Thompsons they carried, and massacre anyone hiding therein. Without the least bit of guilt or hesitation caused by fear, they intended to do murder that night.

Chapter XV

IN KHŌN'S TIPI

In order to feel even the slightest breath of air on this steamy-hot evening, the sides of the big tipi were rolled up, leaving about three feet of the tipi poles exposed. Nine men sat around its circumference, a small fire for light rather than for warmth burned in the center of the circle. The four Kiowa men—Harold, Chester, George, and the elder Charging Horse—sat calmly discussing the course of the evening in Kiowa. The Boyiddle brothers held rifles in their laps. Sheriff Wynn and the Coopers had been untied and were all glaring with unmitigated hatred at Hoolie, the four Kiowas, and Hughes in turn. Hughes said nothing, and Hoolie, with a .45 automatic pistol in his lap, sat chewing a stem of grass, wondering why the chiggers weren't attacking anybody in the tipi.

The Charging Horse family had fed all of them and handed out blankets all around so that each person could nap when he felt like it. None felt like it. The Coopers, Wynn, and Hughes protested long and hard against their abduction and the fact that they were being held against their will.

Although they all glimpsed the automobiles in the distance, it was George that said, "Somebody comin'—two cars."

Hoolie and George got up and walked crouched in a clockwise direction to exit the tipi. The Boyiddle brothers gripped their rifles. Hoolie and George went to the arbor to await the arrival of the two automobiles.

As Benson Tsotigh and his passengers and Mayor Rohrbach and J.D. pulled up next to the arbor, Hoolie raised his hand in greeting. Benson jumped out of the car and immediately went into the Charging Horse home. J.D. had driven the mayor's automobile. The rest of the men got out of the cars and stepped into the arbor.

J.D. made the introductions. He had obviously explained to Rohrbach that Hoolie, George, and the Boyiddles were not to be treated as escapees from the county jail, but as free citizens acting in the aid of law enforcement. The fact that three officers from the Justice Department and the Prohibition Unit and a private detective from the city of Tulsa accompanied him frightened the mayor into a kind of enthusiastic compliance with getting to the bottom of the crime spree that had engulfed his city. The fact that he was an indirect participant in the graft and corruption of the liquor trade was conveniently forgotten—at least for the time being.

Even though the tipi was very large and had been used for several Native American church ceremonies, it felt cramped with fourteen men, some of whom were very broad shouldered, sitting inside the tipi poles. It felt like an important meeting, even a ritual of some kind.

After everyone was more or less comfortably seated, the Coopers and Wynn began to protest again. In answer, Harold and Chester moved their rifles menacingly. Harold raised his voice, "Shut your traps, boys, and listen." They all finally held their peace.

George, acting as the host of the meeting, began. "I want to say that we brought you all here to solve the problems that are plaguing our people and your town, Mayor. These gentlemen"—he paused to look at Shuler, MacGregor, and Hess individually—"are from the government in Washington City. They're law officers and were asked to come here to stop the crimes.

"Now, we don't like havin' guns in this tipi. This tipi is where we hold our religious meetin's. This is the place for Jesus and for Grandfather Peyote, not guns. But . . ."—he looked at the Coopers and Wynn—"we took these men because they have to answer for what they done, and the guns have to be here to keep them here safe. . . . I have to tell you about how things worked in the olden times with our people. That way, you'ins will understand why we did this in that way. This is the good way, the way we brought back peaceful times.

"Mr. Hoolie Smith is gonna say somethin', and I'd ask you'ins to hear him out. He's a humble man. I've talked to my father here, and he thinks that in the olden times Hoolie Smith would be a chief. In our way, a chief has to be brave, truthful, generous, and humble. Mr. Hoolie Smith has been those things. Hoolie, would you speak?"

Hoolie looked up and began to speak in a low voice. "I want to thank George and his father for helpin' clear things up. I want to stop the killin's. I want to stop the liquor from hurtin' Indians. And I think we can do that tonight. . . . J.D., there's somethin' you don't know yet. Violet Comstock was killed in Anadarko several days ago."

J.D.'s jaw dropped for a second. He began to bluster angrily. "What . . . how? . . . By God!"

"I'll tell you about it. But it takes some time," Hoolie said sympathetically. He knew that J.D. had taken a shine to Vi Comstock.

"When J.D. and me came here, we was lookin' for Mr. Shotz. We didn't know that he'd already been dead and buried for a while. I got to look around his campsite and found a couple of papers that said he was lookin' for oil and not going into the cattle business. He was probably workin' for Big Bill Shelby, but he mighta been lookin' on his own. Talkin' to Deaf Bob the other day, I found out that he'd said that there was natural gas under the rock, but it'd cost a lot of money to get out.

"So it seems that Mr. Shotz was tellin' other people that there might be a treasure under the ground, but that it'd take drillin' to get it out. Deaf Bob thought that Mr. Shotz just gave up and was goin' back home—the cost for drillin' that far down was too much.

"But Paul Cooper here said somethin' to us first time we talked to him. Said that he was gonna put Shotz in touch with Mr. Hughes to work out a deal with some of the Indian families who owned the land. That never happened. Why didn't he do it? Shotz knew he had the backin'. Everybody who was in the oil business trusted him. They'da put up the money. I think Mr. Cooper was lyin' about contactin' Mr. Hughes because he already knew Mr. Shotz was dead."

"Hold on there," said Cooper.

"No. You hold on. Let him finish," J.D. commanded.

Hoolie looked at his hands, saw a bit of dirt, and rubbed them together. He continued. "Right at the time I didn't put anything into Cooper sayin' he'd contacted Mr. Hughes. That came later, after I found a couple of scraps of paper out to Shotz's campsite. The papers had been tore up. But one of 'em had 'pest place to dri' written on it. Since Shotz was a geologist lookin' for oil, I guessed it was sayin' 'cheapest' place to drill. Now, if Cooper was puttin' in the word with Mr. Hughes like he said, why would Shotz want to just pull up stakes and go back home? Shotz was on to somethin'." Hoolie looked at Hughes and asked, "Did Mr. Cooper call you about meetin' with Shotz?"

"No. He didn't," Hughes replied immediately.

"Didn't figure he did. Shotz wanted to get the money together to drill for gas. He really wasn't gonna leave. He'da called up people in Tulsa. They trusted him 'cause he was a good geologist. Shotz told Deaf Bob that the Chargin' Horse place was the best place. I think that he meant the cheapest.

"Cooper complained about George here bein' an old fogey. That usually means an Indian who don't give in so quick to what the white people want out of 'im. Cooper wanted control of the Chargin' Horse place for the cattle business and to store Wynn's or Collins's whiskey. Cooper might be temperance, but he knows that liquor brings in the money. He knew—just like Deaf Bob knew— that Shotz had his eye on a deal with George. So he wanted Shotz and George outta the way. Killin' Shotz and guttin' him was to make it out that Indians did it. White people seem to think that we did that sort of thing. You always hear about us scalpin' people and burnin' them alive and throwin' babies agin trees and such. George'd be locked up or put in the electric chair, and Cooper could work a deal with Mr. Hughes to get control of the land. I seen it done too many times out where I'm from."

"You're not bringing me into this sordid affair," Hughes said emphatically.

"I can't say you're outta it. You let the liquor trade go. You coulda called in the prohibition office to help you. But you didn't. I don't know if you're in with Wynn and Cooper, but you ain't workin' against 'em."

Hess, MacGregor, and especially Shuler, the prohibition officer, stared menacingly at Hughes, who, in turn, sat back and closed his mouth.

Hoolie continued. "Now we come to something else. Mayor Rohrbach and Violet Comstock met with J.D. to clean up the town. The plan called for me and J.D. to ruffle all the feathers in town and then, through J.D.'s contacts in Tulsa, to get Governor Walton to call out the national guard and declare martial law in Anadarko like they did in Tulsa.

"That didn't work out too good. J.D. got cut and called back to Tulsa. And the local laws decided to go after me and Miss Comstock. That was even before she tipped us off to the shipment that was gonna be hijacked down on Owl Creek. Somebody musta told about the tip-off, but even before that, somebody went after J.D. I looked at J.D.'s cut. It wasn't deep or dangerous. It caught him between the inside of his arm and his chest. It was a long blade sharpened on both sides. Not too many blades like that, unless it was a old-timey sword.

"I think it was a bayonet. I saw lots of guys in the trenches grind down and sharpen their bayonets on both edges. They said it made it easier to stick into somebody and pull it out again. I don't know about that, but the infantrymen would do all kinds of crazy things with their weapons thinkin' that it'd make 'em better to kill somebody with. Like some of the guys would carve Xs on the tips of their .45 ammunition and make 'em into dumdums. They thought that carving Xs would make the bullet flatten out and kill the enemy quicker—as if a .45 don't do enough damage as it is. Those guys were always doin' somethin' to their knives or even to their entrenching spades. One sergeant sharpened the edges of his entrenching tool and wound barbed wire around the handle except where he held it. The wire was to keep the Germans from grabbin' the handle when he swung it at 'em. I think you'd be surprised at all the things you make up to kill other people. The government even give us things that could kill somebody real easy.

"A bayonet sharpened on both sides would be good for butcherin' somethin'—like Mr. Shotz was butchered. Now, Marty Albright and Moe Tucker had been in the trenches. So I thought of how and why Marty woulda done those things. And he mighta been, but I never heard that he came within a mile of Shotz. Same with Moe. Besides that, I don't know if Marty coulda cut up a guy like that. That takes more than just defendin' yourself in combat. Marty could kill people real easy, but his eyes said that he couldn'a rolled out somebody's insides like you would a deer's. Moe probably coulda—he's mean as hell. But I don't think he was around

Shotz either. But the Coopers knew him. And to tell you the truth, I don't think Paul Cooper coulda done it either."

"Hool," J.D. said, "what do you mean? It sure sounded like you were after Cooper."

Paul Cooper jumped up from his seat on the ground. He took a menacing step toward Hoolie. Chester raised his gun and said flatly, "You take one more step, and I'll shoot you in the leg. You'll be hurtin' so bad you ain't gonna have another word then. Now sit."

Fear clouded over Cooper's face, and he resumed his seat. Eric Cooper stayed seated the whole time. He didn't make a move to help or to hinder his father. His face revealed nothing. He didn't look as if he cared if Chester had killed Paul Cooper dead on the spot. Hoolie appraised Eric Cooper once again. The young man's eyes weren't dead; they were cold yet alert and frightening, like those of a copperhead. A rattlesnake would warn you before he struck. You could smell a cottonmouth and hear him hiss before he bit. But a copperhead was small, swifter, and never warned you before he attacked. Eric was a copperhead and should be treated with just that much more caution.

Wynn and Hughes began to protest. "I'm tired of this," said Wynn. "You can't kidnap a duly-elected county official, by God, and as soon as I get outta here, I'm gonna throw all of you in the pokey. That's right"—he looked squarely at Shuler, MacGregor, and Hess—"you're gonna get paid back too. I don't give a damn about you bein' from the government. Washington City don't have no jurisdiction over me, by God. This is a free country. You can't have Indians decidin' to do what they want with a free white man. That ain't right."

"I want a lawyer," cried Hughes, "and I mean right now. You people have no jurisdiction here at all."

J.D. put an ironic, twisted smile on his face. "I'll remind you, Sheriff and Mr. Hughes," he said, "that right now we're on Indian land. These federal officers are investigating crimes committed—"

MacGregor finished J.D.'s point. ". . . Washington does have authority, Mr. Wynn, especially in cases involving Indians. Mr. Hughes, you above all should know this. In case you didn't know it, Indians have rights too. I'm an investigator with a federal bureau. Marshal Hess and I work for the Justice Department. That means we've sworn an oath to uphold the Constitution. Mr. Shuler is with Prohibition Unit and took the same oath. We will all see that justice is done. So please sit still and hear the man out."

"I'm a federal official as well," Hughes said, "and I protest being held here. These people have kidnapped me, and I have rights too."

"Just a minute, Mr. Hughes," Hoolie said. "Chester and Harold Boyiddle, as Indians, requested that you come here and act as their agent. And you came as your duties called for. They mighta been armed, but you had to come as part of your duties. Please hear us out. I'll be done in a bit."

"I'd like to ask a question," Shuler said.

"Yes, sir," Hoolie answered.

"You served in the war, didn't you?"

"Yes, sir. U.S. Army."

MacGregor looked seriously at each man in the tipi. "So let's all get this straight. Mr. Smith has been a citizen of the United States as a result of the 1919 Indian soldiers and sailors act. Probably before that, if he was allotted land. So he can act as a private citizen to contact law enforcement. And he did. My colleagues here and I are actually acting on a complaint. We have jurisdiction as federal officers investigating crimes on Indian land and in violation of the Volstead Act. So we'll all sit and listen while Mr. Smith explains his complaint."

"Thanks, Mr. MacGregor," Hoolie said. "Like I said, it's just gonna take a few minutes more. Hear me out. . . . All right, now." He paused, gathering his thoughts once again. "I was sayin' that a bayonet coulda killed Mr. Shotz. I think I know where he was killed. That'd be over by his camp down by the creek bed. That's on Chargin' Horse land. But to move his body over here where Mr. Chargin' Horse found him, it had to take a couple of men. Maybe more. They had to occupy the Chargin' Horse dogs with meat or scare 'em off some way. I think they put out some beef for the dogs. This sounds pretty bad, but I looked at the creek bed and didn't find anything. The wolves and coyotes musta took care of what was left of Shotz. And the dogs around here woulda kept them away too. The killers had to carry Shotz and put him under that tree like George said. Then they rubbed out their footprints with brush. Seems pretty clear that they wanted to kill Shotz and make it seem like the Chargin' Horse family did him in.

"To do somethin' like that, you have to be pretty close to your partner. To my way of thinkin', that takes relatives. The Coopers fit the bill. Eric is a strong young man. He don't appear to be too smart. And I can see in his eyes that he don't think that other people are worth stayin' alive. But most of all, he told me and J.D. that he had all his older brother's equipment from the war. And I think that his brother meant more to him than any other person in the world."

"You got no proof!" cried Paul Cooper.

But it was now Eric Cooper's turn to get to his feet in defiance. "You don't know nothin' about my brother!" he bellowed. Chester motioned him down. Eric sat without uttering another word.

"I guess he's smart enough to shut up and keep his peace," George said. He looked at Eric. "Young man," he said, "you're in enough trouble now, so why don't you just let that bad spirit outta your heart. Tell us what happened."

Eric Cooper sat with his knees pulled up. He hung his head and slowly shook it from side to side. "No. I ain't sayin' nothin'," he whispered.

"Leave my boy alone," Paul Cooper said in a low voice. "He don't know nothin' 'cause there ain't nothin' to tell. Now you redskin bastards let us go. You owe me for wreckin' my Packard and for keepin' me here." He looked at the federal law officers. "You people can't keep me here, by God." He looked at Wynn. "Do somethin', you fool! You're the sheriff. You take orders from me. If it wasn't for me, you wouldn't have nothin', let alone that damn badge you carry. Now do somethin'."

"That's enough outta you," said Shuler. Paul Cooper angrily sat back and clenched his fists. "Mr. Smith, please go on with this," Shuler continued. "I'm here because of Mr. Daugherty, and I intend to get to the bottom of all this." He looked around the circumference of the tipi and said, "I know damn good and well most of you are involved in moving and selling illegal alcohol in this state and over state lines. There are going to be some arrests, believe me."

All was silent now. Hoolie began to pick up his narrative, but as he started, the sound of a horse galloping into the yard interrupted him even before he made a sound. George nodded to him and pointed with his lips toward the tipi door. They both rose and exited.

A teenaged boy stood near the arbor holding the reins on a tall buckskin horse. George and Hoolie walked toward him. George asked, "Are you all right, Emmett?"

He breathlessly whispered, "Yes," coughed once, and spit. He looked at George. "I saw it all," he said.

"Before you tell us, I want you to know Mr. Hoolie Smith here," said George. "Hoolie, this is Emmett Tsotigh, one of my nephews. His brother Benson got Mr. Daugherty and the rest at the station house."

Emmett and Hoolie shook hands quickly. The young man dropped his eyes to the ground and started his story.

Fifteen minutes later, Hoolie and George reentered the tipi. Khōn Charging Horse was speaking, and Harold Boyiddle was interpreting. " . . . Those were the days of my grandfather. We solved all these problems in a good way, to set things right again. We didn't take lives except to bring back and fix up what went wrong. . . ." He paused to wave Hoolie and George back to their places. When they sat down once again, Charging Horse looked at George and nodded. George nodded in response and said, "We just had some news from my nephew. I think Hoolie should go on ahead and tell it."

"I think when we came in," Hoolie began, "Mr. Chargin' Horse was in the middle of tellin' you all just how Indian ways sorted crimes and punishment out in the olden times." He paused as if to gather his words. "Cherokee Indians," he said, "had ways of dealin' with crimes too. We had the clan law that settled things. If a person was killed by another Indian, the dead person's clan had the right to take the life of a person in the killer's clan. Sometimes the killer's kinfolks would offer somethin' to settle things, and sometimes the old men of the White Council would step in and settle things. Sometimes a person might be killed, but our Beloved Men would come in and stop the killin's before everything got outta hand. That was the point. To get back to the White Path of peace. Just killin' somebody didn't end it. We had to get back on that road again. Otherwise everything would be outta hand crazy. That would lead to the downfall of our peace with each other. The bumps in the road gotta be smoothed out and life gets back to normal—that's the White Path. It restores everything."

Hoolie looked at the Coopers and at Wynn specifically. "Now you white people just go too far," he lectured. "You kill somebody just to kill 'em for no good reason and not to bring back peace. There's no fixin' things. You think that fixin' things and goin' back to peaceful ways can't be done unless everything and everybody is dead and there's just one man standin' to do more killin'. Just to get your way, you'd kill anybody. Kill just to be killin'." Hoolie's emotions had built to the boiling point. He stopped talking and hung his head. He took a deep breath and said, "It's shameful, just shameful...."

George slowly shook his head in sympathy and, by way of explaining Hoolie's melancholy, said, "Hoolie and me heard somethin' about what happened over near Hog Creek. My nephew Emmett was sent out there to see that the MacFarland brothers got took in. We wanted to know so's we can get everybody down to the courthouse in Anadarko. We sent a message to Marty Albright to go out and arrest the MacFarland brothers. Well, he didn't aim to bring 'em in. Marty went out to kill those boys. We just didn't know that he would be so mean and hate filled.

"Here's what happened. Marty and Moe Tucker and three other boys showed up about a mile away from that o'd moonshine camp over near Hog Creek where the MacFarlands was holed up. They was gonna sneak up on the place. They had a couple of machine guns. Well, Clem was outside relievin' hisself, I guess, when he ran into Moe Tucker. Shot Moe dead on the spot. Then the gunfight started. They killed Clem and started shootin' up the shed. There was a couple of boys in there with Festus. Anyway, a whole lot of shootin' and killin'. Emmett got to his horse and came here. Says Moe Tucker's dead and so's Clem. He saw another two or three go down but don't know if they was killed. We just know that there's probably a lot of bloodshed up there."

Sheriff Wynn sighed deeply. Marty Albright and Moe Tucker were his most important henchmen. With Moe dead, he didn't have the force behind his alcohol trade. Marty would be shell-shocked and beaten if Moe was gone. Wynn immediately tried to save what he could of his own skin. "Paul Cooper done all of this," he cried. "He's been runnin' things—liquor, cattle, controllin' Indian land. The only people who went against him was Collins and the

MacFarlands. Rohrbach and Vi Comstock only went against him when they tried to horn in on the hooch business. See the liquor trade with the redskins makes people rich. You get 'em boozed up, and they sign over the leases."

"Shut up!" Paul Cooper yelled. "I'll see you in hell if you say another word!" He jumped to his feet, and this time Eric followed suit. Chester cocked his rifle. "Sit down," he growled. The years of absorbing abuse by the white people were about to cause Chester Boyiddle to go over the edge. He leveled the rifle directly at Eric Cooper's heart. His brother followed his lead and pointed his weapon at the father. The Coopers stopped and squatted again, both of them looking right and left, back and forth, as would captured animals trying to find an escape route.

"Easy . . . easy," George said soothingly. "Steady boys."

Wynn got in the last words, "You couldn't kill anybody, Cooper. You let your boy do the dirty work."

Harold and Chester relaxed a bit but kept their guns pointed at the Coopers. The elder Charging Horse said something in Kiowa. The Boyiddle brothers put on half smiles and relaxed their grips on the rifles in their hands. Everything went back to a hostile but controlled convention of enemies and arbitrators—the federal officers being the arbiters, and Hoolie the accuser.

Hoolie took up his role more as a storyteller than a prosecutor once again. "Sheriff Wynn, Eric and Paul Cooper, Mr. Hughes," he addressed them in turn. "I can't see how you're gonna get out of goin' to jail for what you done. But we're gonna sit here while I piece this all together. All I want to do is get things back on that White Path I was talkin' about. And to do that, these gentlemen"— Hoolie indicated the federal officers with a sweep of his hand—"are gonna take charge here after I'm done. They gotta know everything before they can do their jobs."

Hoolie sat back and rubbed his chin. He turned to George. "Can I ask what your father said to Harold and Chester?"

"Sure. He said that he would have liked it if they had been with him when he fought the blue coats."

Hoolie smiled and looked around the tipi again. "I'm gonna finish this without bein' interrupted. Then I suspect we're all gonna go back into Anadarko and put a few of you behind bars. We're armed, and you ain't.

"I think Sheriff Wynn just put it all together. The liquor trade around here makes a few people a lot of money, in the end 'cause, like my friends here and my o'd friend John Tall Soldier always says, things are always tied together. The liquor makes people crazy, and then they agree to almost anything, including signin' leases with white people that don't make sense. Mr. Cooper runs the liquor trade and gets cheap leases, and Mr. Hughes helps him out. Wynn helps, along with Marty Albright and Moe Tucker, to keep the liquor trade in their hands.

"Now, there's two things that keep interferin' with Cooper, Hughes, and Wynn makin' money and takin' over everything in Anadarko and the county. That's the Peyote Church and Police Chief Collins. So Cooper goes to war against Collins and his pals Festus and Clem MacFarland. He also goes to war against the Chargin' Horse family because they're convertin' their people to the Peyote Way. And the Peyote Church is legal by federal law. The Peyote Way means walkin' down the path of peace and away from the liquor.

"So now Cooper tried to kill two birds with one rock. George Chargin' Horse is steppin' on his liquor trade and on his gettin' control over more Indian land. When Mr. Shotz shows up and Cooper figures it out that he's thinkin' that the Chargin' Horse place is a good place to drill for gas, he sees a chance to get that land on lease and to get shed of the Peyote Church around here. Gettin' rid of the Peyote people would help his liquor business. But he's still got his war with Collins. Cooper's happy that Harold and Chester beat up Clem for musclin' in on the trade, but it also lets him know that he's losin' control of his plan to get more leases on the cheap and increase his trade in alcohol.

"Then me and J.D. come to Anadarko lookin' for Mr. Shotz. Violet Comstock either don't like Cooper or don't like the war that's goin' on in Anadarko or wants to horn in on the liquor business her own self. She feels sorry for Eric 'cause she thinks he's just a boy. And Eric is sweet on her in his own way. He even tells her that me and J.D. are comin' to town. She's got her hand in a few things around town anyway, and Cooper's war makes for bad business with her. So she talks Mayor Rohrbach into gettin' J.D. to clean up the town. Somehow Cooper gets wind of Miss Comstock's deal and sends Eric to scare off J.D. J.D. gets stabbed but not killed. That scares Mr. Rohrbach into settin' back and not callin' on the governor to send in the national guard or to contact federal officers when things start gettin' outta control. Later on, we know that at least one U.S. marshal, name o' Peeler, is in cahoots with Wynn. Like that fire in the middle of this tipi, Violet Comstock was the center of things. Cooper had to get her out of the way or she might have stiffened the mayor's spine enough to call the governor. Cooper somehow convinces his boy to kill her."

Everyone in the tipi was staring at Hoolie intently, captivated not only by the story he was laying before them but by the way he told it. Hoolie's voice inflections and his gestures mimicked the best orators—both Indian and white—that any of them had ever heard. The whites had grown up in a culture fueled by Chautauqua tent orators, religious revivalists, and persuasive politicians. The Kiowas in the tipi were equally enthralled. Their society, too, was made alive by an oral tradition that gave high status to those who could stand in front of an audience and captivate people simply by their eloquence. Words among the Kiowa people had power in and of themselves.

Hess broke the silence. "We'll take care of Marshal Peeler."

Hoolie nodded his head and continued. "Meanwhile, J.D. gets called back to Tulsa. Then Cooper gets the idea that he has to get shed of me too. So he goes back to tryin' to kill two birds with one rock. He sends Eric to kill Violet Comstock and tells Wynn to pin the murder on me. She's always been nice to Eric and so Eric can get to her easy. I'm pretty sure Cooper told the boy that she's a whore and needed killin' so that Eric wouldn't have no problems killin' her. Since he's already got Hughes and Marshal Peeler on his payroll, he takes them out to the Chargin' Horse place. George shows them where they buried Shotz, and they take him in. George was tryin' to do right by Mr. Shotz and didn't realize that Cooper was after him most of all.

"They got George in jail. Then on the mornin' I get arrested, I see Collins bringin' in the MacFarlands. I don't get it at first—not until that night when Clem and Festus get broken outta jail. All Collins and them were tryin' to do was make it look like Sheriff Wynn and Cooper couldn't keep control, even in the county hoosegow.

It's kind of silly in a way. I just don't think Collins understood just how mean Cooper is or how complicated Cooper's businesses are. Breakin' the MacFarlands and me and George and Harold and Chester out of jail just to humiliate Cooper was pretty stupid.

"Marty and Moe worked me over pretty good after they took me in. They said I shot Miss Comstock dead in the chest with my .44-40 Winchester. Marty Albright told me that I shot her 'up close.' That got me to thinkin'. That o'd rifle is pretty powerful, and if anything, they woulda shot her from a distance or in the back. You shoot somebody up close like that with that rifle, it'll leave a really big hole from the backblast. I seen that. I saw some Germans killed up close with a gun. The blast somehow bounces off the chest bone and opens up the skin like it's been blown out from the inside. Then there's the powder burns. You can't tell what kind of bullet went in at close range 'cause it messes up everything.

"The other thing was while we was out to Deaf Bob's, he asked if there was shootin' in town when Violet Comstock was killed. Deaf Bob said that her and her folks at the café were all armed and would put up a fight. There wasn't any shootin' that I heard, but it got me thinkin' that she mighta got knifed like Shotz or J.D. Now Eric coulda got close to her. I figured if I could see the wound itself, I could figure all this out.

"I didn't do that, but I got to talk to Mr. Merriot, the funeral director. He said that Miss Comstock had a hole in her chest, but it wasn't exactly round. It didn't go in at an angle either. Right then I knew what done it."

Hoolie glanced at Eric Cooper before he continued. "When Eric Cooper drove me and J.D. out to the Cooper place, I saw he was carryin' a trench knife from the war. It was what we called a 'knuckle duster' because it had a hand guard piece on the grip that you could use like brass knuckles. But it had a certain kind of blade. One of the things about the Great War was that a lot of the fightin' was close up. Now, most people got hurt by artillery—like I was—or gunfire. The guys in the trenches went after each other hand to hand. The Germans wore what they called 'great coats' that were pretty heavy. One of the things about them was that regular knives couldn't go through 'em very easy. So the government put a long, sharp pointed blade shaped like a triangle on those knuckle dusters. A lot of the men liked 'em 'cause you can stick 'em through anything. And if you twisted 'em, it would make 'em come out easier and quicker. And that was 'cause twistin' a triangle blade would make the hole rounder.

"Mr. Merriot hisself thought that Miss Comstock's wound looked a little funny, but he let it go. The sheriff was wantin' to put her in the ground as soon as he could. Wynn told Mr. Merriot that they'd done caught me and pinned the murder on me anyways. Eric killed Miss Comstock with his brother's trench knife."

Hoolie looked around the tipi again. Nobody made a move.

"Well, that's it," he said. "That's what went on. That's how J.D. got stabbed, that's why Mr. Shotz got killed, and that's how Miss Comstock got killed." To the federal officers, he said, "Now I reckon you'll want to ask questions."

MacGregor spoke first. "Mr. Smith, I think that's all we need to know right now. We'll need you all to help us transport these people back to Anadarko." MacGregor turned to Shuler and Hess. "Perhaps you gentlemen would like to make the arrests?"

Hess frowned and looked at Hughes, Wynn, and Eric and Paul Cooper in turn. "You're all under arrest for murder, conspiracy to commit murder, and trading in liquor, all on Indian land held in trust by the United States. These are all federal offenses."

Beaten mentally and cowed into accepting what had been said, the four men he arrested sat in their places without moving a muscle. The federal officers stood and, with the help of J.D., Hoolie, and the Boyiddle brothers, got the men to their feet. They led them out of the tipi and to the automobiles by then assembled at the Charging Horse arbor. Mayor Rohrbach followed in their wake.

Agent Shuler paused to talk to the mayor. "Mr. Mayor," he said, "since you'll probably be firing Police Chief Collins when you get back to town, I would suggest that you file the charges of murder against Eric and Paul Cooper based on the fact that Violet Comstock was very likely murdered within city limits. For the time being, I think you'd better find a trustworthy man to fill Collins's shoes, because as soon as I get back to Anadarko, I'll probably put the collar on him for violating the Volstead Act."

Hughes, Wynn, and the two Coopers didn't put up a struggle against being handcuffed, but the federal officers had only one pair of cuffs apiece, so the Coopers were locked together. Everyone except Khōn Charging Horse piled into the automobiles and rode to Anadarko. The old man stood alone next to the tipi, watching as the party drove off into the night. Now the soul of the poor white man left under the blackjack could rest.

>«

A month after the Shotz operation had been settled, Hoolie was sitting on the porch of his mother-in-law's home outside Hominy, Oklahoma. His heavily pregnant wife and her sister, mother, and grandmother were all inside, sitting in the dark front room fanning themselves to stave off the September heat. Even though in many places mid-September brought cool nights, the heat seemed to linger on in Oklahoma. Most of Hoolie's Osage family was sleeping outdoors at night to beat the heat on army cots bought from a surplus store in Tulsa.

Hoolie looked up to see a rooster tail of dust raised by a car coming along the road that led to the house. He knew it was J.D. coming to visit as he always did a few weeks after closing a case. It was just one of those rituals of debriefing they did, partly to sort out the operation, but mostly just to get together as two friends who had gone through trying times together.

J.D. waved as he pulled into the yard. The women had heard the car and came out on the front porch to greet the visitor, whoever it might be. Most of the time it was some relative or John Tall Soldier to visit Hoolie. When they saw it was J.D., they all put on big smiles. J.D. had become like a kindly old uncle. He joked with them and heaped praise on the women's ability to run the place well despite having Hoolie around to mess things up. J.D. also seemed truly taken with Osage cooking. He always ate more puffy fry bread, hominy, and beef stew than anybody else.

The women went into the yard to greet J.D. and walk him back to the house. Hoolie watched as J.D. got out and reached into the backseat to pull out the inevitable gifts he brought every time he visited. When he got to the porch, Myrtle's grandmother told him to sit on the wicker chair next to Hoolie. She herded the rest of the women inside with the admonition that they had to prepare a meal for J.D. Hoolie always grinned at his wife's grandmother's way of putting things. She always said that the meal was for the guest. What everybody else did with the great amount of food on the table was entirely circumstantial to the guest's well-being.

When J.D. was seated and the women had gone back into the house, Hoolie pulled two cigars out of a tin he had sitting on the floor of the porch. The two men lit up and sat for a time without speaking. They were, like old, old friends, simply enjoying the taste of the smoke and their comradeship.

After a few moments and a great deal of smoke, J.D. took off his hat and laid it on the porch swing next to him. "This where Mr. Lookout was shot?"

"It was. It was hard gettin' the bloodstains out. He was a good man."

J.D. looked around to see if anyone was in listening distance. "Does your sister-in-law know?" If there was common knowledge about Mr. Lookout, it was that Hoolie's sister-in-law's white fiancé was one of his murderers and that Hoolie had somehow made the murderers vanish.

"She knows all right," Hoolie said. "She just don't say nothin'. I think Grandma in there helps her along in gettin' over it. She loved that man, evil as he was. But I'm pretty sure she knows that he didn't care for her. He killed her daddy to get control of this land." Hoolie paused for a moment to puff on his cigar. "You know, J.D., it just don't seem to stop. Same thing happened down to Anadarko. They was tryin' to take the Chargin' Horse place for gas, oil, cattle, liquor, and Lord knows what."

"I know, Hool. Greed'll do it every time."

"That was a thing I got a chance to talk to Old Man Chargin' Horse about—with the help of Chester and Harold. There are four things that a person had to be so's he can be a chief. He has to be truthful, brave, generous, and humble. What's terrible is that all the people we run into in the detective business is just the opposite."

"That's true, but we've sure met some interestin' people too. You got to admit that." He paused to draw in more smoke. J.D. crinkled his eyes in a tight half smile and said, "Like Deaf Bob."

Hoolie had to smile too. Deaf Bob was quite a character.

"You know," J.D. said, "I got George Chargin' Horse to take me out to see Deaf Bob when I had to go back to check up on how

Rohrbach's doin'. I woulda never thought that there could be a guy like that.

"I was gonna give him a hundred dollars for the help he gave in the whole operation. I gave a couple hundred each to the Boyiddles. George didn't want none of it, so I contributed to his church. He was okay with that. But Deaf Bob . . .

"First we went out there in a car. Had to stand outside in the sun while he looked us over. And he knew George as well as he knew anybody. He just wanted us to stand out there for a time. Musta give him some kind of enjoyment.

"Anyway, he finally lets us in. I say I want to give him some dough, and he says, 'I don't take nothin' from no white man.' So I tried to explain to him that I was givin' him somethin' for his trouble and help. He says to me, 'Tell you what, boy, I don't need no money, but I'll take that hat of your'n.' I've never been called 'boy' in my life—even when I was a boy. Well, I say that that doesn't make a whole lot of sense since he could take the money, go into town, buy a new hat, and have money left over. No, he says, he wants that hat. So I give him the hat. It was that nice straw boater. As soon as I give him the hat, he pulls out a horse pistol about two feet long. I figure he's nuts and is gonna shoot me on the spot. But no, he turns it around and hands me the pistol butt first. 'Okay, it's yours,' he says. 'Don't go shootin' yourself in the foot with it.'

"That's how I acquired a .44 caliber Remington revolver. I'll probably never carry it—it's too damn big and bulky. I guess I'll just hang it on the wall somewhere. Deaf Bob is a guy I don't understand at all."

Hoolie laughed out loud. "That sounds like him. I was only around him for a few days, but I don't think he's as crazy as he looks. I know that most of the folks I was around thought Deaf Bob was a decent human being, just a bit odd." He looked off toward the creek bed from which his wife's father was shot. "The white people think he's touched. But Indians there believe o'd Bob is just living with a lot of good and bad and powerful spirits. The white people done everything to Deaf Bob that had been done to Indians—wife dead of a white man's disease, sons gone, ears cut off. He lived with death and hurt all around him for years. It must be bad just bein' Deaf Bob."

J.D. sat mute through Hoolie's ruminations about Deaf Bob as if they were a Shakespearian soliloquy. Finally he said, "Hoolie, you're a philosopher. But you know what? By your lights, Deaf Bob's a real chief because he's humble, honest, courageous, and generous. See? I remember what you and Ol' Man Charging Horse said."

"Yeah," Hoolie said after some thought, "I reckon so."

"And, my friend," J.D. said, "so are you."

Myrtle came to the screen door and said, "Mr. Daugherty, would you like to eat something? Grandma says you'd better come before the rest of us eat it gone." The two men rose and went into the house.

EPILOGUE

The judge banged his gavel to get the full attention of the court, waited for complete quiet, and said, "The charges having been read, does the defendant have anything to say before I remand him to custody to await trial and close these proceedings?"

Attorney Miles Shotz rose. "Your Honor," he began, "we would request that you set bail in this case. Mr. Daugherty is over eighty years old and is not a flight risk. My firm has hired a reputable private investigation service that will provide security for my client. There have been rumblings in this city that some parties and relatives of the deceased in this case would like to lynch Mr. Daugherty."

"Who gave you that information?" the judge asked. "Perhaps Mr. Daugherty would be safer in custody."

"Your Honor, no one has specifically said that Mr. Daugherty would be lynched. It's just that the possibility exists, and we—my firm and I—are in the position to provide very good security.

"I would like to impress upon the court that the person my client is alleged to have murdered was openly a member of the Ku Klux Klan, which is, unfortunately, at this point in time still a force in this state. Equally, it is a dangerous organization.

"My client is an elderly man who has a fine reputation in Oklahoma, and in particular Tulsa, as a businessman of impeccable character and a true pillar of the community—"

The judge held up his hand and interrupted. "Mr. Shotz, we're not at trial yet. This is an arraignment, and the crime of which your client is accused is truly horrendous. He has admitted to killing several people, including Bryant Cunningham, Philbert Sooles, Terry Moody, Jesse Poindexter, Ralph Cunningham, and the most recent victim, Roger Ray Elam. I am aware that your client has recanted his original confession. And I don't care if the late Mr. Elam was a member of the Ku Klux Klan or of the Tulsa Bird Watcher's Society—he was gunned down in cold blood. I imply no guilt or innocence regarding your client. That will be decided by a jury trial on another day. This case demands a bond commiserate with the nature of the crime, however. I will, therefore, set bail at ten thousand dollars and remand Mr. Daugherty to your custody and to that of your security organization. Is that understood?"

"Yes, sir."

"Good. Now, Mr. Daugherty, do you have anything to say?"

J.D. stood. "That's a lot of money, Your Honor. Nothing else."

"Very well. Bond is set at ten thousand dollars. The first date for trial we have on the calendar is July 10." The judge rapped his gavel. "These proceedings are adjourned."

Everyone stood as the judge left the bench. The lawyers began to pack up their briefcases. J.D. sat down, put one hand on the defendant's table, and brushed his moustache with the other.

Hoolie Smith leaned over the railing and tapped Shotz on the shoulder. "Mr. Shotz, J.D.," he said to get their attention, "can I talk to you?"

Shotz looked Hoolie over and suddenly realized who he was. J.D. sat knuckling his moustache and smiling at Hoolie. "Hool," J.D. began, "me and Mr. Shotz here are gonna go over to pay off these fools so I can get outta the pokey. I imagine that we'll go over to the Berg law offices." He looked at Shotz, who nodded his head in the affirmative. "Yep," J.D. continued, "that's where we're headed after we get done here. Come on over, you know where it is. We'll talk."

A little over an hour later, Hoolie and J.D. sat in Shotz's office, smoking cigars and reliving old times.

"How'd you get down here?" J.D. asked. "With your eyes, I didn't think Myrtle would let you drive."

"Yeah . . . well, I didn't. John came over and brought me down here."

"That Tall Soldier?"

"Yep."

"He stay?"

"Yep."

"Where?"

"We're camped down by the river. Not too far. I walked over here."

"You boys still haven't gotten used to the fact that this ain't a little Creek town no more. It's a big city, and you two settin' up a Hooverville inside city limits will probably get you both thrown in the can. Go on home. I got a good lawyer. But most of all, I'm eighty-three years old, and they ain't about to throw me in prison or fry me in the electric chair. They don't do that to old successful businessmen, especially if that old businessman knows all about their businesses, private and public. They might put me in the loony bin up in Vinita, but they'll more likely want to put me somewheres I can't get into more trouble, like an old folks' home. That's when Big Bill Shelby'll step in. The Shelbys still have a hand in runnin' this town, and I know that they'll set me up in pretty good style until I croak. And that might not be too long now."

Hoolie stared at the old man for a few moments. He was probably right about his fate.

Out of thin air, Hoolie asked, "Now, Jimmy, did you do it?"

J.D. pulled a frown of disgust and said, "Goddammit, you know I hate to be called Jimmy. You've done that for thirty-five years."

"Okay, okay. I'll stop. But I want to know the whole story. I don't think you bumped off this Elam fella. You ain't gettin' around that good anymore."

"You'd be surprised."

"Well, I'll give it to you that you're pretty spry, but gunnin' down a man like that just doesn't seem like a thing you might do. And that's not even countin' the fact that you confessed to killin' five more men over the years. I just don't see it in you."

"Hool, there a lot of things that would surprise you. You did a lot of things that surprised me. You know, like makin' a couple of men disappear thirty-five years ago. I never got the whole story on that trick. . . . We've had a few adventures together." J.D. took a deep breath and continued, "And I've considered you my best friend for years. You know more about the detective business than any other man in this city. But you don't know everything that goes on."

Hoolie paused for a few seconds. "J.D., I'll tell you some secrets if you'll tell me yours."

"Hool, you sound like a kid."

"Maybe, but what if they do decide to put you in the electric chair. I'm gonna have to do somethin' about that. So I'd like to know what's what."

"Listen, my friend, I'm thankful that you came down to see me. And I'm happy that you want to keep me outta the chair. But you don't have to worry. I'm fine, and I'll be okay. They ain't gonna fry me."

"All right. I'll let it go. But I still don't think you killed all those men."

"Hool, I confessed to bumpin' off all of 'em. And I'll stick by it with you. Now, Shotz entered a not guilty plea and I recanted the confession, and that's okay too. I figure the longer the trial, the longer I get to be free. You know I could keel over and kick the bucket at any time. That trial oughta be a bit of fun for an old-timer like me. They're gonna accuse me of stuff neither one of us can imagine. People are gonna believe that this old man is a monster. They're gonna make me into the Sluagh, a dullahan, and the king of the demons, Balor, all rolled into one. Those are the monsters my dear Irish mother told me about. But don't fret—it'll all come out in the end."

"I just hate to see you go through all this."

"Hool, I got the best lawyer in town," he reiterated. "This is gonna be a good time. . . . And I'm gonna tell you that all those bastards they're accusin' me of killin' deserved to die. And one of 'em got plugged with a .44 that I got in a trade for a straw hat years ago."

ABOUT THE AUTHOR

Tom Holm (Cherokee-Creek) is the author of *The Osage Rose* and several works of nonfiction, including *Code Talkers and Warriors: Native Americans and World War II*, *The Great Confusion in Indian Affairs: Native Americans and Whites in the Progressive Era*, and *Strong Hearts, Wounded Souls: Native American Veterans of the Vietnam War.* He is a professor emeritus in the Department of American Indian Studies at the University of Arizona.